AMISTAD

AMISTAD

DAVID PESCI

MARLOWE & COMPANY
NEW YORK

Published by
Marlowe & Company
632 BroadwayNew York, NY 10012

Pesci, David
Amistad: the thunder of freedom / David Pesci.
p. cm.
ISBN 1-56924-748-X
1. Amistad (Schooner)—Fiction. 2. Adams, John Quincy, 1767-1848--Fiction. 3. Slavery—United States—Insurrections, etc.—Fiction. 4. Trials (Mutiny)—United States—History—19th century—Fiction. 5. Slave trade—United States—History—19th century—Fiction. I. Title.
PS3566.E736A65 1997 96-54050
813'.54—dc21 CIP

ISBN 1-56924-748-X

Manufactured in the United States of America

First Edition

To my parents

†

Acknowledgments

I couldn't have written this book without time, support, and guidance from numerous people, and I need to express to them my most sincere gratitude.

The reference staff at the Homer Babbidge Library at the University of Connecticut in Storrs was extremely helpful in answering my many questions and making a variety of resources available.

Special thanks to my unbelievably patient and wise proofreaders, Nancy Kelleran, Russ Malz, and Susan Campbell. They fixed the typos, offered suggestions, and provided moral support and encouragement from start to finish. Extra special thanks to Carol Hobbs, Esq., who not only proofed many chapters, but offered legal advice on the passages of this novel that dealt with the court trials.

Thanks to my uncle, Don Pesci, the best writer I have ever known. Your suggestions, moral support, and help were invaluable and indispensable throughout this project.

Thanks to Keith Lashley for the introductions and for his

belief in the importance of this book. Thanks also to Raúl da Silva for the title suggestion, the introductions, and his enthusiasm.

Thank you to Roberta Flack for her interest and kind words.

Deep and heartfelt appreciation to my agent, John White. Your enthusiasm, suggestions, editor's eye, and drive made the publication of this book a reality. Thanks again.

Finally, to my family—my parents, to whom this book is dedicated, my sisters, my brother and his family, my grandparents, uncles, aunts, and cousins. All of you have constantly supported me with your encouragement, prayers, and pride. It is a debt I can never repay. Thank you always.

—David Pesci

AMISTAD

PART ONE

The Atlantic
April 1839

Singbe

A cold touch woke him from a dreamless sleep. It was the hand of the boy lying next to him, tossed by the roll of the ship in the night sea. The palm was cold, the fingers stiff. The boy was dead.

Singbe lightly pushed the hand away and shifted his body to face the boy. He could not see him in the darkness of the ship's hold. Groping with his left hand, he found the boy's chest, rigid and still with the lifeless cold. The chain running between Singbe's wrists was connected to another running between his feet and did not let his hand move up any farther. He shifted his body again and reached with his right hand. The manacle grated into his wrist as he stretched it forward. He found the boy's eyes, open. Singbe tried to pull the lids down with his fingertips, but they were fixed and would not move. He said a short prayer and turned away, leaving the dead boy to stare into the darkness.

Singbe closed his own eyes and tried to picture Stefa, and Ge-waw, Klee, Baru, and his father, all together, happy and real. He saw his hut and his farm, the broad field that he and Stefa and his father had worked so hard to clear. They had planted well. The weather had been kind, the sun warm and the rains soft and measured. The birds and small animals had been kept away. There were no locusts or worms. The rice would soon be ready for harvest. After it was in, Singbe would take Ge-waw on his first hunt.

The images were bright and strong. But for the past few weeks, Singbe was finding he could not hold them long in his mind before others began to creep in. At first it was the lion, coming upon Stefa, Klee, and Baru at the river while they were drawing water for the day. The lion gave way to a pack of hyenas, sharp-toothed, quick and bloodthirsty, descending upon Stefa and Father and the children as they tended the fields. But lately these images had yielded to a new one—a man.

He was not a man Singbe had seen before. At first, his features and movements were so thin and sketchy that he was little more than a shadow in the background, barely noticed or seen. But in the past few weeks the face and form had grown clearer, more defined and strong, so that he had become familiar. Confident and smiling, the man moved as one with Stefa and the children, looking back at Singbe with a leering grin as he lay down with Stefa or shared the hunt with Ge-waw. He lived in Singbe's home, sat in his place at mealtimes, and walked his lands. Father was gone.

Each time the man appeared, Singbe saw the light of his own presence in the eyes of his wife and children fade a little more. It had been so long already. How much time would it take before all that was left of him in their minds was a memory living with the ghosts of the dead?

The ship rolled and the boy's hand touched him again. Singbe pushed it away angrily. He closed his eyes again and tried to think of a way to get back home.

Moans and cries, thumps of wood on wood, and a cold gurgle of chains shook Singbe awake. A whiteman held a musket in one hand and slid open the square wooden portholes with the other. Dull morning light filtered in and salt air slowly began to mix with the hold's rancid stink. Two other men, one white and one a light-skinned black, both bare-chested and shoeless, walked down the aisle yelling in that foreign tongue of theirs. They unlocked the links that bound wrists to ankles, then grabbed the wrist chains and pulled the tribesmen to their feet.

Another, a yellow-haired whiteman, stood in front of the deck-hatch ladder, watching. He was tall and lean, sinewy at the neck and forearms, and his skin was whiter than the other whitemen on the ship. He was dressed more completely than the others, wearing a bright white shirt, striped pants, and polished black boots. He had a hawklike nose and wore his thick mane of yellow hair tied behind his head. In his left hand he held a black, sharp-ended walking stick with a dog's head carved in the gold handle. A pistol stuck out from his belt. Singbe looked away from the men. These were the ones who always came in the morning.

The light-skinned black was moving toward him, and Singbe shifted from his side to a sitting position. When the sailor was two men away, Singbe nodded his head to the left.

"The boy is dead. He is dead."

Singbe knew the sailors did not speak Mende or any languages of the tribesmen, but maybe he could get the sailor to understand. The man was over him now. Singbe repeated his words and nodded again. The man unlocked the middle chain, pulled Singbe up hard and pushed him forward from behind the head.

"Shut-up that gibberish and move, Congo."

The push twisted Singbe's feet around the ankle chain and sent him hard to the floor. He started to get up and saw the sailor pull up on the boy's chains. The lifeless body jerked forward, the feet coming off the floor, the head bouncing off the sailor's chest, shit dripping onto his feet. The sailor jumped back.

"Bloody hell."

He threw the boy's body hard, smashing his head against the bulkhead. The eyes, still open, stared back, glazed and vacant.

Singbe jumped to his feet and swung his wrist chains at the

sailor, hitting him square in the side of the neck. The man fell sideways, the deck coming up hard on his elbow. The other sailor pulling up tribesmen exploded with laughter.

"That one giving you some attitude, Paolo?"

"Je-sus!"

The sailor jumped up and struck Singbe with the back of his hand, knocking him face first to the floor. He fell on Singbe's back and grabbed his hair. He pulled it back hard and then smashed Singbe's face into the planking. Singbe felt his head come up again. He rolled his body, hitting the man hard in the side of the face with the wrist chains. He tried to raise his leg to kick, but the manacles snapped it back. He turned and drove his knees up into the man's groin. The man let out a howl. He drew a knife from his belt. Singbe slapped his chains into the man's hand, sending the knife flying. The man shoved his palm up into Singbe's jaw and pressed his knees into the manacled arms. He grabbed Singbe's throat with both hands, thumbs digging deep into the neck, and squeezed.

"Die you bloody-shit nigger! Die!"

Singbe struggled but he could not loosen the man's grip. He couldn't see and he couldn't breathe. There was a cracking in his throat. And then, quite suddenly, the sailor stopped squeezing.

"No, Paolo."

The yellow-haired whiteman held a pistol to the sailor's temple.

The sailor smiled weakly. "But, Señor Shaw, this nigger... "

The hammer drew back with a metallic click. The man pressed the pistol deeper into the sailor's temple.

"Carries a cash value. More than you'll get paid for this voyage. More than you'll ever be worth yourself, I daresay. Leave off and get up. Now."

"But, Señor Shaw, sir. He pushed me to the floor. Surely he is not to get away with it?"

The sailor started to rise. Shaw kicked him back to the floor.

"I'll warn you now not to second guess me or my motives with my property. Your job is to do as you're told. Period."

Shaw stuck his pistol in his belt and pulled Singbe, still gasping for air, to his feet. He gently turned Singbe's head and inspected his neck and bloody nose. Singbe stared at Paolo.

"Get me a wet cloth, Paolo."

The sailor grabbed a bucket of seawater and pulled out a rag. Shaw rung it out and swabbed the blood from Singbe's face.

"I am to say how these blacks are handled. I will give orders for punishment or not. You are to follow those orders. Above all, you are also not to damage my property. Understand?"

"Sí, Señor."

The yellow-haired man pointed to the line of tribesmen going up the hatch and nodded to Singbe. Singbe understood. He stared at Paolo for a second longer and then turned and got in line.

"This black's got strength and spirit," Shaw said. "And that's exactly why I am in this business. The African blacks work longer and better in the fields. They make better breeding stock. That's why we can get twice for any one of these what they get for Creoles. We have already had excessive losses on this voyage. I'll be lucky to break even. What I do not need is some stupid shitfaced scab as yourself busting on my healthy cargo. Now, no harm better come to that particular black unless I order it. If I see a cut to his body, a bruise to his face, if he gets sick, if he catches a bloody cold, it'll be out of your pay. And I can assure you, you useless mulatto scum, it will be out of your hide. Understand?"

"Sí. Sí, Señor."

Shaw took one step toward Paolo, who took one step backward.

Shaw smiled, "Cross me, Paolo, and you will live no longer."

The other sailor, Miguel, had been walking down the line and now had all the tribesmen on their feet and walking toward the hatch. He reached down and dragged the dead boy's body to the aisle.

"Another one, Señor Shaw."

Shaw moved to the boy and poked him in the ribs with the walking stick.

"Take an ear and drag him up with the others once these are on deck, Miguel."

"Sí, Señor Shaw."

Shaw walked down past the line of tribesmen and the sailor with the musket and went up the ladder. Miguel pulled the dead boy onto the pile. There were twelve bodies plus the boy. Paolo picked up his knife off the floor and began cutting off the left ear of each dead tribesman and putting them in the burlap bag Miguel held.

"I'm gonna kill that Inglese son-of-a-bitch. I'm gonna kill him and his precious nigger."

"He's not Inglese, he's American. And if I were you I'd let it go, Paolo. Señor Shaw may walk and talk like some highborn gentleman, but he will kill you or any other man who crosses him. He'll do it without a thought."

"He's a dead man walking."

On deck, Singbe followed the other tribesmen, shuffling to the railing where they were urinating into the sea. All of them were naked, and despite the warm air brought by the ship's southern latitude and the growing strength of the morning sun, their bodies shook with chills. Three whitemen with muskets stood close by. Two others were on the raised deck in the stern.

"Have you lost your mind?"

The words came from a tribesman along the railing, Grabeau, a Mende man like Singbe, with the ceremonial marks of Poro on his back. Many on board were Mende. But there were also Mandingo, Gissi, Timmani, Balu, Bandi, and even Gula. Singbe said nothing.

"Is it not enough that the blackman with the white blood in his skin hates the tribesmen? He would gladly kill any of us. But now you have gone and given him reason to want to kill you, especially."

Singbe stared out at the sea.

"We are in a world of shit."

"Yes, Singbe, it is true. But would you rather be dead?"

"The Gods have not kept me alive through all this just to die."

"Perhaps. Or perhaps they just haven't gotten around to killing you, yet."

"No. I don't believe that. I will return home to my wife and my children and my father."

Grabeau let loose a small laugh and spat into the sea. "How, Singbe? The water is everywhere. The ship leaves no trail in it. We do not even know where the factory or Mende or anywhere is anymore."

A sailor yelled at them. They had been on the ship long enough to know they were being told not to talk. Singbe looked back to the ocean and lowered his voice.

"The ship sails away from the sun in the morning and into it in the afternoon."

"So?"

"So, we need to move toward the sun in the morning and away from the sun in the afternoon."

"And how are we to do that? Slip over the side and walk?"

"No. We take this ship and sail it ourselves."

Grabeau smiled broadly. "I see that mound of shit black-whiteman must have knocked the mind from your head. Have you forgotten these?" He shook the chains lightly. "Or the whitemen on this boat with their guns?"

"I count only twenty-four whitemen on this boat. Even with all the dead they've thrown over the side, there still must be more than three hundred tribesmen in its belly. They bring us up sixty or more at a time. Sixty tribesmen against twenty-four whites. That is more than enough. Guns or not. And all of the whitemen do not have guns all the time. We surprise them, we kill them. The boat will be ours."

"Maybe if we were not in chains or starving or if so many of us were not sick, I might agree with you. But trying it as we are . . . It would be madness. Slaughter."

"No. Spending the rest of our lives in chains, living as slaves at the end of a lash—that is madness. That is slaughter."

The crack of a whip hit the deck a breath away from Singbe's feet.

"No talking! Shut up. Shut up and walk."

A sailor with a musket pushed them forward and they began to walk, slowly, following the railing and the riggings, around the deck. They would do this for an hour then be given a handful of rice and a cup of water, which they had to eat and drink while watched by sailors and the yellow-haired man. It had been this way every day since the second morning, except for the three days and four nights of wind and rain and boiling, heaving seas. On those days they ate below. Many got sick, spilling their food up from their stomachs onto the floor. The stench of that and human waste and the dead drew the food out of most of the others.

Just above the stern, the sun had begun to glow brighter behind the morning mist. Singbe looked out at the sea. He still found it hard to believe its size, that they could sail for so many days without seeing land. Forty-three days so far by Singbe's count. Thirty-five before that in the slave factory at the mouth of the Gallinas River. Thirty-two before that chained in a pen in Genduma. And it was twelve mornings before being brought to Genduma that he was captured by tribesmen on the road.

It was on the road to Kawamende, a Mende village a half day's walk from his farm, where he had gone to look at some goats he might want to trade for. Singbe had never seen the man who stopped him. He was not a Mendeman but he spoke the language and asked Singbe if this was the way to Mawkoba. Singbe was suspicious of the stranger and watched him carefully as he answered. When he finished, the man thanked him and turned up the road toward Mawkoba. It was then that Singbe was hit on the head from behind. The blow was sharp and caught him by surprise. He fell to the ground but he did not lose consciousness. He rolled and then lunged at the man who hit him, tackling him at the knees and striking him on the face. But then others fell upon him and beat him senseless.

When he regained consciousness, he found himself tied to a tree. The men were eating around a fire. Singbe yelled to them but they paid him no mind. After they finished eating, one man came over and tied a rope around Singbe's neck, looped it out to his right wrist, and tied another knot leaving about ten feet of slack hanging. Then he tied another rope around Singbe's neck and freed him from the tree. Singbe stood slowly. A hot, thick throbbing pulsed through his head. His body ached and burned from the beating. Suddenly, one of the men pulled at the rope around his wrist. The noose tightened at Singbe's neck, choking him so hard he couldn't stand. The men all laughed and then pulled him up by tugging on the other rope around his neck. They walked him through the jungle like this. Any time Singbe tried to resist or slow down, they pulled hard at the rope on his wrist, dropping him to his knees, breathless and choking.

Singbe did not know the men. He thought they were Vai, or perhaps Genduma, both neighboring tribes that the Mende had warred with off and on for hundreds of years. It didn't matter. He knew what was happening. Men taking other men as slaves was as old as the tribes. It was practiced in war, as a payment for debts and crimes, and, if it could be arranged, as a way to acquire men's lands, animals, or women. Some slaves were sold and taken away. They could end up as close to their homes as a few days' walk, or be put on caravans and taken halfway around the globe, never to be seen again. In some tribes, slaves could work themselves out of slavery, eventually joining the tribe as an equal, able to take a wife and hold property. In others, the slaves were worked until they died. Singbe had never owned a slave, but he knew plenty of Mende men who did.

The four men who took Singbe sold him to Bamadzha, son of Shaka, the Genduma king. Bamadzha held Singbe in a pen with ten other men for more than a month and then marched them through the bush for three days and nights to the slave factory on the Gallinas River near Lomboko Harbor. There they were sold to a Spaniard, the first whiteman Singbe had ever seen. Whitemen had been buying slaves for a long time, almost three hundred years, trading with rum, fabrics, silver, gold, knives, and even guns. Singbe knew some tribal chiefs had become extremely wealthy dealing captives from rival tribes to the white slave traders.

The slave factory was a collection of huge holding pens which was situated just back from the river in a small hollow concealed by trees. Though they looked crude, the giant cages were nearly impenetrable. The walls were bars made of wooden planks and tree trunks that had been driven deep into the soil. There was barely enough space between each bar for a man to stick two fingers through. Each pen was sealed by a roof of rough, knotty planking and had a single door, chained shut and padlocked. Whitemen with muskets guarded the doors from the outside.

There were whitemen everywhere and they all had guns. Most of the tribesmen held captive had never seen either. To provide an education for new captives, a special demonstration was arranged every week or so. The bodies of four dead tribesmen were tied to trees. The whitemen loaded their guns and took turns shooting at the bodies. Large pieces of flesh were blown off with each shot. The head of one of the dead tribesmen exploded completely. After each volley, one of the whitemen would turn to the pens and say some words. A Genduma tribesman standing next to him translated, first in Genduma, then in Mandingo. Singbe found out later that he said a gun could kill a man or a lion or even an elephant from across a field. There was no escaping its fire and power. Nothing could stop it.

The first time Singbe saw this demonstration, there was an added element. After shooting the corpses, a live tribesman was dragged out from a small shack across from the pen. He looked like a Gissi, but Singbe could not tell for sure. He had been badly beaten and his back and face were bloody. Despite his wounds, the man fought and struggled madly. It took four men, two whiteman and two Genduma tribesmen, to drag him to a tree and bind him. He struggled and screamed despite their repeated strikes to his face and ribs. Singbe watched two men, one whiteman and one Genduma, calmly load guns and aim them at the man. His screaming had become manic, bloodcurdling, heaving cries. There was a flash and then loud crack from the Genduma's gun. The blast hit the tribesman square in the belly. The whiteman fired, snapping the tribesman's head back quick and hard against the tree. Blood flowed from the large hole in his belly. His head sagged forward, the face sheared off. The tribesmen in the pens stared in silence.

By Singbe's count there were almost four hundred men in the pen with him when he was first brought to the factory. Ten to twenty a day were added to their number. They were fed a bowlful of rice and half a fish each day and could have all the river water they wanted. They urinated out through the bars and shit in a hole in one corner. Despite openings in the bars and between the roof planks, the stench was overwhelming. The other captives were from many tribes, some Singbe had never heard of, from as far away as eighty days' walk. Some had been taken in battle, others kidnapped as payment for debts owed by either the man himself or one of his family members. There were others like Singbe who had just been taken for no reason other than the fact that they were strong and healthy and would bring a good profit to their captors.

There were many Mende men in the pens, some whom Singbe had met before at the great harvest gatherings, and two, Grabeau and Kimbo, whom he knew well. Kimbo was taken in his own fields by Bah-rae and five men. He had sold Bah-rae two slaves a few months earlier, in payment of a debt. Soon after the transaction was made, one of the slaves ran off. Bah-rae demanded repayment, but Kimbo said that a slave's actions were Bah-rae's problem once he became the owner. Bah-rae left angry, then came back a few days later with the five men. It was near dusk and they found Kimbo alone in his fields. They beat him and carried him away, bound hand and foot to a pole like an animal killed on the hunt. Kimbo believed that Bah-rae coveted his lands and his wife.

"He is a thief," Kimbo said. "He paid off his friends. They will lie and get people to believe I was taken by Genduma or Vai. Then Bah-rae will steal my property and my wife."

Grabeau had been taken like Singbe, while traveling on a road, except Grabeau was traveling with a companion, his brother Ge-lu. They were on their way back from Fulu, a large

Mende village, nearly a day's walk from their own goat farm. It was midday when they came upon a man lying motionless in the road. As Grabeau bent down to see if he could help the man, he was struck from behind. When he awoke, he was tied as Singbe had been, at the neck and wrist. He asked the men where his brother was, and they said he was killed fighting them. But Grabeau thinks they lied, that his brother escaped.

"He will assemble a war party of Mendemen and follow our trail to this place," he told Singbe. "He will find me and we will kill all the slavers—the whites and the tribesmen who trade with them."

Singbe thought of a war party of Mendemen coming to the factory. It would be a journey of several days that would take them through the lands of several hostile tribes. And even if they made it, they would have to fight against men with guns.

Every few days at the factory, whitemen—slave dealers or ambitious ship captains—would come by, looking through the bars and having certain tribesmen taken out of the pen so they could be inspected more closely. Singbe was taken out like this on three occasions. Men came in the pen with guns and a long stick with a noose at its end. The noose was slipped over Singbe's neck. He struggled the first time, but they quickly tightened the noose and choked him so hard he felt the life nearly go out of his body. They led him out of the pen and the whitemen felt his arms, back, buttocks, and legs, and looked at his teeth and hands. One of these was the yellow-haired man, who was on the ship with them now.

Two days after the yellow-haired man came to the factory, whitemen with guns and their tribesmen allies, armed with guns and clubs, came into the pen. They yelled at the tribesmen to line up. Those who did not do so right away were beaten by the tribesmen with clubs. Many did not understand and were struck with the clubs until they realized what was expected of them. Their ankles and hands were bound with manacles and chains. Then they were lead out along the river's mouth to a beach on the Atlantic. Like most of the captives, Singbe had never seen the ocean or a boat larger than a canoe. Many of them were terrified by it all. They were loaded onto long rowboats, fifteen tribesmen to a boat, with four whitemen pulling at the oars and one sitting in the bow holding a gun.

They were about halfway to the ship when a tribesmen in one of the boats ahead began screaming and trying to stand. The whiteman in the bow put down his gun and drew a whip from his belt. He stood and struck out at the screaming tribesman, hitting him and others. He struck again but the tribesman caught the end of the whip and pulled, jerking the whiteman to the boat's floor. The other whitemen stopped rowing and tried to grab the tribesman. He swung at them with his chains, stumbled to the edge of the boat, and jumped into the water. The chains dragged him down, but after a few seconds he surfaced, his head barely rising above the water. The whitemen tried to reach him with the oars but the tribesman pushed them away. The whiteman with the gun called out to the tribesman, raised the gun to his shoulder, called out again, and then fired. The tribesman disappeared beneath the water just before the musket's flash. He resurfaced a few seconds later in a different spot, farther away, and began laughing loudly. They rowed toward him while the man with the gun reloaded. The tribesman waited until they got close and then rose up a little higher in the water and screamed words in a language Singbe did not understand. Then he threw his arms back and let the weight of his chains pull him down under the waves. They waited several minutes but they saw him no more. Many of the tribesmen in the other boats began yelling and shaking their boats, but a few musket blasts into the air quickly brought silence. They were rowed out to the great ship, the Portuguese-flagged *Teçora*, and taken below. At sunset, the ship headed toward the open ocean.

That was forty-three days ago.

Now, Singbe sat on the deck of the *Teçora* with Grabeau and the other tribesmen, eating a handful of rice.Then he slowly drank from his cup of water. When the yellow-haired man saw that they had all finished, he would give the word and the sailors with guns would herd the tribesmen below and bring up another group. The rice was not cooked and they often found maggots and grubs among the grains. But they had to eat what was given to them. Anyone caught throwing it away or spitting it up later was flogged.

As Singbe ate, he shifted his body slightly out of the shadow of the mast. He wanted to feel the sun's warmth on his whole body.

"That one."

Two men grabbed Singbe's arms from behind and pulled them up and back. Two more men grabbed his feet and together they lifted him off the deck. Singbe twisted and tried to flail with his arms and legs, but he could not get free. The men carried him over to the stock on the raised deck in the stern. Singbe knew what was going to happen. He had seen it before with other tribesmen on the ship. He struggled more, screaming oaths and curses at the sailors. One grabbed a musket and jammed the muzzle into his cheek. Singbe looked up at the barrel and the sailor looking back down at him. He froze. They pulled his legs into the stock's grooves and locked the crossbar down over his calves, just above the manacles on his ankles. Singbe, back flat against the deck, looked into the sun. Two of the men now knelt on his forearms, pinning him to the deck. His feet stuck out the end of the stock. Shaw moved over him, blocking out the sun.

"I own you, buck."

He stood and spoke louder, so that all the tribesmen could hear him.

"I own all of you! You will obey my rules and the rules of this ship! Or you will suffer the con-se-quen-ces!"

He turned back to Singbe, then said,"Neither you nor your friends understand our language, and I do not understand yours. But you will understand this."

He stepped away and again all Singbe could see was the sun. He tried again to move his arms but the men held him tight. There was the rush of air and a loud crack. Singbe bit down on the insides of his mouth, determined not to scream. Shaw struck his feet again. Singbe bit down harder. Two more strikes. Shaw paused. He saw the small trickle of blood running out from the side of Singbe's mouth and let out a laugh.

"Oh, you're a hard one, all right. But I appreciate that, lad. I love the spirit."

He swung again.

"Pride."

Another strike.

"Resolve."

Shaw now took the stick in both hands and drew it back behind his head.

"These are all highly marketable qualities."

He let loose, swinging with all his might. Singbe could not hold back. An anguished cry exploded from his throat.

"But we cannot have you lads jumping the hired help."

Three more cracks. Singbe cried out louder with each strike. Pain burned and ripped through his feet.

Shaw came around the stock, grabbed Singbe by the hair and held the bloody stick up to his eyes.

"Your blood, African. In my hands."

He held the stick high so all the tribesmen could see it.

"Your blood is in my hands! All of you!"

He looked back down at Singbe.

"I think you know what I'm saying here, buck. I think we've reached an understanding. Yes?"

Shaw cleaned the stick with a rag and nodded to the sailors. They pulled Singbe's legs out of the stocks, spun him around, and plunged his feet in a bucket of seawater. He let out another scream.

"Hurts, yes? But it's a healing pain, I assure you. By the time I get you to market there'll be no trace of your little punishment. And I dare say, you'll think twice before trying to get the drop on one of these chaps again."

Paolo had watched the entire episode from the railing. Shaw caught his eye and nodded. Paolo turned away, muttering under his breath.

A sailor tied rags drenched in seawater around Singbe's feet and they lowered him down the ladder into the hold. The rest of the tribesmen followed. They were chained back into the half-sitting position that Shaw demanded for transport of his Africans. It took up less space, which meant more cargo could be fit on board.

In the afternoon, when they were brought back up on deck for more exercise, Singbe was left behind. His feet burned as though they had been scraped raw, and even the slightest move inside the salty rags brought sharp, driving pain. He tried to think of Stefa, and of walking through cool mountain streams. Later that night, word came down the line from Grabeau asking how he was.

"Sixty against twenty-four."

Shaw

The captain lit a pipe and passed the bottle to Shaw. A large oil lamp hanging over the table between them swayed lightly with the ship's motion. Shaw drew hard on his own pipe, poured a small amount of rum into his mug, corked the bottle, and passed it back to the captain.

"The way you treat your niggers, Señor Shaw, I like it."

The captain, Alonzo Frederico Miguel Figeroa, was a short, bald-headed man with a brushy salt and pepper mustache that curved down around the sides of his mouth like a permanent frown. He was thick everywhere, from the thick round face and stumpy neck to the broad barrel chest that ran down to a waist almost as wide, to the large muscled arms with heavy sailor's forearms, fat hands and thick, stubby fingers. It was as though he were an oversized fleshy infant whose proportions never changed through life, but rather became larger, more toughened and weathered. When he smiled, and sometimes when he spoke, you could see the black gap on the left side of his mouth. He had lost three teeth, yanked out long ago during a hurricane off Bermuda, when he was gripping a mastline in his jaw while tying off another. He was also without half the ring finger on his left hand. He cut it off himself after crushing it against some rigging in '09 on the southern passage to Brazil. It was useless; besides, better to lose a finger than to have it go gangrenous and kill him outright. Because of it, though, he wore his wedding ring on his right hand. His wife, a devoted Catholic like himself, went to church every day and kept their home, a bright two-story cottage on a sunny side street up from the Lisbon docks, in perfect order. She had borne him nine children, five of whom had survived to adulthood. His oldest son, Tomás, was a ship's captain, too, and ran cargo from Europe to the Americas and back. Figeroa owned the *Teçora* and had selected its crew, which was mostly Portuguese, but also included a few Spaniards, and Paolo, the mulatto from Brazil. Compared to Shaw, who managed to maintain the glean and bearing of a nobleman about him no matter what the surroundings, the captain looked ugly and inappropriate. Yet Figeroa maintained an aura of authority always. He was a smart sailor and ran a tight ship. There had been many times when he had out-skippered faster British or American cruisers looking to intercept slavers.

Figeroa considered himself a good judge of character, but he had found Shaw difficult to figure. The captain knew that before joining the House of Martinez slave brokerage, Shaw had been an agent of Pedro Blanco, owner of the Lomboko slave factory and the number-one dealer of African slaves in the world. Despite the fact that he was an American, Shaw had become Martinez's chief broker. He was reputed to be shrewd, but also man of his word. Figeroa had met him in January. Shaw was looking to contract the transport of six hundred slaves from Lomboko to Cuba. They haggled for nearly a week over the price. What they agreed to was below Figeroa's usual fee for such a journey, but with a more acceptable payment schedule. Instead of the usual 50 percent up front and remainder upon reaching port, Shaw paid the captain in full, and in gold, the day the contract was signed. True, the price they settled on represented nearly a 20 percent discount, but Figeroa had been cheated on owed sums before and decided it was better to have a little less and have it all in hand.

Aside from business dealings, however, he knew very little about Shaw. No one else he talked to before the trip could tell him more, either. Shaw lived like a gentleman in Havana and frequented only the most exclusive of the city's restaurants and salons. He had no wife or family that anyone knew of. It was rumored that he was a fugitive in America and could not return to that country, though no one could say for sure if this was true.

One thing people did say, though, was that Shaw was not a man to be crossed. There was the story of a ship's captain, who four years ago had promised Shaw a shipment of Africans at a specific price. When the captain arrived in Havana, however, he demanded an additional 30 percent markup. Shaw refused. The captain sold his slaves to another dealer at an even larger profit. Two days later the captain was found in the shithouse of a dockside bar with his throat slit and his balls cut off and jammed into his mouth. A man was found in a similar condition about a year ago in Sierra Leone's Freetown. He was later identified as a slave trader from another brokerage firm. It was rumored that he had cheated Shaw on a deal some years before. There was nothing definite to link Shaw to either murder—other than innuendo and speculation, which served as better than proof for most people in the trade.

Figeroa took a long drink out of his mug, then went back to his pipe. "Some men, they whip the niggers until the life is almost gone from their bodies," he said. "Others, they are too soft, worried about damaging the cargo. They let them get away with anything, which ends up making more work and risk for the ship's captain and crew. But you, Señor Shaw, you know exactly how to walk the line with these animals. You keep them in fear, but you keep them intact."

"Perhaps that is because I don't see them as animals, Captain Figeroa. Rather, I see them as they are. As men."

Smoke trickled out through the broad gap in Figeroa's smile.

"Men? As you and I are men in the eyes of God? Of course, you are not serious."

"Yes, I am. They are men. Oh, perhaps they are not as learned and cultured and scientific as we. Perhaps they are a little closer to Eden in their way of life. But they are men, just the same."

"I do not believe that. I do not believe that you believe it, either. They are ignorant, godless creatures. A lower breed, closer to the monkeys in the trees of their homeland than to any whiteman."

"When you transport female slaves, do you take one to your bed to keep you warm at night?"

"Of course. In fact, I was very disappointed to see that you were not bringing any negresses onboard this trip."

"There demand is stronger for the men, though I never mind giving a wench over to a ship's captain to add comfort during his voyage. After all, it is customary, and, as I see it, a courtesy. However, I detest having my property roughed over by the crew. It can depreciate their value, especially if the females are going to purchased for breeding."

"A good point, Señor Shaw."

"Actually, my point rests on a question, captain. You bed-down female slaves on your voyages, yes?"

"Sí."

"So, do you mean to tell me that you have been fornicating with animals, sir?"

Figeroa's lips parted into a smokey grin.

"Let us say, animals with a human form."

"Nonsense, captain. They can reason, they can speak, they have families and farms and laws. They have governments and wars and take slaves of their own. Show me monkeys that do that. As for ignorance, well, I have seen black servants in America and the Indies who have been taught to read and cipher and speak English, Spanish, and French as well as any whiteman. No, they are men. They are people, as are you and I."

"If you believe such a thing, then how can you do what you do, buying and selling them as cattle, as slaves to other men?"

"There have always been slaves, my friend, in almost every human society since time began. In the Bible, the Israelites were slaves in Egypt, and before that the Jews had slaves themselves. Slaves are the spoils of the conqueror. And, at this point in history, Christian whitemen are masters of the earth. The Africans are men, but their simple ways and societies are no match for our science and weapons or our politics or resolve."

"But why do you do this, especially now, when the trading of Africans is outlawed by treaties with the British and the Americans? There is great risk to you."

"I could put the same question to you, sir. Why do you run slaves when your ship and its cargo could be taken by some pasty-faced British officer who came 'long your side with his deck guns pointed at your hull? Why—when you yourself could be imprisoned for captaining a ship carrying Africans fresh from the bush? It is because we are businessmen. We know the market, supply and demand. We know profit and the advantages it can buy. I can make five to ten times from a raw wild African what I can make from landed stock. And you, you get nearly a hundred times more from running this cargo than from running fabrics or looms or other goods from the continent. Of course, such profits always carry risks. But I think that is part of the attraction, too. The risks. It is a man's challenge—such risks—and there are fitting rewards if the task is pulled off. We are just the type of men who are willing to take that type of challenge. A sad attribute of our own character and nature, no doubt."

Figeroa grinned and nodded, but then he shook his pipe at Shaw.

"You still cannot get me to believe they are men."

"Most certainly they are. And like all men who are in chains, they must be watched, beaten, cowed, and reminded that they are less than their captors. Or they will rise up, and then it is we who will be in chains. Or worse."

The risks Shaw had spoken of were not slight. Trade in African-born slaves had been banned in the Western Hemisphere for nearly twenty years. Britain had ended the importation of slaves to its own colonies during the eighteenth century, and the United States outlawed the importation of Africans to its soil in 1809. That same year, the British drafted a treaty that prohibited the taking of slaves from the African continent or taking part in their importation to English, American, or Spanish colonies. The Americans were willing to sign; in fact, the American minister to England at the time, John Quincy Adams, helped to write the treaty. But the African slave trade was extremely lucrative for the Spanish government and its subjects, and the Spanish prince stated he would not sign the treaty unless his government received payment for "perceived losses." The British complied, giving the Spanish over £400,000 sterling. The Anglo-Spanish Treaty became law in 1819. By signing the treaty, Spain and its colonies agreed to deal only in African slaves purchased before 1820 and in *landinos*, slaves descended from slaves. Britain went even further and ended all slavery in its colonies in 1833.

But the British made a major mistake—they did not include a legitimate mechanism in the treaty to ensure Spanish compliance. The Spanish government recognized this and did what it could to subvert the process. Publicly, they created a bureaucracy that supported the tenets of the treaty. Privately, however, payoffs, often termed "special taxes and fees," allowed the slave traders to go on with their activities. After all, the market had not disappeared. If anything, the treaty increased demand and the prices paid for African-born slaves.

The Portuguese became the main purveyors of illegal slaves, although ships under Spanish, French, Dutch, American, and Russian flags were also involved. The majority of Africans were brought to Cuba or Brazil. Portugal and Brazil had no treaty with the British or United States regarding slave trade, and Cuba, with the winking complicity of the Spanish government, continued importing Africans. By some estimates, more than twenty-five thousand African slaves were brought to Cuba in the first twenty years after the treaty went into effect. More than ten times that number were brought to Brazil during the same period. Such activities were hazardous though.

British cruisers patrolled the shipping lanes in search of illegal slavers. If discovered, the ship, slaves, and cargo would be impounded and the captain arrested. The dealer owning the slaves could be tried on charges of piracy and, if found guilty, hanged.

The fate of the Africans depended on where the seizure occurred. If the ship was taken close to Africa, the slaves were returned to an African port and delivered into the hands of a Christian mission. But for Africans intercepted off the coast of Cuba or another Spanish colony, return to Africa was an expensive proposition. The English, in the treaty negotiations, insisted that the Spanish pay the return transport as a "moral obligation," because the Africans were illegally destined for a Spanish port. The Spanish argued that they had no control over renegade elements of society or the destinations of their contraband. Besides, if the English felt so strongly about the morality of the issue, the price of return passages should be of no concern. Morality gave way to economics and the English agreed to an arrangement. Illegal slaves taken in Spanish waters were to be termed *emancipados*. The Spanish government would be obligated to provide each emancipado with a Christian education and apprenticeship to a viable trade. The emancipados, who had no say in their fate, were to give five to seven years of indentured service in return for their apprenticeship and education. After that they were free.

The British saw treatment of emancipados as a fitting compromise if not an outright reward for the Africans. "These ignorant bush people would be introduced to God and the vestiges of civilization, and turned into functional productive members of society," said one British diplomat.

But the British neglected to enforce or monitor these high-minded conversions. True, the Spanish had to produce paperwork showing the emancipados had been apprenticed, and after the terms of the indenturement were met, give proof of the individual being freed. But no independent office or individual was charged with verifying that actions matched documentation. The British merely assigned an unofficial observer to watch and report what he saw. This left the Cuban administration and other colonial governments free to pervert the already dubious arrangement. They did so, selling emancipados as slaves on five- to seven-year contracts. Emancipados were offered at slightly cheaper prices on the market than African-born slaves, or *bozales*, because the plantation owners were contractually bound to turn them over after the allotted time. Even though this was rarely enforced, many plantation owners were wary that the contracts might be upheld by the government or British interference. As a result, the planters had adopted a proven method to ensure they got their money's worth: They worked the emancipados to death.

† † †

"What say you, lookout?"

The man near the top of the middle mast perched on a platform barely a foot square.

"All clear, deck!"

Figeroa scanned the horizon with a spyglass.

"Have we found our shadow again, Captain?"

"One of the men thought he saw a sail an hour earlier, but now there is nothing," Figeroa said. "Not to worry, though, Señor Shaw. As long as we see them soon enough, they will not be able to catch us."

Singbe braced himself on the railing as he shuffled slowly along the deck with the others. He had barely slept last night, and this morning, when the sailors came to take the tribesmen on deck, Singbe was sure he would be left behind. But after the last tribesman went up the ladder, the yellow-haired man came over and looked at Singbe. He took the rags off Singbe's feet, inspected the wounds, and then pulled him up by the chains. Singbe faltered, his feet tender and burning with soreness and pain. The yellow-haired man motioned for him to walk. Singbe shuffled a few steps and then fell forward into the ladder.

"Right. Good enough. Up you go."

The yellow-haired man motioned up the ladder with his pistol. Singbe stared at him for a moment and then began to climb. He tried to push his feet deep into the rungs and climb with his heels, which were less bruised and raw. At the top of the hatch he fell to his knees, but two sailors caught him by the arms and dragged him over to the side with the others. He grabbed the railing and stood.

The tribesmen walked around the deck in their slow parade. Grabeau stayed next to Singbe, ready to catch him if he fell. But Singbe was worried more about the feeling in his stomach than falling. The pain of his feet, the foul taste of the rice, and the rolling of the ship were all conspiring to create a heaving bilious churning in his belly. The price for vomiting his rations would be another lashing, either on the feet again, or on his back. He looked at the railing, concentrating on just moving forward one step at a time.

Grabeau leaned in close and whispered, "I talked to many men last night about your plan. I could only find seven who said they would attempt it if asked. With myself, who I am not sure we should include, and you, nearly a cripple at the moment, we have nine."

"Why would you not join us? You prefer to submit to this?"

"No, but I do prefer living to dying in vain. Singbe, our chains restrict even the simplest of movements. How could we overpower the whitemen like this? And even if we could, they have the guns."

"We attack the whiteman with keys first, at the proper moment. And we take his gun."

"While the others shoot at us?"

Singbe ignored the comment and looked up and down the line.

"There are nearly sixty of us here now. It sickens me to think that only nine of us would be willing to make a stand against these whites."

"Yes. And how many of those nine do you think would desert you at the critical moment?"

"I count twenty-three whitemen. Twenty-three whites and one half-black. Only ten of them have guns. Two of them, the yellow-haired man and the bald one on the raised deck, only have small guns."

"The small guns can kill as well as the long guns."

Singbe said nothing. He shuffled along. The anger now added to the boiling in his stomach.

"Nine!" Singbe yelled, looking back and forth at the line of tribesmen. "Only nine would stand and fight against the whites! Are you men without honor? Without courage? One blackman from any tribe is worth at least three of these soft-bellied whites. Mendemen would not think twice about this challenge. Mendemen have courage and resolve."

A lash came down hard on his shoulder and brushed Grabeau's face.

"Shut up! No talking!"

Singbe did not look at the sailor with the whip. He stared straight ahead and shuffled through a few more steps.

"We are better than they are—no matter how much they beat and starve us. We are freemen, not slaves. Let us take this ship and sail it back into the morning sun to Africa."

The whip slapped Singbe's face. And again on his neck and shoulders.

"Shut up, damn you!"

The sailor raised his arm for another lash. Shaw stopped him and stepped in front of Singbe, halting the procession. The eight guards with muskets lifted their weapons, aiming them at the line.

"What have we here? Yesterday's bastinado wasn't enough? You feel a need to cry out? Perhaps in protest of your treatment, or to announce the details of some sorry little uprising?"

Grabeau slid in front of Singbe and pointed to his feet and then to his head.

"Please, sir, he is in pain from his wounds. It has weakened his mind."

Shaw watched Grabeau and smiled.

"The pain's gone to his head?" Shaw smiled and turned to the sailors. "Well, that's a shame. We'll have to get him medical attention, eh, boys?"

He wheeled and struck Grabeau hard in the face with the whip's handle, knocking to the deck.

"Take that one to the stocks."

Three sailors grabbed Grabeau by the arms and legs and dragged him toward the stocks. Shaw turned back to Singbe, smiled, and drove the whip handle into his stomach. Singbe dropped to his knees. Shaw grabbed him by the throat with one hand and pulled him up on his feet.

"As for you, I think I shall have to get creative."

Singbe's mouth opened as if to reply, but instead of words, vomit shot into Shaw's face and down his hand.

"Bloody Christ!"

Singbe fell to the ground and heaved again onto Shaw's fine black boots.

"Fucking hell."

He kicked Singbe in the ribs and picked him up by the hair.

"This... will cost you dearly. Miguel! Bring me a coil of rope."

"*Sail!* Sail to starboard!"

The man on the mast pointed to a small patch of white flickering on the horizon. Figeroa aimed his spyglass at the sail. A familiar flag waved above it.

"Get the niggers below and locked up," Figeroa yelled. "The one in the stocks, too. Do it now!"

The sailors scrambled, herding the tribesmen to the hatch and into the hold. Grabeau struggled and yelled for Singbe but one of the sailors swept the butt end of a musket across the back of his head, knocking him unconscious. Shaw paid no heed to the activity. He looped the rope around Singbe's feet and hands and took off the manacles. With the help of two sailors he dragged him up the stairs to the raised deck in the stern.

"Union Jack on the ship!" the sailor on the mast called out. "British ship starboard."

Shaw tied-off the free end of the rope to a cleat and, together with the sailors, pulled Singbe up on the rail.

"You will understand who is in charge here, buck. Even if it's the last thing you do."

Shaw pushed Singbe over the railing. It was about a fifteen-foot drop to the water. Singbe could hear the wind rushing through his ears. His body slapped into water flat, face first, and sank quickly. The rope stretched out and brought Singbe to the surface. His body spun in the ship's wake. Water rushed into his mouth and nose.

"Señor Shaw! What are you doing?"

"Providing an education to my property, Captain."

"Well, cut the line or bring him. We've got a British cruiser on the starboard."

Shaw looked out at Singbe, bobbing and gasping in the surf behind the *Teçora*.

"You are not saying that towing one sorry black behind us will allow that ship to catch up, are you, Captain?"

"What I'm saying is that I need all hands on tackle and sails to outmaneuver that ship. I need these men. And I do not argue with anyone on my ship. Make a decision, Señor Shaw. Now."

Shaw was not accustomed to being told what to do. He looked from the captain to the two sailors, and smiled. He said, "But Captain Figeroa, you must understand . . . "

Figeroa drew his knife and reached out to the rope. Shaw grabbed on to the line.

"My black, Captain. I say whether he lives or dies. Pull, lads. Pull him in now."

It took about two minutes to get Singbe back on board. He fell to the deck, bloated and lifeless. The sailors walked away. The captain looked over from the ship's wheel and laughed.

"Looks like that black had his own say about living and dying, Señor Shaw."

Shaw dropped to his knees and pushed Singbe's belly up into his ribs with both hands. Water bubbled out of his mouth and onto the deck. Shaw pushed again. He turned Singbe on his side and struck hard on his back. He sat Singbe up, reached around from his back with both hands made a fist and squeezed up hard into the abdomen. Singbe's body twitched. An explosion of water shot from his mouth and nostrils followed by a heaving gag. He rolled onto his side coughing, retching, and gagging violently. More water and foam poured from his mouth. On each gurgling, wheezing inhalation, his body shook with a little more life.

Shaw stood soaked with the water and foam from Singbe's lungs. He was breathing hard, but he smiled broadly at Figeroa.

"My black, Captain. I say whether he lives and dies. And when."

Figeroa glanced at Shaw and then back to the British ship, which, although a bit closer, was still far off.

"Such declarations are blasphemy and an abomination to the Lord God in heaven, Señor Shaw."

Shaw knelt back down and began to put the manacles back on Singbe's wrists and ankles.

"Well, I've suffered enough loss on this voyage. More than the usual ten percent or so. If God wants any more of my Africans, he'll have to bid on them at the market in Havana like everyone else."

Figeroa laughed hard and crossed himself. "You are a funny man, Señor Shaw. But I believe you will taste the fires of hell."

"You can buy me a drink when we get there, Captain."

Shaw threw Singbe over his shoulder and carried him across the deck and down the hatch. Singbe lay there for the rest of the day and into the night, spitting up and trying to clear the water from his lungs. Every time he drew a breath it pierced like a crooked blade twisting inside his chest. His whole body felt as if it had been beaten and wrung out. Grabeau sent him messages through the others but Singbe did not reply.

It took a few hours, but the *Teçora* lost the British cruiser. They were near Cuba now, and it was likely that they would see British ships again. Figeroa and Shaw agreed that the Africans should stay below for the rest of the voyage. Two days later they dropped anchor in a secluded harbor about fifteen miles up the coast from Havana. That night, at about eight o'clock, the Africans were put in the long boats and taken ashore.

Havana

Pepe's eyes lingered on the two girls sleeping on the bed while his hands mechanically put on his clothes. The tall one with the hair the color of whiskey had been a devil. Her skin, white like a cloud and soft as a spring evening, seemed to rub against him everywhere. Her green eyes had burned and smiled with fire and mischief, always looking at him, whether she was screaming with glee or cooing with delight. And the other, the raven-haired, cinnamon-skinned one with a magnificent ass that bobbed and arched and shook with pleasure, she had been insatiable. Señora Dionona had not lied. They were worth every cent.

He paused before fastening his collar. It was still early, not even eight. He could wake the girls and begin again. So what if Montes would have to wait a few hours? As he turned the possibilities over in his thoughts he could feel himself rousing below. He smiled and finished his collar. Then he took a slip of paper from his jacket, wrote a short note, and folded into it a gold coin. The dark girl began to stir. Pepe hurried out of the room before she woke and changed his mind. At the main door he gave the note to Dionona's huge house man.

"A deposit, Ramón. Make sure Señora gets it. I want the same two for tonight."

"Of course, Señor Ruiz."

Pepe looked back at Señora Dionona's, then stepped smiling into the street. Havana was alive with movement and brilliant color. The sky glowed deep blue against the rising sun and white stucco buildings. The sounds and smells of commerce and the sea drifted up from the harbor. It was wonderful to be in Havana, and wonderful to be Pepe Ruiz, a rare man of singular advantages. He was just twenty-four and very handsome, with curly black hair, brown eyes, a pencil-thin mustache, and a full, brilliant smile that he loved to shine on the ladies. Slim and above average height for the day—above five-eight, maybe five-ten with boots on—Pepe was born into advantage and educated at private schools in Connecticut. He spoke English as well as any highborn Yankee, adequate French, and Spanish like a nobleman. While his inheritance had left him a comfortable estate, he had increased his lot through shrewd business dealings, mostly in the slave trade. He would buy bozales in bulk at the Havana market, anywhere between thirty and sixty at a time. Then he would charter a coastal bark and take the slaves to cities and larger towns across the island where he would sell them for twice or three times what he paid.

He lit a cigar and walked down the street to the barber. He would get a shave and then go down to the baracoons to meet Montes and see the bozales that Shaw kept bragging about last night.

Grabeau squatted with his back against the baracoon bars and bit into a large uncooked yam. He chewed it slowly, savoring the sweet juice covering the inside of his mouth.

"This whiteman's land is ugly and loud. They are like ants the way they all rush about from place to place. Their city is filled with noise and the smell of horse dung. They treat us like we are less than dogs." He took another bite, "But I must admit, I do like this fruit they call 'papas.'"

Singbe stood next to him. He had already finished his meal—a yam, a banana, half a dried fish, and two cups of water. He stared out of the bars and sighed. The baracoon reminded him of the pens on the Gallinas River. It was a huge oblong cage with wooden bars that rose almost twenty feet from the ground and a mesh of reed serving as a roof. It held only men, at any given time between 1,000 and 1,500 of them, all Africans—the bozales as they were known locally. African women, perhaps as many as 150, were kept in a smaller baracoon off to the left. Landinos—slaves of African descent who were either born on the island or brought there from Africa before 1820—were relegated to barracks-style warehouses to the left of the women's baracoon. In front of these structures, a smaller cage had been created for inspection and viewing. In front of that was a raised platform that served as an auction area.

But unlike the cages in Lomboko, these stood at the center of a city, Havana, and at the convergence point of two great open-air markets. While some of the captives in the baracoons had been provided with burlap loincloths, most remained completely naked. People from all the city's social divisions would pass by and stop to look at the Africans, pointing, laughing, discussing seriously. Young boys often threw rocks at the cage or spit at the blacks through the bars. Four times a day, a train would slowly pass by, terrifying the Africans. Passengers would lean out the cars to see the men and women fresh from the Dark Continent.

Singbe and Grabeau had been in Havana for ten days, coming to the city under the cover of night from the outlying jungle. After getting off the ship, the yellow-haired man and other whites waiting on the shore led all the tribesmen through the jungle to a clearing. At the center of the clearing were five rambling dirt-floored shacks, much like long rectangular warehouses, holding the landinos. Next to them were the baracoons. There were barrels of rice and water, and the tribesmen were allowed to eat and drink and talk as much as they wanted each day. Singbe met other Mendemen he knew who had been held in a different part of the ship. Many felt better about their situation. They were still slaves wearing shackles and guarded by whitemen with guns, but their stomachs were full and the whitemen encouraged them to walk and exercise in the clearing during the daylight hours. Perhaps, some of the tribesmen said, the whites of this land were not as bad as the whites of the ship.

The yellow-haired man stayed among them for only a day. He returned a week later at night and led them all out of the jungle to the city's gates. They were allowed to pass into the city just after dawn. They were herded into the baracoon where the shackles were removed, leaving just the manacles as bracelets around the ankles and wrists. Some recognized faces among the others who were already there. Many were elated just to be without the chains and began turning somersaults, back flips, and other gymnastics commonly performed at tribal festivals and celebrations.

Singbe's feet had healed. His body felt strong and whole again. He ached to tear the manacles from his body and to run free. He spent the days thinking of Stefa and his children and trying to keep the demons from his mind.

He also wondered how they were going to get back to Mende. It was obvious they needed a ship, but he could no longer see the ocean, although he could smell it on the breeze each morning. He talked to the other tribesmen in the pen with him, but not many had any interest in his ideas of rebelling against the whitemen. Most thought it was madness to attempt such a thing in this city of whites. Besides, they could not get out of the pen except through the door, which was locked with chains and guarded by whites with guns.

"It is not so bad," said one Mende tribesman, Be-li, a few days after they were put in the baracoon. "True, we are slaves, and that is a sorry lot. But we are well fed and treated fine as long as we do as they say. And perhaps they will not keep us forever, but only for a few years, as the Timmani do with their slaves."

Singbe did not care for such senseless talk or compromising

sentiments. He had never owned a slave, nor would he serve as slave to any man. Besides, Be-li may have his hopes about a short-lived servitude, but Singbe did not believe it. He saw the way the guards would take out selected tribesmen from the baracoon and lock them into the standing stock at the platform. The white men with high hats and fine clothes would poke and prod and slap bodies as if they were appraising goats or cattle for trade. Slaves to the whitemen were livestock, and Singbe was fairly sure that this arrangement remained until the slave died, escaped, or killed his master. Those were the fates that Singbe had resigned himself to. He would try to flee, try and find a way back to Mende, to Stefa, their children, and his father. He would kill his master or the yellow-haired man, or anyone else who would try to stop him. And he had decided he would rather be killed trying to escape than work as a slave. Sooner or later they will let him out of this cage and put him to work. When they did, that's when he would make his attempt.

Grabeau had finished his potato. He let out a growling belch and looked up at Singbe.

"How goes sowing the seeds of insurrection among these tribesmen?"

Singbe sighed and pressed his face against the bars.

"There are a few, but not enough. Very few even have interest in talking of the subject. I hear the same replies. Many say it is madness. I tell them being a slave to the whiteman or any man is just as much madness. They laugh at me. Their bellies are full and they are afraid."

"And you are not?"

"No. I am terrified. I am terrified that I will be a slave, that I will never see my wife and children and my father ever again. I am terrified that I am trapped in this twisted whiteman's land and will die here."

Singbe turned his eyes back out through the bars and watched the citizens of Havana pass by. They wore fine, elaborate clothes of all colors and patterns. Many of the white women had red paint on their lips and cheeks and wore ruffled hats with broad brims or bright wraps that covered most of their hair. The men wore polished boots like those of the yellow-haired man, and wide, fat hats in shades of black, brown, and gray. They all talked and laughed and walked by on their way to the market or their businesses or homes. The morning sun was about halfway up in the sky. Already, the temperature had risen to near ninety.

"Did you ever face a leopard during a hunt?"

Grabeau laughed. "No. I have killed boar and antelope, as well as many of the small animals. But I have never been on a leopard hunt."

"I came upon a leopard once in the bush, a big male with a large terrible head. I was as far from him as I am from you now. And I was alone, Singbe said."

"Tell me of how this happened, and of how it is that you are still alive after such a meeting."

"It was more than half my life ago. Twelve, no, now it is thirteen, thirteen harvests past. It was my first hunt after my passage to manhood and induction into Poro, the society of men. I was with my father and his brothers and father. We had been in the wilds for three days hunting boar, but all we had killed were rats. Eight of them. I was sick of rat, I tell you. There was no honor in killing such small creatures. And besides, they tasted like sand.

"Each night we would hear the voices of leopards and lions and elephants through the sounds of the bush. Every once in a while, a howl would come from close by, making my heart jump. I was a man now and had to remind myself to think as a man, to not be afraid like a boy. But inside I still held much of a boy's fears, especially of the leopard. I do not know why the leopard scared me more than lions or wild boar or panthers. But in my dreams I would see him come for me over and over again, and rip me apart with his huge claws and teeth.

"After the third night, my grandfather took me aside and told me he had heard me cry out the leopard's name in my sleep. I became very upset. I told him I have dishonored the trial of manhood and Poro. I must not be worthy of being a man because I still carried a deep inner fear of the leopard. My grandfather laughed hard and put his arm around me. He told me there was nothing wrong with fearing the leopard, that it was indeed a great and terrifying animal. All men have such fears, he said, not just of leopards, but of many things. But what makes the difference between a man and one whose body has simply grown into a man's frame is that a man knows his fear and feels it, but he does not let it control him. Instead he meets the subject of his fright face-to-face, eye-to-eye. He may feel dread terror run through his veins, but he does not give himself in to it. He holds his ground, confronts the fear, and takes the proper action, whatever that may be. It was wise advice, but I still felt the terror, hiding in my chest, gnawing at my heart.

"The next day, in the hour when the long shadows of the day draw the sun down from the sky, I found myself face-to-face with my fear, although I tell you, I had not planned it that way. I had been tracking a boar with my father. I was very excited because I love the taste of boar meat, but I also knew him to be a dangerous opponent. My father had gone in one direction and I in the other. We hoped to approach the animal from either side and drive him into our hunting companions. I had only been on a few hunts and had little experience tracking boar. My eyes and mind were focused on the ground, looking for signs of the animal's trail. I do not know how long I stalked him, but I remember taking a step and stopping suddenly with the feeling that everything around me had changed. Exactly what it was that was different I could not say. It was as if the air had turned raw and sharp, the bush more wild and dark. And then I heard it—a low, rolling growl. I looked up slowly. There, on a fallen tree, less than three paces in front of me, was a tremendous leopard. Between his paws he held the lifeless body of the boar we had been tracking. Deep jagged claw marks stretched down the boar's hind-quarters. There was a huge hole in his neck and blood covered the leopard's mouth.

"I do not know how it was that I had been able to walk up so close to the leopard. Perhaps my scent and sounds had been lost in the smell of the boar's blood and the leopard's own feasting. Whatever the reason, there I was. And I knew the great beast could leap at me and tear out my heart in a breath. Already he was rising above the boar and growling louder. I had only my knife and the small spear I had crafted just ten days before. I was so gripped with fright I could not move or breathe."

"What did you do?"

"My instinct was to run and pray the beast did not give chase. Because he would want to protect his prey, it was a good bet he might not follow a skinny scared-to-shit young Mendeman. At least that was my thought. And running may have been the smartest thing to do. I had no bow or arrows. I would have to stab the leopard in the heart with my spear to kill it. That is, if I could pierce its heart. And even then, the leopard would not die right away. It would fight and claw to its death, and probably kill me in the process."

"So you ran?"

"I did not. At first it was because I could not. I was so afraid, my legs had turned to stone. No matter how hard I tried, I could not get them to move. The blood surged in my body and beat loudly in my ears and head. I knew the leopard could smell my fear, and that it would whet his appetite to kill again. At that point I was sure I would die. But somewhere in all of that, I suddenly heard my grandfather's voice, his words from the past night. And I thought, if I must die, I will not die a boy. I will be a man. And I felt my right hand with the spear rise, my left slowly drawing the knife. My feet, still heavy with terror, shifted slightly toward the leopard. If he moved, I would drive my spear and knife into his heart. At least, this was my plan.

"The leopard let out a throaty roar. I screamed my war cry with all my lungs and drew back the spear. The leopard arched his back and crouched. Then he took the boar in his great jaws and slowly backed off the tree. He disappeared into the bush, growling loudly all the way."

Grabeau smiled. He stood and put his arm on Singbe's

shoulder. "Singbe, you are as much a man as any I have met. But here in this land of the whiteman the leopards are everywhere, and they have guns. We have no way out of this cage and no boat to leave this land. And even if we did acquire a boat, I am not sure we could ever find our way back to Mende. We are in a world of shit, my friend. A rebellion here and now would not get us home, it would not get you back to your beloved family. It would just get us killed."

Singbe shook his head. "I will be dead before I am a slave."

A familiar face outside the baracoon caught Grabeau's eye. He spit on the ground and nodded.

"We are slaves, my friend."

Singbe followed Grabeau's glare. It was the yellow-haired man.

"Señor Ruiz, Señor Montes, I own ninety percent of the blacks in this baracoon. Two thirds of them are just off the boat from Africa two weeks ago."

Pepe stood with Pedro Montes. Nearly six feet tall and deeply weathered, Montes had been a minor partner with Pepe on several ventures over the last two years, although today he was acting as his own agent. Montes was twice Pepe's age and had dark brown eyes, thinning salt and pepper hair, and a thick, brushy mustache that reached down nearly to his chin. His skin was dark and leathery, marked from over thirty years as a seaman. He had captained coastal schooners, running cargo through the waters off Cuba and to the outlying islands. But he retired ten years ago for the more lucrative and less backbreaking trade of slave broker. Most of his dealings came on order rather than through the type of speculative buying that Pepe did. Of course he dealt in landinos and emancipados, but it was the African blacks, the bozales, who brought the big profits. And that's what he was looking for today.

"Do you have any children?" Montes asked. "I need three girls and a boy for a client in Puerto Principe."

"Certainly. How old?"

"Between seven and twelve years."

"Let us go to the low barracks on the left."

"In a minute, Shaw," Pepe said, stepping closer to the baracoon. "First I want to take a look at some of these men."

"If Señor Montes has no objections, my assistant can show him the children. Manuel."

Montes and Shaw's man walked over to the small warehouses. Pepe pointed at the baracoon with his walking stick.

"That one. And those two. Are they yours?"

"Of course, of course. Almost all of them are mine. And, if you happen to select a black among this lot that is not mine, I can guarantee you we could find a comparable if not superior specimen from my own stock."

"What about that one over to the left? The one staring at us from just behind the bars."

"Ah, Señor Ruiz, your eye for the merchandise is, as always, excellent. That is a most spirited blackman, I can assure you. In fact I had personal dealings with him on the voyage over."

"Let me see him up close. Him and those three over there."

"Certainly."

Shaw walked over to the gatekeeper and pointed to the men he wanted. The gatekeeper grabbed some metal collars and, backed by five of his own heavily armed men, unlocked the door and walked into the baracoon. The noise and talking among the tribesmen stopped. They all stood still and watched the whitemen. Guards at the bars and in platforms above the baracoon leveled their muskets, hammers cocked.

"Those two there, Luis," Shaw yelled. "That one on the other side. And the taller one over here near the bars."

The men used the long sticks with ropes at the end, tightening the nooses around the necks of the tribesmen. Two men held muskets at their heads while manacles were put on the wrists and ankles. The tribesmen made no move to resist. They were led out and locked into the stocks on the platform.

"Be careful with that next one, Luis. He might struggle. I want no damage or accidents."

"Si, Señor Shaw."

Shaw turned to Pepe.

"Last week one of the bucks made a fuss when they came in

to get him. One of Luis's lads got itchy and pulled a trigger. Splattered brains and blood everywhere."

"Damned shameful waste of property."

"Worse so because he was one of mine."

They both laughed and watched as the men approached Singbe. Singbe did not resist the rope, but neither did he volunteer to walk when the man had set the manacles and pulled at the stick; that is, not until the other man coolly placed the musket barrel against his skull. Singbe looked at him defiantly and then shuffled his way toward the stock. Pepe walked up the platform with Shaw.

"They are all fine choices, Señor Ruiz. Excellent for the fields and for breeding. Get some of that spirited African blood into your lazy, domesticated landino stock."

Pepe began inspecting the tribesmen. They were locked in standing upright and unable to move. He slapped legs and felt arms and shoulders. He ran his hands across their skin looking for whip marks that had been covered with tar. He looked closely at their eyes for signs of jaundice or scurvy, and checked heads for lice. When he got to Singbe, he went around behind and grabbed the muscles of his back and buttocks. He slapped both legs hard with the palm of his hand. Then he walked around front and pried open Singbe's mouth to look at the teeth. Singbe made no sound or move, until Pepe took a step back. Then he spit.

"Bastard!" Pepe slapped his glove into Singbe's face. "Did you see that, Shaw? That black fucking bastard almost hit me with that."

Pepe pulled back his hand so he could hit Singbe full on. Shaw caught it and held him at the wrist.

"A spirited buck, isn't he, Señor? Although he's nothing a seasoned overseer can't teach to fetch and heel. Or perhaps you will do so yourself, when he is yours. However, until then, I can't have you damaging my stock. Besides, like you said, 'almost,' yes?"

Pepe glared at Shaw and then dropped his hand. "Fine. Mark them. All of them. I'll take them all."

Luis put a dash of white paint on the shoulder of each tribesman on the platform and a similar dash on the iron collars around their necks.

"Certainly this won't be all of your purchases, Señor Ruiz?"

"Certainly, it won't, Señor Shaw. I'm looking to buy quite a few of these niggers. Provided the price is right."

"Oh, I'm sure we will be able to do business. Come, show me your other choices."

Pepe spent the rest of the morning having Shaw's men parade tribesmen out into the stocks and inspecting them. Some he liked, others were sent back into the pen unmarked. By noon he had selected those he wanted. Forty-nine in all. Montes had found his four children, too. Loose iron collars were fitted around all of the slaves' necks. Pepe, Montes, and Shaw would meet after the siesta and haggle prices. Then Pepe would pay a visit to the customs officer and provide a "donation" for *trespassos*—papers certifying the Africans were in fact landinos legal for transport and sale.

It was almost night. Singbe had rubbed the white spot on his shoulder with dirt and water until most of it had come off.

Grabeau had watched, not speaking. He tugged at the collar around his neck and gestured at it. "Now wash this one off."

"Grabeau. Always the comedian."

Grabeau smiled. "Well, at least we have the same slave master, unless he trades us again."

"He must. He had tens of tribesmen marked with the white paint. No man owns so many slaves."

Grabeau spit and pointed out toward the others in the baracoon.

"The yellow-haired man does. He owns all in this pen, I think."

"True. But he sells us. He is a merchant."

"So now what happens?"

"They will take us like they took the others. In a wagon, or walking, but to where . . . ?"

They sat silently, watching dark clouds roll in from the harbor to cover the sun setting in the west. A light rain began.

About two hours later, the guard opened the gate, his men carrying guns and torches. The tribesmen with collars around their necks were singled out and made to stand in line. A man threaded a length of chain through the ring in the front of the neck collars, locking it at the first and last man. They were marched out of the baracoon and down the street. The four small children, also fitted with collars and chains, followed behind the caravan.

They walked out of the city and back through the jungle. After about an hour of walking, Singbe felt the mud give way to a more grainy soil. The air, floating through the rain on a light breeze, began to smell different than the air in the jungle or the town. They walked up a small hill and down into a clearing. Singbe could hear the soft roar of waves.

"Grabeau, up ahead."

"I see. I see. But we are in chains."

Singbe stared at the long black schooner sitting at the edge of a narrow dock. "Not for long, my friend," he said.

† † †

Shaw placed the gold in his safe, closed the door, and took a long drink out of his glass. Pepe Ruiz was a good businessman, he would give him that. He had bought all forty-nine of the blacks for $450 a head, about $10 a head cheaper than Shaw thought he would sell them for. He had paid Pedro Blanco $100 a head in Africa, and it cost nearly $30 each to transport them to Cuba, not to mention that nearly a third of those were lost. He had brought the ears back with the manifest as proof, but the insurance would only pay 15 percent, if they paid at all. Still, everything accounted for, he had made a nice profit this afternoon. And he had two other men, a Brazilian and an American, coming to look tomorrow. Business was good. Despite the losses of the voyage, this would be his most lucrative venture yet.

Shaw finished the cognac and refilled the glass. A nice little buzz had begun in his head. He would give it a bit of a boost and then head out. He was to meet one of the city's great merchants, the Frenchman Didreau. Shaw thought it was time to diversify into other areas—precious metals, sugar, fabrics. Didreau had connections in Europe and America. Perhaps, Shaw thought, it may even be time to go back to America. For a moment the sounds and flavors of New Orleans drifted through his mind. Yes, perhaps. But for now it would be dinner, a good meal, and then a trip to a salon. He was considering Señora Dionona's. He had been there the night before and actually preferred a few other houses over it, but Pepe had spoken of a pair who he said were quite talented.

Stepping outside into the rain, he thought briefly of sending a boy for his carriage, but then decided to walk. It was not raining that hard and the restaurant was just around the corner. But after? Yes, after he would want the carriage. He would send for it while he was eating. He pulled his collar up against the rain and gripped his walking stick tightly. The cobblestones glistened in the pale lamplight outside his office.

He was nearly to the corner when he heard his name called from behind. Before he could turn around, a kick to the back of the legs dropped him to his knees. The walking stick flew from his hands. A sharp blow to the head sent him facedown into the street. He reached for the small revolver he kept in his jacket and tried to stand at the same time. A kick to the ribs stopped both. A strike to his hand knocked the gun loose. Two huge hands grabbed his coat, pulled it down around his arms and threw him back into an alley. He landed face first in the mud.

"Remember me, you fucking American pig?"

The voice spoke in Portuguese. Shaw looked up through the blood and mud in his eyes. He could see a large figure of a man, but nothing else. It was too dark. A boot flew up out of the blackness and hit him flush on the chin, knocking him over onto his back. Shaw felt two teeth break off in his mouth. His jaw was numb. He tried to stand but another sharp blow sent him back to the mud. The strength seeped from his body, his consciousness was slipping away. His hands fumbled weakly, seeking any kind of assistance. The left tugged hopelessly at one of his own boots, the right grabbed clods of mud in search of a hold. Another kick hit him square in the ribs with a cracking sound. The figure stepped up closer.

"I want you to remember me, Shaw. Before I kill you."

A hand reached down and pulled Shaw up by the hair. A glint of steel sparked in the rain. Shaw felt a cold, sharp blade pressing against his throat.

"Do you remember? Pig?"

Shaw's left hand had found what it was looking for in his boot. He swung his arm up and drove his own knife deep up into the center of the figure. The man let out a loud, high-pitched animal scream. He dropped the blade at Shaw's throat and let go of his hair. Shaw shook and twisted his knife inside the man, turning and thrusting it in every direction. Hot blood sprayed into Shaw's face and ran down his arm. The man fell on top of him, twitching and writhing. Shaw reached down and drew his knife deeply across the man's throat. The body heaved and turned in a violent gasping gurgle. It rolled forward and then stopped, dead, on Shaw's legs.

Shaw fell back in the mud, still clutching the knife, exhausted and aching everywhere. He turned his head to the side and spit out some of the blood that had filled his mouth. After a few minutes he was able to raise his legs, kick the body off. He found his walking stick and pulled himself up. Fifteen minutes later he was back in his office, bruised and bloody. He called a boy to send for his surgeon. Cracked ribs, a broken jaw, and four broken teeth. It would be months before he would heal.

The next morning a body was found in the alley—throat slashed and testicles stuffed in the mouth. It took several days before someone made the identification—a mulatto Portuguese sailor named Paolo Cotidiano.

Amistad

"Singbe? Singbe?"

"He is not here. We do not know... We are not sure..."

"He is dead. Singbe is dead."

The words shocked Singbe out of his sleep. His body jerked forward trying to sit up, but the chain at his neck slapped his head back down onto the wooden platform. He blinked his eyes but it was all black. For a moment he thought perhaps he was dead. But then the heavy salt breath of the sea and the stink of the hold drifted up into his mind, assuring him that he was still very much alive.

Singbe closed his eyes and watched again the images of his dream—his father walking into his hut calling his name, and Stefa, standing with the man from the other dreams, trying to answer. The man answered for her, saying Singbe is dead. A shiver ran through Singbe's body as the images of the dream danced in his mind. He tried to sit up again, pushing against the chain. It yielded only a few inches and then froze. Singbe let out a great sigh and gently dropped his back onto the platform.

"I need to go! These chains. This ship. This place. I need to go from it all!"

"Shut-up," someone muttered sleepily in the darkness. "Shut up and sleep."

The ship was called *Amistad*, which means "friendship" in Spanish. A sleek, black-hulled, two-masted schooner, it was built and fitted in Baltimore, Maryland, specifically for coastal slave transport. Ruiz and Montes had chartered the ship for the four-and-a-half day voyage to Puerto Principe. Montes's slaves were already sold. Ruiz planned to sell his to owners of sugarcane plantations. The fine male bozales fresh from Africa would bring as much as $1,000 a head; this in a day when the average working man made about $7 a week.

The *Amistad* was captained by Ramón Ferrer, a local sailor who had been running slaves and other cargo around Cuba and the outlying islands for nearly twenty years. The small crew—two sailors, Juan Escondo and Pablo Evangelista, a mulatto cook named Celestino, and Ferrer's slave cabin boy, Antonio—was typical for coastal hauling. Montes had captained coastal slave packets himself for many years and knew Ferrer well. The captain and men were experienced in the handling of slaves and the risks involved with carrying bozales. British cruisers patrolled the waters, and though the dealers held trespassos for their slaves, a boarding British officer would know enough to question some of the slaves. If it was discovered that they didn't speak Spanish, the slaves would immediately be declared contraband. Slaves, cargo, and ship would be seized, and the captain arrested.

Amistad left the small harbor near Havana on the night of June 28. The weather was hot and very humid, even on the open sea. So much so, in fact, that the captain had his mattress dragged up onto the raised deck in the stern where he could sleep under the ocean breezes.

The slaves were kept in the main hold, chained and lying down on slightly inclined platforms that ran down both sides of the hull. The platforms had a two-inch lip on the low side near the aisle, along with a gutter. The lip gave the slaves something to brace their feet against in rough seas. The slight incline also offered somewhat of an escape for human waste; the wooden gutter caught it, making it easier for the crew to clean. Each long line of slaves was held together by a single chain that ran through the neck collars and was locked to a ring in the wall. The ankles were also fastened to the wooden platform lip with a large bolt. Because of this configuration, trying to move more than just a few inches to either side was uncomfortable if not impossible. The heavy stink of the main hold, which would not be cleaned out until after the ship put into port, and the heat and humidity of late June, made lying on the platforms even more unbearable. Along with the fifty-three slaves—which were listed by the names they had been given on the trespassos—the ship's manifest also held $40,000 worth of cargo that included two crates of caning machetes, thirty bolts of fine fabric, ten trunks of finished men's clothes, five kegs of dried beef, a crate of medicines for the doctor in Puerto Principe, and $2,500 in gold coins.

Though Ruiz and Montes preferred to keep the slaves locked down for the whole trip, both men knew it was important to get the Africans some exercise each day. Without it, restlessness could set in. Slaves had been known to hurt themselves or other slaves in such a state. Besides, if the slaves were stiff and tired after a four-day trip, Ruiz would have to keep them off the market for a few days while they recovered. That meant additional food and storage costs. The slave traders decided to bring the slaves out of the hold in shifts of five or six for feeding and light exercise. Montes suggested they restrict their movements to the early morning and late afternoon, making it more difficult for the deck activity to be spotted by the spyglass of a passing British frigate.

Grabeau was in the first group brought on deck. Squinting through the bright sunlight, he could see two other Mendemen coming out of the hatch, Burnah, a muscular blacksmith who was about twenty-three, and Fakina, the teenage son of a village king. They were followed by Furie, a Timmani farmer in his early twenties, and his father Pi-e; both were captured together in their rice field by rival tribesmen. The neck chains were undone on all the men, leaving only the ankle manacles.

Pepe took the butt of his musket and lightly pushed it against Burnah's back. "Walk," he commanded. "All of you, walk. Get some exercise."

The tribesmen took tentative steps. After being locked down in the hold for more than thirty hours, the glare of sunlight stung their eyes. Sore legs, manacles, and the slightly rolling deck made steps and balance uncertain. Pepe tolerated their addled gait and followed slowly behind, crooking the gun in his arms. Even though the sun had only risen an hour or so ago, the heat and humidity were already soaking his clothes with sweat. Montes sat on the foredeck, bare-chested and holding a pistol. One of the sailors, Juan, leaned against a mast with a musket in his hand and stared lazily at the shuffling tribesmen. The other sailor, Pablo, was at the top of the jib mast pounding loudly with a hammer, trying to nail down a loose cleat that held the sail's tackle. He smacked his thumb twice, dropping a few nails onto the deck.

After about ten minutes, the cook, Celestino, appeared at the doorway of the galley, a small room cut into the base of the raised bow deck. He was a moon-faced man with a deep voice, a large Roman nose, and a big, frequent smile of perfect yellow teeth. His great bald head was covered by a bright red kerchief. A silver loop dangled from the lobe of his left ear. His skin was only a shade or two darker than the Cuban sailors. Just under six feet, lean and muscular, he wore a smock apron and a pair of tattered pants cut off just above the knees. He stood barefoot in the doorway straddling two large buckets filled with potatoes and bananas. Behind him was a barrel of water.

"Bring dem sorry niggers over here, Señor Ruiz."

Pepe pointed the gun barrel toward the Africans and nodded his head. "C'mon. Breakfast."

Celestino handed each tribesman a raw potato, a banana, and a tin cup of water. After they all received food, Pepe waved at them on with the gun. "Walk. Walk and eat."

When they had finished eating, Pepe motioned for them to give the cups back to Celestino. Burnah was the last to do this. But instead of handing in his cup, he held out to the cook and motioned for more. Celestino broke out into a great laugh.

"Hey, boss. Dis here nigger wants another drink."

"One cup each is fine."

"You hear dat, nigger. The ownerman says you gots enough."

Burnah smiled, took the cup to his lips as if to drink, and then held it out.

"Stupid nigger. I says no."

Celestino swung to knock the cup from Burnah's hand. But Burnah had worked with iron and the forge since he was a boy. His grip was unshakable. Celestino's hand just bounced off the cup. Outraged, the cook slapped at the cup again, harder. It didn't budge. Burnah smiled, slowly raised it to his lips and then held it out again toward Celestino.

"Contrary fuckin' African! Señor Ruiz, we's gots a contrary nigger here."

Pepe drew up his musket and walked over to the galley door. "What is it?"

"He wants more water. You says no, so I says no. Now da slave won't give back da cup."

"Oh for the love of Christ, here now..." Pepe pulled at the cup but Burnah would not yield. The sailor at the mast lowered his musket, aiming it at the rest of the tribesmen. Montes walked over from the foredeck, pistol drawn.

"Burnah, let go of the cup," Grabeau cautioned. "Give it to the whiteman."

"All I want is some water."

"They don't want you to have any more, my friend."

"It is only water."

"Yes, but..."

Pepe wheeled and cracked a sharp backhand into Burnah's face and barked, "Shut up! Both of you. Shut up that gibberish and give me that cup."

Adrenaline surged through Burnah. He could feel his arms and legs beginning to shake. He turned away from Pepe and leaned forward, trying to dip the cup in the barrel. Celestino quickly pushed him back and drew a knife off the cutting board.

"Get back, nigger!"

"Burnah, no!"

Pepe slapped Burnah and Grabeau.

"I said shut up."

He cocked the musket and pointed it at Burnah's face.

"Now. Give me that cup. Or by the Blessed Trinity you'll breathe no more."

The gun's muzzle was less than six inches from Burnah's face. Blood thundered through in his head and body. Slowly, carefully, he placed the cup in the palm of his hand, held it out to the whiteman, and smiled. Pepe swung the gun down on Burnah's arm, knocking the cup to the deck.

"I think you need to make an example of this one, Pepe," Montes said returning his pistol to his belt.

"Pedro, I think you're right." Pepe raised the barrel, touching the end lightly against Burnah's lips.

Later, Grabeau told Singbe that the whitemen bound Burnah to the mast with his back exposed and took off his loincloth. Then the young slave trader got a whip and took it to Burnah's back and buttocks. By the fourth lash, the whip glistened with Burnah's blood. Burnah kept his head pointed up and bit down on his lip. He did not cry out right away, but by the sixth strike he could not hold back. After twelve lashes the slave trader stopped. Burnah's back was streaked with blood, his lip was split, and his legs wobbled with weakness and pain. One of the sailors moved to cut Burnah down, but the young slave trader made him wait. He yelled to the cook, who gave him a bottle and a rag. The young slave trader soaked the rag with the bottle's brown liquid and rubbed it into the bloody wounds. Burnah's body seized up as soon as the rag touched him, and loud, anguished screams wrenched up from his throat. It was vinegar.

As he rubbed, the young slave trader talked loudly, first to Burnah, and then to the tribesmen on deck. After he was finished, he threw the rag to the deck and ordered the sailors to take the tribesmen below. Burnah was left tied to the mast, his body sagging against the rope, the legs limp, and his back a smeared wash of blood and tatters of skin. Every so often a small, feeble moan oozed out through his labored breathing. This is what the others met as they were brought on deck. After the last group finished eating and walking, the sailors cut Burnah down and chained him below with the others.

On the second morning, Singbe and four others went on deck for their exercise. Among his companions was Konoma, a member of the Kono mountain tribe. Like many men of his tribe, Konoma had filed his teeth into sharp-looking fangs. Over the years, he had also pushed his teeth against pieces of wood to create a large overbite. The look was much admired by the tribe's women and considered essential if a man wanted to attract a quality wife. But the whitemen knew nothing of these practices. When they saw the sharp protruding teeth, they were sure Konoma was a cannibal. As a result, while the other four slaves had been unchained from their neck collars and were allowed to walk on deck, beneath the sight of Montes's musket, the sailors had fixed a ten-foot chain from Konoma's collar to the mast. He was left there to eat and shuffle from side to side. For his own part, the chaining terrified Konoma. Because of his appearance, he had been flogged repeatedly on the passage from Africa. He never knew the reason for the beatings and thought the whitemen simply took pleasure in making the whip crack against his buttocks and feet. Now, being chained alone while the other four were allowed to walk the deck, he was sure he would be beaten again. He stood nervously with his back against the mast, waiting for one of the whitemen to begin the punishment. Celestino stood at the galley door handing out the rations.

"Don't forget the flesh-eater," one of the sailors yelled.

"You feed him, Juan. I is to cook and to clean, not to risk my life with dese savages."

"You're the cook. You feed the cargo."

"Go ahead, Juan," Ferrer said, laughing, from the ship's wheel on the raised stern. "I can't afford to have one of my deck hands eaten, but I can less afford to lose Celestino. No one else among us can cook."

"But, Captain . . ."

"Go ahead. Do it, man. Unless you are afraid."

Juan straightened his back and thrust out his bare chest, and proclaimed, "I am not afraid of any of these animals."

Juan walked over to the galley and put his musket down. He stuck a potato and banana in his pockets and dipped a cup of water from the bucket. He then stepped back out on the deck. Everyone else had become still. Konoma sensed that something involving him was about to happen. He straightened and stepped away from the mast. Juan saw this and hesitated. He drew the knife from his belt and held it out in front of him, blade forward ready to slash, and walked slowly toward Konoma. Juan stopped just short of where he thought the chain's length would reach. He tossed the banana and potato at Konoma's feet and then quickly put the cup of water down on the deck, spilling most of it with his shaky hands.

Juan turned and looked up at the Ferrer. "You see captain, I am not afraid."

"I see also that you have pissed your pants."

Juan looked down and felt his crotch. The captain and the others broke into laughter. Red-faced, Juan picked up his musket and motioned to the slaves.

"C'mon, walk. Walk, you bastards."

They walked around the deck for nearly a half hour. The captain's slave cabin boy, Antonio, sat with his back against the rail and spun a top for the three girls and young boy that Montes had bought. The ship was about twenty miles off shore and a thin gray strip of coastline could be seen from time to time against the edge of the hazy horizon.

Singbe walked over to the cook to hand in his cup.

"Hey, Pablo. Dis one here tinks he king of the lot. You can tell by the way he walk."

"King of shit, more like it."

Celestino laughed. "Hey, king of shit, give me your cup and I tell you a story. Watch dis, Pablo. I going to have a little joke wid da king."

Celestino took the cup from Singbe's hand. Singbe turned to go but the cook grabbed his wrist.

"See dat?" he said, letting go of Singbe's wrist and pointing to the land. "Dat's wheres you going. Understand? We go from Havana to dare. Puerto Principe."

Celestino pointed down the horizon, then to Singbe, and then up the horizon. Singbe looked at Celestino.

"You go dare. Puerto Principe. Four days." Celestino held up four fingers. "Four days."

Singbe slowly pointed to himself and then toward the coastline.

"Dat's right, you dumb fucking king of da shit. And den you knows what's gonna happen to you when you get dare? Huh?"

Celestino picked up a fat-bladed kitchen knife and drew it across his own throat. "Ssssskt. Like dat," he said, and slapped the knife hard on the cutting board.

"Den chop, chop, chop. Like dat." He pulled the top of a barrel and tipped it toward Singbe. "Den deys gonna make lunch outta yous all. Like dat."

Singbe looked at the barrel of dried meat and then quickly back to Celestino. Celestino laughed. He pointed at Singbe with the knife and then to the meat in the barrel.

"Chop, chop, chop, Señor King."

Singbe staggered back, understanding.

Celestino laughed harder. He reached into the barrel, grabbed a hunk of meat, and bit into it.

"Mmmm-mmm! Fresh nigger!"

Singbe had heard 'nigger' enough to know it was the whiteman's word for the tribesmen. He turned and saw the sailor with the musket laughing, too. Singbe's knees buckled and he fell to the deck. The cook and the sailor laughed even harder.

† † †

Grabeau stared into the hold's oily darkness and tugged at the small beard on his chin.

"This cannot be true."

"I tell you it is. They laughed and laughed when they saw I understood."

"It is not that I doubt your words, Singbe. But to take us across the sea, to starve us and beat us and make us lie in our own shit and piss. And for what? So they may eat us? Are you sure that is what they were saying?"

"That is why they fed us so well while we were in the cage in the city of whitemen," cried Bia. "We all regained our strength and the weight we lost on the first voyage."

"But still, to eat us," Grabeau persisted. "This cannot be. The man who drives this ship has an attendant boy who is black, a slave. He speaks the whiteman's language, but he is still black. Why have they not eaten him? And what about the black men we saw in the city who were slaves to whitemen. They wore clothes as the whitemen do. They carried the whiteman's goods and tended to their animals. They were slaves, not livestock being fattened for a meal."

"Perhaps there are different tribes of whitemen just as there are different tribes among the blacks," said Burnah. "After all, the Milawasi in the far south are said to be cannibals. Perhaps we are being taken to a tribe of whitemen who are also cannibals."

"Whatever the reason, I would rather fight these whitemen now and risk death by the gun than be led to slaughter."

"I agree, Kimbo. I have been saying we fight these men all along. Now, even those of you who would not take up this fight, now will you reconsider?"

"I say that perhaps Singbe has invented this tale to get us to fight the whiteman."

"Keep your voice down lest the children hear. Who is that speaking?"

"It is I, Kinna, a Mendeman like yourself, Grabeau."

"Kinna, if Singbe says this is what happened, then it is fact."

"I do not speak untruths, Kinna. If you wish to challenge my honor..."

"What will you do, Singbe? Fight me from across the aisle while we are both chained at the neck? All I am saying is that you have been urging us to rise up against the whitemen since you were brought to the cage in the city. I, too, want to be free, but I do not want to be dead."

"Do you wish to be an evening meal?"

"It is true, Singbe was urging us to rebel even before we were brought to the city," said Kimbo. "All during the voyage from Lomboko he spoke out against the whitemen, too. He was even beaten for standing up to the yellow-haired man. But during all that time he never uttered an untruth to change our hearts. Why start now?"

"Because this may well be our last time on a ship," said Kinna. "And a ship is the only way we can get back to Africa. So he invents this tale of cannibalism."

"It may well be the last time we are on a ship, Kinna. And we do need a ship to get back to Africa. But, I swear to you they mean to trade us to man-eaters."

"I believe the Mendeman. I believe we should rise up."

"Who is that?"

"Yaboi. I am a hunter from the Timmani tribe. I was captured in a battle with the Mandingos of the north, taken as a slave, and sold to a Mende farmer, Qwualimah. He sold me to a whiteman who brought me to the slave island where I was sold again and brought here. I have no love for the Mende, and I never spoke to Singbe before we came on this ship. But I saw him talk to the cook. I saw the cook draw a blade across his throat and then point to a barrel filled with meat. And I saw Singbe fall to his knees with fear. I believe he speaks the truth."

There was a long silence. The sea sloshed thick and heavy against the hull. The muted sound of the huge canvas sails rippling the choppy night breeze drifted down through the open hatch.

"So, what should we do?"

"They only take us up five or six at a time. The whitemen all have guns. Anyone trying an ambush would be killed."

"We would not be fresh, but dead meat is meat all the same."

"Singbe, do you have a plan? Do you have a plan that will not get all of us killed?"

Singbe stared into the pitch darkness. The only plan he had ever considered was using their superior numbers to overwhelm the whitemen. A few tribesmen might be killed in such an effort, but it was a risk he believed they needed to take, and he thought many of the others would make such an attempt. But the way they were being brought on deck now, five or six at a time by three or four men with guns . . . it was suicide.

"We need to surprise them," he said finally. "How we do this I am not yet sure. But we must find a moment, and soon."

Singbe watched the sailor and slave trader the next morning when they came. One unlocked the neck chain from the wall and drew it back enough to let the first five or six tribesmen sit up. The chain was then reattached to the wall and the ankle clip of each man undone. They were sent up the ladder where they were met by the other slave trader who held a small gun. When all were on deck, they were fed, walked around, and brought back down in the same fashion and locked down. There wasn't much opportunity here. They could try to overpower the whiteman and take his gun. But the other whiteman would shoot before keys could be grabbed and anyone could unlock themselves. And the men from above could fire into the hold. Even if Singbe waited until he and a few of the tribesmen were on deck, with their manacled ankles and the whitemen keeping their distance, a surprise attack would be difficult. It would be a bloody affair no matter what, and he wasn't sure they would even be successful.

Singbe walked along the deck, eating his potato and looking out to the horizon. The sky had grayed over and the thin outline of land was no longer visible. Some of the others had talked about jumping over the rails and trying to swim to the shore. But who could swim that great distance with iron on their legs? And even if they could make it to shore, how safe would they be in a land of cannibals?

A sharp pain bit into his heel. He stopped and lifted up his foot. A long black splinter of wood, wedged between the deck planks, stuck out slightly. Singbe rubbed the arch of his foot lightly against the shard. It was hot. Hot from the sun. It was not wood at all but metal. A nail.

"Move along, nigger."

Singbe felt the musket butt press lightly into his back. He started walking. He could hear the sailor behind him, but didn't know if the man had seen the nail as well. The urge to look back boiled in his body. He took another small bite out of the potato and chewed it slowly. They changed direction at foredeck. Singbe looked up casually, glancing at the spot, but he was too far away to see if the nail was still there. He would have to wait until his steps took him back to that part of the deck. He looked down at his feet making sure he wasn't walking too fast or too slow.

As he turned the corner near the galley door, he could see it. Twenty feet away, thick and black. He needed a way to bend down and pick it up without looking suspicious. At that moment he saw Konoma, chained to the mast, sitting on the deck, drinking slowly from his cup of water.

Singbe caught Konoma's eye. He brought his fist up and to his throat and then jerked it down slightly. Konoma watched as Singbe did it again, this time also opening his mouth as if to scream. Konoma turned his hands palm up and shrugged as if to ask a question. Singbe repeated the gesture. Konoma nodded and stood. He faced the mast and let out a nervous sigh. Then he brought his hands up to the chain, pulled hard, and let out a loud frightful scream.

"The cannibal!"

"Je-sus!"

The sailors raised their guns. Montes moved in slowly.

"Easy. Easy."

Konoma let loose another raging howl. He grabbed the chain at his neck and pulled at it, ringing the links against themselves and screamed wildly. Celestino came out of the galley holding a knife.

"What is happening?! What do you do to him?"

The captain walked out from behind the wheel and drew his pistol.

"Ruiz. Control that nigger."

Singbe bent down, picked up the nail, and placed it under his arm and stood. No one had seen.

"Thank you, Konoma," he whispered. Then he made a wiping motion with both hands. Konoma saw it. Just as quickly as he had begun, Konoma stopped. He sat back down on the deck, picked up his cup of water, and drank as if nothing had happened. The whitemen froze, still nervous and bewildered.

"Whatever the hell that was, I don't want to see it again," Pepe said.

"It starting to get dark, anyway. Let's lock them up for the night, Juan."

"Sí, Señor Montes. Sí."

Later after they were all locked down and the whitemen had left the hold, Konoma called through the darkness.

"Was that what you wanted, Singbe?"

"That was perfect, Konoma."

"Why? What was the reason?"

Singbe reached under his left armpit and pulled out the nail. He raised it to the chain link running through his collar and began to pry.

"The reason, my friend, is that now, we have a plan."

Within a half hour, Singbe had broadened the gap enough to slip the link forward and away from the collar. He sat up in the dark and used the nail to loosen the metal bolt fastening his ankle manacles. He found Grabeau in the dark, gave him the nail, and showed him how he had loosened his bonds. A light rain began striking the deck overhead.

"Get everyone free."

"Where are you going?"

"To the other part of the ship where they keep the cargo," he whispered. "Perhaps I can find us some weapons. Make sure they keep quiet."

Singbe walked down the aisle, leaning forward so that he

was nearly on all fours. He went slowly, holding the chain that ran between the manacles. The darkness of the hold was complete. He did not want to stumble or let a sudden roll of the ship cause him to make a sound that would alert the whitemen. He reached the far end of the hold where the cargo was stored. His hands traced the rough splintery outline of a barrel that was roped tightly against the other cargo. He found the lid and slid it aside carefully. His fingers reached inside gently, touching something that felt like a rough fabric. The aroma of salt and spice filled his nostrils, causing his hand to recoil sharply. It was dried meat like the kind the cook had shown him. A sudden wave of nausea pushed through his stomach. He replaced the lid and slid his hands along the rope to the next piece of cargo. It was a large wooden crate. He eased the lid open and felt inside. A thin layer of smooth cloth met his hand. Beneath it sat cool ridges of metal. Singbe pushed away the cloth and tried to find something to grab. Something sharp bit into his fingers. He brought his hand up to his mouth and tasted blood. He reached back in crate carefully. It was filled with caning machetes, wide and sharp with two foot blades.

Singbe took two and made his way back to the stern. Grabeau, Burnah, and four others were free. Singbe handed Grabeau a machete.

"There is a whole box of these swords."

"The spirits are with us. Still, we must get the others free."

"Use the swords to pry loose the neck chain. I will take Burnah and Kimbo and get more. Make sure everyone remains silent."

Grabeau felt his way down the platform until he found the back wall and the cleat where the chain was moored. He wedged the machete blade down between the cleat and the wood and began to work it back and forth. By the time Singbe returned, everyone was free.

"All of you, listen to me."

Singbe squatted down in the middle of the aisle.

"We have the opportunity we need for surprise and the gods have blessed us with weapons. I have found a box of swords over where they keep the barrels and crates. There are enough for all of us. You asked for a plan. Here it is. We kill the whitemen as they sleep, take control of this ship and sail it back into the sun toward Africa. Is anyone opposed to this?"

Singbe paused. All he could hear was the sea and the rain.

"Good. I need two men to stay here and guard the children. Kinna and Yah-nae. The rest of you, follow me toward the ladder. Quietly."

† † †

Singbe balanced his fingertips against the hatch and, very carefully, eased it open. A thick rain, blowing into his face, glistened on the deck in the dull light of the lantern by the galley door. He knelt down and reached back into the hold. Grabeau handed him a machete. Singbe moved to the railing, flattening his body on the warm, wet deck, and looked up to the raised stern. A sailor stood at the wheel under a canvas tarp, his eyes focused on a point beyond the other sailor who slouched near the lantern burning at the bow. Singbe watched them both but neither sailor saw the tribesmen coming out of the hatch, one by one.

The storm, mostly rain, and not much wind, had nearly passed. It was about 4 A.M. The captain had retired to his cabin an hour ago, content that his men could handle the boat until dawn.

The ship hit a swell, dipping the bow down and then up a few feet. Fuliwa, the twelfth man out of the hold, fell forward, his machete slapping against the deck. All the tribesmen froze. The sailor at the wheel did not react. Either he didn't hear it or he discounted the sound as part of the storm. Singbe watched him for a few seconds more and then signaled Grabeau. Grabeau tapped the hatch's frame and another man began to come out, and was struck by a bright flash of light. The galley door was open. Celestino looked out with a lantern in his hand.

"What's dat? Juan, did you hear dat?"

"Shut up. You'll wake the captain."

"I tink I hear someting. I tink some tackle may be loose or someting."

"So check on it."

He took two steps before a swell threw him forward into a bulkhead, just a few yards from Singbe.

"You is de sailor, man. I is just de cook. I ain't going up no mast in dis seas."

"Just do it, Celestino."

The ship dipped again, lurching Celestino forward. He reached out with one hand, catching the rail. The lantern in his hand swung forward, splashing light on Singbe's face.

"Lord Christ! Da niggers is loose!"

Singbe let out a war cry and dove at the cook. The other tribesmen rose up and ran across the deck. Celestino fell back into the galley where he grabbed a knife from the sideboard. Singbe jumped on top of him. Celestino slashed and drove his knee into Singbe's stomach. Singbe rolled with the kick and swung his machete up to block the knife. Celestino let out a shrieking howl as he saw his hand, still clutching the knife, fly from his wrist. He tumbled back into the galley, his other hand desperately searching for another weapon. Singbe rose quickly and plunged his machete up through Celestino's belly and chest. He pulled it out and swung down hard. Celestino's head fell to the floor.

The sailor at the wheel grabbed a musket and fired it at the tribesmen rushing up the stairs. Grabeau, in the lead, lunged at the sailor's knees as the weapon flashed. The blast was deafening and Grabeau felt a hot wind rush past his back. The heavy shot caught the next man flush in the face. Grabeau rose from the deck, only to have the rifle butt thrust into his chest, driving him back down. He rolled as he hit the deck, slashing out wildly with the machete. The sailor screamed and fell, dropping the musket over the railing into the sea. Cut behind the knees, he struggled to stand, grabbing the wheel. Grabeau stabbed again, slicing into the kidneys. Two other tribesmen ran up screaming and hacking.

Ferrer burst out of his quarters with a pistol in one hand and a dagger in the other. He fired into the raging tribesmen. One fell forward, dead before he hit the deck. Others tumbled back. The attackers froze. Ferrer reloaded desperately.

"Throw them some bread!" he yelled to Antonio, who was cowering behind him in the cabin. "Do it!"

Antonio broke a loaf into a few clumsy chunks, flung it at the Africans, and then tumbled back into the cabin. Ferrer held the pistol out ready to shoot anyone who took a step. He kicked a piece of bread to Burnah.

"Eat! Take the bread and get back in the hold, the whole fucking lot of you!"

Burnah squatted down slowly, never taking his eyes off Ferrer. He picked up the bread and stood.

"It is not bread we want, whiteman. We want our freedom. And we will have it."

Burnah bit the bread and dropped to one knee, bowing to the captain. He held out his machete flat on his palms as if to surrender.

"Take it, boy. Antonio! Antonio?" But Antonio had scurried back into the cabin and dropped through the hatch in the captain's floor.

"Shit."

Ferrer shuffled forward a step and motioned slowly with the pistol.

"Okay, nigger. Just put that machete down on the deck. Down I say. All of you."

Burnah leaned forward. Ferrer's foot inched toward him. Burnah tossed the machete lightly into the air, high and flat. Ferrer's dagger hand rose up instinctively to grab the long knife. Burnah lunged forward, knocking the pistol from Ferrer's other hand. They were all on him at once, hacking.

"Stand back, brothers! Stand back!"

Burnah looked down at Ferrer, who was bleeding badly from the face and chest. He held the pistol over the captain's face. Ferrer cried out.

A blast ripped into the night. Burnah pulled the trigger a few more times, but the pistol was empty. They threw Ferrer's body into the water. Across the deck there were wild screams.

Montes and Pablo were pinned between one of the longboats and the deck rail. Montes had killed two of the Africans with his pistol but one of them knocked it out of his hand as he lunged, sending it over the railing. Montes was thrusting at the men with a machete; Pablo was swinging and jabbing at them with an oar. They were holding off about ten of the tribesmen. Singbe jumped on top of the boat and thrust at Montes. Montes parried the strike and slashed one of the lines holding the boat. It tipped and rolled off its mount, knocking Singbe back into some of the other attackers. Montes turned. Singbe stood and dove again. A sharp blow from his machete handle caught Montes behind the ear, dropping him to the deck. The longboat fell on him, covering his body.

Pablo didn't see this. All he saw was the Africans in front of him. And now, from across the deck, Burnah's group was running toward him. A tribesman slashed at Pablo's chest, just missing. Pablo jammed the oar into the man's throat, pushing hard, hoisting his own body onto the railing. He rolled into the sea. It was at least twenty miles to the shore, but Pablo, a good swimmer, figured he could make it. He didn't realize that blood was flowing from a small gash in his side. In a few minutes sharks were swarming.

Pepe was at the bow, holding out his pistol and the keys to the manacles. Grabeau stood over him, holding his head by the hair, the machete's blade raised.

"Please! I beg of you. Spare me!" Pepe pleaded. "With God as my witness I will set you all free. Just don't kill me. Please!"

Grabeau raised the machete to strike but his hand hesitated.

"He cries like a child. Look, Yaboi. There are tears on his face."

"He is one sorry son of a pig. Kill him. Put him out of our misery."

"And he whipped Burnah so hard."

Grabeau slammed Pepe's face into the deck and knelt beside him, still clutching the hair.

"You made him bleed!" Grabeau screamed. "You rubbed vinegar in his wounds! And now look at you! Crying like a whelp!"

He threw Pepe down and raised the machete again.

"No! Please, God, no!"

"This is disgusting."

"You're right, Grabeau. There is no honor in killing such a man."

Grabeau reached down and picked up the keys. He unlocked the manacles, shook them off and rubbed his ankles.

"Bind him with his own chains," he said wearily. "We will talk of his fate later."

Singbe ran up to Grabeau.

"Is he the last of them?"

"Last that we know of."

"The captain, the cook, and the one who was at the wheel are dead. The other sailor jumped into the sea. I do not know where the other slave trader is, or the boy slave. If they are here, we will find them. Regardless, the boat is ours."

Grabeau smiled and hugged Singbe. Singbe jumped up on the raised deck in the bow and held his machete over his head.

"We have done it, my brothers. The boat is ours. We are going home to our families. We are freemen again!"

A great cheer rose up from the tribesmen into the thinning rain. The *Amistad* drifted in the small waves, carried away from the coastline by a light wind from the south.

East and West

"I say we kill them all." After he spoke, Singbe looked down at Ruiz, Montes, and Antonio. All three were bound by chains and shackles to the ship's anchor, which sat in the front of the bow deck.

Montes had been found below, hiding under a tarp. He had fallen into a hatch near the longboat unnoticed after being struck on the head and lay unconscious until dawn. He awoke and dragged his body to the hiding place. But when he heard the Africans searching below decks, Montes could not hold back his fear. His shaking body and heavy breathing gave him away. They brought him topside. His body was covered with several deep gashes and muddy purple bruises. Antonio, too, had slipped below. He had propped himself behind the secured cargo with a musket in his hand. Two tribesmen found him just after sunrise. As they approached, he pulled the gun's trigger. However, the boy did not know how to load it properly. There was a flash and then nothing.

The tribesmen had voted Singbe their leader. He stood over

the captive now with Grabeau and Burnah, who had been made sub-chiefs.

"Singbe, no. We cannot just kill them for no reason."

"No reason? They would have killed us, Burnah. They were getting ready to trade us to cannibals. I think that is reason enough. I say we throw the anchor over the side with all of them chained to it."

"No, Singbe. Burnah is right," said Grabeau. "We have no reason to kill them. They were defending themselves. As for selling us to cannibals, I do not like the idea of that any more than you or any other man among us. But I will not kill for that. It is not right."

"They took our freedom, our lives."

"No. No, they did not," said Burnah. "They were only the last to participate in a chain of events. We were all taken slaves, by different means and by different men. We are all here now because of these two men, but they are just accomplices."

"So, we make them pay for the sins of the others. Besides, how many tribesmen have they bought and sold? How many have they flogged? How many have they seen off to their deaths, either to cannibals or to slave-holders who work their slaves to death? I say we balance the scales with their lives."

"These men may have wronged us, but they no longer can do so. They are our captives now." Grabeau lowered his voice and leaned in close to Singbe. "Singbe, you fought for your freedom, but you are not a killer. You are more of a man than that. It is time to put your anger aside. We are going home now."

"Grabeau, Burnah, listen. I respect your words. I agree to spare the boy. But I do not believe these men deserve to live. Besides, if we do not kill them now, it will come back at us later. They will try to kill us all at their first chance. I am sure of it."

"How?" Burnah laughed. "They have no guns and there are nearly fifty of us. Your hate is clouding your judgment."

"No. It is providing me with clarity."

"Singbe, killing them like this would make us just like the

whites. We would be cowards without honor or dignity. That may be their way, it may be who they are, but it is not who we are, my friend."

Singbe looked from Grabeau to Burnah. Rage and frustration boiled through his limbs. He knew in his heart he was right, that leaving these men alive would only serve to bring everyone pain later on. And Singbe could feel the hate in his belly, hate burning on months of anger, fear, abuse, and humiliation. But this was only a feeling. Grabeau and Burnah spoke reason.

"Fine." He sighed. "We do not kill them. What, then, do we do with them?"

Burnah walked over to Pepe and pried his mouth open.

"He has good teeth, but I think the body is flabby and weak."

He slapped Ruiz's legs and buttocks they same way it had been done to the tribesmen in the slave market.

"He is soft like a baby. Maybe the cannibal whites will trade for him, though. What do you say, brothers?"

A great roaring laughter went through the tribesmen.

"I do not know," said Grabeau. "Perhaps they will be of some use later. But more important I think is that we must learn how to sail this ship. Yes, we know that to get back to Africa we must sail into the sun, but we do not know how to work the sails or the ropes. We do not know how to make the ship sail against the wind. I am not even sure how we steer this thing."

"We use the wheel in the back. That much I have seen," said Singbe. "But you are right. We do not know how to use the sails. Do any of the others know?"

They called the tribesmen together. Some had been busy scrubbing the blood from the decks. Others came up from below where they were cleaning out the stench of the hold. Singbe began asking what they knew about the ship's operation, but no one could offer much. Few of them had ever been in a boat before being taken slaves, and of those who had, their experience was limited to canoes. The sky was clearing and the wind from the west had picked up. The sails were still trimmed for the rough weather; only the jib was unfurled. The ship drifted aimlessly in the choppy surf.

As Singbe and Burnah listened and talked to the tribesmen, Grabeau glanced over at the captives. They, too, watched Singbe and Burnah, perhaps wondering if their fate was being discussed. But he saw something interesting in the older man. While the young man and slave boy followed their every move, the older man was looking about. His eyes moved from the wheel to the sails to the sky. His head turned to the side of the ship where the land had been, and then back to the wheel and the sails. Then his eyes met Grabeau's glare.

The older man quickly looked away, staring down to his own feet. Grabeau stood and walked over to Singbe.

"I think I have found a use for one of the whitemen."

"What do you mean?"

"The older one. While the others watched you, he was looking about this ship and to the skies and the sea. I saw concern and understanding, as if he could see what was right and wrong. I think he knows about this ship. I think he may be a sailor, or at least have an idea of how all of this works."

Montes looked up and found Singbe, Burnah, and Grabeau staring down at him.

"What is he saying, Pedro?"

"How should I know? I don't speak that bushman gibberish. Boy! Do you know what he's saying?"

"No, señor," said Antonio. "I only speak Spanish, like you."

"They are going to kill us," Pepe cried.

"I thought so before. But now I'm not so sure." Montes spoke without looking away from Singbe.

"Yes, they are. They are going to cut us to pieces and feed us to the cannibal. They are going to . . . "

"Shut up, Pepe. Shut up and watch him. Maybe we can figure out what he's saying."

Singbe pointed to the yardarms and the jib. He walked over to one of the masts and undid a rope from a cleat. He slapped a block and tackle and pointed the machete at the ship's wheel. The he turned and pointed the blade toward the rising sun.

"I think they want me to show them how to sail the ship."

"What? Sail it to where?"

"Probably one of the British colonies or some other place where there's no slavery."

"Certainly you're not going to show them."

"I don't plan on it."

Pepe straightened. "Not that I wouldn't welcome their intervention at this moment, but if the British discover where these niggers are from, they'll take everything. The loss would be catastrophic. The ship, the cargo, and slaves. I'll be lucky if I don't come out of this completely ruined."

"If we're not careful, we won't come out of this. Period."

Singbe walked up to Montes and pointed again to the ropes and sails. Montes shrugged and shook his head. Singbe got close to his face and spoke louder. Montes shrugged again.

"I do not think he understands," Burnah said.

"Or maybe he does but really does not know how to do what we ask." Grabeau sighed. "Perhaps I was wrong."

"No. I think your instincts were true, Grabeau," said Singbe. "I think he understands us well enough. He just needs to be motivated."

Singbe unlocked Montes from the anchor and stood him up. His hands and ankles were still bound.

"Don't give in, Pedro. The longer we drift, the more of a chance someone will see us and provide rescue."

Montes said nothing. His head throbbed. The gashes on his side and arms burned. Singbe grabbed him by the collar and led him over to the mast. He pointed to the sails and grabbed the sailropes. He pointed again to the sails, dropped his hand down, and then spread his arms wide.

"Show me how to take these sails down and fill them with the wind."

Montes gave Singbe a confused look.

Singbe drew up the machete and pressed the blade firmly against Montes's throat. He pointed to the sails again with his free hand and drew the machete across Montes's neck, touching the skin but not breaking it.

"Show me now, or I will end your life."

Before Montes could move he heard Pepe screaming.

"Pedro! Pedro!"

Singbe grabbed Montes's hair and turned his head so he could see Pepe. Grabeau had drawn his machete and held it at the base of Pepe's skull, pressing the tip upward into the skin just hard enough to start a small trickle of blood.

"For the love of Christ, Pedro! Do it. Show them what they want."

Montes glanced down at the blade against his own neck and then into Singbe's eyes. He put up his arms as if to surrender. Singbe pulled the blade far enough away so Montes could move, but kept it near enough so that if the move was a rash or wrong one, the head would soon be gone from the shoulders. Slowly, Montes undid the knot tied around the cleat. The topsail began to unfurl. The wind hitting the canvas jerked the ropes forward, almost slicing Montes's neck on the blade. Singbe dropped his weapon and grabbed the rope, helping Montes steady it. Other tribesmen rushed over to help. Montes tied off the line. The ship began to pick up a little speed. The other sails were lowered and tied down. The tribesmen went to the rails and raised decks and laughed at the water rushing past the hull.

Singbe dragged Montes up to the wheel and pointed with his machete at the sun. Montes began turning the wheel until the ship came about and was headed east. He held it there.

"The wheel is direction, yes? Yes?" Singbe said. "Let me try."

Singbe motioned Montes away with the machete and took the wheel. Turning it took more strength than he had thought. He could feel the play of the ocean through the cable that ran down to the rudder. He turned the wheel around several times clockwise. The ship's bow slowly followed around to the right, the deck arching up slightly to the left. Singbe spun the wheel around the other way and felt the ship roll back again. After experimenting for about fifteen minutes he lined the bow back up with the sun and held it there. He nodded to Montes.

"Chain him back up to the anchor with the others."

Burnah and one of the tribesmen locked Montes down.

"We are doomed now, Pedro," Pepe said.

"Perhaps. Perhaps not," Montes mused. "It's still days to any landfall and these waters are heavily traveled by other ships. We may get picked up yet. Besides, these savages may now know how to turn the wheel and drop the sails, but they have no clue about navigation. They seem to be sailing easterly, away from Cuba, but I don't think they have a clear destination. It will be interesting to see what they do when the sun goes down."

"By the love of God, I hope we are intercepted by then."

Singbe showed Burnah and Grabeau how the wheel worked. The three of them took turns piloting the ship and teaching the other tribesmen how to raise and lower the sails. They also created work details to clean the ship and man the sails. Four men were killed in the battle; eight more were injured. Singbe and others helped move them into the captain's cabin. Ka, a Mendeman knowledgeable in the ways of healing, had been put in charge of the wounded. The children were moved into the crew's berth.

Singbe believed it would take them between fifty and sixty days to get back to Africa. He put Burnah in charge of finding out how much food was on the ship and coming up with a reasonable rationing system so that it would last until they got back to Africa. They ate at sunset. The meals were essentially the same as what they had before, a potato, some rice, and water. They had dumped the barrels of meat into the sea, still believing they were filled with human flesh.

Ka came out on deck and walked up to the wheel where Singbe stood eating his sweet potato. He was a small man just under five feet tall, but he had a torso like a water keg and muscled legs and arms. Although he was about ten years older than Singbe, he still had a boyish face. Shaw had ordered his head shaved, though, because wisps of gray hair had begun to appear, a detail which would certainly reduce Ka's value on the slave market.

"Singbe."

"Ka. How are the wounded?"

"Not well. I can find no herbs or treatments on this boat, and I do not know what the whitemen use to stop fever. The men who were shot are especially bad. I pried out the metal from the gun wounds with a knife, but I think its poison has already spread through the men. We will have to wait and see who can survive."

Singbe nodded gravely.

"Beliwa is bad, though he can speak. He said something interesting earlier. Perhaps you should talk with him."

Singbe saw a look in Ka's eyes and nodded. He gave the wheel to Burnah and went down to the captain's cabin. Beliwa was lying on the floor. A broad cloth caked with dried blood had been wrapped over the bullet wound just below his right shoulder. Singbe walked in, squatted down, and took his hand.

"Beliwa. How do you feel?"

"I am strong, Singbe. Soon I will help you and the other tribesmen pilot the boat." He tried to sit up but the pain drove him back down.

"Do not worry, my friend. We have things well in hand. And you fought bravely. If it were not for your courage and that of the others who were wounded, we would not have prevailed. Rest. It will be our pleasure to serve you."

"I am ready to help whenever you need me."

"Perhaps you can," said Ka. "Tell Singbe what you told me about your dealings with the whiteman from years back."

"I told Ka that for two summers I worked for a Bandi trader who had a booth in the city, the one they call Freetown. I tended his pack animals, and helped him maintain his stores. Oh, he had beautiful things. He traded bolts of cloth and wool, fine pots for cooking, knives and grains and even livestock and chickens and fighting cocks. I remember once we had over one hundred hens on a day when the market was filled and the . . . "

"Tell him about your dealings with the whitemen."

"Oh, the whitemen sailors, they loved the cock fights. They would come and wager gold and silver and rum. I knew many of them and learned some of their language."

Singbe dropped one knee down to the floor and leaned in closer to Beliwa.

"You can speak with the whites?"

"Well, some of them. I learned the talk of the British. It was they who we saw most at the fights. The words are different from those of the whites who bought me in Lomboko, or those who brought us on this boat."

Singbe stared off to the side and nodded. He looked back to Beliwa.

"Did you try speaking to these whites?"

"No. No, I didn't. I tried some of the British before, when I was on the long voyage, and later when they put me in the large cage with all the tribesmen. But I might as well have been speaking Mende."

"How much of their words do you know?"

"A little. Enough to get by at a cock fight and in the market. But, as I said, it is not the language of these men."

"Grabeau speaks Mende, Yamani, and Vai. Burnah speaks Mende and two Mandingo dialects. Perhaps these whites know the words of your whites. Can you stand?"

"Of course."

Beliwa tried to push his body off the floor but his legs buckled. Singbe and Ka grabbed him around the waist and lifted. Beliwa took a few steps. Ka handed him a broken oar from one of the long boats to use as a crutch. Burnah watched from the wheel as they came out of the cabin and walked slowly across the deck toward the captives chained to the anchor. Every few steps, Beliwa would take weight off the oar and try to walk on his own. He almost passed out twice before they reached the bow. Ka and Singbe nearly had to carry him up the few steps leading to the raised deck. Beliwa stopped and straightened, absently handing his crutch to Ka. Unsteadiness caused his shadow to waver slightly as it stretched across the anchor. Singbe and Ka stood close, ready to catch him.

"What should I say?"

"Just see if they speak any of the whiteman's words that you know."

Antonio and Pepe looked up at the ragged, defiant warrior standing before them. Montes, chained with his back to the stern, whispered.

"Pepe, what is it?"

"I don't know. The leader, another one, and one of the wounded men."

"Maybe they are going to give him some revenge."

Beliwa began speaking, "Do you talk the An-gleesh?"

None of the captives heard him. Pepe had gone into a frenzy, spitting out Spanish so fast even Montes and Antonio could barely understand him.

"God, no. It wasn't us. I swear. We didn't hurt you. It was the others."

"Do you likes cock fight?"

"I know it wasn't me. It was the others. I didn't wound you..."

"I got fine fabric, rum for trade."

"It wasn't any of us. Please don't kill us. We mean you no harm. Please..."

Beliwa turned back to Singbe.

"I do not understand a word out of his mouth. I do not know what he is saying. I think his mind is gone."

"I didn't wound anyone." Pepe went on. "None of us did. We barely fought back. We were just protecting ourselves...."

Singbe sighed. "How can they hear when this one cries like a child?" He drew up the machete and the tip to Pepe's throat. "Shut up. Shut up and listen."

The machete inspired immediate silence from Pepe's mouth.

"Try again, Beliwa. Just once more."

Beliwa shrugged. "One, two, three, four..."

Pepe's eyes grew huge. His lips stammered, the machete still pressing on his skin. "F-five, six, seven, eight."

"Ya, sir!" Beliwa cried. "He knows the words."

"You speak English!?"

"Ya, sir. I talk good the words An-gleesh."

"For the love of God. Pedro, one of these savages speaks English."

"I didn't know you spoke it."

"Yes. Yes. I went to school in the States. In Connecticut. Oh, thank God. You good sir. What is your name?"

"I Beliwa."

"Belly-wah? Belly-wah? Right. I am Ruiz. Pepe Ruiz. This is my associate, Pedro Montes."

"What's he saying, Beliwa?"

"His name. He is Peperuiz. The other is Pedromontaze."

Singbe nodded. "Tell him our names."

"You are all free," Pepe chirped before Beliwa could begin again. "All of you. You are no longer slaves. I give you all your freedom."

Beliwa looked at him and began laughing. His chuckle spread into a full wide shaking laugh until it broke into a great heaving cough and pain from his wound that drove him back into Singbe's and Ka's arms. He took the crutch and stood again.

"No, sir," Beliwa said, finally regaining himself. "We did that."

Beliwa told Singbe what Ruiz had said, and what had he said in return.

"Tell him this: Tell him I am Singbe Pieh of Mende. Tell him I am chief of these men and we will sail this ship into the morning sun. To Africa. Tell them that we are freemen and they are the slaves, now."

Beliwa repeated the words as best he could.

Ruiz's face paled. "Oh my Christ," he gasped.

"What is it? What did he say, Pepe?"

"Africa. He said we are their slaves, and that they are sailing us back to Africa."

"Good God," Montes whispered.

"YOU SLAVE NOW!" Singbe yelled now repeating Beliwa's words. "You slave now!"

Beliwa's legs buckled again.

"Beliwa . . . " Ka and Singbe reached out.

"I am fine."

"No, my friend," Singbe said. "You will rest now. We will talk with these men later."

"Wait! Where are you going? Belly-wah?"

They said nothing else to the whitemen. Singbe and Ka helped Beliwa back to the cabin. After the sun went down, Singbe sent a man to feed the prisoners. Each was given a half cup of water and a handful of uncooked rice.

Later, Singbe met with Grabeau and Burnah to discuss how to use their newfound form of communication. All agreed that the whitemen and their slave could not be trusted. It was essential, though, that they find out as much as they could about how to operate the ship, especially how to keep it on course at night when east and west were harder to distinguish. That night Burnah stood at the wheel. Singbe slept on deck close by. A canvas bag served as a pillow. He dreamed of Stefa and his children all night. The shadowy man of his past dreams never appeared.

† † †

"Wake up. Wake up now. Both of you."

Grabeau pushed Pepe's shoulder. His body jumped as if to get up, but the chains held him in place. Pepe looked up. The sun was barely breaking into the horizon. Singbe, Grabeau, Beliwa, and Ka stood over him. Beliwa held the crutch under one arm. His voice sounded a little weaker than the day before.

"Tell how to sail ship."

"What?"

"Ship. Tell how it sail."

"I do not know."

"You friend know. Ask him."

Singbe brought the machete in close to Pepe.

"Pedro. They want to know a little more about how to sail the ship."

"What did you tell them?"

"Nothing. I did not tell them you were a sailor."

"Tell them I showed them all I know."

"Pedro, the chief has a machete at my throat."

"Tell them that's all I know."

"He said he showed you all he knows. Really, that was all."

Beliwa relayed the words to Singbe. Singbe stepped in closer to Pepe.

"How do you say untruth in their language?" Singbe asked.

"Lie."

"Lie?"

Singbe pressed the machete into Pepe's throat. "Lie," he said forcefully.

Pepe swallowed hard. They won't kill me, he thought. I'm the only one who they can speak to.

"No, I swear. He does not know."

Singbe looked to Beliwa. Beliwa shrugged. Singbe signaled to Grabeau, who reached down and stood on Pepe's wrist so his hand was pinned to the deck. Singbe squatted down and touched the fingers lightly with the blade and then raised it and looked at Pepe.

"Lie."

Beliwa smiled and pointed the fingers and spoke in English again.

"One, two, three, four."

"God. No. All right. All right. I lied. He's a sailor. We will show you how to sail the ship."

"He says he lied. The other one knows how to sail the ship," said Beliwa. "I think you should cut the fingers off anyway."

Singbe looked from Beliwa to Grabeau and smiled.

"Perhaps. But not this time. Unchain the two white men and bring them to the wheel."

It took them nearly ten minutes to walk from one end of the ship to the other. Infection was spreading through Beliwa and his body was quickly growing weaker. Despite this, they spent an hour, Pepe translating from Montes, Beliwa translating from Pepe, talking about the ship. Singbe heard the basics about handling the sails, tacking, and hardships brought about by crosswinds. Montes saw no problem with this. It was better to give the Africans some knowledge and let them take the vessel into shipping lanes where a British or American flag might spot them and board. But there was one point on which Montes was not forthcoming.

"Tell me how to sail east in the night."

Montes looked up at Singbe.

"I find my way in the stars."

Singbe looked from Beliwa to Pepe to Montes, puzzled.

"He looks to the sky to find path in the sea? He lies."

Montes smiled. "Let me do this. Let me pilot the ship tonight and the bow will be pointed at the sun as it rises in the morning."

Singbe leaned in close and put the blade to Montes's chest. "Tell him we will let him pilot the ship. But if the sun comes up and we are not sailing into it, or if we find ourselves close to the whiteman's land, I will cut out his heart."

Beliwa relayed the message as best he could. Pepe translated, Montes nodded.

Pepe twitched nervously. "Pedro . . . I hope to Christ it doesn't rain tonight."

But as night fell the sky filled with stars and a glowing crescent moon. Singbe had run a chain from the railing to Montes's waist, giving him just enough slack to reach the helm. There were also shackles around his ankles with a chain running between them. Singbe had taken a berth in the galley to sleep. Burnah stood guard, watching Montes.

Montes stood with his hands on the wheel. He looked down at the great compass embedded in a wooden frame in front of him. The glass had been smashed and the compass destroyed, probably during the uprising. All the better, Montes thought. If the Africans knew how to use it the voyage might go against his plans. Once he had enough of their trust to pilot the ship every night, he would see if he could get a look in the captain's quarters for charts and other navigation equipment. For now, he figured they were probably on a rough heading toward the Bahamas. Fine, the British could have them. His losses were minimal on this voyage, and, despite all his moaning, Pepe's personal resources were extensive. Even with this voyage being a total wash, he could handle the hit to his finances. Hell, he would probably be able to make it all back within two voyages. The key was getting back to Cuba alive. They couldn't get back directly. The Africans would know. But if he could keep the *Amistad* in shipping lanes, perhaps they would be spotted and hailed by another freighter or a British or American naval vessel. He wouldn't think twice about going over the side if they got close enough, even with the chains at his ankles.

Montes found Jupiter and the Southern Cross and marked his heading. The wind blew up from the southwest. He turned the wheel slowly, bringing the ship about two degrees every minute or so. Burnah could not have noticed even if he wanted to. The gradual change in direction was imperceptible in the rolling sea. About an hour and a half later, Montes fixed his course and held steady. They sailed on this way, at about 15 knots, through the night. Montes kept an eye on the sky and turned the wheel accordingly. At around 5:30 the sun began filling the horizon. It came up right over the bow. Singbe, Grabeau, and Burnah stood behind Montes watching.

"Fine. He can pilot the boat at night," said Singbe. "But we still guard him and leave him chained to the rail."

"Where can he go?" Grabeau said. "Especially with one of us guarding him?"

"What if he decides to go over the side? He could bring us close to some land, some island, and jump. Then we would have no pilot for the nights."

"So, just keep the ankle chains on him. That will be enough to drag him down if he jumps into the sea."

"I don't know. I do not trust the whites. Any of them."

"I think it will be all right, Singbe," said Burnah. "I do not trust the whites, either. But that does not mean we have to treat them as they treated us. The ankle chains will restrict his movements enough. And if he tries to commit some transgression, we shall kill him. We have two guns and the swords. He cannot escape us."

Singbe gave in. He walked over to the rail, unlocked the chain, and then went over to Montes and unfastened the links from his waist.

"Give him and the other white and the slave boy the same rations as the rest of us, too," Singbe said.

Grabeau smiled.

Ka came up the stairs.

"The sky will be clear and blue today, and I see we are sailing east this morning."

"Yes," Singbe said. "Apparently this whiteman can tell the truth when he has to."

"Good. It will be good to get back home, my brothers."

"Yes. Yes." Singbe nodded. "And when Beliwa wakes we should get him to talk to this one again. If he can read the night sky, then he certainly can teach that skill to us."

"Singbe, Beliwa died in the night. Both he and Lintahma. From their wounds."

Singbe looked from Ka to Grabeau and Burnah. He could feel his rage building. The other men could see the muscles in his jaw rippling, the veins in his neck thickening. They waited, but Singbe was silent. Finally, he spoke, his voice soft and low.

"Take the whiteman down with the other one and feed them. The slaveboy, too. Same rations as us. Throw the dead into the sea."

Burnah led Montes down the stairs. Grabeau followed with Ka. Singbe put his hands on the wheel. Already the sun was climbing in the morning sky.

Later that day, after a nap, Montes ate and talked with Pepe about piloting the ship through the night.

"I'm glad you were able to keep it pointed to the east," Pepe said.

"I wasn't too excited about the alternative."

"Well, the niggers seem to appreciate it. Now we're only wearing shackles and they're feeding us better. Although not by much. This rice isn't even cooked and it's barely enough for a dog."

"I think they're going to let me sail the ship at night from now on."

Montes looked out at the ocean and lowered his voice. Antonio was sleeping but Montes still didn't want to take any chances of him hearing.

"I didn't, you know."

"Huh? You didn't what?

"I didn't keep it pointed east."

"What do you mean? What heading did you take?"

"West. For nearly eight hours. I turned the ship slowly until we were headed west by northwest. About an hour before dawn I brought her slowly back around to the east."

"What's your plan? I mean, other than not sailing us to Africa?"

"We're traveling at between twelve and fifteen knots. That means each day we'll be heading about a hundred and fifty miles toward Africa. Each night I can buy us back about one hundred and thirty-five. At that rate we can sail up the American coast. Within two weeks we'll be in the shipping lanes. In three to four weeks we'll be off the coast of the Carolinas, I think. The American Navy is bound to pick us up."

"The Americans would be more sympathetic to slave owners than the British. Then again, will they believe us? It's our word against the word of these savages."

"Be serious. Who do you think they will believe, white men in chains, victims of a rebellion held against their will, or a bunch of ignorant, half-naked bush natives?"

"True. But if the Americans find out that these aren't really landinos, we could lose everything."

Montes turned back to Pepe. "They may not find out. British or American."

"What do you mean?"

"That little one, the one who spoke to you in English. Bellywah. I think he's dead. The witchdoctor came up just after sunrise and I heard him say 'Bellywah' and the others looked saddened. I think he's dead. So they've lost their translator. Besides, translator or not, the Americans are slaveholders. You are a Christian whiteman schooled in their country, a man who speaks their own language."

Montes looked around at the tribesmen on the deck and shrugged. "Even if they do realize this lot is a bunch fresh from Africa, I think the Americans are reasonable," he continued.

"They will lock them up, give us the key, and an escort back to Havana. Hell, if we do this right we will return home as heroes."

Pepe smiled. "Keep us alive, my friend. Alive and headed west."

Landfall

And so it went.

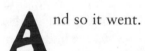

Every night Montes sailed the ship west, bringing it about each morning before sunrise and turning the wheel over to Singbe, Burnah, or Grabeau. Their trust of him was limited, but it grew after the first week when they were overtaken by a huge tropical storm. They rode the gale's raging winds and churning seas for nearly two days, at times with both Singbe and Montes bracing the wheel together. The hard sailing was made more difficult because the tribesmen were terrified by the high seas and roaring winds. Many of them retreated to the hold. Others tried bravely to work on deck, but none knew what to do, and Montes's commands were rarely understood. They had taken down all the sails save for a jib and tried to hold the helm steady as the ship was tossed through the waves at the mercy of the sea. They held their own until late in the afternoon of the first day. The sea had become so vicious and the waves so large that the *Amistad* was being pushed sideways. Montes and Singbe had lashed themselves to the wheel and were trying desperately to bring the ship about. The rain was blowing sideways, stinging their faces like shards of glass. They had almost got the ship pointed into the wind when a huge wall of water crashed down on the bow, driving it under the sea and catapulting the stern forward and into the black sky. In an instant, Montes and Singbe were pinned against the wheel, the entire stern lifted out of the water and thrust sixty feet into the air. They stared helpless down the deck into the sea. Above the screaming skies and pummeling seas, Montes found himself in a second's flash, straining to hear for the sound of the beam shattering, searching to see one of the masts shear off, feeling for the ship to roll over onto its side and break in two. But none of this happened, nor did the sea suck them under the waves. Instead the ocean heaved and exploded, spitting the bow back into the air and slapping the hull down against another wall of water. The *Amistad* rolled starboard as if to list, but the sea shoved the ship over and hard to port. It brought them upright again, though bobbing wildly. The whole exchange between ship and wind and waves had taken less than thirty seconds. Singbe and Montes clung to the wheel stunned and breathless.

That was the worst of it. By morning of the next day, the rains had stopped and the winds lessened, though the seas still swelled and boiled, throwing waves ten, twenty, thirty feet high at the ship. By the evening of the second day, the seas had grown more manageable, and by the next morning the ocean was eerily calm, almost placid. The only traces of the storm were on the ship itself—its ripped jib, snapped lines, and stunned crew. A head count showed that two men were missing, presumably lost over the side. The young boy, Ka-li, had also been killed when he was struck in the head by a tumbling water keg that had been jolted loose in the hold.

But Montes's guidance of the ship raised his stature among the survivors. They realized that his efforts were nothing more than self-preservation. However, they also recognized that without Montes at the wheel during the storm, they would likely have drowned in the wild seas. Many offered Montes their food rations for days after the storm's passing, but he refused. Other squalls and rainstorms came up over the next few weeks, but they were nothing like "The Storm" and were weathered without much difficulty or any loss of life.

More of a concern than the weather were rations. The *Amistad* was only carrying food for a five-day trip, plus a few barrels of meat, bananas, and yams to be sold at market in Puerto Principe, and a few kegs of fresh water which doubled as ballast. They had been on the ocean now nearly fifty days. Singbe had twice ordered the ration size cut for all but the children. Water rations were now at less than half a cup per day. Many drank water from the sea, though it made some sick and others thirstier.

A week earlier, thirst, hunger, and the hot sun had even conspired to drive two men into madness. Ka had found a wooden box in the captain's cabin filled with bottles of colored liquid. He suspected the bottles were medicines used by the whiteman. Some smelled familiar and proved helpful with wounds. But there were bottles which he had no knowledge of and believed to be closer to poison than medicine. He put them aside, but two of the tribesmen, knowing that the bottles were being kept in the captain's cabin, took two of the large bottles without Ka knowing. They believed that medicine would be as good as water at this point. At least it would be something. They drained the bitter tasting liquids into their bodies. Both died within a day. After the incident, Singbe talked with Ka. They decided to throw all the bottles with unknown contents into the sea. It was Ka's suggestion, even though the thought of disposing of possible cures left him uneasy. A fever had set in among some of the tribesmen and Ka was hoping to find a cure. But using what was in the bottles was too dangerous, as was the temptation to some who were becoming "water mad."

The threat of dying from thirst had been abated somewhat, however, from a large three-masted ship. They had encountered it four days ago, about two hours before sunset. It was not the first ship they had seen. They had come across a few others during the weeks past. One was an especially close call. Singbe awoke from his sleep to the sound of a voice hailing. He went on deck only to find that Montes had steered them close to a two-masted ship about the same size as the *Amistad*. Singbe took the wheel from Montes and steered them away from the ship. The ship followed for a few hours but broke off after Singbe ordered the tribesmen to stand on deck and wave their machetes and yell their fiercest war cries. It must have been a curious sight for the crewmen of the other ship.

Singbe had wanted to head away from the foreign sails of the large three-masted ship, too. He feared it may be a slaver or warship from the land of the whites. But Grabeau and Burnah had talked him into getting closer so that they may try to trade for food and water.

"We can put out in one of the row boats and trade with them," Grabeau said. "If they are hostile, then we will sail away."

"What of the men in the rowboat?" Singbe asked.

"They will have to take their chances. I will go. I and three others."

"I will not leave men behind," Singbe said.

"It is our only chance. We are starving and dying of thirst. We do not know how far we are from land. We must do something."

As they spoke, the ship had gotten closer. The tribesmen had become excited and many stood on deck with their machetes in hand. Singbe decided that Grabeau's plan, though dangerous, was reasonable.

"One difference in the plan, Grabeau. I will go on the rowboat. You will stay here."

"You cannot. You are our chief."

"As chief I must assume the risk. It is only right."

"But it is my plan. I am willing to take the risk. Others joining me will be volunteers. No one is going into this with their eyes closed, Singbe."

"If something wrong does happen, Grabeau, the tribesmen

will need your good sense and wise judgment to lead them back home. Besides. I am chief, yes? It is my will that I go and you stay."

"I will go with you," said Burnah. "Yaboi and Bagna will join us."

"Good. Prepare the rowboat and inform the tribesmen of what we are doing. Put an empty water barrel in the rowboat, as well. And take the two guns."

Singbe turned the wheel toward the other ship. As he got closer he could hear someone calling at them from their deck but he could not understand the words. He looked across the deck to Montes and Ruiz who had begun talking together excitedly.

"Grabeau, take the whites below and have Konoma and two others watch them. Make sure they say nothing. I do not want them crying out to this other ship."

Ten minutes later the two ships were within one hundred yards of each other. Singbe and the others climbed down the rigging into the longboat and rowed out toward the big ship.

The other ship was the *Emmeline*, a freighter out of New Bedford, Massachusetts. It was on a return trip from China and had just off-loaded half its cargo two days earlier in Charleston. The captain and crew found the *Amistad* a curious sight, its sails in tatters, some flapping loose in the breeze, and no colors flying from its mast. However, the oddest thing was the all-black crew. The captain had never heard of such a thing, not even putting out of a port in Africa. And this crew, many of whom were nearly naked and stood on the ship's rails holding what appeared to be cutlasses, did not look like a seafaring lot at all. The *Emmeline* had a single small swivel-mounted cannon on the foredeck. The captain had a crewman follow the longboat with the gun as it came across.

As they got within ten yards of the *Emmeline*, the captain called down to them, but Singbe could not understand the words. In response, Singbe stood up in the boat and held the water keg over his head, then turned it upside down to show it was empty. He pointed to his mouth and squeezed his stomach.

The captain nodded and yelled back to one of the crewmen.

After a few minutes two men appeared at the rail of the Emmeline with a large barrel. They looped a rope around it as Singbe and the others rowed closer and came alongside the ship and then a line was thrown down. The tribesmen tied it off through a ring in the bow but the boat bobbed madly next to the ship's hull. Quickly the crewmen lowered the water keg down.

The captain also held up a burlap bag and then threw it down to the boat. Burnah caught it wrong and apples spilled out the top and rained down all over him. Singbe and the others began laughing and bowing in thanks to the captain and his crew. The captain called down to them but he could see they didn't understand. Then two of the crewmen started to lower themselves down ropes to the rowboat. Singbe couldn't take any chances. He cut the bowline with the machete and pushed the small boat away from the hull, bidding Burnah and the others to row hard. As they did Singbe smiled and bowed and waved at the *Emmeline* with his machete. The first mate stood at the ship's rail with the captain and watched them.

"What do you make of that, Captain?"

"You said you saw them through the glass taking two whitemen in chains below?"

"Aye, sir."

"I'm not sure what we've got here. The ship is in a queer state. I can't quite see the name. It looks like 'Hempstead.' And I've never seen a crew like that one."

The captain yelled to the bridge while still watching Singbe and the others row back.

"Get us underway, Hanson. Original heading."

"Aye, sir."

"I think we should get out of here fast. I don't think water and apples is what they really have in mind. My guess is that they're a bunch of black pirates, maybe come up from the Indies."

"Pirates, sir! There ain't been pirates on this coast in more than a hundred years."

"Yeah, well, I don't think we'll be hanging around to see if there's a renaissance in thieving going on. Hanson! Be quick now."

The *Emmeline* lowered its sails and pulled starboard. By the time Singbe and the others were back on the *Amistad*'s deck, the big ship was nearly a half mile away. The next evening, when they weighed anchor, the captain sent out his mate with a message for the local Naval office. It spoke of a suspected contact with a "pirate ship," manned by a crew of blacks. The captain gave the longitude and latitude of the encounter and his best guess of the ship's course. It was the fourth such report in the last three weeks of a suspicious black-hulled ship. The Navy had already dispatched two ships to investigate the reports.

The apples and water satiated the *Amistad*'s occupants for a few days. But Singbe knew their position was tenuous. He also was pretty sure that Montes had been deceiving them and that they were not on course for Africa. He decided to kill Montes. After a long discussion, Grabeau and Burnah agreed, but they would not carry out their plan until Montes could provide them with one more useful service.

Singbe roused Montes from his sleep with a kick. Montes's whole body twitched, startled and awake at once. He looked up. Singbe, Burnah, and Grabeau stood over him, blocking the sunlight. All three held machetes.

Singbe squatted down and drew on the deck with a piece of chalk. It was a crude drawing of the sea, the ship, and a patch of land. Singbe tapped the land with the chalk.

"How long to get to the closest land?"

Montes didn't have to understand the words to know what he was being asked. They were starving and almost out of fresh water. He looked up at Singbe and held up two fingers. Singbe grabbed him by the collar and stood up. He lead him to the wheel, chained him to its base and ran another chain from his waist to the rail.

"Take us to the land."

Montes turned the wheel hard to port. His hands shook. He

wasn't sure if was from hunger or the certainty he would be dead soon.

By noon of the next day a pale thin shadow of land had become visible on the horizon. Montes took them in, finding a small inlet almost right away. They dropped anchor about a mile from a sandy beach. Singbe went into the captain's cabin and came out with two pistols and two small canvas bags filled with gold coins taken from a chest. Burnah, Yaboi, and nine other men waited for him in the rowboat they had lowered into the water.

"We will look for food," Singbe said. Try to trade these coins for it. If we are not back by the time the sun begins to set . . ."

"We will come after you." Grabeau interrupted.

"No. Take the ship and sail up the coastline. Look for a safe place."

Grabeau laughed nervously. "What would that look like, my friend?"

Singbe shook his head. "Just do it."

"I will not leave you behind to become a slave again. Any of you."

"I will not be a slave again. I will die first."

"The spirits did not keep us alive this long to suffer such a fate."

Singbe smiled. "We will find food and water, my friend. I promise."

He lowered himself into the boat and the four of them rowed through the choppy surf to the beach.

Grabeau waited on deck nervously. About an hour after Singbe and the others left, Kimbo came up to the bridge to tell him that Ka had died. It was the fever.

† † †

It was midafternoon when they got the rowboat pulled up out of the water. The beach was long and flat stretching away from the sea about thirty yards before breaking into rolling, high-grassed dunes. It was not like the beach at Lomboko, but neither was it like the whiteman's land called Cuba. There were no huts or dwellings of any kind to be seen. Singbe and Burnah decided to split the group in half. Singbe and Yaboi would take four others and head up to the right. Burnah would take his men down the beach to the left. Both of the leaders had a small canvas bag of gold coins from the captain's chest.

The men were dressed in billowy duck pantaloons and cotton shirts they had found in crates in the hold. Some of the men decided to leave their shirts behind in the boat but Singbe wore his, dull red and collarless, unbuttoned with the sleeves rolled up. He told the men to keep their swords hidden. He and Burnah had each taken a pistol. They would meet up again at the boat when the sun was two fists from the horizon.

Singbe and his group made their way up the dunes through the tall grass. At the top of a small hill they could see the *Amistad* riding anchor in the calm tide. In the other direction, the beach grass and sand gave way to a small thin forest of low pines. They headed toward the treeline. About halfway through the woods they came upon a few small houses set in a circle.

When they returned to the rowboat about an hour and a half later Singbe was worried. Neither group had found much food. His group had only been able to trade for a few chickens, a bottle of rum, and a bag of sweet potatoes. Burnah's group had not done much better. They had two dogs, a jug of apple cider, and four beets. Together they had only been able to find six houses. The people they encountered, all white, had been frightened. One old woman who had two goats would not even look at the gold in Burnah's hands. Instead she took the goats and herself into the house, locked the doors, and stood at one of the windows with an old musket in her hand.

But despite the lack of food, Singbe's group had found a brook that flowed into the sea. The water held only a hint of salt, which Singbe thought would dissipate as they moved back from the stream's mouth. The brook was also filled with fish and crabs, which he was sure they could catch if they could fashion a net of some sort. Perhaps tomorrow. He told the men to get in the boat. They would row down to the brook, fill the water keg, and head back to the *Amistad*. The food they had would have to get them through the night.

It was an odd sight to be sure, Henry Green would later say. A dozen blacks, black as coal and some nearly naked, standing around a rowboat holding a few chickens and a pair of dogs. Green, a local fisherman, had taken his wagon out to the dunes with four friends to shoot birds. They were going down to the mouth of Shelt's Brook, which would be thick with birds of all kinds feeding on the aquatic life stranded in pools left by the receding tide. But when he saw the Africans and the tattered black schooner anchored off shore, he slapped the reins hard. Singbe and the others didn't have time to get into the boat before the whites were upon them.

"What do we do?"

"Give me the coins and have the others hide their swords."

Singbe buttoned his shirt so the pistol stuck in the waist of his pants was hidden. Green and another man, Peletiah Fordham, hopped down from the wagon seat. Green walked up to Singbe slowly, stopped and smiled.

"You fellas lost?"

Singbe smiled as well but took a step back. He pointed to the ground.

"Koo-ba?"

"What?"

Singbe pointed to the dunes and the land beyond it in both directions.

"Koo-ba? Here Koo-ba?"

Green looked around and then realized what the black was asking.

"Naw. America. This is America. The United States."

Singbe had heard the word *America* before. At the slave factory in Lomboko, he had heard it many times. He pointed to the ground again.

"Slave here? Slave?"

Green shook his head.

"No, sir. This here is Long Island. It's part of New York. We don't have slavery here no more."

Singbe stared at him not sure what the answer had been.

"I don't think he believes ya, Henry," Fordham said.

Green turned to the wagon.

"Boys, we got slavery here?

The men all said "No." Green turned back to Singbe and shook his head hard.

"No. Got no slaves here."

A huge smile exploded across Singbe's face. He turned to the other tribesmen.

"The whiteman says they do not have slaves in this land."

The tribesmen broke into laughter and shouts. Some began jumping up and down excitedly and waved the machetes over their heads. Green and Fordham took a few steps back. The others in the wagon had become a bit nervous too and fingered their guns.

Singbe was screaming as loud as the others. But when he turned and saw the apprehension on the face of Green and the others he dropped to his knees and took Green's hand shaking it madly. Seeing this made Green even more nervous, Singbe reached under his shirt, took out the pistol, and handed it to Green.

"We mean you no harm, my friend." Singbe said the words in Mende, but the meaning was clear.

Green looked from the tribesmen and pointed out to the ship.

"Your ship looks like she's seen better days."

Singbe turned toward the *Amistad* and smiled.

"Ship. Ship Africa."

"Africa, huh?"

Singbe looked back to Green and made the motion of turning the ship's wheel.

"You ship?"

Green nodded. "Yeah, I've been fishing these waters since I was a boy. Got my own boat, *Lisa Marie*, up the coast aways." He wasn't sure Singbe understood so he made the same motion of hands on the wheel and nodded his head repeatedly. "Sure, I'm a sailor."

Singbe smiled and walked over to Burnah and the others.

"This whiteman knows how to drive a boat. The driver we have has deceived us. Maybe we can get this one to drive the ship for us."

"How?"

"We pay him with the gold and anything else he wants. He may have the ship for all I care if he can get us back home."

"How do we trust him?"

"He will be on the ship with us. He will have the money once we are underway and can claim the ship when we reach port. It will be different for him than the whites we have. It will be an issue of trade and property. It will be as much in his interest to complete the journey as it would be in ours."

"And what of the two whites and the black slave boy?"

Singbe hesitated. The slave boy had been condescending and contemptuous of them all during the journey, but he hated seeing any man a slave. He would offer to let him come with them, back to Mende or whatever tribe he chose. If the boy did not want that, he would be free to go in this land of the whites without slaves.

The slave traders were a different matter. Singbe wanted to kill them, especially the older one, who had been deceiving them all these weeks. They deserved to die. But Grabeau's words echoed in his head. Singbe knew killing the whites would be justified, but it would also serve no useful purpose beyond revenge.

"I would do this. I would give the slave boy his choice of freedom, either here or in Africa. And I would set the whites free, too, but not right away. A day after we are underway, we give them one of the long boats and enough food to get back to this land. From there they will be on their own."

"Where do we get enough food to finish our journey?"

"We give this whiteman some of the gold for food. He can go among the whites and buy what we need."

Burnah nodded. "This is a good plan. I think Grabeau would agree."

He handed his bag of gold to Singbe. Singbe walked back over to Green.

"You ship Africa? You Africa?"

The statement caught Green off guard and tickled a laugh out of his throat.

"Me sail to Africa? With you fellas? I don't think so, lad."

Singbe took Green's hand gently and turned it over so the palm was up. He opened one of the bags and poured out about a dozen gold coins into the sailor's.

"You ship Africa?"

Green felt the cool heavy coins against his weathered palms. The doubloons were Spanish but they were gold, at least two hundred dollars worth judging from the weight. And there was more in the bags, and probably more on the ship. Green looked at Fordham as he began to speak to Singbe.

"You want to pay me to sail to Africa? In gold?"

Singbe smiled and shook the bag. He pointed to Green and to the gold. He turned toward the *Amistad* sitting in the water, held up the bag and made a motion several times as if to capture it in the bag. He turned and held out the bag to Green.

"Henry. I think he wants to give you the gold and the ship."

"I think you are right, Peletiah."

Green reached out to take the bag from Singbe, but Singbe pulled it back.

"You ship Africa."

"I'm thinking about it, lad."

"Henry, you're not serious."

"Shut it, man. I'm thinking about it, I says."

"Henry! Henry! C'mere."

"Not now, Jack. I'm negotiating."

"Henry, yes. C'mere by the wagon, dammit. I got something to tell you. Before you do any more negotiating."

Green smiled to Singbe and walked back with to Jack at the wagon. Fordham and the other whitemen followed.

"It's the pirates!"

"Where? What pirates?"

"The blacks. They're the pirates they talked of in the paper."

"Jack! Did you drink the whole bottle while we've been standing here talking?"

"They're pirates I tell, ya. There was a report in the news just yesterday. Frederick Blanchard was reading it to me out on the docks while me and Corker were mending nets. He read it right out of the paper. 'Pirates,' it said, running up and down the Atlantic in a low-hulled black schooner with no flag. Ships had reported it to harbor masters in New York, Philadelphia, and Baltimore. And it said the pirates was black."

"These men ain't no pirates. In case you ain't been paying attention, they ain't even sailors. Look at the their ship, for God's sake. It's a shambles."

"Yes, look at the ship, Henry," Fordham said. "Look at it well. A low-hulled black schooner. No flag. And the gold. Them is Spanish coins. Came from a Spanish ship they pillaged, I reckon. And the pirates is black. Well, these men are certainly the blackest coloreds I've ever seen. Like they're fresh from Africa itself."

"Well, of course they are. That's why they want to go there. Bad enough, it seems, to give me gold and their ship. Naw, they ain't pirates. Just a bunch of ignorant savages who've lost their captain. Maybe to illness, maybe to somethin' else."

"Maybe from hunger. From the dogs and chickens and whatnot, it looks like they came ashore to scrounge some food."

"C'mon, Henry," Jack persisted. "Where's a bunch of coloreds get a schooner, no matter what shape it's in?"

"I don't care and I ain't asking. However their case may be, it's sure they're looking for a captain and I'm disposed to taking the job."

"What!? Are you mad?"

"Not at all. In fact, I'm about to become a rich man," claimed Green.

"But goin' to *Africa*?"

"I ain't goin' to Africa. I'll take 'em to New York harbor."

"New York?"

"Sure. It's an uncaptained ship. By law I can claim salvage rights. That means I have rights to a percentage of ship and cargo, whether these boys like it or not. It won't cost me no middle passage to Africa. Just a day's sailing up the sound. You boys help me crew her and I'll cut you in for a percentage."

The men agreed with Green instantly.

"Now, no laughing, no messing about," he cautioned, "no letting on, and by tomorrow night we'll all be rich men."

Green turned to Singbe with a smile. But the smile melted, replaced by a look of anger. Singbe turned following Green's stare to the sea. A large ship with broad white sails and a huge American flag flying from the middle mast had just come around the point and was headed toward the *Amistad*.

"Shit, lads. It's the government."

At that moment all of the men saw a puff of smoke appear just above the big ship's bow. It was followed almost immediately by a loud thundercrack and an explosion of water about two hundred yards behind *Amistad*'s stern.

"Holy Christ," Jack whispered. "It *is* the pirates."

Singbe and the other tribesmen broke for their boat. Green followed after them. Grabeau already had the anchor out of the water and they were beginning to lower one of the big sails.

"Wait! Wait! Take me with you!" Green yelled.

Green ran up to the rowboat as the men were pushing into the water. He tried to get in but a flash of a machete in Burnah's hands changed his mind. The tribesmen got all four oars in the water and began pulling hard. Green watched them, and then turned and began jumping up and down in the water.

"Shit! Shit! Shit! Shit!"

The sun was beginning to burn and bleed just above the top of the dunes. The eight men pulling the oars stared into it, watching the distance grow between them and the raging whiteman on the shore. Singbe stood so far forward in the bow that his front foot was almost in the sea. The big ship, three-masted, wide and solid, had a huge wave cresting from its bow and a fat wake trailing behind. It was gaining quickly and Singbe thought it would be on the *Amistad* soon if they could not get her underway. He had Burnah steer the boat ahead of the *Amistad* so they could meet it as it was moving. Grabeau could throw them down lines and they could scramble on board with the food and leave the rowboat behind.

Another blast roared out of the deck gun, hitting the waves a little closer, but wide. The tribesmen were struggling to get the sails down. The *Amistad* was barely moving. Singbe and the others in the boat were less than one hundred yards away. He yelled with all his spirit for the men on the *Amistad* to throw down lines. In two minutes they were there. Burnah grabbed a line and tied it off in the center of the rowboat. The boat banged against the hull of the slow-moving ship.

"Tie it off with one of the other lines!"

As Singbe worked a knot, the others went up the dangling lines one by one. Singbe was able to tie off the rope, but now the little boat was slamming and bobbing against the hull even more violently.

"Get up on deck. Go!"

Burnah pulled himself up the line he had been holding. All the other men were out. Singbe undid the knot on the rowboat and pulled himself up the rope. There was a loud crack and the sea exploded less than ten yards away. As he got to the top of the rail, he saw the other ship across the deck, about thirty yards out, slowing, angling to come up right next to them. There was a man on the deck with a big hat, yelling through a megaphone. The ship had hatches all along its hull just above the waterline. Each hatch held a cannon. On the bow, a man stood at the deck cannon aimed right at them.

The cannon shots had frightened most of the men. Many had gone down below. Others were running back and forth aimlessly on the deck, screaming and shouting madly. Grabeau was at the wheel, yelling out commands.

"Get the sails down! We must get the sails down!"

Burnah already had the men from the rowboat working on one of the sails. Singbe grabbed a man who was trying to get down the hatch. It was Ba, a Mendeman.

"Ba! Help me with the sail."

"But Singbe . . . !"

"Do it! Or be a slave again to the whites."

"Singbe!" It was Grabeau's voice. Singbe turned. Whitemen

were coming up over the railing. Six of them were already on deck and others were clamoring up the lines. The whites pointed their guns and yelled at the tribesmen. Burnah drew his pistol but one of the whites slapped it from his hand with the butt end of a musket and then swung the barrel around to his face. A loud crack of gunfire ripped into the air. Burnah jumped with the sound. But he was not shot. A tall white with a broad hat had fired his pistol into the air.

"Stand off! Stand off, I say!"

He dropped the pistol so it was even with Burnah's face. There were more than a dozen other whites on deck now, all with muskets and pistols aimed at the tribesmen. A deep sagging ran through Burnah, as if something had reached into him and drained out all hope and spirit from his heart. He dropped his head and sank to his knees. One by one, the other tribesmen on the deck also fell to their knees.

"No!"

The man in the broad hat swung his pistol's sight across the deck to the scream. He found Singbe, still standing, holding a machete.

"Mr. Clifford! Mr. Cobb! Belay that man of his weapon."

Two sailors, muskets leveled, walked over toward Singbe. Singbe backed up as they came. He reached the railing and glanced down into the sea. The whites were nearly upon him now. One was yelling at him. Singbe held the machete out, both hands on the grip and swung wildly.

"I will not be a slave! Never again! Never again!"

Both the whites were yelling now. One of the sailors was less than four feet away. Singbe let out a loud war cry and threw the machete. The man ducked. The other man fired. Singbe went over the railing.

"Man overboard!"

"He's off the starboard bow," yelled the officer in the broad hat.

By now the *Amistad* had been secured to the other ship with lines and drawn close. Three men had stayed in the longboat that had been used by the boarding party. They pulled around

Amistad's bow. Singbe was about one hundred yards away and swimming toward the shore. It was a land without slaves. If he could get there, he might be safe.

"I want him alive, Mr. Jansens!" the officer yelled from the railing.

"Aye, sir! Pull in front of him, lads! Cut him off from the shore!"

Singbe did not look back, but he could hear the boat and the men yelling. The beach, though almost a mile away, looked close enough to touch.

A musket cracked. The volley whistled over his head and exploded into the water about ten yards ahead of him. Singbe turned. The longboat was right there, a man in the bow reloading. Singbe dove beneath the waves and swam away from the boat, away from the land. The water of the Atlantic was thick and green. He swam hard but could see nothing. It was peaceful, quiet, like a cold and heavy cloud all around. If he died here, deep under the sea, would his spirit be able to find its way to the sky, or would it be lost to wander with the fishes? Stefa and the children flashed into his mind. Even now, some part of him still believed he would see them again. He swam until the air in his lungs burned and clawed at his chest and throat to get out. He couldn't hold it anymore. He kicked hard, breaking out of the surf, rising above the waves with a desperate gurgling gasp. He turned only to see the flat of an oar slapping into his temple.

"Welcome to America, you pirate son-of-a-bitch!"

In his mind, Singbe saw Stefa, then darkness. The sailors lifted his limp body into the boat.

The ship, the USS *Washington*, had secured all tow lines on the *Amistad*. Its commander, Lieutenant Thomas Gedney, had listened to the well-spoken Spaniard, Pepe Ruiz, tell his teary-eyed tale about how the cargo of slaves had mutinied and murdered the captain and crew. Where were they headed? Ruiz was not sure. He thought perhaps they meant to find a slave-free port, or perhaps undertake piracy, but they were poor sailors, and if it were not for the other Spaniard—Montes—and his skill at the helm, they all would have been dead long ago. Thank the grace of God that the U.S. Navy had found them. Ruiz, who mentioned that he was schooled in Connecticut, said they were all starving and it would have been only a matter of days before they were dead of hunger. Ruiz also expressed interest in meeting with a representative of the Spanish counsel as soon as they were in port so he could arrange to get his slaves and what was left of the cargo back to Cuba.

Gedney assured the Spaniards that everything would be taken care of when they were in port. He had slaves in the *Amistad*'s hold under guard, except for the leader, who had been chained and put in the *Washington*'s brig, and the children, whom he placed in Ferrer's cabin. Gedney had also ordered his cook to provide full rations for everyone and as much water as they wanted. He gave his own cabin to Ruiz and Montes. It was near midnight before the *Washington* got underway.

"Plot us a course for port, Mr. Tucker," Gedney ordered.

"Aye, sir. New York, sir?"

"No. New London."

"Aye, sir."

Lieutenant Meade, Gedney's executive officer, turned his back to the navigator and whispered, "New London?"

"I know, Richard, it's a little farther away. But I mean to claim salvage on this ship for us and the crew."

"We can do that in New York as well as Connecticut, Tom. I don't understand the difference."

Gedney smiled. "How is salvage calculated?"

"It's a percentage based on the aggregate appraised value of ship and cargo."

"Right. That means if we tow her into New York, we lay claim to the ship and whatever is left in those crates in the hold. But if we tow her into New London, we can immediately increase the cargo's value by a substantial sum."

"How so?"

"Slavery is still legal in Connecticut."

A smile broke across Meade's face and then they both began laughing like men who had just found themselves standing in a pile of gold.

PART TWO

America

The Fuse

Andrew T. Judson believed himself a fair and reasonable man, and many people in Connecticut agreed with this assessment. Judson commanded great respect among civic leaders, politicians, his peers, and the press. He was a devout Congregationalist and rented a front pew at the great church on New Haven's green for himself and his family. He was widely known to be a man of principle and respectable sternness, a man of great intelligence, and, when the situation demanded, a man of relentless perseverance. Judson was also a good Democrat, a rising star in the party which had held the White House for nearly eleven years now. Many attributed Judson's ascension through party ranks in part to his smooth political sagacity and in part to Prudence Crandall.

As people in Connecticut knew all too well, Prudence Crandall was the proprietor and sole teacher at a small private academy for girls in Canterbury, a close-knit village near the border with Rhode Island. Miss Crandall and her school were respected and welcomed members of the community; that is, until 1833. That year the school enrolled a new student, Sarah Harris, the daughter of Prudence's housecleaner. Sarah was black. A few weeks later two more black girls from New York arrived at the school.

The rumblings in Canterbury started very quickly. How dare Prudence Crandall teach blacks side-by-side with whites? Such a thing was unheard of, and in the eyes of many, an outright abomination. And who gave her the authority to teach blacks, male or female, to read, write, and cipher? Who did she think she was, anyway—bringing this kind of controversy and trouble into a good, industrious, Christian town like Canterbury? Surely the town was as tolerant and liberal as any other in the state, but everyone knew that educating blacks with whites would just bring trouble. Never mind the local parents and community leaders who would not stand for that kind of reckless disregard for the natural order of things—what about the others, the people whose anger and righteous indignation would carry them for miles and days from other towns and other states to Canterbury, to right something that was so clearly wrong? At the worst they would bring a level of violence with them. At the very least, the town would be vilified, a soiled mark on the map where few would want to settle or do business.

Prudence Crandall listened to the objections, at first whispered in private, later spat right at her on the streets, and finally shouted at full volume during a packed town meeting. Crandall attended the meeting and spoke—something women rarely did since they were not permitted to vote or hold office. She argued that if the blacks were freemen coming from states that had outlawed slavery, then they had a right to learn and be treated as equals. More abominations! Besides, others countered, if the blacks came from states where they were free, then they should get their education there in black training schools. Prudence could see where all this was going, and she knew the townspeople would never agree to let her continue teaching black alongside white. So she made a decision.

Now, throughout Canterbury, Prudence Crandall was

known as a stubborn woman, principled and resolute in her ways. So when she stood up at the end of the meeting and publicly declared that she would give up her practice of teaching the black students together with whites, more than a few people were surprised. Many broke into applause. Prudence remained standing and waited until the clapping died down. Then she took a took a deep breath and asked to finish her piece. Everyone assumed she was going to apologize to the town for her thoughtless, mule-headed actions of the past few weeks. Instead, she informed them that her academy would now be open exclusively to free black girls from anywhere in the United States.

The outrage that followed flowed out of Canterbury and across the state. Before she could begin enrolling students in her new academy, Connecticut, at the urging of Canterbury's state representative, passed a law forbidding the teaching of students who were not "citizens and inhabitants" of a town. Prudence moved to sidestep this requirement by giving her new students residence in her own home. The state immediately sued. The state's district prosecutor, who was also the same representative from Canterbury, argued that "the founding fathers never intended to include blacks under the term *citizens*."

Two trials, including one before the state's supreme court, ended in hung juries. The citizens of Canterbury decided not to wait for an appeal to the U.S. Supreme Court. Instead, they broke into Prudence's house, and destroyed everything they could get their hands on. There were threats of lynchings and more violence. In fear for her life and the lives of her students, Prudence sent the black children back to their families and moved out west, finally settling in Kansas. She never returned to Connecticut.

The legislator and prosecutor, the zealous proponent and some would say manipulator of the law, the man who had repeatedly told representatives from the press that he was a reasonable person, one with no animosity toward the black race but simply a man who believed deeply in natural laws as God and the founding fathers of this great country had intended, was Andrew T. Judson, now a federal district judge appointed by President Martin Van Buren. He was also the man sitting in the wardroom of the USS *Washington*, conducting a hearing about a curious case of a band of black pirates who had been captured off Montauk Point.

Judson had been summoned by the federal district attorney, William S. Holabird, also an appointee of President Martin Van Buren. Holabird was a nervous, prudent man with a broad, ruddy face, thick, curly hair and a stout, pear-shaped body. He was a competent lawyer, excelling in cases where firm legal precedent had been set and could be cited. His distress was obvious then, when word came regarding the capture of the black-crewed pirate schooner that had been written about in the papers for the last few weeks. He immediately became agitated over why the Navy had brought the ship to his district when the New York office was so much better suited for this type of thing. After all, pirates!? There certainly were laws and cases referring to this type of thing but—for the love of God—pirates had not been an issue in these parts for more than a hundred and fifty years. However, after meeting Lieutenant Gedney and listening to the two Cubans, Holabird felt somewhat relieved. It wasn't piracy at all, simply a claim of property rights.

Holabird was sympathetic to the plight of Ruiz and Montes and the distress their rebellious slaves had caused them. The men had obviously been brought to hell's very gates by these crazed blacks. In fact, Ruiz had assured him that if it wasn't for their superior intelligence and savvy, both he and Montes would have been long dead.

Legally, the case seemed fairly straightforward to Holabird: a formal hearing, depositions for the record, and then the ship and cargo would be turned over to the Spanish consul in Boston for safe passage back to Havana and eventual prosecution of the slaves under Spanish law. However, because foreign nationals were involved, and because Lieutenant Gedney had mentioned salvage, and most important, because Holabird was a extremely careful man, he decided to send an immediate dispatch to John Forsyth, the U.S. Secretary of State. He informed Forsyth of the situation as it had presented itself, mentioned that Judge Judson (whom Forsyth knew well) had been summoned for a hearing, and requested additional instructions regarding international law pertaining to a case of this nature.

Attending the hearing on board the ship were officers of the *Washington*; Wilson Bright, a reporter from the *New London Gazette*; and Dwight P. Janes, a recorder for the court. Judson began by taking the statements of Ruiz and Montes. Though Ruiz's English was excellent, Judson asked Lieutenant Meade, who was fluent in Spanish, to translate for Montes. It would ensure a higher level of credibility for the record. Not that Judson considered that another side to the Cubans' story even existed. The black slaves were after all apprehended in command of the ship. But the judge was an adherent of proper protocol and wanted that to show in the record.

Ruiz and Montes told essentially the same story. Both men had been awakened by screams early on the morning of July 3. They came on deck to find that the slaves had rebelled and killed the captain and were fighting the crew. Montes and Ruiz joined in and fought valiantly but were overpowered by the sheer numbers of their attackers. Montes had been able to convince the blacks that he was a skilled seaman and was permitted to navigate at night. He had steered north hoping to come upon Florida or the Carolinas, but the blacks thwarted every attempt at freedom. It was only by their wits and the vigilance of heaven that they weren't killed on several occasions during their ordeal. The slave cabin boy, Antonio, who also spoke Spanish, echoed the words of Ruiz and Montes.

"It is as they said," Antonio claimed. "They are a bunch of plantation slaves who killed my captain and went wild. They tortured us during the voyage and threatened to kill us almost every day."

"It is only by God's grace and the bravery of the United States Navy that we are alive," said Ruiz.

Judson nodded gravely. He dismissed the boy but asked the two Cubans to stay.

"Bring me the leader."

Two sailors escorted Singbe from the brig. Chained and manacled hand and foot, he still wore the red shirt and duck pantaloons. As he came before Judson, he turned and stared at Montes and Ruiz. Ruiz began laughing and spoke to Singbe in Spanish.

"Still think you are the big chief nigger, eh? Well, Mr. Chief, we shall see how exalted you feel when your black carcass is being burned at the stake in Havana."

Judson looked at Singbe, who stood proud and tall despite the chains, and then spoke to Ruiz.

"For the record, what is this one's name?"

Ruiz's mind reeled through the names on the manifest. He could only remember one.

"Cinqué. Joseph Cinqué.

"Lieutenant Meade, for the record, ask Joseph Cinqué why he rebelled against his white masters and murdered the *Amistad*'s crew in cold blood."

"Your honor, I am afraid these blacks all speak an obscure field dialect," Ruiz said quickly. "It is a crude amalgamation of Spanish and African. I doubt they will be able to understand Lieutenant Meade. I can't even understand them myself."

"We shall try. Mr. Meade."

Meade asked the question and several others at Judson's request. Singbe appeared to listen intently to Meade but offered only silence in response to each question.

"I do not think he is being recalcitrant, your honor," Meade said. "It appears he does not understand a word I am saying."

Judson stood up and walked over to Singbe. He began speaking slowly and loudly.

"Do you know where you are? Do you understand what is happening to you? Why did you rise up against your masters?" Judson swept his arm broadly across the room and pointed to Ruiz and Montes. "Why did you lead the other slaves in rebellion?"

Singbe stared at Judson. Judson let out a little laugh and turned to go back to his seat.

"No slave! Singbe no slave. Africa!"

The room froze. Judson turned slowly.

Singbe pointed his hand to his chest, rattling the chains. "No slave! Africa! Africa!"

"You speak English? Does this one speak English?"

"No, Your Honor. Well, perhaps he learned some on board," Ruiz smiled nervously. "There was a slave who spoke a little English. But he died a few days after the rebellion."

Judson stepped closer to Singbe.

"You speak English? Eh? Come on now, speak your piece. Speak."

"No slave. No slave."

Judson prodded him for more, but it was all of the whiteman's language Singbe knew.

"That's it, is it? Well, you are a slave, my friend, despite your attempts to the contrary. And what you just said sounds like an admission of a rebellion to me. It will be noted for the record. You will have to pay for your crimes."

Judson pointed to the chains and then to Ruiz and Montes. "Do you understand, Joseph Cinqué?"

A sarcastic smile broke across Singbe's face. He pointed to himself and then drew a finger across his throat.

"There, you see," Judson said, returning to his chair and smiling. "He understands well what he has done, what this hearing is about. And I dare say he understands the probable consequences he will meet when he gets back to his country."

Singbe stepped toward the judge. A sailor lowered his musket, stopping the advance. Singbe began speaking loudly in Mende.

"I am a free man, a Mendeman. I will not be a slave again. You can bind me with chains, you can whip my back and my feet until my skin is gone and my blood has run from my body. But I will not be a slave again! I will not be a slave to any man! You will have to kill me first."

If the outburst shook Judson, he made no indication. He stared at Singbe a moment, and then took a pinch of snuff and began writing calmly.

"Right. Mr. Gedney, please have your men take the slave

leader below with the others. Mr. Ruiz, Mr. Montes, I believe your participation in this hearing is finished. Lieutenant Gedney tells me you possess some Spanish currency. There is a bank in town which can make an exchange for you. I will have the federal marshal take you over. The Willow House is a fine inn, and Mr. Barsted, its proprietor, sets out an excellent meal for his guests. It will probably be the most comfortable place for you until we go back to New Haven. The Spanish consul is coming down from Boston and will meet you there."

"Thank you, Your Honor," Ruiz shook Judson's hand several times. "Thank you very much."

"God bless you, gentlemen," Judson said. "You've been through more hell than any men should ever have to endure."

The Cubans left the wardroom. Judson continued the hearing, taking statements from Gedney, Meade, and a few of the crewmen. Holabird tried to persuade Gedney that claiming salvage might unnecessarily prolong the process, and perhaps it would be better to pursue the claim privately and seek recompense from Ruiz and Montes directly. Gedney refused, saying he knew of many men who had tried to settle salvage outside the courts, only to see nothing come of it. He would stick with the proper legal channels.

After they finished, Meade decided he had to add one more thing. "Your Honor. Mr. Holabird," he said. "There is a curious element regarding the slaves."

"What would that be, sir?"

"None of them know their own names, Your Honor."

"I beg your pardon?"

"After we had gotten them all on board and I had the ship's manifest, I began calling out names to catalog which of the original cargo had survived. Lieutenant Gedney and I wanted to use this information and compare it with the purchase price of each black to add it to the value of the full cargo so we could calculate the salvage percentage for ourselves and the crew. However, as I called out the names, no one responded, man or child. I went through the manifest three times. I might as well have been speaking Greek."

"Is there a point to this information, sir?" Holabird asked, closing up his valise.

"Well, sir, I think so. No matter how obscure the field dialect, one would think that a man would know his name, the name he has been called by his masters since birth."

"But what bearing does that have on any of this?" Holabird persisted.

"I think Lieutenant Meade is just doing his duty as a fine officer and giving us complete information. I appreciate your thoroughness and it will be noted, sir," Judson said.

"Thank you, Your Honor. But I think that perhaps..."

"I think that is enough for now, gentlemen," Judson said, standing up. "Since you are adamant in your claims for salvage, I will rule that this is a case of property and must be heard in circuit court. I will set a date and notify you directly. The federal marshal will take the prisoners to the New Haven jail since I believe it is the only one in the state large enough to accommodate so many captives."

"Circuit court! Your honor, isn't it possible we could hand over the ship and cargo to the Spanish officials in the interim and begin the extradition procedures?"

"Not with a property claim by U.S. citizens involved, Mr. Holabird. But we can discuss that later. I'm sure our friend from the press is anxious to go and begin writing this most exciting story, and these brave men from the Navy are probably equally eager to enjoy a little shore leave." Judson moved in close to Holabird and took his arm. "I would appreciate it, Mr. Holabird, if you would walk with me to my carriage."

Holabird tried to renew the conversation about extradition but Judson stopped him until they were at the carriage. At that point Judson asked Holabird to join him inside for a moment.

"William, did you receive any instructions regarding this case from superiors in New York or Washington?"

"I sent a dispatch to Secretary Forsyth when the ship made port, but I have not received a reply yet. Why?"

Even though they were in a closed carriage, Judson lowered his voice. "Do you know what Lieutenant Meade may have been implying when he spoke about the blacks not knowing their names?"

"I would venture that he simply found it quite curious and thought it prudent to mention on the record. As you said, Andrew, he was just being thorough."

Judson went silent for a few seconds. He took out his pocket watch and began flipping it over and over in his hand. "I am considering sending a dispatch to Secretary Forsyth myself, William. Are you familiar with the Anglo-Spanish Treaty of 1819?"

Holabird pretended to think for a moment. "No, I can't say that I am."

"You should look it up. It may prove to be interesting reading, especially in light of recent events."

"Why? What are we considering here, Andrew?"

"If I am correct, we are considering much more than any of us may be able to handle."

What Judson did not realize, and what, in his haste to quickly end the hearing he had failed to consider, was that another man in the *Washington*'s wardroom understood exactly what Meade may have been alluding to. However, if Judson knew Dwight Janes's background and political beliefs, it is absolutely certain that the judge would have never permitted him to serve as court recorder for these proceedings. But Janes did not discuss his political ideas readily with others, especially with men such as Andrew Judson. After all, in 1839, abolitionists were considered occupants of the radical fringe, religious zealots bent on destroying the natural order of things, and, some would say, tearing the United States apart. Publicly proclaiming such sentiments could do damage to a man's career, especially a man who made his living in the courts. So whenever he was asked about slavery or the rightful treatment of freed blacks, Janes smiled and feigned indifference.

But Janes's convictions were deep and strong, and he knew very well the substance of the Anglo-Spanish Treaty of 1819. He also had seen and heard enough to strongly suspect this cargo of slaves was not what Ruiz and Montes would have everyone believe. He wasn't positive, but his heart and mind were ready to jump to conclusions. And now, running down the docks, he was even more ready to help someone else do so as well.

"Mr. Bright! Mr. Bright!"

Wilson Bright had been walking slowly, reviewing his notes and mentally organizing the story in his head. He was twenty-four and had worked for the *Gazette* for six years, the last two as a reporter. This was by far the biggest story he or anyone else had ever handled for the paper, and he was eager to get back and begin writing. He had composed a story two days earlier, when the *Washington* had towed the *Amistad* into port, that was based on interviews with a few of the *Washington*'s sailors. They had told him that the black slaves were traveling with the families who owned them and had killed every soul, twenty-six white men, women, and children, as well as the ship's captain and crew. Before the *Washington*'s crew had apprehended the blacks in pitched battle, the *Amistad*'s buccaneers had spent the last three months on a pirating spree along the eastern seaboard, pillaging, murdering, and sinking unsuspecting ships. The story had run in a special edition of the *Gazette* and was still being picked up and reprinted by papers all over the country. Now that he had heard the facts directly from Ruiz and Montes, Bright was anxious to write the next chapter of this story, as well as set the record straight.

"Mr. Janes. Fascinating hearing, eh?"

"Absolutely, sir. Absolutely. Especially so in what was not said."

"What do you mean?" asked the young reporter.

"By Lieutenant Meade, I mean."

"I'm still not following you."

"Well, the blacks. It's obvious they are Africans."

Bright began laughing. "You don't say? Is that where those fellows come from?"

Janes stepped in front of Bright, blocking his path. "What I'm saying, Mr. Bright, is that's exactly where they come from."

Bright's laughter trickled down and then stopped suddenly. "You mean they're *Africans* directly from *Africa*?"

"That's my meaning exactly."

"But ain't that illegal?"

"For nearly twenty years, I believe. And as you might have noticed, there were certainly more than a few of those men who looked less than twenty. Not to mention the children."

Bright began to write again with his pencil. "Which means..."

"Which means first of all that I am not a source for this information. And if I see my name in print, Mr. Bright, I will deny ever having spoken with you and pursue a suit of slander against you and your paper."

"Certainly, certainly. Being that you are, shall we say, anonymous..."

"Anyway, you don't need me. You have all the facts. Look at how none of the blacks responded to their names despite repeated questioning by Lieutenant Meade. And that language that the leader inveighed His Honor Judge Judson with, that wasn't any amalgamation of Spanish, dialect or not."

"Well, it sure didn't sound anything like the Spanish Mr. Montes and the cabin boy spoke, that's for sure."

"Look at how dark the blacks were, black as coal, not like any home-bred stock I've ever seen."

"No. No, me neither. Well, that is to say, I've never seen but two blacks in my whole life, being from these parts and all. But this lot was much darker, you're right."

"And finally, consider the black leader, this Joseph Cinqué, and his proclamation in broken English, 'No slave, Africa.' The man learns but a few words in English and this is what he chooses? Certainly that combined with a desperate rebellion points to something more that what we saw represented today."

"Perhaps you're right, sir."

"Mr. Bright, if these are Africans fresh from Africa, then there may be an even bigger story behind this than your writings about pirates a few days back."

"Well, I'm not so sure there, Mr. Janes. Pirates was a big story. The biggest we've ever seen around here. But there may be a point to what you are saying here."

"I didn't say anything."

"Right, sir. Right. I've gotta go. Good talking with you, Mr. Janes." Bright turned and ran down the dock and went up the road to the *Gazette* office. Janes went around the corner, in the other direction, and headed to his office. He needed to write a letter as quickly as possible.

† † †

The tribesmen had been receiving food almost from the moment of their capture. Many were sick, and nearly all were suffering from malnutrition. The night after the hearing they were given a meal of fish stew, corn on the cob, and as much water as they could drink. Many of them had been wearing only loincloths when the ship was taken. The marshal saw to it that each was given at least a pair of pants and a shirt; some bright country dresses had been found for the girls. On the morning after the hearing, the captives were given a breakfast of biscuits and gravy. Then the men were chained together and seated in three open wagons, the girls remained unshackled and were allowed to sit up front with the drivers. The forty-mile journey to New Haven would take nearly all day.

From his seat, Grabeau could see Singbe alone in the fourth wagon, the lead wagon, not only wearing manacles, but chained to a ring in the wagon's floor, as well. Across from Singbe sat a white man wearing a thin-brimmed hat and holding a long musket. Despite the chains, Singbe sat straight, defiant. From time to time he would look back at the other wagons and smile as if they were going on some sort of picnic. His bravado warmed Grabeau's heart, but at the same time he couldn't help but think that soon they would all be dead.

† † †

Secretary of State Forsyth left Cobble House, the little tavern in Georgetown, and told his driver to take the carriage to the White House at a quick pace. As he rode, Forsyth's hand twice absently reached up to the pocket inside his suit jacket, the pocket that held Holabird's letter.

In his late fifties, Forsyth cut an impressive figure in Washington. He was well-dressed and handsome with sharp, chiseled features, thick hair still mostly dark, and long sideburns that nearly reached his chin as was the style of the times. A former member of the U.S. House of Representatives and governor from Georgia, he had also served as U.S. Minister to Spain from 1819 to 1829. He had been a key adviser to Martin Van Buren during the election of 1836 and appointed Secretary of State soon after the contest was won. Outwardly he was hailed as an excellent addition to any social gathering, a good Christian man, and, being single, a dandy with the ladies. Political insiders knew him to be a shrewd negotiator and a prescient political mind. John Forsyth was also an owner of slaves and a staunch advocate of slavery and state's rights.

In many ways, President Martin Van Buren's career had mirrored Forsyth's, though Van Buren's progress had been achieved along a higher plane. Also in his late fifties, Van Buren, too, had served in the Congress, but as a senator. He had also been elected governor of his state, in this case, New York, the most populous and economically powerful state in the Union. He had served as Secretary of State during Andrew Jackson's first term, later resigning to become ambassador to Great Britain. But he was refused confirmation by an increasingly truculent Senate. Jackson responded by making Van Buren his running mate in 1832.

Four years later Van Buren had ridden to the White House on a promise to continue staying Old Hickory's course of democratic reforms and bold individualism, as well as a vow to implement a laissez faire policy toward business. However, the economy soured in early 1838, taking the country into a deep recession. The inevitable scattered political scandals that seem to accompany every administration took their toll, as did growing charges of soft leadership and a lack of vision for a growing nation. These factors, coupled with the increasing popularity and vocal denunciations of the new Whig party led by Henry Clay, were quickly eroding popular support. Van Buren's chances in the next election, less than a year away, were troubled at best. Still, he was a strong campaigner and knew the power of the presidency. If he could navigate through the next few months without encountering any serious disasters, and if the economy showed a little life, he was confident he could retain the White House in 1840.

With regard to slavery, Van Buren publicly walked a careful line. Though he was accused by many anti-slavery proponents as "a Northerner with a Southern heart," he professed no strong opinion one way or the other to the holding of slaves, saying only that it was totally up to each state to decide the legality and propriety of the issue. There were events in his administration, however, that on the surface would cast doubt as to where his own sympathies lay.

One involved the American consul to Havana, Nicholas Trist, who had been accused of accepting cash payoffs in exchange for allowing foreign ships sailing with African-born slaves to sail under the American flag. American flagged ships were rarely hailed or detained by British and American anti-slaving patrols. Though there was substantial evidence implying guilt, Trist denied any such involvement. Not only did Van Buren support him, he also permitted Trist to retain his post despite the controversy.

Van Buren had also instructed Forsyth to avoid involvement in a joint Anglo-French effort to conduct regular, coordinated patrols of Africa's western coastline as a way of suppressing illegal slave trading. The refusal to join the effort was controversial since American ships were already involved in this type of activity via the Treaty of 1819. However, the Anglo-French agreement would permit mutual search rights and Van Buren did not want to cede any maritime rights of sovereignty onboard American-flagged ships. He also didn't want to risk an incident where an American ship was found carrying contraband Africans. That would certainly cause a very public debate at home about slavery, an issue that was rapidly becoming more heated and emotional. This more than anything was the crux of Van Buren's stance. Whatever his personal sympathies toward slavery may have been, they were greatly outweighed by his certainty that an event which thrust the question of slavery directly into the public spotlight would be akin to putting a match to a powder keg. Slavery was an issue that Van Buren was sure could shake the Union to its very core, and one he would do almost anything to keep at bay and muted during an election season, if not throughout his presidency.

Forsyth also knew well the danger of letting any issue regarding slavery slip into the public arena. Still, he was not at all distressed after reading Holabird's letter. It did seem like a simple case of property rights, and if handled quickly, this affair of rebellious Cuban slaves hauled into New London should dissipate by early September. But after his meeting at Cobble House with the Spanish ambassador Frederico Calderón, Forsyth realized that the *Amistad* situation must be resolved immediately, which is why he moved with a certain urgency as he walked down the White House halls toward the Oval office.

Forsyth laid out the basic details of the case to the President and read aloud parts of Holabird's letter. Van Buren was attentive and interested. Like most Americans, he had been intrigued by the accounts of pirates appearing in newspapers during the summer. Discovering it was a wayward ship captained by rebellious slaves was less exciting, though perhaps more agitating, especially now that this ship had come to rest in an American port. However, it appeared that Holabird had the situation well in hand, and, as long as it was handled properly, Van Buren saw no far-reaching problems.

"It could get worse, Mr. President."

"How so?"

"Just before coming to see you, I had a private lunch with the Spanish Ambassador, Señor Calderón. I wanted to make sure nothing existed regarding the *Amistad* that had escaped Holabird's eye."

"Well, you wouldn't have come in here this afternoon on short notice unless you discovered something."

"The slaves, sir. They are contraband Africans direct from the black market."

Van Buren got up and walked over to the window. He looked through the glass out onto the rolling green lawn and the carriages traveling in the street far beyond. "Calderón is sure of this?"

"Apparently his office had been alerted some time ago that the *Amistad* was missing. A wreck had been suspected, but there have also been a number of slave uprisings over the past few years, so that type of thing could not be ruled out. When the reports of black pirates began reaching the newspapers, he began to have his suspicions. When I indicated what Holabird had seen on the New London pier, Señor Calderón came forth with the information."

"Holabird has no knowledge of this?"

"No. Neither do the Navy officers who apprehended the ship. However, if the claim for salvage is pressed it will almost certainly mean a court date. That could take weeks to resolve. The longer those blacks are here, the more likely it is someone will discover their origins. And if that happens, well, sir..."

"...The Northern press will go berserk with the story," the President said, finishing Forsyth's thought.

"There are also the fringe groups to consider, sir, especially abolitionists. They would most definitely see this as a call to arms, so to speak."

"Abolitionists. Christ. The last thing I wish is give those lunatic rabble-rousers an opportunity to assert any shred of legitimacy."

Van Buren turned back to Forsyth and sat down. "God, we do not need this. Not now of all times. I can see it turning into so much shit and feathers."

"I fully agree, sir," Forsyth responded.

"Can we resolve this now, without the salvage trial or any other sort of public pageantry?"

"I believe, sir, that if we act quickly, we can turn the ship and its human cargo over to the Spanish immediately and expedite its passage back to Cuba. I will recommend to Señor Calderón that the salvage claims be handled quickly and privately."

"Following that course will sidestep due process. The press will surely raise a row."

"Regardless of the event, what can the press say once the ship and the blacks are gone? Besides, I believe we can claim that the actions of the blacks are covered under Pickney's Treaty. Their taking of the ship can certainly be construed as an act of piracy. It appears on the surface to be a cut-and-dried case. And no matter what a man's feelings about slavery, the facts as presented show that these savages killed the ship's crew and held their white masters in a heinous state of captivity for nearly sixty days."

"Unless it's discovered that the rebelling slaves are actually freemen illegally pressed into bondage. Then, this whole thing could light a fuse that would burn very brightly."

"Yes, and might well blow us all to kingdom come."

"Agreed. Send a direct dispatch to Holabird directing him to stand down from having a hearing and avoid any legal proceedings. Inform him that this situation will be handled via diplomatic channels through the executive."

"Yes, sir. Immediately." Forsyth shifted, ready to act.

"Also, contact Señor Calderón and inform him of our intentions. I'm sure he will want to keep this transaction as quiet as we do, however, you may want to remind him of our desires toward maintaining complete discretion."

"Yes, sir."

Forsyth sent the message to Holabird via special courier. It arrived in New London the day after the hearing. Wilson Bright's story had already run that morning. The headline mentioned only the hearing regarding the *Amistad*'s slaves. But in the third paragraph, Bright pointed to pieces of evidence that cast serious doubt on whether the blacks were slaves or freemen, "stolen from their homes and families, and enslaved against treaty and convention."

The fuse had been lit.

Friends and Enemies

The line stretched out the door, around the building's corner, and flowed out onto the New Haven green. A rough estimate put the number at more than one thousand people—men, women, and children, elite members of local society, farmers from the outlying communities, merchants, sailors, clergy, journalists from across the nation, and others. It was reported that some people were traveling more than one hundred miles by foot just to see this incredible sight. It was only 8:00 A.M. and, as it had done for the last two days, the line would surely grow longer.

The occurrence of such a line, a line that quickly formed in the first hours after the new prisoners' arrival and that had grown steadily since, was equally incredible. It was, after all, a jail, one that had seen its share of murderers, thieves, corrupt politicians, and wrongly accused men. But no one in Connecticut could ever remember having a chance to see a sight such as this—Africans! Men as black as a moonless night, people said, and fresh from the wilds of Africa.

The story in the *New London Gazette* detailing the hearing had reached New Haven before the tribesmen, and the idea that the slaves might actually be Africans caught the eye of both the New Haven papers' editors and their readers. The excitement that followed spread quickly throughout the community. That Connecticut was a slave state did nothing to dampen the public's interest. Slavery was legal, but also was in the process of being grandfathered into extinction. The sale of slaves had been forbidden in 1795, and when the last of the approximately forty slaves left in the state died, so would slavery. Connecticut also had about 350 free blacks living within its borders. But these people were lighter skinned than the *Amistad* blacks and spoke English as well as any natural-born Yankee. In fact, free blacks were just as interested as their white neighbors in seeing "the Amistads," as they were being called. From what people said, it was quite clear that the prisoners from the mysterious ship were unlike anyone who had ever been seen in these parts within memory.

The jailer, Stanton Pendelton, a state militia officer who insisted on being called "Colonel Pendelton," was a perpetually grumpy man with a limp that seemed to grow more pronounced with stormy weather or his own personal level of aggravation. He claimed the limp was the result of a battle wound from the war of 1812; in reality, he received it several years after that conflict when he took an ill-advised step on a rickety ladder after one too many pints.

Pendelton was upset that he would have to care for so many prisoners without so much as a day's forewarning to prepare. He was peeved that the federal marshal spent several minutes reinforcing that these prisoners must receive no treatment that would embarrass the United States government. He was angered that none of his new charges could understand a word he said. But most of all, he was outraged that federal payment for the prisoners' food and comfort would not begin arriving for another two weeks.

Pendelton limped hard around the jail and instructed his men to do what they could under the circumstances. They decided to split the Amistads into four large cells. There were no cots, but every captive was given a blanket and each of the rooms was equipped with four chamber pots. The chains and manacles were removed from all the blacks, and they were allowed to walk freely within their cells; visiting from cell to cell was not permitted. In all, the Africans were to be locked down but kept comfortable and well fed until their extradition to Cuba.

The only one excluded from this treatment was Singbe, who had been deemed by Judge Judson "a cunning, dangerous, and deadly murderer." He was placed with the prison's general population and remained in wrist and leg irons.

When the line began forming, Pendelton saw no reason why the general public, who were mostly county taxpayers, should not have an opportunity to view the strange new captives. And yet, Pendelton reasoned, these were extenuating circumstances. People had never queued up before to see anyone in his jail. This could possibly lead to a need for extra security, and would most certainly mean more work for him and his men. Pendelton decided the only proper thing to do was charge admission. Twelve and a half cents, or "one New York shilling," in the slang of the day. People would be allowed to file by the cells and pause for a few moments. They would also be allowed to see the murderous, savage leader, Joseph Cinqué, in chains among the jail's general population. On the first day the colonel had collected nearly $65; but the second day this had increased nearly sevenfold, a tidy sum considering that Pendelton's salary for a month was only about $45.

The tribesmen were troubled by the steady parade of people staring into their cells. They were sure it meant they would soon be executed. It was all Grabeau could do to keep everyone calm, especially the children, who kept breaking into tears at the sight of black-frocked clergy members, who they were sure were executioners of some sort.

"It is a lot like being in the cage back in the other city of the whites," Burnah said to Grabeau after the first day. "They feed us well, people stop and stare, point and talk. I even had one old white woman offer me a piece of bread."

"Yes, but the feeling is different. We are not among other tribesmen. This is not a slave market. It is a prison of sorts. Between you and me, I do not have good feelings about our future. And I wish I knew where Singbe was."

Antonio sat in a corner of the cell, occasionally pointing and laughing at the tribesmen. Every once in a while he would rattle off a long stream of Spanish, berating the Africans and saying, "Wait until we get back to Havana. I will smell your flesh burning in the fires." No one could understand him and, for the most part, they ignored him. Later that day, Ruiz was able to convince the marshal to entrust Antonio to his care and the boy was released.

On the second day, a group of whites, mostly young men, entered the cells and began talking to the tribesmen. They carried thick, black, leather-covered books and a few held up small pieces of crossed wood and iron. They made long emotional speeches, not a word of which was understood by any of the tribesmen. They also smiled a lot and often reached out to touch the tribesmen on the tops of their heads.

The whitemen were members of the Yale Divinity School in New Haven. When one of the school's professors, Dr. Gallaudet, had read that native Africans were being brought virtually to the school's gates, he was immediately convinced that this was a sign from God to not only Christianize the poor souls, but to begin a crusade of bringing Christianity to the entire continent of Africa, as well. Other faculty members and the school's students agreed with his appraisal and appealed to Colonel Pendelton to permit them access to the blacks immediately. Being a God-fearing Christian man, Colonel Pendelton held great sympathy for the sentiments of Dr. Gallaudet and his students. Pendelton agreed to allow them daily access to the Africans, and for a reduced rate of only three cents per man per day.

Accompanying the members of the Divinity School into the cells was Dr. Josiah Gibbs, a renowned Hebrew scholar and philologist. Though he also wished to save the Africans' souls, his immediate interest was focused on their tongues. In addition to English and Hebrew, Gibbs was fluent in Latin, Greek, French, and Italian. He also had a passing knowledge of Spanish and six other foreign languages. And yet, as he listened to the blacks speaking among themselves, he heard nothing, not a shred, which sounded familiar.

Gibbs watched and listened for more than an hour. He noticed that the blacks on the whole seemed respectful of their visitors. Though they obviously could not understand what was being said, they remained quiet and attentive, sitting on their blankets and listening as the students and faculty members spoke. After a particularly stirring sermon by one of the students on the redemption of wayward souls, Gibbs picked out the black whom he thought the most intelligent looking of the lot, sat down in front of him, and held up a single finger.

"One."

Gibbs drew a line in the dirt floor.

"One."

He continued for a nearly five minutes, holding up the finger, pointing to the line on the floor, and holding out an apple.

"One."

Grabeau looked back at Gibbs, a little whiteman wearing a crisp black small-brimmed hat and spotless linen jacket. Gibbs's smiling, gentle face was framed by bristly, wild-looking white sideburns that reached almost down to his mouth. Grabeau held up one of his own black fingers slowly.

"Wwwone?"

"Yes! Yes, one! One! One! One!"

Grabeau took the apple from Gibbs hand and bit it.

"One."

Gibbs pointed to his own mouth and then to Grabeau.

"One?"

Grabeau chewed the sweet meat of the apple, swallowed it, and smiled.

"E-tah."

"E-tah?"

"E-tah."

Gibbs held up two fingers and said, "two." Grabeau repeated the word a few times and then held up his two of his own fingers.

"Feh-lee."

Gibbs and Grabeau sat there repeating each other's words over and over. Burnah walked up and sat next to Grabeau.

"What are you doing?"

"I am teaching this whiteman how to count in Mende and he is teaching me the same in the white language."

"Why?"

"He seemed bored."

Burnah moved to get up.

"From the numbers we can go to things and thoughts," Grabeau said. "If we can speak to these men, perhaps we can convince them that they should not kill us."

Burnah nodded. Soon he was counting along with Gibbs and Grabeau.

After nearly an hour Gibbs decided to see how many of the other blacks spoke this language. He stood up and walked over to one of the other tribesmen, Ka-le.

"E-tah. Feh-lee. Saw-wha. Nah-nee. Thlano. Thataro. Shupa. Hera-Mebedi."

Kale looked with amazement and then fell to his knees.

"This whiteman speaks Mende! This white speaks Mende!

All the men in the cell immediately jumped up and ran to Gibbs, everyone yelling and screaming. The spectators outside the cell thought that Gibbs was being attacked and began yelling and screaming, as well. It took nearly fifteen minutes for Gibbs and Grabeau to calm everyone down and explain.

Singbe sat in the back corner of the general prisoners' cell. Night had fallen and the crowds of whites that had filed by all day, looking at him like some captured animal waiting for the slaughter, had at least temporarily disappeared. Only the barest hint of light crept into the cell, flickering wisps made by a single lamp in the hallway. But now that light was gone, too.

"Hey, nigger."

Singbe looked up. Two hulking forms stood over him.

"Nigger, we're talking to you."

Singbe slowly began to stand, sliding his back up against the wall.

"We heard you killed a bunch a white folks. Hacked them to death with long knives. Is that right?"

"You musta thought you was a pretty damn high and mighty nigger to do somethin' like that, eh?"

"Yeah, well he don't look so mighty now. He just looks like a scared to shit nigger to me."

"I wouldn't know, Jack. He's so black, all I can see of him is the whites of his eyes."

Singbe saw one of the forms twitch. He ducked and felt the wind of a fist go by his ear. The man screamed as his hand slammed into the wall. A kick came up and caught Singbe in the jaw knocking him back into the wall. He began swinging the chains on his wrists wildly from side to side. The iron sang with the cries of the attackers each time the chain found its mark. The other prisoners, about a dozen or so, were screaming and pushing the attackers and Singbe back into each other.

"What the hell is going on here!?"

The cell was filled with light. Three guards stood inside the bars, pistols and muskets drawn and cocked.

"It was the African nigger, Mr. Colton! I swear!" said a big man lying on the floor. His face was splattered with blood from the gashes that the chain had made.

"Jack's right, captain. This crazed nigger he just starts swinging them chains and screaming like a wild jungle animal."

Colton looked at Singbe crouched in the corner. His jaw was swollen, his body shaking. He looked like a cat surrounded by a pack of hungry dogs.

"Go wake the colonel, Tim," Colton said. "Now."

One of the guards ran out. The man on the floor began to stand but Colton kicked him back to the floor.

"You just hold there, Murtaugh."

Colton walked up to Singbe and motioned with the pistol.

"This way, African."

As he passed Murtaugh, Colton let loose with another kick to his ribs.

"No more shit outta you, Murtaugh. Or you either, Spivey. Otherwise, I'll be back."

He walked Singbe down the hall to a small empty cell and unlocked the door.

"In."

Singbe stayed standing for nearly an hour after the men with guns had left. He wasn't sure if there would be another beating. He finally drifted off to sleep and dreamed again of his home and family. In the morning he woke up to the sounds and gestures made by a new blur of staring white faces walking by his cell. Later in the afternoon, a man named Nathaniel Jocelyn was allowed in the cell to paint Singbe's portrait.

† † †

Roger Baldwin was a dependable sight for the people of downtown New Haven. Forty-two years old, a little over five and a half feet tall, and gaunt with dark, thinning hair and small round spectacles that almost never left his face, he was distinguished in a schoolmaster sort of way. But in his case, Baldwin would be a schoolmaster of means. He always wore fine dark business suits, silk bow ties, and polished black boots; in the winter he was partial to long, heavy frock coats. He was a man who, despite his political leanings, commanded great respect from the community, a man of great intelligence, principle, and conviction. He was known as a gentleman, always courteous and polite. You could see it in his walk, straight, proud, confident, and perhaps a half step quicker and sprier than the average man's. There was no doubt that he was the essence of propriety. Which is why people were aghast when late on the afternoon of August 29 they saw Roger Baldwin in his fine black suit and shiny boots, running madly down the middle of York Street.

If he had stopped to think about it, he would probably not have believed it himself. He had not run at all since his days at Yale. And even then it was a rare occurrence. But as he left his office near the town green for Reverend Simeon Jocelyn's church, he found himself walking more quickly than usual. His mind began moving faster and faster, spurred on by the possibilities of what he had just read. He was more than halfway down the street before he realized he was running. He hesitated only for a moment at the discovery, and then let his legs continue at their perilous pace, deciding that they were being moved by a force greater than himself.

He reached the church fifteen minutes later, drenched in sweat and gasping for breath. Jocelyn was next door at his house trying to rescue the roses he had planted on the sunny side. They had bloomed late and lingered huge and bright, but the sweltering heat and dense humidity of the past week had wilted many of them. Jocelyn looked up to see Baldwin run his last few steps before staggering, stopping, and nearly falling into the church doors.

After Jocelyn had helped his friend into the house and given him a mug of cool well water, Baldwin was finally able to speak.

"Simeon. I received this letter from New London less than an hour ago. It was written by a friend, a dedicated man of the cause. He tells of Africans—*Africans*!—illegally captured and pressed into slavery, coming into his port. A federal judge has ordered them to be brought here, to New Haven."

"Your friend is right. They are here. They came in yesterday morning. Their story was in all the papers. In fact, my brother was allowed to paint the leader's portrait. Where were you?"

"I am just back from New York. On the afternoon train," Baldwin answered.

"Well, it is good that you are here. In fact, I have been approached by several people to speak to you about this issue in hopes that you would take sympathy with the Africans and perhaps hire yourself out in their defense."

"Hire myself? I will do no such thing."

"But Roger, don't you find their situation compelling? At the very least it will draw attention to the cause."

"I think their situation is beyond compelling. So much so that it made me run here from my office. If the facts are as my friend has set them down, then I do not think I could face myself if I took one dime for their defense. I will do the job, yes, but money will not be a factor here."

"Bless you, Roger. You are a man of irreproachable principle, and the best attorney in Connecticut. I have always said it. But your generous offer aside, we will need money if we are to build a defense team around you, as well as to fight this in the press. Van Buren will want this to go away quickly and with as little public debate as possible. Which is why I wrote Mr. Lewis Tappan this morning after I read the accounts in the newspapers."

"Tappan?"

"If anything has come to us that will finally draw the questions of slavery and abolition into public debate, it is this event. And if any one thing can increase the interest and attention that will be given to the event itself, it is the presence of Lewis Tappan."

Baldwin took a long drink from the mug and then let out a chortling laugh. "I do not think Connecticut is ready for our friend Mr. Tappan."

Jocelyn smiled. "Neither is the rest of the country."

"What if these black men were white!? What if they were Americans or Englishmen or Spaniards, held by native Algerians or Arabs? Certainly those cultures still ascribe to the practice of slaveholding. What, then, would be their fate, my friends, if an American brig waylaid them at sea and boarded? Would they be here, behind bars in a jail with the most vile of criminals? I think not. They would be heroes, honored in parades, wined and dined by politicians and society's elite. But in our great wisdom we have not judged them by the virtue of their actions or the purity of their souls, but rather by the color of their skin. Their skin is black. So naturally, they are immediately treated as criminals. They are put on display as freakish carnival attractions. And yet, we live in a country built on the phrase, 'All men are created equal.' *Equal*? Please! We are a nation of hypocrites. For even if we do not personally own slaves, even if we do not hold prejudices against the darker races, if we permit such things to occur, we are as guilty and as sinful in the eyes of the Lord as the perpetrators of such heinous acts."

The crowd outside the jail erupted, some with cheers, some with cries of hate. Many others just stared, not quite sure what they were seeing. A dozen Connecticut militiamen stood nervously ready, muskets in hand, facing the crowd and separating them from Lewis Tappan and his small entourage. A potato, launched from somewhere in the crowd, landed just to the left of his feet. This sent the crowd into a new explosion.

Lewis Tappan stood defiant. If not for the attention focused on him, he would be an unremarkable man, a healthy white New York businessman, average in height, face, weight, and dress, average-looking in every way, except for the hair. It was thick, wild, bushy and flaming red, streaked with patches of white, a frozen cloud of flame and smoke, a raging, burning thunderhead. The hair was completely immune to combs and brushes, and Tappan kept it free of oils or balms. Instead he let it grow on its own course, trimming it every so often, but not enough to damage its personality. He understood completely its effect and importance.

Tappan was used to such treatment and spectacle. Wherever he went, crowds and boiling emotions seemed to follow. Sometimes only a few people would stop him for a debate or to listen to his words; sometimes it was dozens. Occasionally he drew a mob.

Such was the case in 1834, in his native New York City, when more than a thousand angry people descended on Tappan's Dry Goods, the largest such store in the city, calling for the heads of Lewis and his brother Arthur. Both men had been the founders of the American Antislavery Society and were conducting a membership meeting that night at the store. The mob outside had stomached enough of the agitating pamphlets, the probing articles in the Tappan-supported abolitionist newspaper *The Emancipator*, and the scathing street-corner stump speeches given by the Tappans and their followers. The filth and lies they were spreading about abolishing slavery and the equality of races had gone far enough, and the mob was there to put a stop to it all once and for all.

But they hadn't anticipated the massive iron shutters the Tappans had installed outside—which, when closed and locked, made the store as impervious as a bank vault—or Arthur and thirty of his clerks armed with muskets. Lewis spoke at length to the crowd from a second-story window and had to duck several times to avoid hurled rocks and rotted vegetables, but he and Arthur were eventually able to turn away the angry rabble without anyone having fired a shot.

This is what open, honest talk about abolishing slavery did in New York during the 1830s. In the South, such talk never occurred, at least not in public. It would have been lunacy and courting almost certain violent retribution, if not a public lynching.

Though often portrayed as a strictly North-South controversy with clearly defined pro and con camps, the issue of slavery was much more complex and muddy than its geographical delineations. At this time most Americans believed as firmly in the superiority and ruling destiny of the white Christian race as in the inevitability of the sun rising each day. Many of those same people had great sympathy for blacks. Some felt slavery was unfortunate but an inevitable consequence of the natural order of things. Others wished to see slavery eliminated.

But anti-slavery sentiment did not always, or even frequently, translate into a desire for immediate abolition. There were those who believed that the "peculiar institution" of slavery should be subject to a gradual extinction, permitting the blacks to be freed slowly. Once free, they would enjoy the same rights other free blacks experienced in the United States at the time. These "rights," which varied from state to state, often denied blacks educational and employment opportunities, and uniformly forbade voting or running for elected office. Other people held that free blacks should be sent back to their motherland of Africa. In the early 1800s the American Colonization Society was formed to do just this. They purchased land in what was to become Liberia and paid to transport free blacks there. Many saw the society as a thinly veiled attempt to eliminate free blacks from American soil and bring the U.S. one step closer to being a wholly white and completely Christian nation. U.S. Senator and Whig Party leader Henry Clay held little of his feelings back, saying that the society's work was a blessing because it would eventually "rid our country of a useless, pernicious, and dangerous portion of the population."

The ideas of giving blacks limited freedom or directed resettlement were seen by most people opposed to slavery as reasonable positions. They also saw a gradual end to slavery as the most prudent way to solve the problem. But a very small percentage of the anti-slavery proponents went further. They were the religious extremists, the abolitionists. Abolitionists believed in immediate cessation of slavery and complete emancipation of all slaves. Though few in number, abolitionists were well organized, vocal, passionate, and possessed by a fervent, religious zeal for their cause. Many of their leaders were in fact members of the Protestant clergy who believed that enslaving fellow human beings was a sin and an abomination unto the Lord.

To the vast majority of the American population, such talk of abolition was not only nonsensical claptrap, it was patently dangerous. Many recognized that if the abolitionists were permitted to spread their emotionally volatile dogma and rage, it would only be a matter of time before the country degenerated into some sort of civil war. Awareness of the incendiary capacity of such rhetoric was so acute that in 1837 the U.S. House passed a "gag rule" that prohibited petitions or discussions regarding slavery. But though attempts were made by the Congress, and even by Andrew Jackson during his presidency, to end public discourse regarding slavery, their efforts failed. And so the activities of abolitionists persisted.

The Tappan brothers were early supporters of the abolitionist cause as well as grand-nephews of the founder of America's first abolitionist society, Benjamin Franklin. They were despised in the South, so much so that a South Carolina plantation owner had put up a $100,000 bounty, for the delivery of the bodies of Lewis and Arthur Tappan to any slave state.

But while both brothers believed strongly in the cause and worked tirelessly toward spreading its doctrine, it was Lewis who embodied abolition—word, deed, and spirit. He was righteous indignation incarnate, a man who not only walked his talk, but took every opportunity to share his beliefs with the world. Lewis had formed a committee to raise the money for Prudence Crandall's defense. He had paid to send several promising young black men to Oberlin College, the only American college of the day that accepted black students. He had also once offered $5,000 to the American Bible Society to print 5,000 Bibles and distribute them to blacks across the country. The American Bible Society politely refused.

Lewis Tappan believed that slavery was wrong on moral terms, an affront to God Almighty, and that anyone who permitted slavery or racial prejudice to occur without protest sinned as greatly as those who embraced the evils of oppression. He believed that the most important thing in a marriage was not social station, love, or commercial opportunity, but rather adherence to a Christian religion. As a result he saw nothing wrong with the intermarrying between races so long as both partners were confirmed in their belief in Jesus Christ.

"In fact," he once said, "if religious unity could be spread throughout the world and intermarrying between races accepted, then, within a thousand years or so, the planet will become peopled with a single copper-colored race of human beings, and the whole issue of prejudice and oppression based on skin color will fade away forever."

Regardless of a person's beliefs about slavery, this last statement was enough for many people to label Lewis Tappan as thoroughly unbalanced and uncivilized, as well as dangerous. He received threats on his life regularly, and had more than a few times been confronted by angry men or surly mobs bent on doing him harm. But while Arthur was reputed to carry a small revolver in his vest pocket, Lewis claimed that he ventured out each day only armed with his Bible, which he kept in a pocket close to his heart.

Simeon Jocelyn's letter asking for help from both Tappan brothers had reached Lewis in New York. The Tappans were good friends with Jocelyn, a white pastor of an all-black church in New Haven. However, Arthur was abroad on a business trip to England and wouldn't be back for nearly six months. Lewis immediately wrote his brother to brief him on the events and then took the next available train to New Haven.

And now, on the third day of September, 1839, he stood speaking to the crowd outside of the New Haven County Jail. While he spoke, the men surrounding him, Simeon Jocelyn, *The Emancipator*'s editor, Joshua Leavitt, and nearly a dozen other men who had become members of his newly formed Amistad Committee, watched the agitated spectators and fidgeted nervously.

"I can feel your rage at the injustice that is being perpetrated here, my friends," Tappan continued. "That is why we are here. I and these gentlemen with me have formed a committee, the Amistad Committee, to ensure that the devilish machinations from the morally bankrupt presidential administration in Washington will not impede a just outcome for these poor African souls."

This hit another nerve with the crowd, provoking more outcries. Connecticut was a Democratic state and Van Buren enjoyed strong support among most of its citizens. Tappan waited, smiling, until the yelling subsided.

"I'm glad you share my displeasure with Mr. Van Buren. Please feel free to show how much by making a donation to the Africans' defense through our committee. Thank you, and good day."

Two militiamen ushered Tappan and his entourage into the jail through a door, away from the howling crowd. Once inside, he was allowed to enter the cells and meet with all the tribesmen, including Singbe and the three girls. He stayed nearly three hours and spoke at length with the divinity students and faculty from Yale. After leaving, he accompanied Jocelyn to Roger Baldwin's office to discuss the Amistads' defense.

Forsyth had seen enough. Daily reports of the Amistads had run on the front page of virtually every major newspaper in the country. Reporters had descended on New Haven like a plague of flies, gobbling up and spitting out every available detail. More troubling was that many Northern papers were canonizing the rebel leader Joseph Cinqué. The *New York Tribune* called him "a bold and courageous man reminiscent of Othello, proud, intelligent-looking, and of noble bearing." The *Boston Light* declared, "Cinqué is obviously a chief whose veins are filled with royal blood. He has the mannerisms and appeal of all great leaders." And the *Philadelphia Daily Sunbeam* stated, "Joseph Cinqué is definitely superior to others of his race. He has an air of intelligence and destiny about him, he is of calm humor and great pride. It is obvious that he was a prince or a king of his own tribe." Forsyth was heartened to see that some of the editors still had sense, though. The *New York Herald* said Cinqué was "as miserably ignorant and brutalized as the rest of them, a rubber-lipped, sullen-looking negro not half as intelligent-looking as every third black you meet on the docks of New York." The *New York Daily Express* said he and the other Amistads were "hardly above the apes and monkeys of their own country." The Southern papers concentrated on the fact that the blacks, whether Africans or not, were seized on a Spanish ship and should be tried under Spanish law; there was little or no mention of Cinqué or any of the other captives as being in any way remarkable.

In truth, however, Forsyth did not care one way or the other about the printed appraisals of this Cinqué or any of the other blacks. His concern was focused on the fact that the Amistads had captured the imagination of the country. That, and the fact that no one seemed to be denying that they were in fact Africans. With a trial scheduled, there seemed to be no way to avoid public discussion regarding the slaves, and more important, slavery. And now Lewis Tappan—Lewis Tappan!—and his horde of lunatic abolitionists had descended upon the scene, conjuring up a defense team that would no doubt do all they could to prolong the judicial proceedings for as long as possible. If something was not done, this whole affair could drag on well into the fall, giving the journalists and the Whigs plenty more fodder for pot shots at the Van Buren Administration.

Forsyth met with Calderón earlier in the day. Coming from an authoritarian monarchy, the minister had a difficult time understanding how the legal maneuvering of a small group of political radicals and an impending hearing by some provincial tribunal could take precedence over the will of the country's chief executive.

"If her Catholic Majesty or one of her ministers ordered prisoners to be delivered, then, by God, they would be delivered."

Forsyth went on to explain the separation of powers within the government and how even an order from the President could not extricate a person or persons from the right to due process.

Calderón erupted into laughter.

"Well, certainly your Constitution is written in that way, but you do not mean to tell me that in reality it supersedes the will of your leaders?"

Forsyth explained that it did. When Calderón realized the Secretary of State was speaking in earnest and that the President of the United States was unable to intervene in such a piddling affair, he nearly stormed out. It was all Forsyth could do to calm him down.

"You know, it is just something like this that the British have been waiting for," Calderón hissed. "They have had eyes for Cuba for many years now. If this gets out of hand..."

"Trust me, Señor Calderón, it will not. It should all be resolved within a few weeks."

"A few weeks? Your papers are filled with stories about contraband Africans. Why are you not controlling that? Why isn't your president forbidding such stories?"

"Unfortunately, the government cannot suppress journalists,

no matter how reckless or irresponsible they become with conjecture and fabrication."

"Preposterous! All of this is just preposterous. Why, in Spain, such denunciations would be handled immediately. This, this flaccid government of yours will be your ruin. Trust me, Señor Forsyth, you will never be a power in the world if you cannot impose the will of your leaders at home."

Forsyth raised a single eyebrow. He was a man of great control and could usually restrain his temper, but right now it was all he could do to keep from slapping Calderón's words back into his mouth.

"We call it democracy, Señor Calderón. And we much prefer it to the tyrannical ravings of a whimsical monarch, or in your case, a child queen."

"Señor Secretary! You will apologize immediately for any disparaging comments you have just made to her Catholic Majesty or I will lodge a formal protest with your government!"

Forsyth smiled. "Señor Calderón, I certainly did not intend to slight your queen in the least, nor did I in any way mean to imply that she was either a tyrant or whimsical. I merely pointed out that she, though certainly a most wise and beneficent ruler, is in fact a child. But if you find this fact disparaging, I certainly do apologize."

Calderón measured the words in his head. They sounded sincere, and believed he had a fair comprehension of English. Yet he could not help but feel he had been insulted again. But before he could say anything, Forsyth spoke up.

"Now, with regards to the press. Though it is true we cannot control the newspapers, I believe we can use them to our mutual benefit."

"How so?"

"My government's aim is still to resolve this situation between ourselves, between the executive and your ministry," Forsyth said. "I know it was in both our interests to keep negotiations on this hushed, but events have taken a very public turn. Thus, it might suit our purposes if we, too, added fuel to the flames of public conjecture."

"What do you mean?"

"I think it would be best if you composed a letter protesting the trial and the handling of the affair. Emphasize that the blacks are in fact Spanish subjects. Cite the Treaty of 1795, Pickney's Treaty on sea commerce. We will let a copy of your letter fall into the hands of newspapers sympathetic to our cause. At the same time we will issue the administration's position, which will be virtually identical. What the public will see is two different governments coming to the same conclusion on the issue. If we can create enough public perception that the *Amistad* incident is in fact covered under that treaty and is best left to the executive, then it will be easier for a judge to draw a similar conclusion."

"Why don't you simply instruct the judge how to rule?"

"I'm afraid the courts do not work that way. The lawyers for both sides have to make their arguments and precedents must be adhered to. However, the President asked a highly placed attorney to render a written opinion about the case. The attorney also focused on Pickney's Treaty, the Treaty of 1819, and the fact that according to the documentation taken, the slaves are Spanish subjects. This will be the basis of our argument in court next week. It's a strong case. We are very confident the judge will find favorably for our side. I've noted the salient passages."

Forsyth passed a copy of the document to Calderón. The Spanish minister thumbed through the document and shrugged.

"This all seems like so much work for something that in my country could be done with just a wave of a hand. But I will do as you say."

An hour later Forsyth met with the President.

"He is a whining, petulant little peacock." Forsyth sighed. "But Calderón agreed to write the letter."

"You did not mention that the opinion was written by the Attorney General?"

"Mr. Grundy's name or title never came up, sir. I simply said it was the opinion of a high-placed lawyer."

"How long before we receive Calderón's protest?"

"I would think we shall have it by tomorrow at the latest."

"You know, John, in addition to all the problems this case can cause domestically, I'm also worried about the British."

"Señor Calderón expressed similar sentiments. He believes that if the slaves are found to be contraband Africans, it will be all the British need to begin an incursion in Cuba."

"I agree. And you know, if they take Cuba, Texas will be next. We cannot grant Sam Houston statehood at this point, but I think it would be impossible to avoid involvement in the event of some sort of Anglo invasion. Not that this will happen tomorrow, but it certainly sets up all the pieces."

Forsyth sensed the opportunity to take a new course. It was something he had been hoping for. "What would you like me to do, Mr. President?"

Van Buren paused. He had read Grundy's opinion and was confident that the circuit court would rule in their favor. But he also knew that courtrooms held no guarantees. However, if he and Forsyth began discussing alternatives, it would certainly lead them down a path of dark shadows. It was not a direction the President wanted to take. At least, not yet.

"Don't do anything. Let the hearing go on and let us remain confident that justice will take its proper course."

Circuit Court

"Singbe! Singbe!"

The tribesmen sat in wagons under the rising morning sun. The sky was blue and clear, but the air held a crisp fifty-degree chill. It was much cooler than any of the tribesmen were used to. Many shivered under the prison blankets they had wrapped around their bodies. But the sight of Singbe, though he was chained and manacled and flanked by two armed jail guards, lifted their spirits and warmed their bodies. It was the first time they had been reunited with their leader since coming to New Haven more than two weeks before. Many feared he had been executed, tortured, or sold as a slave. Seeing him emerging from the jail, proud and defiant, was like seeing hope. Their cries and greetings quickly broke into loud cheering. It infected the thousand or so spectators who had gathered by the jail to watch the prisoner transfer and soon they were cheering and yelling "Cinqué! Cinqué!" The half-dozen guards stood nervously, but the federal marshal was unimpressed. Singbe smiled and waved as he was led to an empty wagon. The marshal motioned for him to sit on the floor. As he did he was surrounded by four armed guards.

The caravan of wagons would make the short trip across the city to the canal locks and the tribesmen would be put on a barge for the forty-mile journey to Farmington, a small town just outside Hartford. From there wagons would bring them to the Hartford jail where they would wait two days until the trial began.

Within a half hour they were on the barge and away from the landing. Two mules pulled the flat wooden hull up the canal at a pace of about three miles per hour. Along the way they would pass through sixteen different sets of locks. In all, it would take them nearly twelve hours to reach the Farmington landing.

The marshal let Singbe sit with the others during the canal ride. It was a move of convenience rather than leniency as the deck of the barge could barely hold all of them. The tribesmen surrounded him and told of their days since they had been brought to the jail. Singbe was saddened to hear that two of the tribesmen, Fulwie, and Kinae, had died of the fever during the week. He told the others that he had been well fed and, except for the chains, believed he had been treated fairly. He did not mention the beating. Grabeau sat across from Singbe but said little for the first few hours. He was just happy to see that his friend was safe. But after a lunch of bread and beans, most of the tribesmen were napping on the deck. Grabeau thought it was a good time for a few questions. He slipped down next to Singbe and kept his voice low.

"What do you think this is about?"

"I do not know. When I saw all of you in the wagons, I thought for sure they were taking us out to be executed. But we have been on this boat now for more than half the day. It seems like a lot of traveling and effort for a killing."

"I agree. The whitemen with the black books brought a tribesman into the cells with them yesterday."

"Yes. They brought him to me, too. Congolese?"

"I think so. I tried to speak Mandingo with him, but he only knew a little, and only the northern dialect. Still, I think he said something about judgment or laws."

"You understood more than I did. I only know how to say hello in that language. And I know no Congolese."

"I have learned a few words in the language of the whites. All of us have. But it is difficult."

Singbe watched the lush Connecticut countryside pass by. The cool September nights had already begun to breathe touches of yellow, red, and orange into the leaves of some of the larger trees.

"If it is a trial, then what will that mean?" Singbe asked. "How can we defend ourselves if we cannot speak the language of the whites? The slave traders will tell their lies and that will be all."

"I have thought the same thing. But not all the whites seem to be on the side of the slave traders. Perhaps some will speak for us."

Singbe shrugged and dropped his head. "How can they speak for us when they don't know our story?"

† † †

A few miles from the canal locks in New Haven, the *Edna Louise*, a two-level back paddle steamboat, had just departed for a trip up the Connecticut River to Hartford. On board were Lieutenants Meade and Gedney, Pepe Ruiz, Pedro Montes, their lawyer William Hungerford, and District Attorney Holabird. They had all ensconced themselves in the ship's lounge to sip drinks and hold an impromptu conference with the more than three dozen journalists from newspapers across the nation who were also on board. It was a smiling, self-congratulating, laughing affair, with Pepe Ruiz exuding great charm and conviction as he told again the tale of the rebellion, and of the courageous rescue by the gallant U.S. Navy.

"I thank the United States for giving me and my friend Señor Montes our lives. My only wish now is that we are permitted to return home with our property."

"And my only wish, sir, is to see you thoroughly prosecuted and hanged for piracy, kidnapping, and murder."

The booming voice burst across the lounge, turning the loose chatter and laughter into silence. There at the doorway stood Lewis Tappan and several members of the Amistad Committee.

Later that night some of the journalists would speculate on the possibilities of such a coincidence: the claimants and prime sympathizers of the defendants ending up on the same boat for the nearly five-hour trip upriver, especially when ample rail and stage service to Hartford, as well as other steamers, were readily available. However, if they knew him at all, the journalists would have been assured that Lewis Tappan never left events to the chances of coincidence, especially when substantial representation from the press was guaranteed.

"I would further assert that you, Mr. Ruiz, and your compatriot, Mr. Montes, are the most contemptible, cowardly, and vile breed of criminals," Tappan continued. "For by your actions, by knowingly trading in African slaves—and do not deny that you were unaware of their true origins—you perpetuated a chain of events that is so completely immoral and unjust that all the consequences, including the tragic subsequent occurrence which transpired during your ill-fated voyage, rest firmly on your shoulders."

Hungerford, a portly and distinguished looking man of about fifty, spoke to the room, rather than directly to Tappan, through a bemused grin.

"Mr. Tappan's indignation has obviously affected his cognitive abilities and clouded his grasp of the facts. My clients were not contracting in any actions that are illegal. Slavery, as all of you in this room know, is completely legal in Cuba, as well as several states in this country, including Connecticut. It was the black miscreants who perpetrated mutiny, murder, and the repeated torture of my clients during a harrowing voyage of more than eight weeks."

Ruiz laughed and held out his drink saluting Tappan. "A toast, to the madhouses of the world. May their doors soon be secure, and their inmates not allowed to roam so freely."

Laughter rippled through the room but Tappan's voice rose above it. "The whiteness of a man's skin or the misguided customs of his land do not exonerate him from hideous deeds, no matter how they have been rationalized and legislated into feigned legitimacy. But since the law has been broached, let us talk of the legality of stealing people into captivity. Let us consider that the *Amistad* blacks, though cast as Spanish subjects living in Cuba for more than twenty years, speak not one word of that language. How is that so? They have been on American soil for less than two weeks, and yet my friends from the Yale Divinity School tell me that many of the blacks have already learned to speak a few words of English. If they were slaves in Cuba for twenty years, certainly they would at least recognize the barked orders of their masters. But the transcripts of the hearing showed that none could even answer to his name. How do your clients explain this simple fact, Mr. Hungerford?"

"This is not a court and my clients do not have to answer to you or your ridiculous theories, Mr. Tappan."

"A refusal to answer the truth is as good as a lie," Tappan quipped with a grin. "Take note, gentlemen! If you ever commit a crime and wish to avoid just prosecution, Mr. Hungerford is the man to see. It is obvious that he views the truth not as indelible fact, but rather as a malleable suggestion which can be twisted, manipulated, and shaped to fit his own needs or the needs of his clients."

Hungerford forced out a laugh. "Mr. Tappan seems to view himself as someone to whom confessions should be made. Perhaps, sir, it is time for you to join the papist Catholics and fulfill your life's true aspiration of dispensing forgiveness and penance at your own leisure and discretion."

"My life's aspiration is to not rest until the noble blacks of the *Amistad* are freed and returned to their native soil, and your clients are made to pay the highest price for their transgressions against God and the natural right of all men to maintain their own freedom."

"He is mad," Ruiz said, draining another glass of whiskey.

"It is a shame you have to put up with such ridiculous persons in your country. In Cuba we have sanitariums for such slack-witted fools."

"The only fools in this room are you and your co-conspirator if you think you can avoid judgment of your crimes."

"The only ones to be judged are those savage, insane slaves, the ones you call noble," Ruiz countered. "They will be judged in Havana and burned at the stake, I dare say."

Ruiz was smiling, but there was a slight tremble his voice, a tiny spark of anger being held back by an awareness of propriety and appearances in front of the press. But Tappan heard the tremble, he could feel the heat, and his heart leapt at the opportunity to draw out a flame.

"If there is any more death, any more blood spilt or men killed, it will be produced by your hands, Mr. Ruiz, as has been all the carnage and cruelty of this affair. After all, you knowingly bought Africans on the black market. You perpetuated a series of illegal actions that enslaved free men. And because of your ignorance, greed, and malicious, arrogant disregard of the law, the captain and crew of your ship are dead. Thirteen innocent blacks are dead. And now you would have the lives of the others snuffed out merely to satiate your own personal indignation. You are less than a man, sir, less even than a vile gutter leech. You are simply filth and evil without restraint."

The Cuban's glass flew across the room. Tappan ducked. The glass shattered on the wall behind him. In three quick strides Pepe Ruiz was standing within inches of the abolitionist.

"I was practicing a trade that is completely legal in my country, as well as yours. I followed the laws of my country to the letter and did nothing wrong. Nothing! The blame and all the punishment should lie where it rightly belongs—with that blood-thirsty brute Cinqué and those other black beasts whom you call 'noble.' If you take issue with that, then you can settle it now as a man with me."

Tappan did not flinch. "I will not dignify a murderer, thief, and pirate with the satisfaction of sinking to his own level. The level of sewage."

Ruiz drew back his fist but Hungerford and Gedney grabbed him and pulled him back.

Tappan shook his head paternally. "Gentlemen of the press, I think you can see what kind of man Mr. Pepe Ruiz, slave dealer, truly is."

Hungerford spoke to Ruiz and Montes and then the three of them quickly left the lounge. Ruiz leveled a long stare at Tappan on the way out, but Tappan just smiled. After they were gone, he took a seat in front of the press, had a cup of tea, and continued to speak at length about the innocence of the Amistads.

Two days later, on the morning of Thursday, September 19, 1839, the Circuit Court of Connecticut began hearings on the *Amistad* case. The city was packed and crackled with a carnival air it had not witnessed since a triple public hanging nearly ten years before. Every hotel, rooming house, salon, and brothel was filled to capacity with guests. Dignitaries and society folk traveling from as far as Boston, Providence, and New York had tried to secure seats inside the courtroom. It was rumored that over one hundred members of the press were in attendance. On the green outside the Hartford courthouse more than three thousand people walked about or sat on blankets with picnic baskets. Vendors were hawking engravings of Nathaniel Jocelyn's portrait of Joseph Cinqué, as well as lithographs and sketches of the Africans and the infamous slaveship. A few days earlier a play titled *The Black Schooner: The Pirate Slaver "Amistad"* had opened at New York's Bowery Theatre. It took in nearly $1,700 in its first week and would run throughout the fall to packed houses.

The courthouse, a proper two-story brick building with a peaked roof, sat just down the cobbled street from the State House. Inside the courtroom, the tribesmen had been seated behind their lawyers and in the jury box. Antonio, though indignant at being lumped in with the tribesmen, had also been commanded to sit with the Amistads. Ruiz and Montes sat across the aisle with Holabird and Hungerford. Gedney, Meade, appearing in full dress uniforms, and their lawyer, retired militia general Mark Isham, sat at a table near the far wall. Spectators and press filled the other seats and the gallery and overflowed into the aisles and out the courtroom door.

The presiding judge, the Honorable Smith Thompson, was also a U.S. Supreme Court justice. Seventy years old, pale and thin, white-haired, clean-shaven and immaculate in his flowing black robes, Thompson's face was fixed in a look of sternness and skepticism that should be required of all high judges. Though he believed slavery to be a disgusting institution, Thompson was a steadfast proponent of legal precedent who would never let personal opinions interfere with the judgment of a case. Because it was a circuit court case, he would be serving as grand jurist and pronouncing the final judgment.

Joining Roger Baldwin in the defense of the Amistads were Seth Staples and Theodore Sedgwick. Staples, a tall, lean, well-dressed man not quite thirty with whiskey-colored hair and a broad Roman nose, was a Democrat from an affluent family and an admitted abolitionist. Sedgwick, also a known abolitionist, was a thick unkempt man with a ruddy complexion, fat and reaching sideburns, and a rapidly receding dark brown hairline. Closer to fifty and a resident of Philadelphia, Sedgwick was the son of a former slave trader and had worked as his assistant early in life before turning to the law. Barrel-chested and broad-shouldered, his frame strained against the fabric of his suit, giving him the appearance of a hardscrabble farmer or blacksmith wedged into the only set of Sunday clothes he had ever owned. His huge, beefy hands folded on the table in front of him looked like a twisted mound of gnarled, raw muscle being squeezed into submission.

Staples and Sedgwick were respected lawyers in their own right, but both knew Baldwin to be the superior litigator and agreed that he should lead their team. Baldwin's reputation as a savvy and intelligent defense attorney was well established. A direct descendent of Roger Sherman—one of the signers of the Declaration of Independence and later a congressman who was instrumental in preserving slavery in the newly created United States—Baldwin had graduated from Yale at age eighteen and was admitted to the bar three years later. Soon after beginning his practice, he had won a writ of habeas corpus and eventual freedom for a runaway slave.

Despite being an ardent supporter of abolition, he was respected throughout the state's political circles as an articulate, principled, and fair-minded man. He had been a state legislator from New Haven since 1834 and many people agreed that if he chose to throw his hat into a statewide political race, he would be a daunting challenger to any opponent. It was also widely believed that he was the best defense attorney in the state and could be a very wealthy man if he opted to take more cases involving clients of means. But Baldwin was a man of firm morals and strong convictions, and though he did handle cases which brought him fair compensation for his services, he took many more that involved, as he put it, "pronounced injustice and injury perpetrated against the downtrodden and less fortunate." By their nature, these cases paid little or nothing. Regardless of the fee, Baldwin was a relentless defender and rarely lost in court.

Despite their legal prowess, the case of the Amistads would be a difficult challenge for Baldwin and his team. Along with having to fight the resources of Holabird, Hungerford, Isham, and the Van Buren administration, they were facing the prospects of defending a politically charged case that was devoid of any established legal precedents which could work in their favor. Baldwin agreed with Tappan that the primary objective would be to try to win the Africans' freedom. Short of that, the defense team would use appeals and any other legal maneuvering they could muster to keep the plight of the Amistads in the public eye for as long as possible.

The moment court was declared in session, Holabird stood and made a request that surprised no one.

"Your Honor, I move that this case be immediately dismissed on the grounds that the disposition of the *Amistad* and its cargo are covered under Articles eight through ten of Pickney's Treaty of 1795. As such, ship and cargo should be turned over to the President of the United States promptly for delivery to a representative of the sovereign nation of the ship's occupants, in this case, Spain. I have prepared a brief to that end and will submit it to the court."

Baldwin was already standing.

"I oppose this motion, Your Honor. The Treaty of 1795's coverage of this event is dubious at best and should be subject to trial within the auspices of the court. I further object to the blacks being referred to as 'cargo.'"

"The black slaves are mutineers, thieves, murders, and Spanish subjects," Hungerford, also rising to his feet, countered. "As such they should be turned over to the crown representative of Spain for trial under the laws of that country."

"Gentlemen," Judge Thompson said, raising his voice. "It has already been ruled that the case will be heard before this court."

"What about my other objection, Your Honor, to referring to my clients as 'cargo'?"

"Mr. Baldwin, the disposition of your clients' condition will comprise a substantial part of this tribunal's inquiry. However, I, too, dislike the terming of men as 'cargo', even if they are the legal property of another man. Therefore, from hence forth in this case, when referring to the blacks taken with the ship *Amistad*, all parties involved speak of them as 'blacks,' 'negroes,' or 'the colored occupants of the *Amistad*.' Now, let us proceed."

"Then before going any further, Your Honor," Holabird said, standing again, "I request that if the court finds the black slaves subjects of Spain, they be handed over to the President for prompt delivery to the Spanish authorities. Alternately, if they are found to be free men, I request that they be handed over to the President's care so they may be safely transported back to their homeland."

"I will take these requests under advisement, Mr. Prosecutor."

"I most strenuously object, Your Honor!" Baldwin cried.

"To what, now, Mr. Baldwin?"

"Mr. Holabird referred to my clients as slaves. Yet, I believe we are still in a country where men placed before judgment are innocent until proven guilty. I presume that to mean all men, Your Honor. I therefore submit that my clients should be considered freemen until proven otherwise. To that end, I petition the court for a writ of habeas corpus for the blacks taken from the *Amistad* when it was boarded by the crew and officers of the *Washington*."

"Your Honor," Hungerford protested, "these negroes are certainly slaves, legally purchased and paid for in the slave market of Havana. My clients have the documentation to prove it. A writ of habeas corpus would only be an invitation for them to flee prosecution for their crimes of mutiny, murder, and thievery, prosecution for which should rightly take place back in Havana."

"These men have committed no crimes and your client's documentation is spurious at best," Baldwin snapped back. "And we will show conclusively that there is no possible way that these men or the children could be legal slaves of Cuba or any other country subject to the Treaty of 1819. Furthermore ... "

"Enough!" Thompson's gavel slammed down on the wooden pallet. "Mr. Baldwin, Mr. Hungerford, Mr. Prosecutor. Each of you will be allowed to make your opening statements to this court and present your cases accordingly. I shall overrule Mr. Baldwin's objection regarding the disposition of the negroes. I will rule, however, that this court will entertain petitions for a writ of habeas corpus. Now, let us get on with procedures. Mr. Prosecutor, please, present your opening statement."

Holabird stood and delivered an opening statement that lasted nearly three hours. Forsyth had provided a copy of the opinion written by U.S. Attorney General Felix Grundy and Holabird followed it to the letter. He pointed out how the "rescuing" of the *Amistad*, whether from pirates, a mutiny, or damage due to weather and malevolent seas, was covered under Articles 8, 9, and 10 of Pickney's Treaty. These articles permitted the rescuers to claim fair compensation for their efforts based on the appraised value of ship and cargo. They also granted power to the executive to return the ship, crew, and cargo to the care of the country of origin, in this case Spain, for prosecution of whatever crimes may have been committed by its subjects on the open seas. The treaty was clear, and thus the *Amistad*, its cargo, and the negro slaves, should be surrendered to the President so that all may be properly delivered to the Spanish minister.

In addition, he cited the case of the *Antelope*, a slaveship bearing the flag of a Spanish colony, La Plata, that had been taken by the U.S. Coast Guard off the coast of Florida. The Coast Guard suspected the slaves were to be sold illegally in the U.S. They demanded prosecution under the treaty of 1819 and salvage of the ship and slaves. A legal battle ensued regarding the disposition of the slaves and the right of salvage. Eventually, however, the slaves on board the *Antelope* were surrendered to the Spanish government under Article 8 of Pickney's Treaty. Because the conditions surrounding the *Amistad* appear to be nearly identical, the same provisions should apply. Holabird closed by saying that issuing a writ of habeas corpus was ill-advised because it would pave a road for escape, a road that would most certainly lead these slaves away from proper justice under the laws of their homeland, Cuba.

Isham stood. He stated that he agreed with Holabird and went on to repeat virtually all of the prosecutor's assertions. He then paused and began an impassioned description of the brave and daring actions of Gedney, Meade, and the crew of the *Washington* in apprehending the wild, dangerous, renegade blacks. His long, often wandering, soliloquy presented numerous accounts of unrelated acts of naval heroism and seemed as though it would never end until, as if suddenly prodded, he said:

"So in conclusion, my clients seek their full rights of salvage on the ship and all its cargo as delineated by its manifest, bills of sale, and other documentation presented herewith to the court."

After this performance, Hungerford's opening came off as refreshingly focused and brief. Though he shared many of the same points as Holabird, his argument was more impassioned.

The blacks were clearly the property of his clients, Ruiz and Montes. They had rebelled against their masters, murdered the captain and crew practically while they slept, seized the ship, and forced the defendants, free whitemen, into bondage. During the ensuing journey they perpetrated torture upon Ruiz and Montes, including regular beatings and deprivation of food and water. The slaves were Spanish subjects and committed their crimes on board a Spanish-flagged ship upon Spanish citizens. Thus they should be tried and judged under Spanish law. Granting a writ of habeas corpus would be denying rightful justice, as well as opening the door for mass escape, a course the slaves certainly would pursue in light of their previous actions of murder and mutiny.

As to the question of salvage, Ruiz and Montes heartily thanked the bravery and intercession of Lieutenants Gedney and Meade and the crew of their ship. However, the salvage claims of $40,000 were exorbitant since most of the manifested cargo had been destroyed or hefted overboard by the mutineering slaves. Amended documentation would be presented and it was hoped the judge would decide on a fair figure that was more representative of the ship's value at the time of boarding.

During the openings, Staples and Sedgwick had taken notes furiously. Baldwin, on the other hand, had sat straight and still, watching the presenters and the judge, and only writing down a few occasional lines. The tribesmen, sitting under guard to the left of their defense team, also sat quietly, although many looked back and forth among themselves, as well as to the Yale Divinity students sitting in the gallery. Lewis Tappan, for his part, had made a few well-timed yawns and sighs during the openings, not at a volume to draw the wrath of Judge Thompson, but certainly loud enough to make his presence, and his views toward specific points, well known.

The court recessed for lunch after Mr. Hungerford had finished. When they returned, Baldwin was allowed to make his statement.

He began by stating that the defense would refute the claims made of the applicability of both Pickney's Treaty and the *Antelope* case. He questioned the government's warrant for the arrest of the blacks as runaway slaves guilty of mutiny and murder based solely on the testimony of two slave owners. He also challenged Gedney's move of bringing the *Amistad* to Connecticut when it was taken in waters off New York, saying that it was an attempt to bend the law in order to satiate aspirations of greed. Finally, Baldwin pressed the point of habeas corpus.

"I find it extremely odd, Your Honor, that we hold these men prisoners as presumed slaves even though when they were found by the U.S. Navy, none were in shackles and each was in command of his own liberty. It was solely due to the darkness of their skin that Mr. Gedney immediately presumed them as property, as slaves and criminals who were perpetrating nefarious acts. He did not even wait for corroboration of this fact from Mr. Ruiz or Mr. Montes. No, Mr. Gedney, seeing their black skin, presumed them wayward property and immediately imprisoned them until they could prove otherwise. In essence, Your Honor, these men are being held captives so that we may ascertain if they are free.

"But as the Court ponders this wretched irony and injustice, let it consider another question of equal if not greater injustice. If these men are property—and we dispute this point wholeheartedly—are they as property no longer men? Please look at them, Your Honor, Mr. Prosecutor, Mr. Hungerford. Everyone in this courtroom, please look at the blacks held under guard. They have human form, they wear clothes, they speak a language, though certainly not Spanish or some sort of contrived 'field dialect.' They have thoughts and emotions. They walk and talk and breathe and feel in the same manner as every other person in this room. They are persons, men. And yet, the court has asked that we petition to see if they be granted the basic rights of men as guaranteed under the law. The federal government holds them captive until they can prove they are free. The law holds them as beasts, as property, until they can prove they are men. I say that justice has been perverted here from the outset, validating without question certain prejudices against the color of a man's skin. But we shall make it right, Your Honor. Rest assured. We shall make it right."

At the conclusion of Baldwin's statement, Thompson adjourned the court until 8:00 A.M. the next morning.

That night Tappan and Jocelyn met with Baldwin, Staples, and Sedgwick in the lounge of their hotel.

"I must admit, Lewis, that it is highly unlikely that the judge will issue a writ for the blacks," Baldwin said. "It is too politically charged. Thompson certainly realizes that if we get a federal court to admit that these men have rights as guaranteed by the Constitution, and if Holabird succeeds in proving they are slaves, the precedent set would strike at the very heart of slavery. Ostensibly, such a ruling would create legal grounds to grant Constitutional rights to every slave in the nation."

"What a glorious thing that would be," Tappan mused.

"Gloriously impossible," Sedgwick said with a sigh. "Holabird would appeal in a second."

"That may be as it may be," Tappan continued, "although an appeal will suit us just as well, since it will keep the case in the public eye."

"I'm afraid, Mr. Tappan, that we will likely be the party filing an appeal," said Staples. "As it stands, now our case is rather thin."

"Nonsense," Tappan cried. "Not a one of those blacks speaks a lick of Spanish. That should be proof enough. And what of the man from the Congo, Mr. Ferry? Won't his testimony validate that they are, in fact, Africans?"

"Mr. Ferry's affidavit won't hold as much validity as the ship's papers, I'm afraid," Sedgwick said. "The documentation they have is legally stamped and verified by Spanish officials. As corrupt and falsified as they may be, those papers carry weight in a court and with a judge. They grant possession of the blacks as property to Ruiz and Montes, and in the eyes of the law, possession weighs heavily, despite what Thompson said about burden of proof."

"Well, certainly we can pray for the best," Tappan said.

"And besides which, I can attest that most of the journalists in attendance were very impressed with Mr. Baldwin's opening statement. Let us hope that in the next few days we can further impress and inspire them. At the very least, this trial should create a national polemic on the evils of slavery."

"Even if we do not get the writ, I am confident we can cast enough doubt upon their case to unsettle their sureness of its outcome," Baldwin said. "Certainly their reading of Pickney's Treaty is open to debate."

"Well, if anything will turn events in our favor, it will be Seth's motion tomorrow," Jocelyn mused. "Let us hope for providence in that area."

The men talked further about the next day's strategy until nearly 1:00 A.M. When he got to his hotel room, Baldwin was exhausted. He undressed and was nearly in bed before he realized he had forgotten to take off his spectacles. As he rose to put them on the bureau he noticed a letter by the washbasin. The envelope had been posted from Washington, D.C.

Mr. Baldwin,

I admire you wholeheartedly for taking this case of the Amistads and shall be watching these proceedings with great excitement and anticipation. I wish you the best of luck and the blessings of providence in your defense. May justice prevail.

A Friend

P.S. Note well that the Treaty of 1819, which the government will certainly cite throughout its case, contains barbs that can be used against their position as well. Specifically, in the fifth paragraph of the second section, and the third paragraph of the eighth.

Baldwin turned over the envelope but there was no return address. He stared for a moment at the spot near the washbasin where he had found the letter and then glanced around the room. Shaking his head he took the oil lamp and quickly walked down the hallway to see Sedgwick. They had been able to secure a truncated copy of Pickney's Treaty, but the federal government had yet to provide the defense with any part of the Treaty of 1819. Baldwin's team had been forced to work from notes and cribbed transcripts. It was frustrating but yet another example of how much control the government had in this case. The defense had divined what they could from the notes but had given more time and weight instead to Pickney's Treaty, the *Antelope* case, and their proposal of the writ. Baldwin woke up Sedgwick and had him pull the notes on the Treaty of 1819 from his valise. They looked for the portions of the treaty cited in the letter, staying up until nearly sunrise to incorporate it into their defense.

Court was set to resume at 8:00 A.M. on Friday morning. At 7:00 A.M. Pepe Ruiz decided to pay a visit to the tribesmen. They had been placed in six different cells in the Hartford jail, all within sight of each other. As the jailer watched, Ruiz walked down the line, stopping at each cell to look inside. He saw that his blacks were being fed and treated well. They looked good in the outfits that had been supplied by the Amistad Committee, and he was sure that when they returned to Havana, he would be able to get top dollar for each of them. He got to the cell holding Singbe, Grabeau, and seven of the others. He stepped up to the bars and began speaking in Spanish.

"So, Joseph Cinqué. Soon this will be over and you will be entrusted into my care again. We will go back to Havana where you will all be put on trial for proper justice. But you know what I think? I think I will tell the Spanish Consul that only you are to be tried. I will sell your friends to recoup my losses. After all, burning them would be a waste of some really fine niggers. I think it will be enough to see your black skin sizzle."

Singbe lunged at the bars. He did not reach out or make any other threatening moves. But it was enough to startle Ruiz into jumping back. He raised his hand as if to slap Singbe, but then he lowered it and began laughing.

"You have spirit, Cinqué, I'll give you that. But I think it will be the death of you."

He drew his finger across his throat slowly and laughed even harder. The three girls were in the cell next to Singbe and had been watching intently. When Ruiz made the slashing movement, the oldest one, Margru, began screaming. The others quickly became hysterical.

"What are you doing in here!?"

Ruiz turned to see Tappan and Jocelyn standing at the far end of the hallway.

"Mr. Tappan. Good day, sir. I am simply inspecting my property, making sure they are well taken care of until this little affair is done with."

Tappan rushed down to the cell holding the girls. They were cowering against the back wall, screaming and shaking. The tribesmen were yelling to them, trying to calm them down. Singbe's grip on the bars of his cell tightened as he stared at Ruiz.

"What did you do here?" Tappan asked. "Why are these girls so frightened?"

"It was not me. It was Cinqué. He scared them. The children delight in my presence, I assure you."

"You are monstrous, sir," Jocelyn hissed. "Without scruples or any kind of human heart. These are just children, for God's sake."

"They are property. They are all property. Mostly mine. And soon I will be taking them back to Cuba. Although, I must say your countrymen have not treated them all that well. I heard two of the bucks died on Sunday last. I am deciding on whether to sue for losses or not."

"Get out of here!" Tappan screamed. "Jailer! Jailer! This man is unsettling your prisoners! I implore you to expel him immediately from the premises unless you want to have a riot on your hands."

"Here, now, Mr. Ruiz. I think the gentleman is right," the jailer said. "These is your slaves, sir, it's true. But it don't benefit no one to have 'em screaming and chattering on like wild monkeys."

"They are not monkeys!" Tappan yelled. "They are men, damn it!"

Three reporters burst into the hallway. They had come to watch the prisoner transfer to the courthouse but had rushed down the stairs when they heard the yelling. The area was in chaos. Ruiz decided it was time to leave. He walked up to the reporters and pointed to Tappan.

"Wherever this man goes, he causes trouble. Look how he has scared the slaves. It is a disgrace that his kind are let to run free and stir up such problems. It should be criminal."

Tappan heard Ruiz but ignored him. The jailer had let him in the girls' cell. He tried to calm them down, but they were too far gone with terror to respond to any white face, no matter how kind it had been in the past.

Nearly an hour later, the tribesmen were led out of the jail and into the courthouse by the guards. The jailer, who was adamant that "the slaves was belonging to Mr. Ruiz and the court'll prove it," nonetheless did admit to a reporter that it was Mr. Ruiz who appeared to cause the row down in the cells. The three girls came out last, clinging to Tappan, and still sobbing.

Court reconvened soon after. Holabird began, opening with an examination of Pickney's Treaty. His reasoning followed the logic and strategy set out in Attorney General Grundy's opinion. Accordingly, Articles 8 through 10 were cited by Holabird as the passages most pertinent to the case.

"Of these, Your Honor, it is Articles 8 and 9 which contain most of the salient points relevant to this case. I quote for the record and those in attendance, Article 8: 'In case subjects or inhabitants of either party with their shipping be forced through stress of weather, pursuit of pirates or enemies, or any other urgent necessity for seeking shelter and harbor belonging to the other party, they shall be received and treated with all humanity, and enjoy all favor, protection and help. They shall in no way be hindered from returning out of said port, but may remove and depart when they please without any let or hinderance.'

"And Article 9: 'All ships and merchandise whatsoever, which shall be rescued out of the hands of any pirates or robbers on the high seas, shall be brought into a port of either state and shall be delivered to the custody of the officers of that port. There they shall be taken care of and restored entire to the true proprietor as soon as due and sufficient proof shall be made concerning the property thereof.'

"Hence, Your Honor," Holabird continued, "it seems quite clear that the situation of the *Amistad* fits these conditions and thus should be treated accordingly."

"Your Honor," Baldwin spoke while rising slowly, "I wonder if the Prosecutor can provide some clarification regarding the government's disposition toward my clients?"

"Which would be, Mr. Baldwin?" Thompson asked.

"If it please the court, Your Honor, I think we would all like to know whether the prosecutor is saying that the United States of America is charging these men, and these little girls, with piracy?"

The gallery instantly filled with a wave of whispers and rumblings. Many in attendance knew that if piracy was charged, Thompson would have no course but to refer the case to a trial by jury, a move that would certainly provide months of proceedings as well as a source of entertainment for the entire state, if not the whole country.

Thompson brought his gavel down to quiet the courtroom. Holabird had been trying to speak from the moment Baldwin had finished his question.

"No, Your Honor, not at all," Holabird spurted. "For the record, the Federal Government has no wish to pursue charges of piracy. We are only entertaining the issues of mutiny, murder, and property. As to the first two, we freely admit that the girls were nothing more than witnesses."

"Satisfied, Mr. Baldwin?"

"Completely, Your Honor."

Holabird collected himself and continued. He cited the decision of the *Antelope* case and pointed to passages of the Treaty of 1819. In particular he cited the Treaty's provision permitting America's armed vessels to cruise in search of suspected slavers. By intercepting the *Amistad*, the government not only rectified a mutinous situation, but also verified that the slaves were in fact rebellious property. He also submitted as proof of the Cubans' claim of rightful ownership the original bills of purchase, customs documentation, and the manifest from the *Amistad*.

"They are Spanish subjects and, in the eyes of Spanish law, they are most assuredly slaves."

Hungerford's presentation was almost identical. He also followed Grundy's opinion, deviating only in his much stronger emphasis on Article 10 of Pickney's Treaty which dealt with reimbursement. He stressed that his clients were willing to pay salvage on a refigured value based on the condition of ship and cargo when boarded, but certainly not the exorbitant sum of $40,000.

"So we mean to cheat our benefactors, is that it?" Isham said, standing. "Lieutenant Gedney and Lieutenant Meade risked their lives to save these men from almost certain death and weeks of torture."

"Objection!" Sedgwick stood. "General Isham is postulating about supposed 'certainties' and other events which either did not occur or have yet to be proved in this court."

"Sustained. General Isham, you will kind keep your mind and your words to the established facts."

"It is a fact that my clients risked life and limb to extricate these men from harrowing circumstances, Your Honor," Isham said. "Now, these men, Spaniards of Cuba, though reputed to be gentlemen, are trying to deprecate the value of their holdings. It seems an odd and crass way to treat your saviors, Your Honor."

"Quite frankly, Your Honor, my clients wish nothing but the best for the brave officers and crew who saved them," Hungerford said. "However, to award such exorbitant sums as claimed by the Naval officers would be the equivalent of robbery of my clients, as this voyage is already a total loss for them."

Hungerford finished his presentation and sat down.

"We will now hear from the defense," Thompson announced.

All eyes in the courtroom turned to Baldwin. But it was Seth Staples who stood and began speaking.

"Your Honor, we have a strong case to present in defense of these men. But before we begin, I would like to enter a second petition for habeas corpus."

"For whom, Mr. Staples?"

"For the three girls, Your Honor. This would be separate and alone from the other petition."

"On what basis?"

"Your Honor, Mr. Montes claims that these girls are Spanish subjects and have been raised in Cuba. And yet, though their ages are listed as being between seven and nine years, not a one of them speaks so much as a single word of Spanish. The record shows that they could not even answer to their given names when put to them by Lieutenant Meade."

"Your Honor," Holabird objected, "it is also in the same record that Mr. Ruiz and Montes clearly stated that the slaves speak an obscure field dialect."

"I wonder if either of the slave traders would care to swear to that fact in open court, Mr. Prosecutor?" Staples countered. "Mr. Hungerford, what say you? Will your clients swear to the existence of this obscure field dialect today? Your Honor, I respectfully request that the court asks them to do so. And as this request is made, perhaps we should apprise them of the penalties in this country for perjury. Also, I think we should let them know that, according to Section 8 of the Treaty of 1819, any persons found to be in the possession of contraband Africans shall be prosecuted as pirates. As you well know, Your Honor, under American law, piracy carries a penalty of death."

"Your Honor," Hungerford blurted, "I request that we break for a short recess so that I may confer with my clients and the prosecutor."

"I second the request, Your Honor," Holabird said.

"I will grant a fifteen-minute recess."

Holabird and Hungerford retreated with Ruiz and Montes in an anteroom and scoured their copies of the treaty. Ruiz translated for Montes who, when he heard all the factors and possibilities, shook his head over and over again.

When court was back in session, Hungerford declared that his clients would not testify at this point in time, nor were they compelled to do so by law.

"Your Honor, my clients have already made depositions under oath regarding all of their activities, which were well within Spanish law. The documentation regarding the disposition of the slaves is clear, Your Honor, and sanctioned by Spanish authorities. All transactions took place in Cuba, a Spanish possession. The U.S. government has no right to intercede in this area. We are only concerned with issues of salvage and the return of my clients' property. The rest we leave to Spanish law."

"Your Honor," Holabird said, standing, "The United States urges that a writ is not granted for the children on the grounds that they are witnesses to the events on board the *Amistad*."

"So for that they are to be held in jail, Your Honor?" Staples said. "Since when are innocent witness interned in jailhouses in these United States?"

"Your Honor," Holabird continued, "the girls are being held for their own safety. As the court is aware, abolitionists have made themselves cozy with the *Amistad* negroes. It is well known that abolitionists are responsible for spiriting runaway slaves out of the country through the so-called underground railway. The government is concerned that if the children or any of the other negroes are provided with a writ of habeas corpus, they will very quickly disappear, perhaps even against their will. Therefore we ask that if a writ is granted for the children it be accompanied by bail of one hundred dollars per child."

"$100! Your Honor, that is an outrageous sum! For the love of God, these children have not even committed a crime!"

"Mr. Staples!" Thompson said slamming his gavel down. "You will control yourself before the court. I said I will rule on motions for a writ, but I am not ready to do so now. Submit your second petition and I will review it. Mr. Prosecutor, prepare your points in a brief and submit them as well. They will also be considered. It is past noon. Court shall recess sixty minutes for lunch."

As soon as Thompson left, the room exploded into chatter. "Bail for innocent children? And one hundred dollars at that!" "Yes, but Holabird's right, those abolitionists can't be trusted." "The Spaniards won't take the stand. They must be lying." "Perhaps not. Would you set yourself at the mercy of foreign laws?"

As the crowd filed out, Tappan sat, watched, and listened. His face remained inscrutable but inside he glowed with pleasure. At the very least, their strategy was winning over most of the spectators and some of the press.

An hour later, court resumed. Baldwin rose and asked if Lieutenant Gedney had any problems testifying under oath.

"Or are you of the same disposition as the Spanish slave dealers?"

"Certainly not!" Gedney said confidently. "I stand by what I saw and reported in my log."

Gedney was sworn in and Baldwin began leading him through a recounting of the events concerning the *Amistad*'s seizure and boarding. Gedney had been through this several times already with depositions and interviews to the newspapers, but still he was on his guard. He knew lawyers were tricksters, aimed on bending the truth to suit their needs. Still, as the questioning went on, he became more relaxed. This lawyer, Baldwin, seemed harmless, perhaps even a bit distracted, for he made Gedney repeat himself more than a few times:

"Your orders again were what, Lieutenant?"

"To survey the coast, although we had also been warned to keep an eye out for a black ship reported to possibly be a pirate ship."

"But you were never formally ordered to track down pirates or apprehend a renegade slaver?"

"No, sir."

Then later:

"Were any of the blacks in chains when you boarded the ship?"

"No, sir."

"Was anyone in chains?"

"No. Mr. Ruiz and Mr. Montes and the slave boy Antonio were being held down below, but they were not bound in any way."

After Gedney finished his testimony, Baldwin thanked him and then walked over to the defense counsel's table and picked up two small stacks of paper.

"Your Honor, I would like to submit these documents. The first is an annotated account of the *Antelope* case. While the prosecutor has said that the case of the *Amistad* is nearly identical, I believe we have heard Lieutenant Gedney's testimony to reveal a major discrepancy. The negroes on the *Antelope* were bound and chained as slaves when the ship was taken. Yet, as Lieutenant Gedney has just stated, twice, the men on the *Amistad* were not. They were free when found. As such they were 'prima facie' free in the eyes of the law and hence should have been, and should be, treated as *persons*, not slaves. Mr. Ruiz and Mr. Montes were found by the naval officers to be just as free, just as unbound by shackles or chains. They were accorded every right and afforded every comfort by Lieutenant Gedney. However, simply because of the color of their skin, my clients were immediately locked up. For all Lieutenant Gedney might have known, they were the rightful crew of the vessel. But he let his prejudices make the decision regarding rights. It was he who chose to consider my clients slaves, even when there was no immediate evidence pointing to this fact.

"I also have here a pieced-together copy of the Treaty of 1819. Let the record note that it is in such a state because the federal government has not as yet provided us with a complete copy of the treaty. However, I do have enough of the document's content to have been following the prosecutor's suggestions. He has cited certain passages repeatedly. Let me add to his notations. If he will look to the fifth paragraph in the second section, he will find that it clearly states that in order to cruise for slavers, the ship's captain must be 'instructed, commissioned, or authorized by presidential order.' Mr. Gedney's stated mission was to survey the coast. He had no written orders to detain suspected slavers or to chase down presumed pirates, for that matter. I wonder, Your Honor, when the United States' Naval officers got into the business of chasing down wayward ships for other nations on a freelance basis?"

"That will be enough of that type of speculation, Mr. Baldwin," Judge Thompson warned.

"Yes, Your Honor. But it is clear that this seizure of apparently free men is completely illegal. They were not seeking port as argued by the prosecutor when he pointed to Article eight of Pickney's Treaty. They were not waylaid by pirates or enemies of state. They were in fact, exercising their natural rights to extricate themselves from illegal kidnapping. They were trying to return to their homeland."

"Objection, Your Honor," Holabird said. "Documentation has shown that these slaves were legally paid for."

"Your Honor," Baldwin implored, "we have submitted the affidavit by a British seaman located by the Amistad Committee, a Mr. John Ferry, who is fluent in Congolese. He testified that these men did in fact speak an African language and not a Spanish-inflected dialect. The documentation submitted by the Spanish slave traders is obviously falsified."

"Objection again, Your Honor," Holabird cried. "The documents are clear and we are not here to impugn them. Also, Mr. Ferry's affidavit further states that he was not able to communicate with the blacks beyond a greeting and a few cursory words. That does not constitute fluency of an African language by the slaves."

"It is more than my clients know of Spanish," Baldwin cried.

"Mr. Baldwin! Mr. Prosecutor! That is enough!" Judge Thompson said. "Mr. Holabird, your objections are sustained. Mr. Baldwin, you will remain true to the facts as they have been laid forth to the court."

"I would like to, Your Honor, but the facts as laid forth

before the court are not true."

Many in the gallery broke out into laughter. Some even began applauding. Thompson slammed his gavel down repeatedly.

"Quiet in the court. And you, Mr. Baldwin. Once more, sir, and you will be cited for contempt."

Baldwin apologized emphatically to Judge Thompson. He went on to reemphasize his points as carefully as possible. He also stated that, if anything, the trial's location was wrong because the ship had been seized in waters off Long Island and thus should be tried in New York. Gedney had simply been trying to increase the value of salvage by bringing the ship to Connecticut. Isham objected, saying his clients took them to Connecticut because they believed it would be easier to get to the bottom of the incident without all the press scrutiny and public curiosity that would have surely befallen them in a larger port such as New York. Holabird also objected, knowing New York would provide the defense with a more sympathetic arena than Connecticut. But Thompson overruled them both and said he would take the matter under consideration. Baldwin finished by imploring the court to grant the writ of habeas corpus.

"Regardless of whether they are ruled property or not, these men, these children, are persons. They deserve the same rights as any person in this country as guaranteed by the Constitution. To do less is to deny any semblance of justice."

Baldwin had sat down. Judge Thompson asked Holabird, Hungerford, Isham, and Baldwin to file closing briefs with the court.

"I will render my ruling on Monday," Judge Thompson said. "Court adjourned until 8:00 A.M. two days hence. Monday, the twenty-third."

As the weekend passed by, the city was abuzz with predictions on how Thompson would rule. But when he issued his judgment on Monday morning, the public was more miffed than anything else.

"Personally, slavery is as abhorrent to me as it is to any man here," he began. "But I must, on my oath, pronounce what laws are subject to this case. As such, I can render little because the proper answering of the questions of property brought here are clouded by claims of murder and mutiny. Those are issues properly taken up in district court. That is where I will refer this case. Because of this I will not grant writs of habeas corpus for either the men or the children of the *Amistad*. I will rule, however, that they be kept in preferred incarceration, that the shackles be removed from Mr. Joseph Cinqué while he is in lock-up, and that the negroes be allowed regular outdoor exercise and visitors from the Yale Divinity School without barrier or surcharge. I am also ordering a surveyed measurement of the point of seizure to determine whether district court proceedings will be held in Connecticut or New York. That is all."

Tappan stood up and immediately congratulated Baldwin and his team. Though they had not won, important points had been scored. And the prospect of bringing the trial to New York warmed them all. A few days later, however, the survey came back and diminished some of their optimism. It was found that the *Amistad* was taken more than a mile off the New York shoreline, and hence was in the open seas. According to maritime law, Gedney was within his right to bring his ship to a port of convenience and safety, in this case, New London, without affecting salvage claims.

The news got worse. The district court date was set for November 19 in New Haven. The presiding judge would be Andrew T. Judson.

Counter-Offensives

A frosty October wind blew off the water, curling its icy fingers quickly around the posts and planks and corners before rushing off along the docks and into the city. Josiah Gibbs tucked his chin down deeper into the high collar and angled his broad-brimmed hat so that it covered more of the back of his neck. He followed the wind, walking away from the French freighter and toward the public house the sailor had mentioned. In the distance, the graying skies had already begun to burn and smolder with the setting sun.

The pub, known as The Hold, was about three blocks up from the bowery docks on a narrow dirt side road, an alleyway really, that was framed on both sides by low and sad, sagging clapboard buildings that looked like they couldn't stand another minute of the stiff winds that had been blowing all day on the New York City waterfront. There was no sign hanging outside and Gibbs almost passed the place but he noticed the chipped and faded yellow door, which the sailor said marked the spot. Gibbs turned the knob, thinking to knock only after he had opened it halfway. But the dark faces inside, and the immediate silence that his own appearance caused, told him he was in the right place.

Since the end of the circuit court trial, Gibbs had been wandering ports and waterfronts from Boston to Bridgeport. Baldwin and Tappan were sure that if they could find a translator for the Africans, they would stand a much better chance in the district court proceedings. Gibbs had learned only shreds of the tribesmen's language over the last few weeks, but he figured it was enough to find someone who was fluent in the tongue. Both he and Baldwin agreed that the best bet would be to scour the docks of major ports. Certainly there would be a sailor, probably a black one, on some ship, that spoke the language as well as English or some other dialect of the west. Gibbs had spent nearly all of the last four weeks along the water or in seaside pubs for "Negroes Only," looking for such a man, but to no avail. The trial was less than a month away and he was starting to lose hope at the prospect of finding anyone who could help.

Gibbs shut the yellow door. About a dozen black men, some smoking pipes and cigars, stared at him from the tables scattered through the narrow dim room. A few lanterns burned with a smoky oily smell. In one corner, two black women wearing very little clung to a huge black man in a striped jersey. Gibbs smiled weakly and walked quickly over to the bar. The dirt floor was uneven and soggy in spots. The bar itself was nothing more than rough planks crudely hammered together. A few bottles sat on a shelf along with two dark wooden casks. The bartender, a rotund light-skinned man with two small gold rings in one earlobe, a fresh, broad scar scratched across the bridge of his nose and a crooked grin on his face, stood back near the bottles with his arms crossed.

"My good man, I'm wondering if you can help me. I am looking for a man who speaks an African dialect."

"Sorry, constable, we gots none a them here."

"Oh no, sir, I'm not a constable. I'm a college professor," Gibbs said.

The bartender raised one eyebrow and snorted.

"And . . . and a minister, as well," Gibbs added quickly. "I wish this man no ill will. In fact, I don't even know who he is. You see I am in need of a translator."

"Translator? For what?"

"Well, I do not know exactly what language, but I believe it is a western African dialect, though not Congolese. We have attempted that. Perhaps Mandingo."

"We gots none a them here, Mr. Minister, sir."

"Yes, well, perhaps you wouldn't mind if I asked around? You see my need is rather urgent as I am working with the blacks taken with the *Amistad*. Perhaps you've heard of them."

The bartender stepped forward until his great stomach was touching the bar. "You been with the slaves of the *Amistad*?"

"Yes. I and my colleagues are trying to communicate with them. We hope to . . . "

"Phillip! Jean-Paul! This man spoke with the slaves taken off the *Amistad*!"

"No! It is not true!"

"He says so. And he is a minister. You are telling us the truth, yes?"

"Absolutely." Gibbs smiled. "I have met with the men several times trying to learn their language and teach them ours, as well as trying to introduce them to Christianity. Our discourses were daily until about three and half weeks ago. That is when I began searching for a translator who could speak in their tongue."

"Will they be hanged?"

"Do you think the government give them back to Spain?"

"Is it true that Cinqué is a king?"

"I hear one of them is a fierce cannibal."

"Gentlemen. Gentlemen," Gibbs said. "I can see you are interested and well informed. Let me see what I can add to your knowledge. No. There is no cannibal among them, although there is one who certainly has sharp, terrifying teeth. But he has proven to be quite tame and friendly. We do believe their leader, Joseph Cinqué, is a tribal chief or prince of some sort, although we cannot confirm this because we cannot make ourselves understood to him. As for the government, all I can say is that we have assembled the finest defense team for the *Amistad* blacks. Our attorneys will pursue every avenue that may help these fellows. However, we know we can present a better case if we can get the Africans' side of the story. To that end, gentlemen, do any of you speak an African dialect in any degree of fluency?"

The men looked at each other and then about the room. They all shook their heads. Gibbs sighed. He thanked them and turned to leave.

"Mr. Minister."

Gibbs turned back. The words came from the corner. The big man in the striped shirt was now standing, though his broad black hands still clung to the two women's scantily clad breasts.

"What language these men speak?"

The man's words were thick with an accent that Gibbs had never heard wrapped around the English language.

"I do not know. But I know a few words."

"Speak them, then. We see if they too are my words."

Gibbs gathered himself and took a deep breath.

"E-tah, feh-lee, saw-wha, na-nee?"

The black man asked to hear them again, slowly. Gibbs repeated. The black man sat back down shaking his head.

"I am sorry. I know those words not."

Gibbs smiled. He thanked them all and walked to the door. As he opened it, a black man from the street was reaching to grab the knob. He almost fell into Gibbs. The black man smiled for a second at the moment. But then, as the realization washed through him that Gibbs was white and was coming out the yellow door of The Hold, the black man straightened and moved out of Gibbs's way with an air of servitude and a flicker of fear. Gibbs tipped his hat politely and was nearly past the man when he stopped and turned quickly.

"E-tah, feh-lee, saw-wha, na-nee?"

"Thlano, thataro, shupa, hera-mebedi," the man replied

matter-of-factly.

Gibbs grabbed the man by the arm.

"One, two, three, four!"

"Five, six, seven, eight," the man said, now backing up.

"Praised be God!" Gibbs cried. "Praised be Our Father in Heaven!"

The man turned into the bar, only to see all the men in there rushing at him. He wrenched his arm free from the little whiteman and began to run down the alley. Gibbs and several men from the bar took off after him, yelling into growing darkness for the man to stop.

Seth Staples poured over the more than two dozen notes that Baldwin had received over the past few weeks. Each was short, at most only a few lines, and contained a suggestion or question for the defense team to ponder: "How could the government justify holding the blacks for piracy and murder?" "What grounds existed within the law to hold the children since they had been declared witnesses and not perpetrators?" "How could the court hold the blacks simultaneously as property and criminals?" "If the blacks were in fact slaves accused of murder and piracy, then the law required forfeiture of property on the part of the owners." Other notes pointed out passages of the Treaty of 1819 that might aid their case and talked about contributing factors of state that might affect the President's overall strategy. All the notes had been posted from either Washington or Boston. All were written in a flourishing, educated hand and bore the same simple signature: "A Friend."

The most recent of the series had arrived yesterday and cautioned Baldwin to note well the comments being made by the Spanish Ambassador in official documents and the newspapers. "He has repeatedly expressed himself in terms that clearly identify the blacks as people rather than property. This disposition may be used effectively against the Federal Government's case in court."

Staples had been systematically exploring the implications of the suggestions. As he did, he found for the most part that each was extremely well reasoned and insightful. Neither he nor Baldwin nor Sedgwick knew the identity of their "friend," but it was apparent that whoever it was had a considerable grasp of the workings of the state department and the presidency, as well as a sharp legal mind.

"Perhaps it is old Van Buren himself." Sedgwick had laughed. "He's giving us the keys to the kingdom through the back door so that we may tidy up this mess and end the public spectacle."

Staples had actually spent half a night and a few glasses of wine considering that very proposition. He was sure that the administration was growing increasingly agitated with the publicity the case was drawing, and they had to know that the defense would do everything they could to draw the proceedings out, no matter how dismal the prospects for a victory looked. The best thing for Van Buren would be for this whole thing to go away as quickly as possible. But helping the defense toward this end seemed ludicrous. It would mean a very public loss for the President and risk raising new questions about slavery on the domestic front. Not in an election year, Staples concluded. Not ever, if Van Buren could help it.

All of which left him puzzling as he continued to research the clues being provided: Who was sending the notes?

† † †

It was a sunny day in London, an occurrence that Arthur Tappan had discovered was not as rare as the city's reputation would have most people believe. He still much preferred Manhattan and America, though, and in that order.

Tappan had been in England nearly three months and had found most of his time had been used productively. He was working to create distribution, import, and export arrangements with a number of manufacturers. The negotiations were going slowly, but progress was being made. He was certain that by the end of his trip, The Tappan Dry Goods Company would have exclusive export customers for dozens of different specialized American products, from finished fabrics and women's hats, to steam boilers and precision instruments. He also anticipated that his store would become the premier place in New York City to find the finest in British and European fashions, fixtures, and notions.

However, his dealings and discussions on English soil had not been limited to business. He had been invited to several discreet meetings with various upper-level British government officials to discuss slavery in America and the abolition movement. The British seemed to be greatly interested in supporting efforts aimed at destabilizing and ultimately eradicating American slavery. The parliamentarians and ministers he met with almost immediately broke into long moralistic tirades about the evils of slavery and the need to abolish it worldwide. They would invariably point with pride to their own advances, how slavery was no longer permitted in the Empire, and how so many blacks had been "reclaimed" through Christian education and schooling in the trades.

Tappan listened and smiled and made the appropriate comments, but he was no one's fool. He knew that despite their claims to occupying the moral high ground, much of the British government's concern with U.S. slavery was economic. They had eliminated slavery, yes, but at the same time they had escalated their own colonization efforts, apparently preferring to exploit whole countries and their resources rather than simply slapping chains on the unfortunate few. For the most part this had reduced the costs of exports and opened up foreign markets. However, countries that embraced slavery and maintained large agricultural concerns could still undercut the Crown and her possessions in several areas. Nowhere was this more true than with American cotton.

Cheap, high quality, and seemingly endless in its supply, American cotton was king; it was also the fuel that drove the British textile industry. However, the cut taken by the U.S. government through duties and tariffs drove up prices to what many British manufacturers claimed were outrageous levels. Despite this, U.S. cotton still came in well below the prices demanded by plantation owners in British colonies. Many British businessmen and legislators believed, though, that a negative alteration of the American production system, such as an increase in labor costs brought about by the elimination of slavery, could make the British-controlled colonial growers more competitive and increase their market share worldwide.

But others in the British government foresaw a different scenario, one where America's slavery problem would eventually cause a fissure that would split the United States into two countries. These men were looking, ever so delicately, for an opportunity to drive a wedge into that fissure. They believed a second country hewn out of the U.S., one perhaps made up of America's southern states and relying heavily on cotton and agriculture, would be eager to secure a reliable cash influx. This situation would make the new country willing to negotiate more acceptable import arrangement terms. It would also be a country less likely bent on expansion to the south and west, leaving Cuba, Mexico, and even Texas more accessible to annexation by the British Empire.

Tappan was not a trader. He believed in America and the country's ability to change and grow. He constantly heard talk that pressing abolition could cause civil war, but he didn't believe it would ever happen. He had more faith in the American people than that. He was sure that if slavery could be exposed for what it truly was, and if its proponents who were so deeply burrowed into the federal government could be rooted out, then a grand bloodless policy shift could occur in America as it had in England. So he listened at these meetings and remembered; and when he got to his lodgings he penned out notes and then slipped them through an intermediary to the American ambassador. The ambassador, who did not even know the source of the notes, would place them on a ship in a diplomatic pouch to Washington.

Because mail was carried over the sea, Arthur had just begun receiving letters from his brother, Lewis, regarding the

Amistads. He wished he could go back home and take part, for he was sure this was the catalyst they had been seeking to detonate an open, nationwide polemic on slavery. But the future of the brothers' company depended on him staying in London for several more months and finishing what he had started. And he knew in his heart that Lewis was more than up to the task of keeping the case in the public eye.

Still, there was one element that he was sure Lewis had not given enough thought to, and so he wrote out another note for the diplomatic pouch.

> *Have heard talk about an incident involving blacks taken from a ship called* Amistad. *One of the men in a recent meeting postulated that it would be unfortunate, even dangerous, for the government, if the blacks fell into harm's way before the court system was done with them and they could be returned to Spain. It might be useful to increase security for these men until they are out of the country.*

Later that night, Tappan passed on the note to his contact. He had little confidence in the prospect of leaving the blacks' security in the hands of the government. But for now, it was the best he could do.

In the great room of his Washington town house, Secretary of State Forsyth sat in a thickly padded wide-backed chair, the one with the polished mahogany frame that had handcarved claws on the ends of each leg and beautifully detailed swan's necks for arms. His feet rested on an equally ornate footstool. He held his favorite pipe in his hand, drawing on it slowly while his eyes focused on the dull glowing embers in the wide white marble fireplace. A light knocking broke into his concentration. Forsyth grunted and a black servant walked in carrying a silver tray with a single snifter of brandy.

"Thank you, Paul. Tend to the fire, please."

"Yes, sir, Mr. Forsyth."

The servant threw a thick cut of birch and a smaller one of cherrywood on the dying heap and stirred the coals until the flames licked the logs quick and bright.

"Anything else, Mr. Forsyth?"

"No, that will be fine for now."

"Yes, sir."

The servant closed the door quietly on his way out. It was nearly midnight and Forsyth's body longed for sleep, but his mind raced, analyzing events and recounting the day. There had been a small food riot in one of Philadelphia's poorer neighborhoods yesterday. Nobody killed, but the police arrested over forty people who were protesting the rise in the cost of bread. During the morning cabinet meeting, Vice President Johnson said it was an aberration, the grousing of dirt Irish immigrants looking for free food, perhaps trying to scare a few honest men out of their jobs. Van Buren agreed, but Forsyth was not so confident in the assessment. If the economy did not pick up soon, he was sure there would be more such altercations.

The thought of Van Buren as president was troubling him more as of late, too. He was an excellent manager, an intelligent politician, and a good strategist. His creation of an independent treasury system that eliminated the federal government from direct operation of the banking system was an inspired move and should have stimulated investment and spending. It didn't, however. If anything, the domestic markets had weakened, and foreign trade was dismal. Forsyth was convinced that it was a confidence factor. The country's financial barons simply didn't see Van Buren as a forceful leader. He didn't have any of Jackson's public charm or private temper, mannerisms that seemed to singlehandedly carry the country through eight years of prosperity. No, Van Buren was more even, an administrator dedicated to consensus-building and compromise. Excellent traits in a civil servant, but they were proving to be suicidal for a president. Public perception, which was solid during the campaign, now appeared to be mixed and declining, as well. There was concern that the President was capricious, afraid to assert his will or remain committed to the issues he took up. Increasingly he was a man seen by the public as trying to please everyone and instead satisfying no one. It didn't help that he had been in the White House for nearly three years and still had yet to cast a single veto. Meanwhile, the Whigs seemed to be gaining momentum, and the opposing press was becoming more and more vicious every day.

At least the press was making less and less of this *Amistad* case. Where it had been front page news in September, it was now not even mentioned in most papers—even with the district court case coming up in just two weeks. Forsyth had met with Holabird last week to go over the details. Despite the points that Baldwin had made in circuit court, the case seemed fairly certain to go the government's way. Judge Judson had agreed during a lunch meeting yesterday. Though he was not sure what new evidence the abolitionists would marshal, he assured Forsyth that a writ of habeas corpus would never be granted in his court. Further, despite the fact that there was some doubt as to the validity of the Spaniards' claim regarding the blacks' origins, the documentation was in order. "Of course, I have not seen everything," Judson said. "But it appears the abolitionists will have to present something that was neither seen nor heard in the circuit court proceedings, something very different and indisputable in the eyes of the law, to change the course of this case."

However, despite his confidence in both Holabird and Judson, Forsyth still held a degree of uneasiness over the case. Some of this was the product of a recent addition to the mix: Pedro Alcántara Argaiz, the new Spanish minister. Unlike the more discreet Calderón, who had been recalled to her majesty's court, Argaiz's overtures were aggressive, relentless, and extraverted. He was eager to make an impression on his superiors and establish himself with the American government as someone who was not to be trifled with. He had begun filing very formal, and very public, diplomatic protests regarding the *Amistad*. The text of these protests had been supplied to a variety of newspapers. A few—mostly those sympathetic to the Whigs, slavery, and states' rights—reprinted portions, including the demand to "immediately surrender the ship, cargo, and slaves to the Spanish government so that justice can be carried out under Spanish law." Argaiz also pressed for meetings with Forsyth and the President at almost a daily rate. Forsyth assured him that all would be resolved within a few weeks. The minister expressed his doubts about this haughtily and continued to repeat his demands. Forsyth was sure that the press would quickly discover Señor Argaiz to be the bore he truly was and ignore him accordingly. Still, he was someone who needed monitoring.

Of more concern was Lewis Tappan, who Forsyth heartily wished would drop dead this very moment. Tappan was a pompous, persistent snake, who no doubt sensed the lull in the press coverage of the *Amistad* case, as well. Forsyth was certain that the twisted abolitionist was at this very moment planning some contrived event to give fresh blood and juice to the journalistic hounds. Whatever it was, it probably would not change the outcome of the case. But it would renew the talk of the slaves, with whom the public seemed to have grown more sympathetic. It would also stir up more talk about slavery in general, talk which might fuel embers that could burn through the winter and into the spring when campaigning for the election would begin in earnest. That, more than any boatload of African slaves, was the most dangerous element in this whole affair for the Democrats and the Van Buren Administration.

Forsyth drained his brandy glass and stood, tapping the pipe on the side of the fireplace until ashes of the spent tobacco fell into dying flames. He stared into the coals for a few seconds, turning over the fate of the *Amistad* in his mind.

"I think this is something we shall have to take care of ourselves," he mused half aloud.

† † †

Singbe sat patiently in a small room at the New Haven jail as a man stretched brass calipers around his head. The instrument's pointed tips touched lightly, one in the middle of his forehead, the other at the base of his skull. The man held the calipers up against a long brass stick with numbers and Latin words embossed on it and then scribbled on a piece of paper. He took one more such measurement around Singbe's eye sockets and then put the calipers down.

"It's obvious this one is the leader," the man, Dr. George Combe, declared.

"You knew that before you began the examination," Simeon Jocelyn sighed.

"Precisely. The measurements bear this out. Phrenology is, after all, an exact science," Combe said.

"What does your examination show about Cinqué, Dr. Combe?" an excited journalist asked.

"His behavior as leader of the mutineers was totally in character and in fact might have been predicted had he been examined previous to the voyage."

"Really? Remarkable! How so?"

"His head measures twenty-two and three eighths inches in its circumference, sixteen inches from the meatus auditorias to the occipital protuberance, and six and one third inches through the head at the outermost from the point of nominal destructiveness. It's all fairly obvious that these observations, when properly analyzed, show a man in the possession of abilities suited for spirited leadership."

"What else do you see, doctor?" another journalist asked.

Combe let out a long breath, took up his notes, and began walking slowly around Singbe, who was sitting on a low wooden stool.

"This is a man steeped in hope, determination, and resolve. He is relatively fearless, prone to taking action, and not troubled by committing destructive acts to reach his goals. He can be ruthless, although there is also a great capacity within him for justice and even mirth. He is an individual of strong motivation, will, and perseverance, qualities not often seen in members of his race. No doubt he is the tribal chief or prince that reports have postulated."

"All this can be determined by measuring his head?" a third journalist questioned.

"*I* can determine this. But then again, *I* am a trained scientist, the personal phrenologist to Queen Victoria herself."

"Hogwash," Jocelyn hissed. "I don't believe a lick of it."

"Oh no, parson," said yet another journalist. "It's hard science. I've seen it done dozens of times. A good phrenologist can tell a criminal from a gentleman just by taking a few measurements."

"What if they are one and the same?" Jocelyn asked.

"That, too, can be foretold by an expert," Combe said smugly. "Although let me caution all in attendance that the science of phrenology simply gives indications of predispositions, of how it is natural for a person to act. We are all human, and hence subject to human inconsistencies or behavioral modifications that, in one way or another, may cause us to act against our nature. I can, however, tell what is natural to an individual's character. And by leading the mutiny, this man followed his destiny."

"Well, you'll never get me to believe that you can tell any of this by fiddling about with the bumps on a man's head, sir," Jocelyn persisted.

"Pity, Reverend," Combe said donning his hat. "But I'd venture to say that your reaction is totally predictable. In fact, you must let me examine your head some day. I believe I would be able to discern that the evidence of your skepticism is entrenched in the short line from the root of your nose to your central diameter. I'm sure it would reveal a crooked nubibus pathway indicative of lifelong reliance on dogma and aversion to change."

Combe left the cells with the journalists trailing him asking for more facts about Cinqué and the other blacks he had examined. They took no notice of Dr. Gibbs coming down the other hallway, or the thin black man walking next to him.

Singbe stood up. This room where the examinations had taken place reminded him too much of the small solitary cell he had been kept in before the trial. He wanted to get back to the general cell with the others. Jocelyn smiled as if reading Singbe's mind and took him by the arm in a friendly way and opened the door. Gibbs burst in, almost knocking both of them over, and began speaking excitedly. Singbe tried to listen, but he had still only learned a few of the white words, and this man was rambling on far too quickly to understand. Besides, from what Singbe had seen during his time among the whites, loud, quick talking seemed to be a habit common to many of their kind. He barely noticed Gibbs stopping, or the black man coming around from behind him. So when he heard a greeting in Mende, he assumed it was one of the other tribesmen. He stepped out into the hallway but saw no one.

"I said, 'It is a good day to be alive and a Mendeman.'"

Singbe turned. His body began to tingle and sweat. His heart edged up through his chest into his throat.

"It is a good day to be alive and a Mendeman," he whispered.

"What is your name, brother?" The man said, smiling.

"You speak the words of The People? And the words of the whites?"

"Yes. I speak their English. And I am a Mendeman, born in Kawamende and raised in the shadows of dark hills, among other places. I am here so that you may tell your story and seek justice from the Americans—the whites."

Singbe's knees shook and then gave way. He reached out with both arms and grabbed the man's hand, kissing it softly. He could feel his heart pounding as if it would break through his chest, but he could not breathe.

The man that Gibbs had brought to the jail was James Covey, the same man he had bumped into at the doorway of The Hold. Covey was a sailor on the British man-of-war, *Buzzard*, which had come into New York for supplies. When Gibbs had finally convinced him that he was not mad but rather a college professor on a quest for a translator, Covey consented to help if he could. Knowing well of the *Amistad* case, the commander of the *Buzzard*, Captain James Fitzgerald, granted Covey leave to serve as interpreter for the Amistad Committee and the blacks held in captive, saying it was the least the Crown could do in the situation.

Covey, barely twenty years old, was a native of Mende. He was born Kaw-we-li and raised inland until three Genduma men kidnapped him from his parents when he was eight and brought him to Freetown. He was sold to an old Mandingo goat trader and worked in the bazaar for the man until two Vai tribesmen killed the trader, stole the goats and Kaw-we-li, and sold him to a Dutch slave trader. The Dutch man brought him to Pedro Blanco's Lomboko slave factory and sold him to a Portuguese ship captain who was running a slaver to Brazil. The captain put to sea, but two days out of Lomboko a British cruiser on slave patrol overtook his ship and liberated all aboard. Kaw-we-li had learned English in the bazaar and immediately became favored by the British crew. By the time they returned him to Freetown, he decided to enlist in the British Navy and took the name James Covey in honor of the lieutenant who cut the slave chains from his feet and hands. He had been serving on the *Buzzard* for four and a half years, believed in Jesus Christ, and considered himself a good Christian.

Jocelyn sent for Tappan and Baldwin immediately. He also asked one of the divinity students on hand to record what they would hear. Then he gathered all the tribesmen into the biggest cell and brought in Covey. Covey greeted them has he had greeted Singbe and told them quite modestly that he was here to help them as best he could. Many of the tribesmen stood in stunned silence. Others began shouting with joy or breaking down in tears. Grabeau had his body wedged in a corner. He was laughing so hard he couldn't stand on his own.

While the excitement was still rippling through the room, Singbe leaned into Burnah and whispered a few words. The smile faded slightly from his face as he listened. Singbe stood back and smiled. Burnah nodded and began moving through the others. Within two minutes, everyone had heard and nodded. Grabeau walked over to Singbe.

"Why tell them this? That we are of tribes other than Mende?"

"I am glad that we finally have someone to talk with who can make our story known to the whites," Singbe said. "But I do not trust the whites, at least none outside of this room. If they find out where we are from, perhaps they will try to go to our villages and steal or kill our families and clansmen. So let them think we are Mandingo or Genduma who can speak Mende."

Grabeau nodded. Covey walked over and put his hand on Singbe's shoulder.

"Mr. Tappan would like to speak with you. He wants to hear your story in your own words."

Singbe stepped forward. The room became quiet. The tribesmen squatted down or sat on the cell's dirt floor.

"What is your name?" Covey asked. "They call you Joseph Cinqué."

"They may call me what they like, but my name is Singbe-Pieh. And I am a free man."

"Tell us how you came to this situation, how it is that you are among the Americans now?"

Singbe told them everything, the story of his capture, of his time in the Lomboko factory and the voyage on the *Teçora*, how he and the others had been kept in the baracoons, seized the slave ship, and tried to sail back home. Tappan, Jocelyn, Baldwin, and Sedgwick stood in the cell's doorway and listened in rapt amazement. It took nearly two hours for Singbe to provide all the details.

"All I want is to get back to my wife and my family. That is all any of us want. To get back home."

When Singbe had finished, Tappan walked up and gave him a great hug.

"We are your friends, truly. And we shall do all we can to help all of you get back to your homes and families."

Covey translated the words. Singbe shook Tappan's hand firmly.

"I will trust you, my friend."

It was decided that Covey would interview each of the tribesmen while the Yale divinity students served as recorders. The stories could then be compared and elements used for the court defense as well as to bring out more facts to the public about the horrors of the slave trade.

Later that night, Sedgwick, Tappan, and Baldwin discussed the events over dinner.

"Though he says his name is Singbe, I should like to keep referring to him as Cinqué in court and whenever we speak of him," Tappan said. "That identity has been built in the press and in the minds of the populace, and we should do nothing to confuse or alter that."

Both Sedgwick and Baldwin nodded.

"I also like the fact that he is a rice farmer and not a warrior chieftain or prince," Tappan continued. "It shows a certain commonality that everyman in the street can identify with."

Sedgwick skewered a huge chunk of steak with his fork and shoved it in his mouth before he began speaking.

"If anything, I've found the man to be more noble and heroic because he isn't highborn or a chief. Hell, he just wanted to get back to his wife and little ones. Anyone can lend sympathy to that."

"Exactly. This will be a boon to our defense," Tappan said, smiling and raising his burgundy glass. "To our much improved chances."

Sedgwick drained his mug of ale and signaled the tavern keeper for another. He said, "I will drink to that, but we still have quite a fight. The court will take these words into account, sure. But they are the words of black men against those of white men. We know who wins that one, court of law or not. And regardless of what these men have said today, Judson will still be looking at them as slaves, especially with the documentation held by Ruiz and Montes."

"I'm afraid Theodore is right, Lewis," Baldwin said. "This is good information, but it is not a lever that will move this case in our favor."

Tappan was undeterred. He knew that this would play well in the papers. He could see the headlines in his mind: "Cinqué speaks!" "Africans Tell of Atrocities!" "The Amistads' Heroic Odyssey Revealed!" But he sensed that there was something more that could be extracted from all of this. Something that would be unprecedented.

"How can we use this to our benefit?" Tappan asked. "Other than in the district court, I mean?"

Baldwin and Sedgwick looked to each other and then back to Tappan. Both lawyers were tolerating the public relations carnival that Tappan had brought to the case. After all, they, too, believed in the cause and wished to see slavery ended, and they knew how important this case could be in bringing that about. It had already instigated debates nationwide of varying intensity on slavery. In many communities, sympathy with the Amistads ran high, which could only help when the court convened in November. But it was going to be a considerable task to redefine their defense and anticipate the prosecution's response when they discovered the blacks would be testifying. The idea of further "usage" was beyond them.

Tappan read their faces. He smiled and reframed his question. "Suppose for a moment that the Amistads are white. This has been the basis of our defense thus far, correct? Equal treatment under the law with disregard for color. Well, then, let us continue to think in those terms. Now, we have the information we heard today from Cinqué, Grabeau, and the others. What else do we put in the tray to make the scales tip even further in our favor?"

Baldwin sipped his wine, lost in thought. Sedgwick took a whole potato in his hand, bit it in half, and washed it down with some ale.

"How far do you want them to tip, Mr. Tappan?"

"If possible? Further than they've ever gone before, Mr. Sedgwick."

Sedgwick winked at Baldwin and held his tankard over his head so the tavern keeper could see it was empty. "Then, sir, I think I have an idea that may satisfy your needs."

† † †

Two nights later, at a posh Manhattan restaurant, Pepe Ruiz,

Pedro Montes, and two female escorts were sharing dinner with one of New York's City Councilmen and his wife. They had just begun their third bottle of champagne when a city sheriff approached the table, flanked by Lewis Tappan and a dozen reporters.

"Mr. Pepe Ruiz?" The sheriff said. "Mr. Pedro Montes?"

Ruiz tipped his glass to Tappan. "Mr. Tappan," he said, "defender of pirates, murderers, and runaway slaves. I would ask you to join us but they do not serve from the swill trough at the tables. Perhaps if you went around back, accommodations could be found that are suitable for yourself."

The group at his table fluttered with laughter. Tappan smiled and turned to the sheriff.

"These are your men, constable."

"Mr. Ruiz and Mr. Montes, I have here warrants for your arrests, pending appearance in New York Superior Court."

"What! On what charges?" scoffed the councilman.

"Assault, battery, and false imprisonment," the sheriff continued. "The claims are made by a Mr. Joseph Cinqué and a Mr. Grabeau."

"I beg your pardon?" Ruiz said, still laughing.

The councilman snatched the warrants from the sheriff's hands.

"Let me see those! This is outrageous! These are spurious claims. It's all a sham. Trumped up charges made by that man. By Tappan."

"I am happy to say that everything here is legal and true, Councilman Hyde." Tappan smiled. "And before you utter a single word more, please consider that these gentlemen represent some of the city's finest newspapers."

"What does this mean?" Ruiz asked.

"It means, sir," the sheriff said, "that you and Mr. Montes are under arrest and to be escorted to city jail pending hearing before a state judge."

"What!?"

"You heard the man," Tappan said. "You're being sued. Welcome to America."

Judson's Court

Pepe is a fool, Pedro Montes thought.

Montes tried to walk quickly, but the cold November rain made the cobblestone street slick and slippery. The wind blew up from the water, spraying his face with its wet, icy breath. He was sure the sun had been up for over an hour but the hard black sky had barely brightened since the dawn. He pressed his hands deeper into the pockets of his great coat and hugged his body for warmth. God, how he hated this country. Foul laws, prudish women, bland food, and bad weather. It was all so uncivilized. It would be a blessing to leave.

The situation was becoming untenable, anyway. Pepe had convinced him that the trial would vindicate them and they would be treated as heroes, and for a while it seemed as if his predictions would come to pass. But with the lawyers and the judges and the courts having say over the country's president, and now this, a lawsuit brought by the slaves—slaves suing their owners! What kind of a country was this? Were the Americans truly mad? It was all too much.

Their lawyer had persuaded the judge to reduce the bail to a nominal fee, but they had spent three days in jail in the interim. And for what? For surviving savagery and almost certain death at the hands of their own property, only to have that same property sue them? It was insane!

Pepe was insane, too. Pedro was sure of it. The Spanish minister told them they should both stay in jail, make an issue of the matter, and embarrass the Americans. He said Her Majesty would look favorably on such a sacrifice. It could lead perhaps to a knighthood when this was all over and done with. That was enough for Pepe. He refused bail and instead called in members of the press to say he would endure confinement because the fact that he, a white slave owner, was being sued by his own slaves for the conditions of their captivity, was a "national matter with which all Americans should heed and take notice." Of course, the federal government had persuaded the New York officials to make his confinement extremely palatable. They gave Pepe a private cell and allowed him to come and go during the days and early evening as he pleased. The American Secretary of State had also instructed the New York District Attorney to provide legal services for both of them free of charge.

Still, Pedro thought, it is all madness. None of it is worth contesting ownership of three brat slaves, or a knighthood, or one more day in this wretched country. He had resigned himself to cutting his losses long ago. Pepe may have more at stake, but he is a rich man and could well absorb all that has happened. He would do best to leave, too, and let the Americans do what they would with the niggers. May they all burn in hell together.

Pedro got to the gangplank of the ship, the *Texas*, and showed his bill of passage to the porter. He went down to his cabin and shut the door, not opening it again for anything except to receive food and pass the chamber pot until the ship weighed anchor in Havana harbor.

Sedgwick's idea had worked to perfection. The lawsuits brought by Cinqué and Grabeau were a masterstroke. The suits hinged on whether the blacks were the legal property of Ruiz and Montes, and hence would have to wait until the district court rendered a decision on that issue. But a little time in jail and the prospects of having to mount a defense would give the Cubans a taste of their own sour medicine and offer a harsh counter-perspective to the rest of the country. As Sedgwick saw it, the Amistads were foreign nationals seeking refuge and justice just as the Cubans were, and the defense's claim all along had been that the law did not specify difference based on color. So, why not let the Amistads pursue the same action any white man would follow if the tables were turned? Sedgwick didn't expect to win the suits. Then again, if the cases were dismissed, he had thirty-three other clients who could bring identical actions against Ruiz and Montes, one by one. Sedgwick could tie the Cubans up in court until the end of the century.

Tappan was equally pleased with the lawsuits, but for a completely different reason. It had thrust the *Amistad* case back into the front pages of virtually all the newspapers in the nation. It was also receiving notice in England, France, and Spain. Unfortunately, most of the stories sided with the Cubans. The Southern papers lambasted both Tappan for being a "puppet master who uses ignorant savages," and the federal government for permitting "two foreigners seeking asylum from murderers to be enslaved by their torturers once again." The *New Orleans Times Picayune* ran a large derisive front-page story with a thick black headline: TAPPANISM! Even the more liberal Northern papers expressed outrage at the action and identified it as an obvious manipulation by Tappan and the abolitionists. One paper, the *New York Express*, went on to pose a most prescient question: "How long will it be now before a Southern gentleman traveling with his servants is immediately sued by his property as soon as they cross over into a Northern state where slavery has been abolished?"

Tappan was undeterred, as were most of the abolitionists. The most important thing was that people were talking—about the case, about slavery, and about the virtues and vices of abolition and the current American system. Sure, right now the effect was tumultuous and perhaps even a little dangerous. But danger was not a consideration when doing the Lord's work. And besides, when the frenzy calmed, the issues would still remain. A smart man would know how to use all of this—how to cultivate it, shape it, perhaps even control it to a certain degree—to spur it on and forward. The great debate they had been trying to ignite for a decade was finally burning. Tappan would do everything he could to keep the coals hot and glowing.

The morning of November 19 blew into New Haven gray and windswept with a raw stiffness that had been gripping Connecticut and the other New England States through most of the shortening late autumn days. Despite the weather, the green held a crowd of thousands. Every seat and place fit for standing in the courthouse had been filled. People cheered and jeered as the tribesmen and Antonio, bundled in blankets and donated coats, were led from the jail to the court building. Off to one side, a man with a large wooden sandwich board draped around his body stood on a small platform lecturing to the nearly one hundred people who had gathered around him. The sandwich board read: "Equal Treatment for Whites!" As the full crowd reacted to the tribesmen emerging from the jail, the man turned and pointed.

"Look, now! There they are! Look at how they are dressed! Fine coats, wool pants, socks and shoes on their feet. Gloves and hats they've been given, too! And have you seen their quarters? Every man has a blanket and plenty to eat! I say the white men in this jail or any other jail in this state ain't been treated near as good. Why not? Ain't they citizens of this state? Don't they deserve as good if not better than a bunch of motley niggers fresh from the bush?"

As the tribesmen passed, the man spit in their direction and continued to yell, "Equal treatment for the whites in jail! Equal treatment for the whites!" Many in the crowd joined in with his chorus until well after the tribesmen had disappeared into the courthouse.

The three girls were brought in through the back door by Colonel Pendelton. When preferred incarceration had been declared in the last trial, his wife had offered to take the girls into their home rather than have them exposed to the filth and "criminal elements" of the jailhouse. Judge Thompson had readily agreed so long as the Yale students were allowed in on a regular basis to provide tutoring.

Andrew Judson convened his court at 10:00 A.M. and asked for opening statements from all parties. As he listened to the arguments he took special note of where Lewis Tappan and the other abolitionists sat. He planned to cite any outburst from that group as an action in contempt of the court and have the offending person or persons dismissed for the remainder of the trial.

Before they even opened, the district court proceedings generated a substantial amount of new excitement. Henry Green had added his name to the claimants for salvage and obtained as his lawyer William Ellsworth, who was also Governor of Connecticut at the time. It was unusual but not unprecedented for a sitting governor to be involved in active litigation during his term. The Amistads had been big news since they had set foot in the state, and being a smart politician, Ellsworth had tried from the beginning to become associated with the case in some way. He was also friends with Lewis Tappan, having served as the defense lawyer for Prudence Crandall. Even though he was seen by many state residents to have been on the "wrong side" of that case, the counsel he provided was admired. Many say that the notoriety he gained propelled him to the Democratic nomination and the governorship. Ellsworth had approached the Amistad Committee asking that he be allowed to lead the defense. They declined, preferring Baldwin and also believing that Ellsworth's presence would be more about his needs and lust for attention than the needs of their clients. Undeterred, Ellsworth then approached Gedney and Meade, and later Ruiz and Montes. All had found suitable council. Ellsworth could do nothing except attend the circuit court proceedings. But when he did, he heard about Green's encounter with the Africans. He had also heard through a New

York friend that Green felt he was entitled to the salvage, or at least a percentage, since he had "discovered the Africans and their ship." Ellsworth contacted Green, listened to his story and, convinced the man had a case, filed the necessary papers to be included in the salvage claims before the district court.

Along with entertaining the claims of Ellsworth and Green, the court would also be hearing the testimony of Dr. Richard R. Madden, the British Superintendent of Liberated Slaves in Havana and a self-appointed observer of the Cuban slave trade. A staunch anti-slavery man, Dr. Madden was returning to England after ten years in Cuba. He had heard about the *Amistad* case and had written to Tappan offering to testify about the conditions of the Havana market, as well as to offer his own evaluation as to whether the blacks were bozales or landinos. During a trip to the States five years before, Madden had gained a reputation as a fine writer and orator and a passionate opponent of slavery. He had even been invited to dinner by President Jackson, who nearly laughed the old Irishman out of the White House when he suggested that the President work to abolish slavery in the United States.

Finally, and most intriguing, would be the testimony of the blacks themselves. Tappan had reportedly secured the services of a translator and during the two weeks leading up to the trial a few teasing snippets of accounts by Cinqué and the others had been released. The blacks insisted they were in fact Africans stolen from several African nations, that they had rebelled because they had been threatened with cannibalism by the mulatto cook on board the *Amistad*, and that their only wish was to return home to their people and families. Though the prosecution had said the translator was a ruse being used to obscure the true facts, Judson had met with Covey in the presence of all counsel and was convinced that seaman's ability to understand the blacks was genuine.

Despite these new wrinkles, the case would still hinge on the authenticity of the documentation held by Ruiz and Montes, the claims of salvage, and Judson's rulings on the applicability of Pickney's Treaty and the Treaty of 1819.

"We will be going against entrenched sentiment regarding the black race and a system which has legally condoned slavery for more than two hundred years," Baldwin said. "Despite what the law says, we will have to make each of our points so that no hint of doubt exists. And even if we prove our case, it is Andrew T. Judson who ultimately will decide the fate of our African friends."

"Anything left to Judson is left to the devil himself," Sedgwick told Staples that morning about an hour before they went over to the courthouse. "He is the same man who declared in the Prudence Crandall case that, 'Though they may aspire to equality, it is folly to think that the African race occupies the same pedestal of development and intelligence as white men.'"

The opening statement by Holabird was almost identical to what he offered two months earlier in circuit court. However, added to the documentation found on board the *Amistad* were the several formal letters of protest written by Calderón and Argaiz that cited specific passages in the treaties. Baldwin and his team sat and listened as Holabird's entire presentation took the full day. Hungerford, Isham, and Ellsworth used up all of the next two days making their statements. Ellsworth was particularly dramatic, saying that he would prove beyond a shadow of a doubt that the Navy officers had used their command of firepower and Marines to cheat Henry Green and his friends from rightful salvage. It wasn't until the afternoon of the fourth day that Baldwin was allowed to speak. He intended to review in detail the points that had been made during the circuit court trial. He was also ready to put strong emphasis on the new evidence that had come to light. However, his opening volley was aimed squarely at the actions of his opposition.

"Before I begin, Your Honor, I would formally like to protest the United States government's extreme prejudice in this case."

"I object, Your Honor," Holabird said wearily. "The U.S. government is only concerned with discovering the truth in this case. There has been no prejudice exercised whatsoever."

"I beg to differ, Your Honor," Baldwin snapped. "It is

November of eighteen hundred and thirty-nine. I have been involved with this case since August. And yet, the U.S. federal government has not yet provided me, the other attorneys with whom I am presenting this case, or my clients, with a copy of the Treaty of 1819. Nor did we ever receive a full copy of Pickney's Treaty. Further, when my clients were incarcerated, it was left up to them to find counsel. Yet, when Mr. Ruiz and Mr. Montes were arrested in October as a result of legal action taken by my clients, the U.S. Secretary of State instructed the Federal District Attorney of New York to extend, and I quote, 'every courtesy and measure of legal assistance,' end quote, to both of those gentlemen. Mr. Ruiz and Mr. Montes also received a very lenient form of incarceration, of which Mr. Montes took advantage and appears to have left the country. None of these courtesies or advantages has been extended to my clients, Your Honor. And we still do not have full copies of all the documents we need to properly defend our clients' interests."

"Your protest has been noted and entered into the record, Mr. Baldwin," Judson said.

"To that end, Your Honor, I move for another cessation of this trial until said documents are provided to me and my fellow attorneys, and we are given enough time to examine them with an eye toward our clients' defense."

"Motion denied, Mr. Baldwin. This court will not brook a halt in these proceedings if it can be at all helped. However, I will take your request for documents, specifically the noted treaties, under advisement, and strongly exhort Mr. Holabird to use his contacts within the government to procure copies for you."

"I have been doing all I can," Holabird said. "There have been some problems with transcription at the proper offices in Washington, however. But I am assured that headway is being made. My apologies to Mr. Baldwin for any inconvenience this may have caused."

"There, now, you see, Mr. Baldwin, the government is doing its best. Proceed with your opening."

"But Your Honor..."

"Proceed, Mr. Baldwin. Or be cited for contempt of this court. The choice is yours."

Baldwin made a dramatic pause. Judson's response was what he had expected, but there was no reason to let the gallery, or the journalists in attendance, know this. He let out a deep sigh and then spoke.

"Very well, Your Honor. I will proceed. And I am sure that after you hear the testimony of linguistic experts, Dr. Richard Madden, and the men of the *Amistad* themselves, you will have no other choice but to conclude that the blacks on board the *Amistad* are in fact residents and citizens of African nations, and as such are subject to immediate release and guaranteed return to their nation as stated by the Treaty of 1819."

Judson leaned forward from the bench and for the first time since court opened three days earlier interrupted a lawyer making an opening statement.

"Well, that all remains to be seen, now, doesn't it, Mr. Baldwin?"

Baldwin, not missing a beat, smiled and nodded to Judson.

"As well you shall, Your Honor. As will everyone in this court."

Baldwin went on to ask Judson if Dr. Madden could be called as the first person to offer testimony as his official duties required that he begin his return trip to England before December. Judson said he would take the request under consideration and pronounce a ruling tomorrow. Court was adjourned at 4:35 P.M.

In the evening, when Tappan was finished talking to the press and had returned to his hotel, the desk clerk handed him a small package that had been delivered by an express cargo carrier. Tappan brought the package up to his room and unwrapped the burlap and string, revealing a small wooden box. He opened it and immediately felt a rush of nausea. Inside was a single black ear, roughly hacked and covered in dried blood. His shaking hands dropped the box on the bed. The ear fell out on the quilt, along with a note, apparently written in blood:

No matter what happens, your niggers will not leave this country alive.

It was signed, "Justice."

Later that night Tappan, who was still rattled by the incident, had a private dinner with Simeon Jocelyn.

"Simeon, we are both praying for a favorable outcome to this trial. But, according to Mr. Baldwin, there is a strong chance the judgment will go against us."

"He will appeal that decision, of course, Lewis."

"Of course. But perhaps it is time we talked about some insurance for our African friends."

Jocelyn raised an eyebrow. He was pretty sure he knew what Tappan meant. "There is a station in Farmington, and another in Stonington," Jocelyn said. "But how do we get them to either place. I mean, moving thirty-five blacks would be difficult enough in this state. But these men are practically famous."

"This 'preferred incarceration' has left me less worried about that. I think a diversion could be created, or perhaps because of the way spectators are being let to come and go through the jail, we could simply walk them right out under pretense of their daily exercises and spirit them away. New Haven has a harbor. Besides, we don't have to use the underground railroad stations here. We could take them to Boston, Portland, or any of a hundred inlets along the way. We could take them straight to Canada for that matter. The important thing is that we must devise two plans, a main strategy and a backup. They should be tight and simple and ready to implement at virtually any moment should the need arise."

"I will talk to some friends of mine. This may take some money. Perhaps a hundred or so."

"That is manageable. Get me an exact figure, though, so that we can have the cash on hand. I don't want to leave anything to chance. I will be damned in hell before Van Buren or some bloodthirsty maniac gets their hands on any of these blacks."

"I will get to work on it right away."

"Oh, and Simeon. Not a word to Baldwin or any of the others. God willing, we don't even have to carry any of this out. But I don't want to compromise their integrity or trust."

"I understand."

Judson decided to let Madden swear out a deposition in chambers, but only after Holabird paid him a visit. Judson was not disposed to give any preferential treatment to the Amistads during the trial. However, Holabird assured him that under cross-examination, Madden would do more to harm the defense's case than good. Forsyth had told the prosecutor that Madden was a prejudiced zealot and that he would be forced to admit that all of his assessments are based on conjecture and gross extrapolations. When put to the test, Holabird smugly said, his "expert" testimony would easily be exposed as the ravings of a fanatical lover of negroes.

However, as he listened to the old Irishman, Judson was sure Holabird had made a serious error in judgment. Madden told of the baracoons and how Africans were off-loaded regularly at small harbors surrounding Havana. He examined the purchase papers and documentation taken from the *Amistad* and insisted that there was no way on earth the children and the majority of the male slaves could be landinos as the trespassos said.

"None of them speaks a lick of Spanish, Your Honor."

"Yes," Holabird said, "but as I understand it, many of the slaves, especially those on back country plantations, retain the African language of their ancestors or speak a field dialect that is an amalgamation of Spanish and tribal languages."

"I'm afraid you have been misinformed, Mr. Prosecutor," Madden said. "In fact, in my experience it's been just the opposite. I've yet to meet a true landino who didn't speak Spanish as well as any native-born Cubano. What's more, the ones they bring in from Africa pick up the language fairly quickly, too. They certainly have the rudiments of communication down within a month or so."

"But really, Dr. Madden," Holabird continued. "How much actual experience do you have with visiting the plantations, especially those in the outlying areas? And remember, sir, you are under oath."

"I remember it well, sir," Madden bristled. "As for my experience, as part of my official capacity, I tour the plantations throughout the islands four to six times a year. That for the last four years. Does that satisfy your criteria for experience, sir?"

Holabird got tripped up again when he pointed to the bills of sale obtained by Montes and Ruiz for the blacks. "It is clearly stated here that they are landinos," Holabird said.

"Yes, sir, but you will also note that Ruiz and Montes had to acquire that documentation from the authorities themselves. Why was it not provided by the seller? I'll tell you why: Because he didn't have their documents. Do you know why he didn't have them? Because they were Africans. Do you want to know how I know that, besides, of course, for the obvious fact that Africans are who they are?"

"Let the record show that Dr. Madden is expressing an opinion," Judson said absently. "Continue, Dr. Madden. Tell us how you presumed you knew they were Africans."

"The seller of record, Mr. Shaw, whom I know quite well, and who, I might add, is the principal agent for the House of Martinez, a slave brokerage that deals almost exclusively in Africans. Well, Mr. Shaw passed on to Ruiz and Montes the port tax in his bill of sale. One doesn't pay a port tax on domestic goods, gentlemen, only imports."

"Is it possible that these slaves were imported from another place where slavery is legal?" Holabird asked quickly. "Perhaps one of the outlying islands?"

"Possible but not probable, sir. They wouldn't have to pay a duty on slaves from a Spanish port. And all the island ports controlled by the British Empire have abolished slavery."

"Is it possible that this Mr. Shaw himself never paid such a tax but passed the cost onto Mr. Ruiz and Mr. Montes to elevate the price a few dollars per head?"

"Absolutely," Madden said. "But then, being experienced slave traders themselves, Ruiz and Montes would have seen the tax on the bill and knew what it meant. Thus, sir, by paying a bill with the tax declared is a tacit admission by these men that they believed they were buying African bozales. Their purchase of Africans was not an unwitting act of ignorance as some have claimed."

Judson sighed. Holabird attempted to backtrack and concentrate on a few other points, but Madden had unshakable answers for every question.

After the deposition, Madden asked if the court reporter could make a copy of the deposition so that it could be presented to Queen Victoria when Madden returned to London. Judson said he would consider the request.

When Madden left the chambers, Judson sat back in his chair and shook his head. "William, if I allow that testimony to be entered into the record it will not help your case in the least," Judson said. "It all but confirms that these men are Africans."

"So what if they are, Your Honor? The federal government has no jurisdiction to intervene in domestic affairs of foreign nationals."

"That depends on one's interpretation of the Treaty of 1819," Judson said. "In this case, the government may be forced to intervene."

"You wouldn't think of ruling that way, would you?"

"Mr. Holabird," Judson snapped. "Make no mistake that my mission and primary responsibility in this case is to render a ruling which follows the letter of the law. I will not jeopardize the integrity of legal process or the future of my career on a ruling that will be exposed as careless or biased and overturned by a higher court. Do you understand that, sir?"

"Yes, Your Honor."

"Now, I shall consider whether, in the eyes of the court, Dr. Madden's testimony is acceptable and I shall rule on that on Monday morning. I will inform Mr. Baldwin of my decision to consider this deposition. That is all, Mr. Holabird."

Holabird left the judge's chambers. Judson slammed his hand down on his desk and cursed. The court reporter got up to leave.

"Mr. Janes, I'd like you to hold off on Dr. Madden's request for a copy of his deposition until I have ruled whether his testimony is admissible in court. Leave the deposition here so that I may consider it. Please inform Dr. Madden of my decision on the way out."

"Yes, Your Honor. Good day."

Mr. Janes, who was Judson's favorite court reporter, was the same Mr. Dwight Janes who had recorded the proceedings on the *Washington*, and who had sent the letter to Baldwin announcing the plight of the Amistads. Judson had personally selected Janes to handle the recording duties of this case.

Janes did as the judge said and then went directly to his hotel room and began writing. Within an hour he had reconstructed what he remembered from Madden's testimony. He placed the pages in an envelope and sealed it. Later that night, while most of the city slept, he walked down the frigid streets and slipped the envelope under the door of a darkened building.

Court was back in session on Saturday, as was the tradition of the times. The day was uneventful until a few hours after adjournment when Judson was having his dinner. He unfolded the *New Haven Express* and nearly spit out his evening coffee. The headline read: "Exclusive—Dr. Madden's Deposition." Underneath, the subheads went on: "Slavery Conditions in Cuba Revealed in Detail. Africans Regularly Imported. Widespread Corruption Among Cuban Officials."

By Monday morning, the New York and Boston papers were running reprints of the story. Neither Judson nor Holabird knew how the information had gotten out. It was a crude transcript with some major omissions and a few inaccuracies, but in general it was factual. They suspected it was some conspiracy between Tappan and Madden. In truth, the information printed was nothing Madden hadn't said in print in the past. But the addition of Holabird's question lent the information an air of heightened credibility. It also showed that there was nothing about the testimony that Judson could declare inadmissible. So, grudgingly, the judge consented to allow Madden's deposition to be entered into the record. He also released the full text to the press so that misconceptions and inaccuracies produced by the bootleg copy could be allayed.

The rest of the week saw testimony by Josiah Gibbs and other members of the Yale Divinity School's faculty. Gibbs testified that the men and children were speaking an African language. The cross-examination by Holabird, who pointed out that Gibbs was not an authority on African languages and in fact did not even speak any African languages, seemed to make an impact with Judson.

However, during rebuttal questioning, Baldwin scored an important point when he asked Gibbs about the Africans' ability to speak Spanish.

"Among all of them I only could get a few words," Gibbs said. "One, Grabeau, knew the word for potato. Another, Burnah, knew the word for water. All of them appeared to know a word that, loosely translated, means 'nigger.'"

"And yet, the documentation submitted by the prosecution says my clients were born and raised in Cuba," Baldwin said. "That means that some of these men have been in that Spanish-speaking country more than twenty-five years, and yet they have only picked up one, perhaps two words?"

"Your Honor," Holabird said, "while certain members of this band of blacks have shown themselves to be cunning and clever, it is well known that the black race is not a very bright one, and it is entirely possible that these men only comprehend the field dialect that they were raised with."

Staples shot to his feet.

"Objection, Your Honor! Mr. Holabird's statement is not only crass and derogatory, it is totally without merit and slanders my clients."

"On the contrary, Mr. Staples," Judson said. "As much as some of us may hate to admit it, I believe what Mr. Holabird has said has strong basis in scientific facts and observations. Though some blacks do quite well, the race in general is not highly intelligent. Your objection is overruled."

"Your Honor," Baldwin said. "I would like to follow up on Mr. Holabird's point, if I may."

A low roar of surprise ran through the courtroom. Judson slammed his gavel down hard.

"Quiet in my court. You may proceed, Mr. Baldwin."

"Dr. Gibbs, have any of the blacks learned to speak English since they have been tutored by you and the other representatives of Yale?"

"Yes, sir."

"How many?"

"All of them."

"Objection!" Holabird said standing. "They do not speak English. If they did, why, then, have their defense attorneys enlisted the services of an interpreter?"

"I must say, Mr. Baldwin, that I was called on board the *Washington* when these blacks were brought into New London," Judson said. "The leader, Cinqué, knew a phrase or two but none of the others questioned by the ship's officers could speak any English."

"They have all improved their abilities, Your Honor," Gibbs said. "They cannot speak English as well as you or I, it's true. But virtually all of them have learned a number of words and sentences over the past few weeks. And they comprehend what they are saying, too."

"How many words, Mr. Gibbs?" Baldwin asked.

"I would say the average is perhaps between fifty and one hundred."

"So these men have been in this country less than three months and they have learned between fifty and one hundred words, but the prosecutor claims that they lived in Cuba for as much as twenty-five years and couldn't learn Spanish at all," Baldwin stated.

"Objection! Objection, Your Honor!" Holabird cried. "This is ridiculous. We have seen no display of any of this ability by any of these blacks to speak English."

"Mr. Baldwin, would you care to put your clients to a test before the court?" Judson said.

"Absolutely, Your Honor. Select a man, or better yet, Mr. Holabird, select any man from among my clients."

Holabird looked to Judson. Judson nodded. Holabird walked over to the tribesmen. Most of them sat in the jury box or in chairs placed around it. Some squatted on the floor or leaned against the wall. Holabird stopped in front of the one he thought looked like the dullest and slowest of the group and pointed.

"You. What is your name?"

The tribesman stood slowly from his squatting position and looked from Singbe to Tappan to Covey. Holabird snorted.

"Name?"

The tribesman said nothing. Holabird smiled.

"Fifty words indeed."

Holabird turned to the bench and opened his mouth to say something to Judson.

"My name Burnah."

The people in the gallery gasped. Holabird wheeled.

"Who said that? Was it him? Was it you?"

"I Burnah."

"Bur-nah? Bur-nah. Fine. He knows his name. That is hardly English."

"It is more than the Spanish he knew when they were taken by the *Washington*," Sedgwick said.

"Bid him say something else," Judson said. "Bur-nah. Speak."

"I Burnah. Burnah. I come Africa. I learn from Dr. Gibbs and Dr. Gal-a-det. I learn Jesus and God. Halleluia!"

Burnah looked around the room. He could see that every person had turned and was looking at him. He smiled and raised his right hand.

"One, two, three, four, five. God bless Amer-ca."

Holabird's face boiled with anger and embarrassment.

"Your Honor," he hissed, "this man is simply repeating phrases that have been fed to him by his tutors. He has no comprehension of what he is saying."

"Comprehension is not the issue here, Your Honor," Baldwin said. "All we were trying to establish was that these men had learned some English during their very short stay in our country. Yet, they have learned no Spanish over a supposed lifetime in Cuba. It is simply another fact that casts aspersions on their alleged origins as landino slaves. Please, feel free to question any of these men. You will find they have all learned some English."

Holabird was still skeptical and asked to interview more of the blacks. Judson consented but stopped the interrogation after the third tribesman. All who were questioned spoke at least a few sentences of English. None of this was doing the government's case any good. The day was growing late but there was much anticipation among the observers. It was rumored that Cinqué was scheduled to testify soon with Covey as a translator. Judson was aware of the excitement among the people in the gallery, but he thought they and the press had been given enough to talk about for one day. He adjourned the court until the next morning.

The defense had planned to call Singbe the next day, but the slight cold that Covey had caught had degenerated into a deep-fevered, body-shaking, debilitating flu. He had shivered through the court proceedings over the last two days and had nearly passed out twice during the questioning of the tribesmen by Holabird. Now, on Friday morning, his condition was so severe he could not get out of bed. The tribesmen were extremely concerned, but Tappan kept them away, afraid that whatever it was that Covey had contracted would spread to the others.

Baldwin had juggled the witness list to accommodate the growing severity of Covey's illness. He had hoped for a reversal of symptoms. But now, with Covey incapacitated, Baldwin was running out of people. Virtually all of the Yale faculty involved were called, as well as some of the students. Gedney and Meade had already testified. Antonio had been called as a prosecution witness and would add nothing to the defense. Aside from the tribesmen, Green and Fordham were the only ones left.

Green went first. He claimed that, despite the court survey, he believed the *Amistad* was less than five hundred yards from shore. He said the blacks had offered him the ship and chests of gold to sail them to Africa. He admitted that his plan all along was to sail the ship into New York harbor and claim salvage. Baldwin asked what condition the men were in when he came upon them.

"They were getting in a long boat. They looked like a hungry bunch. I could tell they ain't had much to eat as of late."

"How were they dressed?"

"Some wore pants. Others just looked like, well, like savages. Practically naked with just their privates covered by some rags."

"Did any wear chains?"

"Chains? No, sir."

"So they were free?"

"Aye, sir."

Holabird stood and stated for the record that pirates and mutinous slaves do not wear chains, either.

Ellsworth went into extensive questioning of both Green and Fordham, trying to establish that they had come across the *Amistad* first. He insinuated that Gedney had perhaps run off with the chests of gold supposedly contained in the *Amistad*'s hold. Isham objected, saying such chests had never been seen nor were they listed on the manifest.

"Just because we have never seen them, does not mean they did not exist," Ellsworth exhorted.

He went on to emphasize that Green did not wish to claim salvage on the slaves.

"My client is a resident of the free state of New York and wishes no truck with slavery. He is a true humanitarian and is interested only in his rights to a percentage of the value of the inanimate cargo and the ship."

Testimony ended and court was adjourned. The next day Covey was no better. Baldwin had the dubious task of approaching Judson to ask for a postponement.

"For how long?"

"Until Mr. Covey is well enough to provide translation services for my clients. He is hard hit. I would say perhaps a week to ten days."

"A week!" Holabird protested. "These are stalling tactics, Your Honor."

"I cannot help it that Mr. Covey is ill," Baldwin persisted.

"And I cannot help it that this court's docket is full," Judson said. "I have another case scheduled in a fortnight. This trial is near completion. We have already had one shortened week due to Thanksgiving. I can ill afford to grant any sort of extension. It would push the whole docket back."

"Your Honor, Mr. Covey's participation is essential to my clients' defense."

"I'm not completely convinced of that, Mr. Baldwin, but I am feeling generous today. I will grant a postponement. Until Tuesday. If you interpreter cannot present himself to the court by then, you shall have to press on."

"But Your Honor, that is only three days!"

"Don't test me on this, Mr. Baldwin, or we will continue on today without interruption."

Baldwin started to speak but he caught himself. He bowed his head.

"Thank you, Your Honor," he muttered.

Judson slammed his gavel down. "This court is adjourned until Tuesday, December fourth."

Covey's fever grew worse. He became delirious late Sunday night and shook uncontrollably. Tappan sent to New York City for his personal physician but Baldwin and Sedgwick thought it was too late. The local doctor who provided services to negroes predicted Covey would not live to see the morning. He did, but his condition was unimproved. The fever persisted. Covey actually tried to get out of bed early Tuesday morning, but his legs were too weak to hold him and he fell to the floor. He suggested they put him in a chair and carry him over to the courthouse, but even sitting up made him nauseous. His presence in court was just not possible.

The defense team entered the courtroom with heavy hearts. Baldwin walked over to Judson's chambers and knocked on the door. Inside, the Judge and Holabird sat in front of the small fireplace drinking hot cider.

"Come to gloat, have you?" Holabird sneered.

"Gloat? No, I came to speak to the judge about the postponement."

"Well, you shall just have to live with it. There is nothing I can do. Both Governor Ellsworth and General Isham are as ill as that sailor. Ellsworth's doctor says he'll need at least two weeks. That takes us into the holidays. The earliest date I could set that was agreeable to the claimants and the prosecution was January the seventh. Are you here to tell me that doesn't satisfy your clients, Mr. Baldwin? For if so, spare your words. You'll get no quarter."

"January seventh? January seventh. No. No, Your Honor. The seventh will be fine, sir. Gentlemen, good day."

Baldwin stepped out of the chambers only to see the huge grin on Staples's face.

"The clerk came over to tell us while you were in with the judge." Staples laughed. "Providence is smiling on us."

"Let's hope her smile is big enough to cover James, as well," Sedgwick said.

† † †

Two days after Christmas, Forsyth paid a visit to the White House at the invitation of President Van Buren. The weather all along the East Coast had been unusually cold and stormy. Though Forsyth's home was only a few blocks away, he decided to be taken to the White House in a sleigh rather than walk. Upon entering, he was escorted to a room near the back of the building. Van Buren had pulled two chairs up very close to the fireplace and was drinking from a mug of steamy liquid.

"John. I'm glad you are here. Would you care for some blackberry tea?"

"Certainly, Mr. President."

Van Buren signaled the butler who quickly came back with a large mug of tea. The butler left the room, closing the door behind him.

"John, the Attorney General has told me that the *Amistad*

case looks like a lock."

"I fairly well agree, Mr. President. Despite the delay, I believe we will have a verdict soon after the court reconvenes. And with Mr. Judson sitting at the bench, I dare say a proper verdict, at that."

"Very good. I've also considered your suggestion about making this disappear thereafter. I wholeheartedly agree. What would you think if, as soon as the verdict is declared, we stick that whole pack of renegade negroes on a U.S. naval vessel and get them the hell back to Havana?"

"Mr. President, I think that is an excellent idea, save for one detail."

"I know, I know. It denies the blacks their right of appeal. But for Christ's sake, John. They're not even U.S. citizens. For the love of God, if they're slaves then they're not even citizens, no matter where they're from."

"I agree, Mr. President, and I can see the sense in what you're saying. You and I both know, however, that the abolitionists will raise a major row."

"We're returning Spanish subjects to Spanish territory for trial under Spanish laws. If they are in fact free men, then they can prove it in a Spanish court. We can even send Gedney and Meade down there as witnesses."

"Plausible. But we will still feel considerable heat from the press sympathetic to the abolitionist cause."

"A distinct minority. And no matter what we do, short of nationwide emancipation, they will never be with us anyway. Besides, we've given them due process. They will have had their trial and lost. What I want to know is how long would you say this whole thing will take to run its course in the papers, other than the abolitionist rags, I mean?"

"Three to four weeks, I would wager. If that."

"And the diplomatic rumblings?"

"Well, the Spanish, of course, would be extremely pleased and in fact beholden to us for a great favor. The British may lodge a protest with us regarding the illegal seizure of blacks, but they really have nothing to base it on since this can be portrayed as a domestic issue for the Spanish. And once Spanish justice gets through with the slaves, I believe they'll have no illegal blacks alive to point to. None from the *Amistad*, anyway."

Van Buren stood and picked up a large brass-handled poker. He jabbed it hard into the biggest log in the fire, sending an explosion of sparks up the chimney.

"Well, then, I'd say this will do the trick nicely. I will have my secretary send a memorandum to the Secretary of the Navy, Mr. Pauling, to cut orders to have a ship standing by in New Haven harbor. As soon as Judson pronounces his judgment, we will be rid of this odious problem once and for all."

Forsyth held up his glass. "Here, here, sir."

† † †

Andrew Judson sat at the large oak desk in his study reading depositions for an upcoming trial. His head was tilted slightly back so he could see through the small half-crescent wire-rimmed spectacles that sat at the end of his nose. Two large oil lamps, fashioned to look like candelabra, burned brightly from the corners of the desk. Outside in the winter darkness, the temperature was well below zero, and despite the broad blanketing warmth that was being thrown from the wide brick fireplace across the room, the inside of the study's windows glowed with a fine, white, frosty glaze.

Aside from the light crackling and the occasional pops of the flames and wood burning brightly in the fireplace, the room was silent, except for every few minutes when a grunt or a sigh would seep from Judson's mouth. The sounds escaped in nearly regular intervals and it was difficult to tell whether they were a response to something he was seeing in the transcripts or if the man's body simply produced throaty spurts and hisses by habit with his silent reading. Whatever the case, it had been nearly two grunts and a loud dwindling sigh before he realized someone else was in the room sitting in one of the broad velvet-seated oak chairs by the fire.

"Good evening, Andrew. This is a lovely fire. Would you mind if I threw another log on?"

Judson took off the glasses and stood. "Thadeus! Good God, sir. When did you come in?"

"Your man Michael let me in out of this deuced cold about twenty minutes ago. I've been sitting here ever since. You were working so hard I didn't want to bother you. And in truth, I was happy to take a moment to try and get some heat in my bones. It's been so blasted cold outside for so long, I swear I'll never be completely warm again."

Judson smiled. "Brandy?"

"If you can spare a drop."

Judson walked over to a cabinet, took out a bottle and two snifters and poured three fingers in each.

"Would you like this warmed?"

"No, no. It's fine as it is, Andrew."

Judson sat down in the other chair and the men toasted the New Year, which had come in two days earlier.

"So, Thadeus. What brings you out so late on such an evening?"

"God, it is awful, Andrew. They say hell is all flames and boiling heat, but I swear to you that Satan's kingdom is a frozen, desolate place. However, I am not here to present my views on the hereafter or pilfer from your fine brandy stores, or even to test your always pleasant hospitality. I wish to discuss the *Amistad* case with you."

Judson held his gaze at his friend while sitting back in the chair and taking a long sip from the glass. He said, "You know I am not at liberty to discuss particulars of the case."

"I am not interested in particulars. I'm interested in the future. Your future, Andrew."

Thadeus Moss rose. He still wore his greatcoat but it was unbuttoned now and revealed a fine English suit with a deep blue jacket and black pants. A bright red silk ascot was in his collar, a gold pin with a single diamond stud holding it in place. The glow from the fire washed his steel-colored hair with dark flickering orange and red. His face, which must have been devastatingly handsome in his younger days, was still stunning.

"You have done well," Moss continued. "From selectman to prosecutor to congressman and now a federal judge. You have ambition for more still, yes?"

"Certainly there are other positions that I am sure I could execute adequately."

"Andrew, it's me! You need not be so modest. I am one of your most vigorous supporters. As I see it you should be able to choose your way from here, be it to the Senate and beyond, or the Supreme Court."

"An appointment to the court has been in my mind."

"And why not? You are certainly more than capable. The country would benefit greatly from your wisdom and fairness, especially in these troubling times." Moss paused by the fireplace and stared into the flames. "However, this *Amistad* thing could challenge that ambition."

"Yes. I've considered the implications. They could be quite significant."

"Terrifying, if you ask me. Do you have any idea of how it will go?"

"There is still more testimony to go. It is difficult to tell."

"Difficult to tell? Andrew, you're the judge."

"Yes, and as the judge in this case it is my responsibility to render a decision that is sound and that will hold up under the scrutiny of an appeal. At the same time, I have a certain responsibility to my party and the President."

"The only responsibility you have is to yourself."

"In this case I believe one may be inextricably connected to the others."

Moss set down his glass on the small table and walked over to Judson's desk. He raised the glass from one of the lamps, took a cigar from his jacket, and lit it on the flame. He turned and looked across the room and Judson and slowly began walking back to the fireplace.

"Personally, I don't care what decision you render, Andrew. I am a businessman first and a Democrat second. No matter from where the political winds blow, I make money and will continue to do so. But you are a political animal, and your advancement depends strongly on who is in power. So I have come to give you a bit of political advice. My contacts in Washington believe that Van Buren will not make it this fall."

"How can they say that? The election is more than ten months from now."

"True. But the President does not hold the confidence of the people. They don't see him as a leader. This whole *Amistad* affair is proof of that, too. If the man had anything between his legs he would have shipped the whole lot of them back to Cuba on the first tide. Instead he fumbled and wavered. As a result, he's got Tappan and the rest of those mad religious fanatics trying to whip up the country into some sort of frenzy over slavery. And all because of some wretched black murderers. Really."

"It's more complicated than that."

"Yes. Now. But it didn't have to be. A man must look at the facts, assess the risks, and make a decision. Van Buren does none of those things. He vacillates, halfheartedly initiates, and then draws back and regroups. All the while he never gets anything done. Trust me, Andrew, the man and his administration are done for."

"I don't believe it. But even if I did, what does the *Amistad* case have to do with all of it?"

"What I said before about the court is true. I have been told that your name has been mentioned both by Democrats and Whigs. You have respect. But there are a lot of people who are concerned about the prospects of a decision which would grant a slave the right to challenge his captivity. Such a decision would cause tremendous unrest, even though I am sure it would ultimately be overturned by the Supreme Court. Furthermore, leveling this type of a ruling would almost certainly keep your dreams from becoming a reality."

"Regardless of how my decision goes, I strongly doubt that I would write it in such a way as to permit that interpretation."

"You tell me this in confidence but also in truth, yes?"

"Yes. But I will also tell you that my decision will be based first and foremost on propriety under the law, party alliances notwithstanding. As any man with experience in these things will tell you, Thadeus, the only way to get on the Supreme Court is to have a sound record based on precedent, legal scholarship, and prudent judgment."

"No, Andrew," Moss said, leaning in. "The only way to get on the Supreme Court is through presidential appointment."

† † †

The raw, grating cold continued to draw its brittle gray fingers tightly across the Northeast. No one could ever remember anything like it. Rivers and shallow bays froze solid. Snow fell nearly every other day. In many places the rails were impassable, halting trains and testing the wills of numerous towns and cities already short of food and coal. People stayed indoors if at all possible. Traffic along the docks of the seaside villages was nonexistent.

So when on the morning of January fifth, two days before the trial was to resume, the USS *Grampus* made its way through the ice flows into New Haven harbor, it was a conspicuous event. The small two-masted ship was fresh from patrolling the western coast of Africa for illegal slavers and not outfitted for ice-breaking or frigid weather. Three shivering sailors stood at the bow rails with great pointed pikes pushing away ice from the hull.

A reporter from the *New Haven Herald* managed his way out to the ship by walking on the bay's ice while pushing a rowboat in front of himself. When the boat broke through the ice he got in it and rowed and sculled and drove the little craft until it came alongside the Navy ship. He was not allowed on board, though. All the commander would say was that the *Grampus*'s mission was subject to "special orders."

The orders, which were tucked tightly in the coat of the ship's commander, Lieutenant John S. Paine, were personally signed by the President of the United States. But it was because of Paine's concern and attention that their execution hadn't been botched from the outset. The *Grampus* was chosen by Secretary of the Navy Pauling to ferry the tribesmen back to Cuba because of its previous mission as a slave catcher. What Pauling did not consider was that the *Grampus* was built for the chase rather than transport. As such it was small and had limited crew and cargo space. There was no way it could accommodate nearly forty prisoners and a full crew. Paine explained these facts in a dispatch after receiving his orders. The word came back to "store as many of the negroes below decks as possible and chain the rest on deck, rotating them above and below as he saw fit." Paine was horrified and wrote another dispatch saying that, if the weather up north was as reported, it would be inhuman to have anyone on deck for a prolonged period of time. He added that if a storm was encountered, it could "produce a serious loss of life for the blacks on deck, as well as a potentially damaging political disaster for the President." This last bit seemed to touch the proper nerves, for when Paine went ashore in New Haven he was met by Holabird with additional orders to "reduce his crew as he saw necessary so all the blacks could be accommodated below decks for the entire voyage."

But there was another problem. The warrant signed by the Attorney General instructed Paine to take the blacks on board, stipulating that it was for "apprehension of the defendants, Spanish negro slaves taken from the *Amistad*, currently on trial in Circuit Court." With the proceedings occurring in district court, Paine was concerned that his warrant was invalid. He showed it to Holabird, who nearly fainted. The prosecutor summoned an express courier and charged him to go to Washington for a new warrant. Generally, the trip would take a full day by train. However, with the weather making passage questionable all the way down to the Carolinas, it was doubtful the courier could deliver the message before the trial reconvened. Holabird informed Judson, who assured him that Baldwin would probably take two or three days to simply present the final elements of his case.

Court resumed on Monday, January 7, a sunny but frigid

day. Despite the fact that the great coal furnace in the basement had been fired four hours earlier, the courthouse had yet to warm up. People entering the building could still see their breath in the air.

James Covey had recovered, as had the lawyers for the opposition, and the gallery hummed with anticipation of what they would hear that day. They were not disappointed. As soon as Judson entered and convened the proceedings, Baldwin stood.

"Your Honor, I ask that Joseph Cinqué be called along with the interpreter James Covey."

"Call Mr. Cinqué and Mr. Covey," Judson said, "and let the record show that the court recognizes and accepts Mr. Covey's ability as interpreter for the *Amistad* negroes."

Singbe walked up to the stand and took the oath. He was dressed in black cotton pants, a plain checked shirt, tattered field boots without laces, and a thick wool winter coat that reached down to his knees. He also had on fingerless wool gloves and held a gray knitted wool cap in his hands.

"Now, Joseph," Judson said. "I know you're not a Christian. But we expect you to be on your word here."

Singbe looked from Covey to the Judge, nodded, and spoke in English.

"I tell truth only."

A murmur went through the courtroom. Judson banged his gavel twice. Sedgwick winked at Staples, who had spent several hours of the last week helping Singbe to master the phrase he had just spoken.

"Proceed, Mr. Baldwin."

"Yes, Your Honor. Mr. Cinqué, tell the court how you came to be here, in America."

Singbe told the tale of his odyssey that had begun nearly a year before. Sedgwick provided a rope so Singbe could show how he was tied by his captors. Later, when Singbe got on the floor and got into the half-sitting position that he held for most of his time on the nearly fifty-day voyage of the *Teçora*, the silence in the courtroom was tangible. Holabird objected, asking what bearing this had on the case, but Judson, who even appeared to be moved, overruled. Singbe also told of his time in the baracoons and how he was appraised by Ruiz.

"Would you show us exactly what you mean?" Baldwin asked.

"He will need a man," Covey said. "To serve as a prospective slave."

"Mr. Holabird, would you care to volunteer?" Baldwin asked.

"Certainly not, sir!"

"Fine, fine," Baldwin smiled. "I will submit. Appraise me as a prospective purchase, Mr. Cinqué."

Singbe got up from the stand and walked over to Baldwin. He stopped in front of him, reached out tentatively and gave the lawyer's arm a soft squeeze.

"Really, Mr. Cinqué. Is this representative?" Baldwin said. "Were the slave traders this gentle?"

Covey translated. Singbe shook his head. Covey told him in Mende, "Show them. Show them how it was."

Singbe unbuttoned his coat and set it aside on a chair. He took a deep breath and turned Baldwin around so he faced the gallery. Singbe slapped the lawyers' arms and back hard. He felt his legs and buttocks. Then he spun him around and inspected the teeth. The gallery gasped at nearly every move Singbe made. They were not used to seeing such practices, nor had they ever see a white man treated so by a black man.

When Singbe was done, he turned to Covey and whispered a few words.

"He says he is sorry, Mr. Baldwin, sir."

"Quite all right," Baldwin said, though it was obvious he was somewhat unsettled by the experience.

Singbe retook the stand and told about his time in the baracoons and how he had met the other tribesmen. He explained how after a few days they were loaded onto the *Amistad*.

"And when did this occur?" Baldwin asked. "At what part of the day were you and the children moved?"

"Late at night," Singbe answered through Covey. "After darkness had fallen."

A great roar of unrest exploded through the spectators. Late at night! Late at night! It was unthinkable! Judson banged his gavel several times.

"Quiet! Quiet! There will be order in my court! Mr. Baldwin. Does your client understand the question of time?"

"Yes, he does, Your Honor."

"And it was after dark? Late at night?" Judson spoke now to Singbe.

Covey relayed the message and repeated Singbe's words.

"Yes, sir," Covey said. "Late at night."

The courtroom again was in turmoil. Judson slammed his gavel down again calling for order, but he knew what they were hearing was scandalous. Slavery was one thing, a horrible thing, but legal nonetheless. However, keeping children up late at night—why, in New England such a thing was widely recognized as an appalling, outright cruelty. Baldwin had scored a crucial point. More important, Holabird could not respond. Ruiz was not in attendance, for he still refused to take the stand, calling the proceedings a mockery. Until now, Holabird had not minded Ruiz's and Montes's absence, preferring instead to work from the Spaniards' sworn deposition. But there was nothing in there about what time the slaves were loaded, so there was no way to refute Singbe's testimony.

Singbe went on to tell of the mutiny, and that, yes, they had killed the captain and crew, but that it was in self-defense. The captain had fired upon them. Besides, they had been kidnapped, beaten, and tortured. Now they believed they were to be killed and eaten.

"What would you have done if it were you?" he asked rhetorically.

Baldwin also asked about his capture by the Navy. Were they in chains when they were boarded? "No." Were Montes or Ruiz or Antonio in chains? "No. But they were under guard." What did they intend to do with the captives if he could get Henry Green to pilot the ship? "Give them a long boat and point them toward land."

The testimony went the day. When Baldwin had finished,

Holabird stood up to cross-examine, but Judson stopped him. "I think we have heard enough for today," he said. "You may step down, Joseph."

Singbe looked to the Judge and then to Baldwin. He stood, but then stopped and turned back to Judson.

"Please. Me just want go home. Go Africa. Be with wife and childrens and fah-ter. Want be with Stefa and childrens. Please."

Sedgwick looked to Staples, who shook his head. They had not heard this before. Not in English, at least.

Judson grunted and pointed with his gavel toward the other tribesmen. "Get back now with the others, Joseph. This court is adjourned until ten o'clock tomorrow morning."

Judson banged the gavel hard on the pallet and got up and walked out quickly.

Later that night, Tappan sat in his hotel room, worried. Surely the Van Buren Administration wouldn't be so bold as to kidnap the Africans. But why, then, was the *Grampus* riding at anchor in the harbor? He had asked Baldwin and the others if there was any chance the blacks could be spirited off by the government.

"Highly unlikely," Staples said, "unless, of course, the President wants to ignore the U.S. Constitution and deny the blacks their right of appeal."

"It wouldn't be the first time a president has thumbed his nose at the Constitution," Tappan said.

"Yes, but they try not to do it publicly in an election year"—Sedgwick chuckled—"not unless it can win them votes."

"Which getting the blacks out of here and back to Cuba certainly would in many quarters," Tappan said in exasperation.

"Perhaps Van Buren is ready to concede and provide the Amistads with passage back to their homeland," Staples sneered.

Baldwin laughed and assured Tappan that there was nothing to worry about, that the ship was nothing more than some sort of scare tactic, perhaps to get the abolitionists to make a rash move.

"What kind of a move?" Tappan asked.

"There's been talk that the underground railroad may be employed to move the Amistads," Baldwin said. "You wouldn't know anything of that, would you, Lewis?"

"Now, Roger. Do you think I would endanger the case with such a folly?"

"No. So why should the government make the same mistake, especially when it appears they may have the case won?"

"What happens after we leave the courtroom, that's what has me worried," Tappan said.

Baldwin waved his hand as if to dismiss the whole idea of a conspiracy. But Tappan remained concerned. Jocelyn's plan to get the blacks out to an underground railroad station depended on passable roads or seas. The frozen bays and inlets, and snowed-over roads made a quick, inconspicuous escape improbable. And a diversion would be nearly impossible if the blacks were seized by the government in the courthouse at the conclusion of the trial. Tappan considered trying to make a break that night, getting the Amistads out on sleighs and taking them north to a barn of a sympathizer in Farmington. But Jocelyn talked him out of such rash action.

"The government would never do such a thing," Jocelyn said. "It would be beyond scandalous. It would be the downfall of Van Buren's presidency. They want this affair to disappear, but to kidnap the blacks and deprive them of the rights under the Constitution? Why, it would create a deafening public outcry. No, Lewis, they will keep it in the courts. Remember, there is an election this year. Van Buren covets vindication in the eyes of the law as much as we do."

What Tappan and Jocelyn did not know was how close the trial had come to ending that day. Isham had met with Holabird, Hungerford, and Judson after court was adjourned and offered to drop Gedney and Meade's claims if the trial were immediately discontinued. Isham did not say so, but the Spanish government had offered to pay the two officers $20,000 in lieu of a salvage claim. The arrangement would be dubious in the eyes of the law but all involved felt comfortable enough as long as a certain level of discretion was maintained.

Holabird and Hungerford knew of the Spanish offer, though Judson did not. Isham insisted to the judge that his clients were having second thoughts and did not want to impede their government's desires to resolve the issue of the blacks. Judson nodded and said that if the Navy officers wanted to withdraw their claims, he would allow it, but that it would probably not accelerate the case since Henry Green still had a claim pending. This pronouncement caused Isham to immediately back down on his offer, saying he would only tender it if the judge could guarantee a cessation to the trial. Judson said that the trial would go on unless Green withdrew his claim as well.

Holabird moved quickly, trying to work as an intermediary for the Spanish. He met with Ellsworth that night and explained that cash could be found for Green as well if his claim was withdrawn. Ellsworth, however, refused to even hear of such things, knowing that if a secret deal were discovered by the press, it would mean political disaster. The Spanish decided to withdraw their offer to Gedney and Meade when they saw it would not produce the desired results. It was a disappointment to the Spaniards but no great loss. The *Grampus* still rode at anchor in the harbor.

The next day, Holabird began his cross-examination of Singbe.

"Joseph, is it true that you were a slaveholder in your native land?"

Holabird's question froze all the movement and coughing in the already chilly courtroom. Baldwin stood. "Your Honor..."

"Instruct your client to answer the question, Mr. Baldwin. "

Baldwin shrugged and nodded to Covey who relayed the question to Singbe.

"No. I have never had a slave," Singbe said through his interpreter.

"But isn't it true that you told James here that you had owned a slave?" Holabird continued. "Two slaves, in fact. And that you owed a man a sum of money and agreed to settle by selling him the slaves. But one of your slaves ran off, so the man took you and your remaining slave as well?"

"No. This never happened," Singbe continued.

"So he says under oath," Holabird said smugly. "We shall see the value of his word. No further questions, Your Honor."

As Singbe stood to leave the stand, Holabird asked to call the U.S. federal marshal, Norris Wilcox, who had been assigned to the slaves. Wilcox took the stand.

"Mr. Wilcox, tell the court what you heard on December 14."

"The interpreter was talking to Cinqué, taking a statement. And Cinqué said that he had traded two slaves to pay a debt. But one of the slaves run off after the deal was done. So the man took Cinqué as payment for the debt. That's how he come to be a slave."

"Are you sure of this?"

"I was standing right at the bars when I heard it. Yeah, I'm sure."

"No further questions, Your Honor."

Wilcox stood and began to walk off the stand. Baldwin met him in front of the prosecution table. "Would it interrupt your day terribly if I asked you some questions, too, Mr. Wilcox?"

The court broke into laughter. Judson was not amused. He knew Wilcox was well apprised of court proceedings. He pointed to the chair and reminded Wilcox he was under oath.

"Mr. Wilcox, was there anyone else in the room with Mr. Cinqué and Mr. Covey?" Baldwin asked.

"Sure. About ten of the other blacks."

"Any other white men?"

"Yeah. There was one of those fellas from Yale."

"Would you know him if you saw him again?"

"Sure."

"Is he in this courtroom today?

Wilcox took a moment and scanned the crowd. He stood to see better and then pointed to a man near the back.

"That man, the short one in the black coat."

"Are you sure?"

"Yes, sir."

"No further questions, Your Honor. But I would like to call that man, who is, in fact, one of the Yale Divinity faculty who helped us record the oral testimonies of my clients."

Baldwin was taking a chance. One of the Africans, Kimbo, had in fact said that he was taken because of a debt for which he tried to repay with two slaves. Wilcox had heard the story right, he had just gotten the face of the defendant wrong. The key was not to let those facts come out in court if at all possible.

Baldwin questioned the man Wilcox had pointed out, George E. Day, a professor at Yale. He testified that he had recorded statements from Cinqué. Had Cinqué ever said he had owned slaves or sold them? No, in fact he went out of his way to mention that he had never owned a slave. Was this reflected in his statement? Word for word. Baldwin then offered to submit the testimony from Cinqué as Day had recorded it, as well as all other testimony from Cinqué taken down by others from Yale. Judson accepted the offer. Holabird cross-examined Day asking again about the slave incident. He did not ask about any of the other tribesmen holding slaves. Day left the stand without relaying Kimbo's story. The transcripts later confirmed Day and Singbe's testimony.

The next day Burnah and Grabeau were called to testify. Both told their stories through Covey. Burnah went into great detail about being beaten for asking for more water. In his cross-examination of Grabeau, Holabird asked how the slaves had been treated since they had come to America.

"Good," Grabeau said in English.

"Better than you were treated on the plantations?"

"I have not been on a plantation," Grabeau said through Covey. "And no matter how well we are treated, this is not our home. Cuba was not our home. We are African blackmen."

Holabird asked to recall Antonio. Judson consented. Holabird asked Antonio when the slaves were loaded on the *Amistad*.

"Just after dark," Antonio said through a Spanish interpreter. "Perhaps eight o'clock."

"Eight o'clock, Your Honor!" Holabird said triumphantly.

"Not the 'late at night' that was asserted by Cinqué."

Baldwin asked if Antonio had seen a watch or clock. Antonio said no, but that the slaves were loaded just after sunset, which, he thought, would be around eight o'clock. Baldwin had no further questions. Holabird beamed.

The prosecution rested, as did the defense and the claimants. Closing statements were made. Holabird emphasized the documentation and the passages from the two treaties. Hungerford said that this was a case for Spanish law and demanded immediate release of the blacks to the Spanish authorities. Isham and Ellsworth talked about their clients' rights to salvage.

Baldwin stood and summed up the major facts as they pertained to the Amistads. He then turned to the questions of the blacks' disposition and their origins.

"They are men, Your Honor, not cargo. Even the Spanish Ambassador, Señor Argaiz, has admitted as much. In his diplomatic protest to the United States Government, which Minister Argaiz so kindly supplied to the nation's newspapers, he said, and I quote: 'I therefore request that the United States immediately surrender the ship, cargo, and slaves to the Spanish government so that justice can be carried out under Spanish law,' end quote. Note he said 'cargo and slaves.' They are people, men, not inanimate objects. As men they are entitled to the same rights guaranteed to 'all men' in our Constitution.

"But this case is also about the natural rights of all men who were born free and have lived as such throughout their lives. These men are citizens of African nations. I am certain we have proved at least that much. They were free men until they were illegally abducted and pressed into servitude. As free men illegally bound, they did what any free man would try to do. They exercised their rights to wrest themselves from false imprisonment and servitude. This is not an issue of race or property. It is an issue of natural law and a free man's inherent right to maintain his liberty. The facts hold to this. It is only proper that their freedom be restored to them and that they be permitted to return to their homeland."

Judson adjourned the court until 10:00 A.M. on Monday, January 14, at which time he would issue his decision.

Baldwin was trying to be optimistic but conceded that they would probably lose. In fact, he and Sedgwick had already begun drawing up the papers for an appeal.

Tappan was now completely convinced that the government would be trying to get the blacks out on the *Grampus* the first night after the decision. He said as much to Baldwin and the others, but they refused to believe it. For the next two days, Tappan and Jocelyn tried to pull together the resources to get the tribesmen out of New Haven as soon as the trial ended. Their plan was to use a hundred or so devoted followers to start a commotion across the green as the tribesmen were being led from the courthouse to the jail. Upon seeing the commotion, Tappan would urge the guards to rush the tribesmen back into the jail. Once there, men posing as federal marshals would present the jailer with forged orders to transport the blacks out of the city to ensure their safety. Six large sleighs would be waiting at the back of the jail, and by the time anyone was the wiser, the blacks would be halfway to Farmington. It was a daring plan, more so because they had no backup. Much could go wrong and they would probably be traveling in broad daylight. But it was the best they could come up with, considering the limited time and the conditions.

Holabird was also trying to leave nothing to chance. He instructed Lieutenant Paine, who received his revised warrant the day before, to have an armed contingent of Marine guards from the *Grampus* waiting outside the courthouse. When Judson read his decision in favor of the government, Holabird would request a meeting with Baldwin, Tappan, and the others to propose a "deal." While this was happening, the blacks would be escorted back to the jail. Paine and the Marine guards would meet them at the courthouse doors, present the warrant, and take possession of the blacks. They would be loaded on the ship and be on their way out of the harbor within an hour. The plan had to be altered only slightly when Paine noted that, because of his abbreviated crew, he had no Marines on board. In fact, he only had thirteen men including himself. Holabird decided this would be enough, but instructed Marshal Wilcox to have ten more men ready to assist.

"This whole thing will finally be out of our hair tomorrow," Holabird said sighing.

On Monday, though the sun shone brightly, the air was so cold that the beards of men waiting in line to get into court had turned white from their frozen breath. Judson entered the courtroom at precisely ten o'clock, sat down, and took out a small stack of paper from his valise.

"To all in attendance, this is how I rule on the case of the U.S. government versus the occupants of the *Amistad*. First of all, with regards to jurisdiction. As it was discovered by survey, the seizure of the vessel *Amistad* took place on the high seas. As such, the commander, Lieutenant Gedney, was within his right to bring it to port in Connecticut, giving this court jurisdiction over the case.

"With regards to salvage, I find that Mr. Green's claim has no substance. He has no rights to salvage because he was never on board the *Amistad*. Further, Mr. Green believed he had a verbal agreement with negroes on shore, including their leader, Joseph Cinqué, to take command of the ship and sail it to Africa. However, Mr. Green's intentions were not to honor that agreement, but rather to seek immediate salvage in New York."

As Judson read on regarding Green's claim, Tappan felt someone tap him on the shoulder. He turned and saw Jocelyn, who had a look of horror on his face. Jocelyn pressed a note into Tappan's hand. Tappan opened it slowly.

Armed Navy guards outside the door. What do we do?

An electric agitation surged through Tappan's body. It was all he could do to keep from standing on his seat and begin screaming at the top of his lungs. Instead, he leaned back to Jocelyn and whispered as quietly as he could.

"Go to the door. On my signal, leave and have our people

begin their action, but at the courthouse door instead of across the green. We will take them out the back instead."

Jocelyn nodded, stood, and made his way to the back of the courtroom. Tappan folded the note carefully and passed it over to Staples. Staples held the paper for a few moments and listened to the judge. Finally, he glanced down at it absently. His face grew white and he quickly passed the note to Sedgwick with a hard push to the big man's arm. Sedgwick read the note, looked from Staples to Tappan and then over to the tribesmen. His great back seemed to strain even more against the suit's seams. He shook his head slowly and passed the paper to Baldwin. Baldwin looked down and his whole body straightened. He moved to the edge of his seat, getting ready to shoot to his feet and declare the government conspiracy as soon as Judson had finished.

"With regard to the claims of Lieutenants Gedney and Meade," Judson went on, "I find that their actions were in fact meritorious and saved a wayward, uncaptained ship from certain peril. It was in the hands of men who knew nothing of navigation or seamanship, and it was supposedly bound for Africa, a destination I believe would have never been reached given the state of ship and crew. I therefore rule that Lieutenant Gedney and his associates receive the fair compensation of one third the appraised value of the ship *Amistad* and its cargo as it appeared in New London harbor.

"As for the question of slaves and cargo . . . "

Covey had been translating quietly for Singbe and the others. He paused, listening to Judson's words making sure that he got this part absolutely right. Singbe watched the judge as he spoke.

"The slave Antonio, having been born in Cuba, should be restored to the heirs of his former owner under the Treaty of 1795, also mentioned in this court as Pickney's Treaty. The Spaniards, Mr. Ruiz and Mr. Montes, have submitted genuine documentation that states the other negroes in question are in fact slaves, legally purchased on the Havana market. The court recognizes the validity of these documents and believes Mr.

Montes and Mr. Ruiz thought they were purchasing domestically bred 'landino' negroes. However, this court has been influenced by the presentation of facts and compelling testimony by the defense. The evidence offered has convinced this court wholeheartedly that the men and children taken on the *Amistad* are freeborn Africans, who were illegally kidnapped from their homeland and unlawfully sold as slaves. Their alleged actions of mutiny were committed in a desire to win back their liberty and return home. While Mr. Ruiz and Montes may not have known that the negroes were freeborn and illegally imported into Cuba, it does not validate their purchase of said negroes. I therefore urge both men to return to their homeland and seek redress of this falsehood through refund of the money used to purchase the negroes from the party which sold said negroes to them.

"As for the charges of murder, I rule that in the first part, the actions took place on a Spanish ship in Spanish waters and thus should be subject to Spanish law. In the second part, however, I rule that I will not order extradition to Cuba of the negroes participating in the mutiny, since, as stated, these men were trying to wrest themselves from illegal bondage and thus in the eyes of this court, acting in self-defense. Instead I rule that the negroes of the *Amistad* be handed over to President Van Buren under the guidelines stipulated in the Treaty of 1819, and be safely returned to their homeland."

A loud cheer went up from Staples. The tribesmen also began cheering. Sedgwick brought his hands up to his face and leaned back laughing. Baldwin was so stunned by the verdict he nearly fell off his chair. Judson banged his gavel trying to restore order. Holabird ran up to the bench, demanding an appeal.

At the door, Paine heard of the verdict and began laughing.

"Come on, lads. All this for naught," he said. "Back to the ship with us."

That night the *Grampus* sailed out of New Haven harbor with only its skeleton crew on board. Two days later, on leave from his jail cell in New York City, Pepe Ruiz jumped bail and boarded a ship back to Havana.

The Friend

A week after Judson's decision, a new painting was unveiled in New Haven titled, *The Amistad Massacre*. The canvas, more than 135 feet long, was based on "actual testimonies of the survivors." It showed a variety of scenes on board the *Amistad*: the tribesmen using machetes to wildly hack away at two terrorized sailors; Pepe Ruiz standing in the bow, desperately fighting against seven savage tribesmen; Konoma baring his sharp "cannibal" teeth and leering hungrily over the blood-soaked and dying Captain Ferrer; and, in the center of the canvas, Singbe, insane with anger and a thirst for blood, being restrained by three other tribesmen from striking at a severely wounded Pedro Montes.

It was decided after the trial that the Amistads would be moved to the new jail in the village of Westville, about two miles outside New Haven. The jail had just been completed and contained a single large holding room, thirty feet by forty feet, that had yet to house a prisoner. Marshal Wilcox believed that all the African men could be kept here comfortably under a reduced guard. City officials also thought that locating the blacks outside New Haven proper would cut down on the number of spectators and protesters that their presence kept drawing.

On the night before the tribesmen were to be moved, a few minutes after the great bell of the Congregational Church on the green had signaled midnight, Colonel Pendelton walked into Singbe's cell and poked him with the butt of a musket.

"Cinqué! Cinqué! Get yer ass up. Now!"

Singbe jumped as the gunstock went into his ribs. He looked up into the flickering light being thrown by a lantern held by one of Pendelton's men. The oily smoke mixed with the sticky smell of whiskey.

"C'mon, boy," the man said. "Do as the Colonel tells ya."

Singbe stood. Other tribesmen began standing too, but Pendelton jerked the musket around wildly.

"Just Cinqué. The rest of yous stay put."

Pendelton pushed Singbe out of the cell and led him down the corridor past the common prisoners' cells, down a small stairway and into a musty, windowless room rancid with the stench of urine and vomit. It was a part of the jail Singbe had never visited. As the lantern light filled the room he could see Grabeau and Burnah standing in a corner, naked from the waist up. Their hands were chained to a pole that ran floor to ceiling.

"Get over there, nigger."

Pendelton pushed Singbe toward the pole. He could see fear in the eyes of his two friends. He turned back to Pendelton only to have the old man slam the gun butt into his crotch. Singbe dropped with the pain, nearly passing out. The cold steel of the gun barrel bit pressed into his temple as the other man placed manacles around one of Singbe's wrists. He dragged Singbe over to Grabeau and Burnah and connected the chain to the other wrist, locking his hands around the pole.

"Stand up!" Pendelton yelled. "Stand up, I say. Tim, stand that murderin' pile a shit up."

The man jerked Singbe up and made him grab hold of the pole.

"Now, I was in court for the whole thing," Pendelton said. "Ev'ry day. An' I heard the evidence. You niggers surely did get away with somethin'. And I don't need no evidence to tell me this, either. No sir. I sees guilty men ev'ry day. All the time. White or black, I know when they're guilty and when they're not. Just like that English peacock that come in here and played with the bumps a yer heads. Right, Jack?"

"Much better than that rickety fool, Colonel," Tim snickered.

"Right. Now, as I sees it, yous, all a yous, are guilty, filthy murderers. However, the law is sometimes prejudiced and don't sees things right. Politics an' all. Your Mr. Tappan, with his almighty attitude and nigger-lovin' ways, he swayed the courts and the papers. Hell, he bought 'em off with all his money. That's a truth as sure as we're standing here this night. So, as I sees it, someone 'round here has to dispense some justice. That someone'll be me. Tim!"

Pendelton handed the man the musket. The man handed Pendelton a whip. The jailer cracked it in the air a few times and let out a creaky laugh.

"We flogs the attempted escapers 'round here. The way I sees it, you fellas are tryin' to escape proper justice."

He staggered forward a few steps and sent the whip into the three men. The first lash struck Grabeau on the back and Singbe in the neck. Pendelton swung the whip twice more, hitting Burnah as well, and then staggered around them, taking up a new stance just behind Singbe. He let out a yell and cracked the whip hard into them five more times.

"Stop yer moving, ya black sonsabitches," Pendelton slurred, staggering a little to the left. He drew back his arm quick, catching the rest of his drunken body by surprise, especially the feet, which twisted, shook, and then flew out, sending Pendelton onto his back.

"Colonel! Colonel?"

The other man, Tim, ran over to Pendelton. The old jailer rolled over on his side and vomited.

"Tim," he gagged. "Give 'em what for."

Pendelton passed out. Singbe, Grabeau, and Burnah watched Tim take the lamp and help Pendelton out of the room. The thick wooden door slammed shut. The room's darkness was complete. The only sound they heard was their own shaking, gasping breaths. About a half hour later Tim came back, holding the musket. He unlocked the chains and led them to their cells. A few days later, when one of the divinity students discovered welts on Grabeau's back, the story of the flogging was told. Tappan went back to Pendelton to ask what happened.

"They must've given someone a hard time," was all the jailer would say.

Tappan promised an inquiry and charges.

"You can look into it, Mr. Tappan," Pendelton said. "But I have a feeling nothing will be uncovered. Besides, how do you know them blacks didn't get surly one night on my night guards and deserve a little flogging? We'd do the same if they were white."

Tappan reported the incident to the committee, which decided to present a report to the New Haven City council. An inquiry was launched but the council found no evidence of mistreatment.

† † †

Secretary of State Forsyth paced in the White House parlor while President Van Buren sat in front of the fireplace puffing on a pipe. As Forsyth saw it, Judson's decision was not the sudden enlightenment that the abolitionist papers were claiming. If anything, it was a shrewd ruling that walked a razor's edge between judicial propriety and political expedience. He had granted the Amistads their freedom, but in no way had he granted them rights as persons under the U.S. Constitution. In returning Antonio to the heirs of Captain Ferrer, Judson was also affirming that foreign slaves could not look to the United States for asylum. Finally, in putting the Amistads in the care of President Van Buren, he had given the government control over their destiny. True, Forsyth admitted, the Administration had been officially charged with returning the blacks to Africa. But what happened after a ship left port and reached the open ocean was always a dicey proposition.

"A storm could blow them off course and force them into a nearby port for refuge, a port such as Havana, say," he said. "Then again, everyone knows how upset the Spanish are about the entire incident. It is not unforeseeable that they would overtake the ship on the high seas, board it, and take all the blacks back to Cuba for trial. Certainly we would lodge a protest. But in the end, what could we do, especially if no American citizens were harmed and no ship was taken?"

"Are you suggesting we drop our appeal?"

"My sources tell me Tappan and his crowd would accept such a gesture if we promised passage for the blacks back to Africa."

"Albeit with stipulations for verification of their safe delivery to Sierra Leone, no doubt."

"I would expect so, yes sir."

"That is a barrel of shit," Van Buren said, slamming his fist down on his desk. "I will not make treaties with abolitionists, nor will I be seen as compromising on this issue. That would be disastrous to our Southern strategy in the fall."

"To not do so might prove equally disastrous with the Northern contingent."

"I believe Northern sympathizers will look at the court decision as the ultimate yardstick. They will know that we must cede to the judiciary's demands."

"I met with Minister Argaiz this morning."

"That bilious little runt Argaiz. He has not stopped whining since Judson made his ruling in January."

"Yes. He continues to lodge protests both with my office and in sympathetic newspapers. Although I have noticed a shift in content and tone. He has gone from calling the blacks 'slaves' to 'murders and mutineers.' No doubt the shift was inspired by Holabird's advice on what will play better in the courts."

"I'm less worried about the Spanish than the election. We need a court-sanctioned vindication for our position in this matter. It is essential. At the very least it will halt the gossip. Christ, look at the papers. It is April and they are still filled with *Amistad* and Cinqué."

"That's because the appeal will be heard next Monday."

"Yes, and by Smith Thompson. He is no friend of ours, that's for sure. Mark my words, John, this is headed for the Supreme Court."

"It would appear so, Mr. President. However, if that proves true, all the better. No doubt we shall finally see proper justice done."

"Yes, yes. But in all likelihood the court wouldn't take it up until its winter session. The election is in November. I want it gone now. We have too many other distractions to deal with."

"Mr. President, trust me. This *Amistad* affair is not affecting any sort of drag on your election prospects. Win or lose, you have been doing the right thing in the public's eye. Any unrest out there is solely hitched to the state of the economy."

"The economy has been improving slowly and steadily since last October. I wish someone would take notice of that."

"Some people have taken notice, sir. But you know how perception always trails reality."

A heavy sigh hissed out of Van Buren. He stood and walked over to the window near his desk.

"Do what you can to strengthen our cause with the *Amistad* case. If the appeal does not go our way, I shall take Holabird off the case and order Attorney General Gilpin to present it before the Supreme Court. We will prevail in this matter, John."

"Yes, sir. I'll see to it."

† † †

Ten days later, on a cool and foggy Washington morning, a well-dressed man stopped another man on the street, a proofreader from a local print shop, and said, "Excuse me, my good man. I'm wondering if you can help me?"

"Sir?"

"I wonder if you could take a look at this?"

The man handed the proofreader an envelope. Inside was a hundred dollars. The proofreader had never seen so much money in one place.

"You see this word?" the man said, holding up a small sheet of paper with the word *landinos* on it.

"Yes, sir."

"You will see it in your work in the next few weeks. It is a typographical error. I would like you to substitute these words instead," the man said, holding out another piece of paper. "Understand?"

"Yes, sir."

"That's all. The money is for your troubles. Of course, if you do not fix the error, I will have to send a friend to retrieve the cash."

"Oh no, sir. That won't be necessary."

"I'm sure it won't. But I will know if the errors are corrected, so pay close attention to your work in the next few days."

The proofreader looked down at the envelope and gently fingered the money, still not believing. His voice came out almost as if in a dream. "You can count on it, sir."

The proofreader looked up, but the man was gone. He looked up and down the street. There were dozens of men walking to work. Any could be the one who had just handed him the envelope. The proofreader turned and quickly stuffed the envelope into his pocket and went off to the print shop where he worked.

The defense team had been working hard to put together their case for the appeal and perhaps beyond. The task was made more difficult because Staples was being pulled away by work for other clients. He declared that after the appeal he would have to leave the Amistads. Sedgwick and Baldwin did not feel any animosity toward Staples for this. Both men had a number of cases that they were also working on besides *Amistad* and could sympathize with the young lawyer. But Sedgwick had pledged to stay until the end despite the minimal pay. For Baldwin, who had still not taken a cent for all his work, there was never a question of whether he would remain with the case. For him it was a cause of virtually religious proportions.

The defense was still receiving no help from Washington in getting copies of government documents. Still in England, Arthur Tappan had acquired a copy of the Treaty of 1819 from the British and sent it over in the U.S. ambassador's diplomatic pouch, but the Secretary of State's office informed the Amistad Committee that the copy had somehow been lost between the ocean voyage and the pouch's arrival in Washington. The process of sending word back to England for a second copy, getting it made, and having it brought to the United States would take another six or seven months. By then a hearing before the Supreme Court might be over. Baldwin wrote a letter to his friend William Storrs, a Congressman from Connecticut, to see if any pressure could be brought to bear on the executive from more formal channels. Storrs turned to John Quincy Adams who, in addition to being a former President of the United States and a current member of the House of Representatives, had also been Minister to England when the treaty was written. In fact, Adams was the architect of much of the treaty's original text. Despite having not worked in the executive for nearly twenty years, Adams maintained a few contacts within the State Department. He sent a note to Baldwin saying simply: "With regards to securing documents for your case with the Amistads, I will see what I can do." Baldwin stared at the note for a few moments. It stirred something in his mind, a reminder of something he thought he should remember. But nothing came forth, so he put the note in a file and carried on with his work, hoping something would come of Adams's efforts.

A few days before the appeal opened, Senator John C. Calhoun, a Whig from South Carolina, proposed a resolution that in part read:

> *If a ship should be forced by stress of weather or other cause into a port, she and her cargo, and persons on*

board, with their property, will be accorded all the rights belonging to their personal relations as established by the laws of the state to which they belong, and would be placed under protection of the laws of nations which are extended under such circumstances.

The resolution, which was worded vaguely enough to include any such incident, was clearly aimed at the *Amistad* case. It passed in the Senate 99 to 0. Meanwhile in the House of Representatives, John Quincy Adams put forth a resolution specifically stating that the blacks of the *Amistad* were being detained unlawfully by the U.S. Government and should be returned immediately to their home state in Africa. The resolution failed miserably.

† † †

On April 21, Smith Thompson opened the appeal of the U.S. government by hearing the presentation of William Holabird, who was now also representing the interest of the Spanish government in the case. Holabird's opening was followed by Baldwin's motion to dismiss the federal appeal on the grounds that the U.S. government's representative, Holabird, had no right under the Constitution or international law to represent the interest of Spain or any other foreign nation. Thompson was unimpressed with both Holabird's appeal and Baldwin's motion to dismiss. After four days of hearings, he ruled in favor of Judson's decision, declaring that the case properly belonged in the docket of the U.S. Supreme Court for ultimate resolution. The Court would hear the case during its winter session, which began in January, 1841.

After his ruling, Thompson was approached by Seth Staples with a motion to set bail for the Amistads.

"Motion denied. These blacks shall remain within the custody of the law until this case is decided by the Supreme Court."

"But by Judge Judson's ruling they are free men."

"No, Mr. Staples. By Judge Judson's ruling they are residents of Africa and remanded to the president for return to their native land. This disposition has been appealed by the government, and thus, ultimately, the rights regarding freedom will have to wait until the Supreme Court issues a final ruling."

"Your Honor, this is unprecedented. Are you telling me that if these men were declared by Judge Judson to be citizens of France or England, you would hold them in jail pending the appeal?"

"If they were citizens of France or England, I would issue writs of habeas corpus, Mr. Staples. However, they are not citizens of those or any other such nations, nor can American law in its present incarnation view them in such a light. Such as the Amistads are, they will have to remain in custody."

"Because they are black, correct, Your Honor?"

"Because of the way the law is written, Mr. Staples. I can honestly say I wish it were not so, but it is. And I must follow the law. Court adjourned."

The next day, Baldwin went with Tappan to the jail to explain what had happened to the tribesmen. Singbe, Grabeau, and the others listened carefully. When Baldwin had finished they sat silently for a few moments until Burnah stood and spoke.

"So we not be hanged yet?" he said in English.

"Not ever, if we can help it, Burnah," Tappan said.

"How many more court have to hear case?" Grabeau asked.

"Just one more," Baldwin said. "No other court can rule above them. Their word is final and must be carried out."

"President no change court's word?" Grabeau persisted.

"No," Baldwin said. "The Supreme Court has power over the President in this case."

"Why not we go to this court first, then?" Burnah asked.

Baldwin stood and smiled. He knew the tribesmen's English wasn't good enough to comprehend an explanation of the American judicial system. He nodded to Covey who stood up and began translating. When Baldwin was done, he asked for questions. None of the tribesmen said anything. Either they fully understood the progression of the case through the courts, or more likely, they didn't care. Finally, Singbe stood.

"Mr. Tappan. When we go home?"

Tappan looked at Singbe for a moment and then forced out a smile.

"The Supreme Court will consider our case in the winter."

"It spring now. Why they wait so long?"

"I am afraid that's just how things are done, Joseph."

Later, after they had finished their afternoon exercises on the lawn outside the jail, Singbe sat with Grabeau on the grass listening with the group to a sermon by one of the Yale Divinity students.

"I was taken on the road to Kawamende two springs ago," Singbe whispered in Mende. "Now Mr. Tappan says the high court won't hear our case until next winter."

"I know. We have been a long time among the whites."

"I am confused by the white's system of justice. One judge is overruled by another. Why not just have a council of judges whose word is final, like in Mende?"

"I do not know," Grabeau said. "It is odd, though, you are right. There is much about the whites that makes me think their culture is not well developed. But at least we are being allowed another chance at receiving our freedom."

Singbe nodded and said nothing for a long while. When the sermon was done, the divinity students split them into groups and began the reading lessons. Before he joined his group, Singbe turned to Grabeau again.

"I know I will return to Mende, but I fear Stefa will be with a new husband. She must think I was killed or taken as a slave. Either way, I am dead to her. She is long past the mourning period. She has a new man, now. I am sure of it."

"Singbe, you must not think that way. You must keep your mind and heart filled with hope."

Singbe smiled a little and nodded, but Grabeau could see a tired despair in his friend's eyes.

"I will return to Mende, Grabeau. We all will. That is my hope. Anything more is just a dream."

"Singbe..."

Singbe walked away and sat down with a small group of others who were reading from a first-grade primer.

Since the trial, the tribesmen had been receiving more intensive instruction in English and Christianity. This was at Tappan's request. He agreed with Dr. Gallaudet and others at the Yale Divinity School that the tribesmen were delivered to America's shores by the Lord God Himself in an act of divine providence so that the full Christianization of Africa might begin in earnest. When the case was resolved and, in Tappan's mind, when justice prevailed and the blacks were set free and allowed to return to their homeland, they would do so as shining examples of Christianity and civilized culture.

"I want them to all become God-fearing, devout Christian gentlemen," Tappan said. "They shall become missionaries to the cause, much like the Apostles themselves, enlightening the dark continent from shore to shore with the words of Jesus Christ."

The English lessons were going well. The tutors were particularly impressed with Burnah, Kinna, and Ka-le, whose reading and writing skills were progressing rapidly. One day, after being treated to a demonstration of the progress made by the tribesmen, Sedgwick took Baldwin aside.

"What do you think old Andy Judson would say if he knew these Yale boys were doing exactly the type of educating of blacks that he ran Prudence Crandall out of the state for?" Sedgwick said with a big grin on his face. "And doing it all under the auspices of judicial orders from himself."

Baldwin smiled. "Not too loud, Theodore. If your words fell into the ears of the wrong people, this could turn into an even bigger nest of hornets than the case at hand."

But while the English lessons were going well, the conversion to Christianity was more problematic. The teachings were coming primarily out of the New Testament, and most of the tribesmen thought Jesus and his father were wise and benevolent, much like their own great spirit Ngewo who lived far above the clouds. They were puzzled, however, that Christian religion was devoid of lesser gods such as the ones that inhabited the jungle and rivers and earth. After all, it was through these gods and the spirits of dead relatives that the tribesmen communicated their concerns to Ngewo. How was it that the Christian God and his son allowed themselves to be petitioned directly by people of the earth who did not live in the spirit world? Despite this confusing discrepancy, most agreed that it was a good religion, and some, Burnah and Kinna in particular, had accepted Jesus Christ as their savior. But for most of the tribesmen, full conversion was being held up by one important point.

"One wife?" Yaboi the Timmani tribesman laughed. "Some clans in Mende do such a thing. Singbe's is one, I hear. But even that is a voluntary condition, and one that is not always followed. I myself think only taking one wife severely limits the benefits to the tribe. A man should be able to have as many wives and children as he can afford. It is much more generous."

"I used to think so," Burnah said. "But Dr. Gibbs says it is a sin of the flesh and an abomination unto the Lord to have more than one."

"Perhaps it is because he doesn't know any better."

"Perhaps. But I want to be a good Christian. I do not have any wives now, but when I return to Mende I plan to take only one."

"One is a good start," Yaboi agreed. "But what if you prosper? It will be expected of you to take more wives and have more children. You can increase your prosperity by marrying into the right families. And the bloodline of a wise and prosperous man is continued and strengthened. It is the right way, the way of nature. Tell me, does not the strongest lion have the biggest pride?"

"I understand all that. But it is different when you are a Christian. You follow the Christian ways. No. I will have one wife and many children. They will be Christians, too."

Yaboi wondered if Burnah was joking, but his face was sincere.

"Well"—Yaboi smiled—"by taking only one wife, Burnah, perhaps in your own way you will be providing the women of Mende with a service."

As part of his inquiry regarding the documents for the *Amistad* trial, John Quincy Adams was able to have the President send the transcripts from the previous trials to the Congress so they might be entered into the official record. These would also be the official transcripts used by the Supreme Court as part of their evaluation of the case in the winter. The government printed over ten thousand copies. Interest in the case was so strong among the public that the copies sold out in a matter of days.

However, a few weeks after the transcripts, jointly labeled "Document 185," reached Congress, Adams discovered a serious discrepancy. On the Cubans' original bills of sale, on the trespassos, and on other identity documents, the word *landinos* appeared in each referring to the disposition of the blacks. However, in all the documents prepared for the Document 185, the word *landinos* had been translated to "sound negroes." In the eyes of the law, and especially the Supreme Court, this translation would greatly weaken the claims of the defense. Adams was a savvy enough politician to know that this type of "error" was too convenient to be a product of coincidence. He strongly suspected tampering by the administration and expressed his views on the House floor. The White House issued a statement denying any involvement with "alterations or unforeseen discrepancies." Adams was unconvinced and requested and received permission for a Congressional inquiry into the affair. With the election just ten weeks away, the opposition newspapers played the story up as big as they could, but there was little that could be written beyond speculation. And despite Adams's best efforts, the inquiry produced little substance. The only smoking gun discovered was a proofreader at Blair and Rives, the printing firm that produced the documents. The committee was able to confirm that the man had made alterations to Document 185 before it was set in type. However, that was an acknowledged part of his job—to correct grammatical imperfections and spellings. He admitted as much to Adams's committee. Yes, he had changed "landinos" to "sound negroes," but only because that was what the word looked liked to him.

"On my oath, sir, I did not think I was making a change in meaning," the proofreader testified. "The documents were written in a bad hand. I thought it said 'sound negroes.' And to be honest, Mr. Adams, sir, I never heard of the word 'landinos' before in my life."

Adams produced the original court documents for the committee. The word 'landinos' was clearly legible as such wherever it appeared. The proofreader was unshakable. Adams didn't believe the man, but there was nothing to disprove his story, nor could any kind of trail be found that led to the White House. The best Adams could do was send a formal letter to the Supreme Court, calling their attention to the error and issue a public notification as well.

Tappan remained very hopeful that the Supreme Court would find for the blacks, but he was not abandoning his plan for a quick evacuation in case something went awry. He had also been approached by Antonio with a request. Since Ruiz had fled the United States, Antonio had been forced by the court into incarceration with the tribesmen. The tribesmen still disliked him, though they were not mistreating him. Mostly they just ignored him. For his part, Antonio continued to believe that the Africans were contemptible because they were not, in his words, "as well-bred or civilized" as he was. But while Antonio saw that these men might be able to return to the place of their birth, he had no desire to do the same.

"I do not want to return to Cuba," he said. "I do not want to go to Africa, either. I see the free blacks in America and I decide that I do not want to be a slave anymore. Is there anything you can do for me, Mr. Tappan? Please."

The boy asked the question nearly every time Tappan visited the jail. Privately, Tappan was positive something could be done. Antonio could be smuggled off to Canada in a heartbeat. But he would not attempt such a thing until after the Supreme

Court hearing. He was also wary about Antonio's motives. It could well be that his plea was inspired by Holabird, someone in the Van Buren administration, or even the Spanish Minister. Perhaps someone promised him his freedom if he could get Tappan or another member of the committee to expose the abolitionists' contacts with the underground railroad. It would bring down a net of criminal charges on Tappan and the others and most certainly scuttle the *Amistad* case. For these reasons, Tappan sadly shook his head each time Antonio asked, telling that they would have to let the law dispense freedom and justice.

As summer turned to fall, Tappan became increasingly concerned with the trappings of a Supreme Court hearing. The abolitionists were still widely perceived as religious extremists by most people in the country. Tappan believed that it was essential for their credibility to have a nationally known and respected man arguing their case. Though both Sedgwick and Baldwin were exceptional, neither carried the kind of standing Tappan craved. He wanted someone whose presence would, in his own words, "infuse their cause with an immediate tremor of awe and legitimacy."

Tappan's first choice was Daniel Webster, the best known and perhaps most respected lawyer in the nation. Webster, a native of Massachusetts, had presented cases before the Supreme Court over thirty times. Having him argue the *Amistad* case would be an incredible coup. But though he had no love of slavery, Webster desperately wanted to be president one day. Taking up the defense of this case would be an unwise step for anyone who would eventually need to forge a coalition between Northern and Southern states. Though he did not trust or like abolitionists and believed their agenda would ultimately divide the union, he had a sneaking admiration for Tappan and his abilities. And when Tappan approached Webster personally, it seemed as if the abolitionist's powers of persuasion might win out. But Webster stood firm and sent a note along a few days later that expressed regrets at not being able to take up the case due to a full schedule. He assured

Tappan, however, that in Baldwin and his team, the Amistads had outstanding representation.

Tappan next turned to Rufus Choate, another lawyer with an impeccable reputation, anti-slavery sentiments, and experience before the Supreme Court. But Choate had no desire to become involved with the abolitionists or their extreme beliefs. Always gracious, Choate turned down Tappan's advances with a letter that claimed his health would not permit an "undertaking of such a formidable, though no doubt honorable, task."

Tappan had seen these men as his best chance for making a national statement and generating extensive press coverage—two things his instincts told him were essential to furthering the abolitionist cause. But with both Webster and Choate refusing to become involved, Tappan believed that there was only one other man who commanded both the notoriety and the legal ability needed for this case.

"But," Tappan said to Jocelyn, "he is probably too old and wise a fox to throw his lot in with us."

Still, Tappan decided to try his powers of persuasion one more time. He got in touch with a friend, Ellis Gray Loring, who was also a friend of the man in question. Within a few weeks, a meeting in Boston between the three had been arranged.

It was not an easy sell. The man had been following the case in the papers and thought it was a most noble and just cause. He wished Tappan and his defense team well, and believed that Baldwin was a most capable presenter. However, the man continued, he had no wish to become personally aligned with the abolitionist movement.

"I believe in the ideas that constitute the foundation of your cause, Mr. Tappan, and would love to see slavery abolished in this country this very instant. But I also believe that the methods of the abolitionists as a whole have been dangerously close to sedition on a number of occasions. There are those among your ranks who are dangerous and would gladly see this country split in two."

He also spoke of his advancing age—he was nearly seventy-four—and a busy schedule that got him up at dawn every day and kept him working until nearly twelve each night. The man listed reason after reason why he should not and could not take the case.

Tappan listened closely. But instead of hearing reasons why the esteemed man couldn't take the case, Tappan was hearing excuses, the kind of excuses a person makes when he is trying to convince everyone in the room of his point, and trying to convince himself most of all. Tappan saw the opening, and he knew if he could lay things out just so, the excuses would crumble beneath the weight of the man's true desire to take up the case.

Tappan took his time, going back and forth with the man. Each excuse was refuted. When the man pointed to his age, Tappan pointed to the man's daily schedule—one that would quickly put much younger men in the grave. When the man suggested that it was outside of his interests, Tappan listed achievements and current work by the man that were directly related. When the man mentioned that he had not appeared before the Supreme Court for more than thirty years, Tappan said no one doubted his legal acumen or skills of oratory. Tappan further assured him that statements would be made letting the press know unequivocally that the man's involvement was in no way an endorsement of the abolitionist cause. The sole intent was to achieve justice for the Amistads. After four hours like this, the man finally consented, saying he hoped his involvement would not do the Africans' case harm. Tappan, barely able to contain himself, assured the man that his involvement was exactly what the Amistads needed.

On the way back from Boston, however, Tappan was forced to consider how to solve another problem. Bringing on the new lawyer meant Baldwin would no longer be senior counsel.

Three weeks later, on November 17, the defense team was called together in New Haven for a special meeting. The new senior counsel was coming to the city to meet the Amistads, the committee, and his new colleagues. Tappan had broken the news to Baldwin soon after returning from Boston. If Baldwin was upset at being dropped as senior counsel, he did not let on. After being informed of the situation, Baldwin's first response to Tappan was, "What a great stroke of luck for our cause." He went on to compile an exhaustive brief on the case to bring the new counsel up to date. However, Tappan suspected that Baldwin was extremely disappointed. After all, it was Roger Baldwin who had brought the case farther than anyone could have dreamed possible. But Tappan knew that Baldwin's desire to win the case, his unapproachable professionalism, and his high regard for the lawyer coming on board had helped to temper his discouragement.

On the day of the New Haven meeting, Staples had stopped by Baldwin's office to drop off the last of the files he was working on. As of today he would be officially off the case. Staples could have sent the files over with an assistant, but he was hoping for a chance to meet the distinguished guest in person.

As Staples came in, Sedgwick and Baldwin were discussing a point about one of the trespassos issued to Ruiz. Baldwin asked Staples to hand him the copy of the trespassos from a file on the shelf near the door. Staples opened the file and began looking for the document. As he did, he came across a short note in the hand of their "Friend." Staples glanced through it, realizing it was not one he had seen before. However, when his eyes reached the end, his heart nearly stopped. Instead of the familiar signature "A Friend," this one had a name.

"Roger, when did you get this?"

"What is it? Is it the trespasso?"

"No, it's a note. From him. Only it's signed!"

At that moment, the door of Baldwin's office flew open. Tappan walked in over the threshold with Jocelyn, two professors from Yale, and the new senior counsel.

"Mr. Baldwin, Mr. Sedgwick. And Mr. Staples! Good to see you, sir." Tappan beamed. "Gentlemen, it is my most sincere and honored pleasure to introduce our new senior counsel. The Honorable John Quincy Adams."

"It's our Friend!" Staples cried waving the note. "Roger, Theodore! It's Him! Our 'Friend.' The one who's been helping us all along!"

Mr. Adams and the Court

John Quincy Adams was a man of high intelligence, strong convictions, and ideas that were well ahead of their time. He was also a man of action who lived by his words, a philosophy that had more than once put his life in danger.

Son of the second president of the United States, he was fluent in German, French, Latin, and Greek, in addition to English. He lived in Massachusetts and was elected to the U.S. Senate as a Federalist at age thirty-five. He later served as Ambassador to Russia, Ambassador to London, and was the Secretary of State under James Monroe. As such, he was responsible for acquiring Florida and drafting the Monroe Doctrine and the Treaty of Ghent, as well as the Treaty of 1819.

In 1824 he was elected President of the United States in a tight race that, because of no clear electoral majority, was decided in the House of Representatives. As president he worked to implement such policies as uniform currency, a national banking system, a national university, and a nationwide federally funded canal and highway system. Two years after losing the 1828 election to Andrew Jackson, Adams was elected to the House of Representatives. He had been reelected every term since and spent much of his time working for civil rights, public works, the advancement of science, and was instrumental in the founding of the Smithsonian Institution.

Though not an abolitionist, Adams was a vehement opponent of slavery and became the prime crusader against the "gag rule," a parliamentary order passed in 1836 by the House that forbade discussion of slavery on the House floor. Adams argued that the rule was an abomination upon the Constitutional rights of not only the members of the House, but also of their constituents. His stance on slavery and the gag rule won him respect in the North and a level of hate in the South generally reserved for abolitionists. It also nearly got him censured from the House and brought him several threats of injury, violence, and death—the most recent coming just before he took up the *Amistad* case. Adams had received a framed portrait of himself with a fresh bullet hole shot through the head. The portrait had been anonymously posted from Georgia. Adams hung it on the wall behind his desk.

Adams's reputation as a gripping orator was unequaled—this in a nation whose residents regularly turned out to hear lectures and debates that ran two to four hours. He loved to speak publicly and could do so on a variety of subjects, often going from one to the next easily and without notes. In fact, after visiting the Amistads, their lawyers, and members of the Amistad Committee, Adams gave a free lecture to a standing-room crowd in New Haven's great Congregational Church on "Society and Civilization." But despite his great legal mind and speaking abilities, Adams quickly began wondering if he had taken up more than he could handle with the *Amistad* case. He had been following the proceedings closely since news of the black schooner had first hit the papers. His keen insight into the case was witnessed by the anonymous notes he had penned as "A Friend" and sent to Baldwin's team from Boston, Washington, and through his close friend Loring. Although not being intimate with all the court documents associated with the case, Adams's attention to the details as reported by the papers and friends had been so sharp that the nearly two hundred-page brief Baldwin sent him offered few new facts to consider. Still, an argument before the Supreme Court was not something to be taken lightly, especially when it was on behalf of a case that carried so much controversy and potential for far-reaching actions. If able to give all his time, or even half of it, Adams was confident he could, as he put it, "carry his portion of the load." But Congress would soon be back in session, sapping up much of his time and energy. And he was frequently heard to remark that his aging constitution was slowing him down, though he still managed to work eighteen hours a day, rising at dawn to walk the mile from his house on F Street to Congress and returning by the same route each night.

On the way back to Boston from New Haven, Adams wrote a note to Baldwin thanking him for such a warm welcome to the defense team. "I only hope that my involvement will not in any way damage the chances of our African friends or cause detriment to a positive outcome for this case." Though Baldwin and Sedgwick read the passage as an example of the courteous modesty embraced as a custom of the times, the hesitancy and nervousness expressed by Adams was completely sincere.

Four days after Adams agreed to defend the Amistads in the Supreme Court, Martin Van Buren lost the presidential election to William Henry Harrison, a Whig. The electoral victory had been huge, 234 to 60, but the popular vote was much closer. In fact, after the final tally was in, Forsyth noted that a shift of only 8,500 votes would have put the necessary electoral votes in Van Buren's camp to win a second term. Though the *Amistad* case and Van Buren's apparent pro-slavery sympathies may have produced a minor decline in his popularity, his loss was attributed to the economy and a lack of public confidence in his leadership.

Van Buren was crushed by the results. Publicly he appeared magnanimous and promised a smooth transition of government. Behind the White House doors, however, he brooded for several days, taking no visitors or nourishment save for a few cups of blackberry tea. When he finally emerged from his quarters and held a meeting of his cabinet, he declared that the execution of Democratic policies that had been taken up or initiated by his administration would continue until the last day of his term. He also gave orders for zealous pursuit of the *Amistad* case. In late December, word was received from Harrison's camp that they, too, were anxious to see the district court's decision on the *Amistad* case overturned. Van Buren's attorney general, Henry Gilpin, was given permission to continue on behalf of the new administration if the case went beyond Harrison's March inauguration.

Though the addition of Adams swelled the members of the Amistad Committee with confidence, opinion across the country seemed to be running against them. In part, this appraisal hinged on the perception that, no matter what the facts, it would be very difficult for blacks of any nationality to defeat whites in a court of law. General consensus also had it that the court would not want to go against the will of the executive on such an explosive issue. Finally, there was the composition of the court itself. Chief Justice Roger Tanny, a former slave owner from Maryland, was an acknowledged supporter of states' rights. Four of the other eight justices were either Southerners or known as pro-slavery sympathizers: Philip Barbour from Virginia, John Catron from Tennessee, John McKinley from Alabama, and James M. Wayne from Georgia. Barbour, McKinley, and Wayne were also slave owners. In fact, the only justices on the court who were strong anti-slavery advocates were Smith Thompson of New York, who had presided over the original circuit court trial and the district court appeal, and Joseph Story of Massachusetts. The deck, it seemed, was stacked decidedly against the Amistads.

A few weeks before the Supreme Court hearing, Adams, on his way from Boston to Washington, stopped in New Haven for a scheduled meeting with Baldwin and Sedgwick. Adams had still not been able to spend much time with the case and had yet to even begin formal notes or a brief in preparation for his argument. He listened as Baldwin and Sedgwick outlined their strategy and offered some advice on specific points. Adams said nothing about how he would present the case to the high court and was thankful that the two lawyers held enough respect for him not to inquire. After the meeting, however, he did have a request.

"Might we go out to Westville to visit the Africans? I had only met with them that once, and then it was a decidedly brief encounter."

Baldwin and Sedgwick gladly consented. Despite the chill January weather, Adams suggested they walk the two and a half miles but then recanted, remembering his tight schedule would not permit such a luxury. So instead they made the short ride in his carriage.

Adams spent more than an hour with the tribesmen. He talked to all of them and was impressed by how much their command of the English language had grown in just two months. Before he left, Adams spent a few minutes with Singbe talking about the conditions.

"Well," Adams said, "I am glad that you are all well fed and that the rooms are kept warm in the winter. And I must say, you all appear rather happy."

"We smile all the time when whitemen come," Singbe said. "Until whitemen leave."

Adams raised an eyebrow. "Why? Why do you smile until the whitemen leave?"

"Colonel Pendelton tell us whitemen fear African blackman. They want to hurt us because of fear. So we smile and make whitemen feel better. So they no afraid."

Adams nodded.

"Mr. Adams, Mr. Tappan say you can help us. Please help us, Mr. Adams. We need get back home."

Adams stood and shook Singbe's hand. "I shall do my very best, my friend."

† † †

On February 22, 1841, the case of *The United States vs. Cinque and Others* opened in the Supreme Court of the United States. The small, semicircular courtroom located under the Senate floor was filled to capacity. There were only three windows in the room, which were located behind the judicial bench. The morning light streamed through the long, thick-paned frames, rendering the judges into eight foggy silhouettes to anyone who faced them—eight silhouettes because the ninth, McKinley, was in ill health and had been ordered by his physician to remain in bed. The abolitionists considered the pro-slavery judge's absence not luck, but a direct intervention by God to improve the odds in the case.

Tappan and Jocelyn sat nervously in the front row of the court. The tribesmen had been left behind in Westville. Sedgwick, Baldwin, and Adams entered and took seats at the long, dark table to the justices' right. Henry Gilpin and Holabird sat across the aisle from them. Neither of the government's attorneys made eye contact with any of the lawyers from the Amistads' team.

The judges entered and the opening formalities were performed. After calling the court to order and going through the business of the day, Chief Justice Tanny commanded Gilpin to begin.

Henry Gilpin stood. He was a thin man with a close-cropped tuft of tired brown hair covering the top of his head. His face was so bony and gaunt that at times his sallow skin appeared transparent, but his pale blue eyes were sharp and belied a canny stealth and intelligence. He was a Philadelphia lawyer and had been the city's chief prosecutor, handling more than a few cases where Sedgwick was the adversary. Appointed Attorney General midway through Van Buren's term, Gilpin was well-known to the justices of the court and respected as a highly capable attorney.

Gilpin began his presentation by setting forth the same basic arguments framed in the opinion written by Grundy in 1839. As the government's case unfolded, it was clear that the meat of Gilpin's argument would be a reiteration of the familiar points made in the previous court cases: The government was bound by both Pickney's Treaty and the Treaty of 1819. The President believed it was his duty to place the blacks, the ship, and the cargo in the hands of the Spanish authorities, who would then assess whether criminal charges for murder and piracy were warranted. The question of whether the blacks were legally slaves was also a matter for the Spanish courts. Gedney and Meade had acted valiantly, saving the ship and all aboard from certain peril, if not a complete demise. The officers and their crew deserved salvage on ship and cargo; however, the U.S. government would leave it in the court's hands whether the slaves should be included in that formula. Gilpin further declared that the executive was within its rights in attempting to secure a court order permitting the return of property to the documented owners of the ship's cargo.

Gilpin went on to question much of the "supposed evidence" brought forth by the defense that cast aspersions on whether the blacks were slaves or not and hence acting as men attempting to wrest themselves from unlawful imprisonment. Gilpin insisted that the district court was unduly influenced by the emotional testimony provided by Dr. Madden.

"This testimony was complete hearsay," Gilpin asserted, "and, even though Dr. Madden never fully admitted it under oath, his impressions were highly prejudiced in favor of the blacks and against the Spanish slave owners."

As he spoke, Gilpin paced the courtroom, often disappearing behind the huge Roman pillars that ran from floor to ceiling. At no time during his presentation did he acknowledge any of the testimony made by Singbe or any of the other tribesmen. After almost four hours, Gilpin sat down.

The Court adjourned an hour and a half for lunch and then Baldwin began. Though he spoke for two hours that afternoon and six more the next day, his presentation was little more than a careful listing of the facts surrounding the case. As he listened to his colleague, Adams wondered if such a low intensity display was typical of the Connecticut lawyer or if the man was simply clearing the way for the defense's senior counsel.

Regardless, Adams congratulated Baldwin at the end of his presentation for a making such a "clear and eloquent argument."

With Baldwin finished, Chief Justice Tanny adjourned the court until the next day when Adams would offer his defense. Before Adams left the courtroom, Tappan handed him an envelope.

"I brought this for you from a friend in Connecticut." Tappan smiled. "Best of luck tomorrow."

Adams thanked Tappan and put the note in his valise. He left the courtroom and walked over to his office at the House to look over his notes and to see what had transpired in Congress that day. At quarter to midnight, he began his mile walk back to his house on F Street.

After getting home, Adams continued to work in his study, preparing his notes for the next day's presentation. Some time after 3:00 A.M. he was too bleary-eyed and exhausted to continue any longer. He pushed away from his desk, took an oil lamp, and walked upstairs to bed. As he entered the room, the lamp's dull light caught a small white square beside the bed. It was the envelope Tappan had given him. Adams had placed it on his nightstand so he wouldn't forget to read it.

Dear Mr. Adams,

People say we bad. We kill cook and captain and sailor. But if white man come to Africa and he taken slave, then what he do? He not try to get free too? Please make court understand we free men who want be free again. We want go home. We pray you to win our case. You our friend. We trust you.

Joseph Cinque

Adams had seen and done much in his life, so much that very little surprised him anymore. But the lump that had formed in his throat while he was reading the letter caught him completely off guard. He let out a long, slow breath and then carefully folded the letter and placed it back in the envelope. He extinguished the lamp's flame and waited for sleep to come. Instead, his impatient body tossed fitfully through the night until a sliver of dawn's light pried through the space between drawn curtains.

Court was back in session at 10:30, Tuesday, February 24. Adams stood slowly, greeted the justices and said it was truly an honor to be able to stand before the distinguished court after an absence of more than thirty years. He also hoped aloud that his absence from legal work of any sort over the same long period of time, and his advanced age, would not detract from his performance in court today.

Adams smiled to the gallery, put on his round wire-framed spectacles, and walked toward the bench to begin his presentation.

"I derive, in the distress I feel for both my clients and myself in this case, consolation from two sources. First, the lives, rights, and liberties of my clients have up to this point been so ably and completely defended by my colleague, Mr. Baldwin. Second, I derive consolation from the thought that this court is a court of justice. And in a court of justice, each party has a right to expect and secure justice from the court. We seek nothing more than that, Your Honors. However, as I stand before the court, I do so also with great sadness and outrage, for I am obliged to take this ground because another department of the government of the United States has used its power to pursue a course of utter injustice. I charge that the present executive administration, which was bound not less than this honorable court to uphold the principles of justice, the rights granted by our Constitution, and the laws of our great land, instead from the outset acted with pronounced sympathy toward one party and antipathy toward my clients—antipathy, I might add, that was solely inspired by nothing more than the color of their skin."

With that opening, Adams went on to provide a precise and detailed account of how from Gedney's initial boarding of the

Amistad, to Holabird's actions in the hearing, to Forsyth's instructions to the prosecutor and communications with the Spanish minister to orders issued by President Van Buren himself, representatives of the U.S. Government acted at every step to deny the Amistads their right to due process.

"Rights, Your Honors, which I'm sure we would all agree would certainly and immediately be afforded to them had their skin been of the same complexion as our own."

Adams's presentation was staggering in its precision and organization. He produced quotes from correspondences between Forsyth and Calderón and Argaiz. He noted that early on, Calderón had referred to securing return of "ship, merchandise, and negroes," which showed a differentiation between men and cargo, and yet in later letters, he demanded return of the blacks under Pickney's Treaty because they were "part of the ship's manifested cargo." Argaiz made similar distinctions in his communications as well. Adams presented as evidence the letter Forsyth had sent Holabird, insisting that a hearing be avoided and the negroes be turned over immediately to the President for delivery to the Spanish consul. The letter, a formal document, had been added to the case files during Holabird's last appeal.

Adams then moved to Gedney, castigating the officer for his actions in boarding and seizing the *Amistad*.

"The Africans were in possession of the ship and had the presumptive right of ownership. They were acting peacefully and, the courts have decided, were not in any way engaging in piracy. And yet, Lieutenant Gedney, without any charge or warrant or authority from his government, by force of firearms seized the vessel, boarded it, and, upon seeing the color of my clients' skin, imprisoned them. At the same time, upon seeing the color of the skin of Señors Ruiz and Montes, Gedney took them in, afforded them every comfort, and, without question, immediately assumed the legitimacy of their claims."

Adams went on to outline and examine the events of the circuit court proceedings and the first portion of the district court hearings, including the testimony of Dr. Madden, whose credentials, Adams reminded the justices, had been reviewed and accepted by Judge Judson.

At 3:30, with the winter daylight beginning to wane, Justice Tanny asked Adams to break off his argument and resume it the next day. Adams agreed and court was adjourned. The next morning, however, Judge Tanny entered the courtroom alone and made a stunning announcement.

"The proceedings of this court have been interrupted by the solemn voice of death. One of the learned and honorable justices who sat here yesterday, Judge Barbour of Virginia, has died last night. This court will be in recess until Monday, March second."

Barbour, who had not been ill, died in his sleep of an apparent heart attack. He was discovered by one of his slaves who entered the bedroom at dawn as usual to wake the judge. Tappan commented to a friend that the incident, complete with its inherent ironies, made it probable that it was nothing less than divine intervention by the Almighty on behalf of the cause.

On the morning of March 2, court was brought back in session and Adams renewed his attack. Along with continuing to point out that Forsyth's repeated promises and assurances given to Calderón and Argaiz showed a contemptible disregard of the Constitution, Adams added a new element: the direct participation in these activities by Van Buren himself.

"The court will notice that the orders provided to Lieutenant Paine, orders signed by President Van Buren himself, authorize Mr. Paine to take into custody the blacks. Also notice the form and phraseology employed in these orders not only permits Paine to do so despite the fact that a trial regarding the disposition of the blacks was pending, but also that there was no stipulation that this action of apprehension had to wait until after a decision had been rendered by the district court. We can only wonder at what the President's intent truly was. Did he intend to deprive the blacks of all their rights and have the U.S. military kidnap them and force them back to Cuba, or did he wish to first let the court make its decision, then deny the blacks their right of appeal, and then kidnap them? Or is it even remotely possible that the President of the United States was completely ignorant of the rights of personal liberty and the laws of our nation as guaranteed by the U.S. Constitution? Whatever the case, the issuance of these orders is a contemptuous, vile, and unnerving example of the executive acting in a dictatorial fashion, and, in its appearance, clearly grounds for an extensive inquiry by the legislative branch."

Adams also provided an extensive examination of the Treaty of 1819, a document that Adams had negotiated and co-written.

"The Government is trying to stretch both the language and the intent of this treaty. However, as one of the treaty's writers, I can assure the court on my word that at no time did any of the parties involved intend to equate people with merchandise, be they slaves or otherwise."

Finally, Adams gave a detailed analysis of the *Antelope* case, which had been pointed to by Gilpin as justification of the Government's attempts to send the blacks back to Cuba. It was preposterous to attempt to use the *Antelope* case as any sort of foundation for the case of the *Amistad*. As it had been pointed out and verified, the blacks of the *Amistad* were free when they were found, not slaves bound in chains and marked for sale on the American market as were the unfortunate black men of the *Antelope*. Nor had the *Washington* any warrants or orders authorizing a seizure. The two cases were covering indisputably different legal territory.

Nearly five and a half hours after he had begun, Adams let his voice trickle into silence. He paused and took off his spectacles.

"May it please Your Honors. On the seventh of February, 1804, now more than 37 years past, my name was entered on the rolls as one of the attorneys and counselors of this court. Five years later, in March 1809, I appeared for the last time before this court in defense of the cause of justice. Very shortly afterward, I was called to other duties, first in distant lands, and later within our own country. Little did I imagine that I should ever again be called to appear in the capacity of an officer of this court to plead the cause of life, liberty, and justice. I stand again, I trust for the last time before the same Court, although not the same judges, asking for justice once more. I pray to you that it shall be served."

Adams returned to his table and sat. A wave of exhausted relief flowed down over his body, draining so much strength from his limbs that he could barely stand as court was adjourned.

The next day, Gilpin was allowed a rebuttal. He spoke for nearly two hours but Adams, Baldwin, and Sedgwick didn't hear anything that hadn't been said by the prosecution before. In fact, Adams mentally noted a few instances where, had Gilpin been more attentive, he might have scored a point or two. At noon, Justice Tanny banged his gavel and declared that both parties would be notified to appear before the court when a decision was rendered.

Sedgwick returned to Philadelphia, Tappan to New York, and Baldwin and Jocelyn to New Haven to wait for the court's pronouncement. A week later, on March 9, the court summoned Adams and Gilpin. Justice Story from Massachusetts read the decision. As was the custom of the time, the judge recounted the major facts of the case, a task that took nearly an hour. Then he spent the next two hours reading the text of the court's decision.

Story declared that on a vote of six to one, with Judge Henry Baldwin dissenting but not rendering a written opinion, the court found the following: Neither Pickney's Treaty nor the Treaty of 1819 applied to this case except in the instance of the slave boy Antonio, who was to be returned to the heirs of his former owner. It was ruled that the passports obtained for the negroes by Ruiz and Montes were accurately proved to be fraudulent in district court and as such were invalid as proof of ownership. Gedney and his crew had acted meritoriously and were entitled to salvage in the percentages and within the stipulations declared by Judge Judson. However, when the *Amistad* was boarded, the blacks on board were in possession of the ship. They were not slaves nor did they purport to sell themselves as slaves within the borders of the United States. As a result, their seizure by Gedney and his crew was not valid under the Treaty of 1819.

"Thus," read Judge Story, "Judge Judson's decision regarding this point must be reversed."

Adams held his breath and leaned forward slightly, waiting for the next part. Gilpin, too, was nearly standing with expectation.

"This court rules that the blacks on board the *Amistad*, save for the slave boy Antonio, were acting as free-born men, who were attempting to wrest their liberty from false imprisonment. The court does not dispute this status nor impugn their actions. As such, they are free, and this court orders them to be discharged immediately from incarceration. They may go as they please and return to their nations as free men."

Adams stood and thanked the judges and immediately left the courtroom and penned a letter to Baldwin and Tappan.

"God has smiled upon us," he wrote. "Our friends, at last, are free."

Baldwin received the letter a week later. For the second time in two years he was seen running down the streets of New Haven.

The Gentlemen

The celebration in the Westville jail was marked by laughing, prayers, and a great feast. During the festivities, Burnah, Grabeau, Kinna, and a few of the other tribesmen ran outside, back into the jail and outside again several times to prove their freedom. Late at night, when the festivities were still carrying on, Singbe slipped out barefoot and shirtless and dropped to his knees in the moonlight and wet March snow. He offered up tearful prayers to both Ngewo and the Christian God. He prayed for them to send a message to Stefa and his children that, soon, he would be home.

Or would he?

If the Supreme Court had upheld Judson's original decision, Singbe and the other tribesmen might at that moment actually be on a ship headed for Africa. However, because the judges ruled that neither Pickney's Treaty nor the Treaty of 1819 applied to the tribesmen, the federal government was under no mandate to return the Africans to their home.

Lewis Tappan had appealed to the new Secretary of State,

Daniel Webster, to see if the President could be persuaded to provide transportation to the tribesmen anyway. Webster spoke to President John Tyler, who had been sworn in when President Harrison died of pneumonia, just within a month of his inauguration. Privately, Tyler, a Virginia plantation owner and slaveholder, had no sympathy for the Africans. However, he instructed Webster to tell Tappan that if Congress voted the appropriate funds to charter a ship and supplies, he would sign the legislation. Tyler was confident that the Southerners in the House would never let such a measure pass. He was right.

"The Africans are free men," Webster said to Tappan. "They will have to find their own way home."

This left Tappan to devise his own plan for returning the Amistads. Chartering a ship, captain, and crew for passage to Africa would cost nearly $2,000. Supplies would run another $300. There was also the matter of the mission.

Tappan and the other members of the Amistad Committee had decided that when the Amistads returned to Africa, they would do so as Christian gentlemen and missionaries. Land would be purchased and a mission built with the aim of converting first the people of the immediate area, and later all of Africa, to Christianity. It was also hoped that the mission would be the first step in a counteroffensive aimed at the efforts of the American Missionary Society, which the abolitionists saw as a tainted organization because they were associated with the American Colonization Society, a group which worked to send freed American blacks back to Africa.

"The Colonization Society is composed of racists, pure and simple," Tappan said. "They want nothing more than to rid our country of all negroes, mulattos, and any other people of color. I am sure that if they had their way, all the Irish, Chinamen, and Catholics on our shores would be among their deportees, as well."

The missions of the American Missionary Society were also reputed to teach only Christianity, not bothering to provide instruction in reading, writing, and other formal subjects for their converts.

"Our organization will be different," Tappan insisted. "We will provide to the people of Africa not only the endless joys and rewards of our Christian faith, but also the knowledge and culture of our civilization. This way they can learn how to help themselves and join the rest of the Christian world as equal partners in faith, custom, and civility."

Not everyone on the committee agreed with Tappan's goals for the people of Africa, but most believed in the basic principles he was proposing, and all agreed that "true" missions must be established to check the fraudulent work being done by the American Missionary Society. However, the Amistad Committee was nearly broke. Tappan pledged to personally provide half of the funds needed. The rest would have to be raised by donations and demonstrations.

"Demonstrations of what?" Jocelyn asked.

"Why, of what good we have already done," Tappan answered, beaming.

† † †

The three girls screamed and cried loudly. The youngest one, Ke-ne, who was now being called Charlotte by Mrs. Pendelton, clung to the old woman's skirt, terrified. Colonel Pendelton stood with his hand on the hilt of a pistol stuck in his belt, looking at Tappan.

"I say they're not going," Pendelton growled. "They don't want to go with you, Tappan, and I can't blame 'em. This is their home, and we provide a good Christian living here. You're bringing them back to live with those murdering savages."

Tappan stood defiantly holding a warrant sworn out by Judge Smith Thompson ordering the release of the girls from the Pendelton home. Behind Tappan stood Marshal Wilcox, two federal deputies, and several reporters.

"Home, sir?" Tappan bellowed. "You have turned these poor innocent girls into house slaves. We heard testimony in court yesterday by some of your friends and neighbors saying just that. Why, you've got these girls of seven, ten, and eleven years doing your laundry, cleaning your home, mending your clothes, and even doing your cooking."

"We's just helping them learn the civilities of womanhood and letting them assist us for providing for them."

"May I remind you that the state has been paying you and your wife to provide for them," Tappan said. "However, the 'service,' such as it is, that you have been providing is now officially terminated. The U.S. Supreme Court has freed all the Amistad Africans and this warrant from Judge Thompson relieves you and your wife of these girls. They will come with me to join the men."

"No! No!" Te-me screamed. "Mrs. Pendelton, say it's not true, ma'am!"

"It isn't, Marie," Mrs. Pendelton said. "The Colonel will keep you here safe with us."

"Hardly," Tappan said, and he stepped toward the door. Pendelton tightened his grip on the pistol.

"Another step, Tappan, and I'll blow a hole right through that big mouth of yours."

"Here now, Stanton," Wilcox said, stepping up next to Tappan, "He's got a warrant from the court. You know how it is. You gotta give him the girls."

"Not likely, Norris. And don't you go helping him or I'll have to plug you, too."

Tappan stepped forward, undeterred.

"The Lord Jesus Christ is my God and my Savior," he said confidently. "Because of that I fear no man or his empty threats."

Tappan took another step. Pendelton drew his gun and cocked the hammer. Wilcox pushed Tappan to the ground and leapt at Pendelton. The gun went off just as the marshal collided with the jailer. The pistol ball ricocheted off the doorway of the house, narrowly missing Mrs. Pendelton and the girls, and buried itself in the soft dirt by the foundation. Wilcox held Pendelton as the girls were led away sobbing. They turned back several times with reaching arms and searching eyes to

Mrs. Pendelton and her husband. The next day, the *New Haven Express* ran a blistering article that excoriated Tappan for his "inhuman actions of dismembering what appeared to all present was a supportive family and genuinely safe home." The article went on to question if the girls were better off, even if they had been made to work as house servants, than they would be in the "wild bush of Africa where they were destined to return."

As Tappan left the scene, Pendelton warned him that the Amistads may not live to see their return home.

"There are many men who believe you abolitionists pulled one over on the government, Tappan," he yelled. "I wouldn't be surprised if you woke up one morning to find Cinqué and your other niggers with their throats slit!"

Though Tappan appeared unfazed, he believed Pendelton was not far off with his sentiments. The decision was made to move the tribesmen from New Haven to Farmington, a small town west of Hartford. Many of Farmington's residents were openly anti-slavery in their sympathies. The girls were placed in private homes in the town to be educated and cared for. A barn on the outskirts had been outfitted to accommodate the men until enough money could be collected for their passage home. It was no coincidence that the barn sat on a sprawling, bucolic farm that was also an underground railway station. It was through this same farm that Antonio had passed, two days after the verdict was made known in New Haven, on his way to Canada.

The scene at the Pendelton home was not the type of "demonstration" Tappan spoke of to Jocelyn. In fact, it may have been Tappan's only media-witnessed miscalculation of the last two years.

What Tappan was hoping for was the production of a carefully orchestrated tour of the Amistads throughout sympathetic locations of New England. Town halls, churches, and even factories would host the Africans that people had read and heard so much about. But these were no longer the savage-looking, ignorant blacks fresh from the jungle that had been on display in the New Haven jail before the circuit court trial. These were finely dressed, Christianized, English speaking, reading, and writing black gentlemen who would go back to their country and spread the word of the Lord Jesus Christ's Holy Gospel. It was Tappan's hope that such a display would not only draw attention to what could be done with rough materials straight from the dark continent, but also serve as an example of what kind of transformations could be made if American-born blacks were emancipated. The members of the Amistad Committee agreed with the plan. It was decided that Singbe, Grabeau, and eight of the others who had shown the most progress in speaking, reading, and understanding the Scriptures should comprise the touring company.

Tappan called on Singbe to explain what they would be doing over the next few months.

"Why we have to do this, Mr. Tappan?" Singbe asked.

"Because we do not have the money yet to send you back to Africa and to start our mission. People are interested in you and your countrymen, Joseph. They will pay money to see you do things that are natural to your culture and to see how well you have adapted to ours."

"How much money you need, Mr. Tappan?"

"Well, enough to charter a ship and crew, get us supplies and purchase land in your native country for the mission. I'd say it will be quite a sum. Nearly $5,000 we suspect."

Singbe stopped for a moment, and thought, but he had not been taught to count in English past 100. Thousands sounded like an unattainable number.

"How long we do this, Mr. Tappan?"

Tappan looked at Singbe and smiled broadly. "Oh, not too long, I hope, Joseph. Perhaps six months or a year or so."

Singbe bowed his head. "That long time, Mr. Tappan. We need get home. We here two year now. And many of us taken slave much time before that."

"I understand, Joseph, and I know many of you miss your families and your home in Mandingo. But we cannot take you back there without money."

Singbe nodded. Tappan patted him on the back and assured him that, with hard work, the money would be raised. He stood to go but Singbe stopped him.

"Mr. Tappan, sir. Something we no tell you before. We no from Mandingo. We, most of us, we Mendemen from Mende. Like James Covey. Kaw-we-li."

"Mende? You are from James's Mendeland?"

"Yes. It up river and over hills from Freetown. That where we live. That where you build mission."

"Why, then, did you tell us you were from Mandingo and that you just spoke Mende?"

"When we come here, you and Mr. Jocelyn and Mr. Baldwin very kind to us. Show us great love. But we still very much afraid that if bad whitemen find where we from, if Peperuiz and Pedromontes find where we from, they go there and take our wifes and childrens slaves. So we say we Mandingo. But now court says we free. And president and no court can lock us in jail again. Now we no slave no more. We go home. So now I tell you, we, most of us, we Mendemen, strong and proud."

Tappan nodded slowly. "It is no sin what you did, Joseph. You did the right thing."

"I know," Singbe said.

Along with Singbe and Grabeau, Tappan's traveling Amistads included Burnah, Kinna, Fabanna, Ka-le, Mo-ru, Ses-si, James Covey, and the oldest girl Margru, who now called herself Sarah. Tappan made sure that the men were outfitted in tailored suits and top hats, and that Margru wore simple but elegant dresses. Tappan and Jocelyn used a network of abolitionist sympathizers and clergy to identify the best places for the Africans to appear. A firm list of towns and cities was made, and a schedule created that was loose enough to allow for side trips if events permitted.

They left Farmington in mid-April, stopping in Hartford and Windsor before going to the Massachusetts cities of Springfield, Northampton, Holyoke, Worcester, Lowell, and Boston. Other towns and cities would follow.

A man was sent ahead to each stop to alert the press and the townspeople that the Amistads were on their way, but there was no telling how they would be treated once they arrived. One restaurant manager in Springfield allowed them to select whatever they wished off his menu at no charge; however, the next day, as they walked through the city's streets, a riot nearly ensued when angry men and women began swearing at them and throwing handfuls of horse manure taken from the streets. A hotel owner in Northampton offered his vacant rooms to the Africans, a gesture that made many of his white boarders check out immediately. In Hartford, when papers reported that a local hotel had refused the Africans rooms, several families of the city's elite quickly stepped forward and offered beds in their own homes. The owner of the Nashua & Andover Railroad provided free passage to the Amistads on any of his trains.

When they did arrive, the Africans quickly asserted their authenticity by doing their flips and somersaults, all while remaining in their fine dress clothes. Then Tappan would speak about the reclamation of souls for the Lord God, the need to "take our black brethren to our breast and provide them with the jewels of Christianity and civilized knowledge." After Tappan's speech, which generally lasted nearly an hour, the tribesmen would read from the Bible or any book that an audience member cared to hand to the stage. There were also tellings of their ordeals on board the *Amistad*, in the Havana slave market, and of their capture and voyage from Africa. Kinna, who had become fluent in English and memorized most of the New Testament, would field theological questions from local ministers and churchgoers and dazzle them with his Yale-tutored answers. The highlight of the presentations, however, was Singbe's retelling of their voyage on the *Amistad* in his native Mende, with James Covey interpreting. Spectators were transfixed by the rolling, melodic sound of Mende, Singbe's easy oratorical style, his dramatic pauses, and the plea he always finished with in English:

"Please, we just want to go home."

There was never an outright charge to see the Amistads, but a hat was passed after each performance. The amount of money that would be donated by a crowd was always a mystery. A gathering of nearly 200 people in Worcester yielded a little over $20. A collection among workers after a short tour of a rug factory in Lowell produced nearly $60. The reception by the crowds varied as well. Many people wanted to shake Singbe's hand and would wait in line for an hour to do so. More than a few men, however, reaching the front of the line, tried to punch him. One woman in Hartford attempted to empty a chamber pot on him. Subsequently, Tappan began positioning two faithful abolitionists next to Singbe at each stop for protection.

Stories in several New England and New York newspapers described the Amistads' activities and their need for money to return home and start a mission. These accounts inspired people to send donations directly to the Amistad Committee. Each day the mails brought in hand-written notes containing as little as ten cents or as much as $20 for the Amistads. One note, penned by a Maine farmer, read:

> *Here is four dollars and a half for the Amistad blacks. I intend to make it a full six after my crop comes in. God bless them all and your work.*

Tappan was heartened by the sympathies being expressed and theorized that the Africans' tour may be extended to generate more interest and funds exceeding the $5,000 needed. He realized that once the Africans left America's shores, public interest in them, and in the continuing work of the Amistad Committee, would quickly wane. For that reason he hoped he could keep Singbe and friends in the United States for as long as possible. But this did not mean the mission would have to wait for the Amistads. In fact, the committee, which had decided to change its name to the American Missionary Association, was actively interviewing candidates to begin work in Mende. Leading the mission would not be an easy task. During the last fifty years, the British missionaries had attempted to create ten separate missions in and around Freetown. Nine of these had failed. Climate, disease, tribal wars, and the incursion of Islam from the east had all played a part.

Despite these hazards, a candidate was selected in late July—William Raymond, a Massachusetts man who had experienced a vision that in the Far East would be called enlightenment but in the West was known as receiving the call of God. Raymond's vision, in which he saw "the sinners of the world descending into the flames and ravages of hell," left him weeping for three straight days. When he recovered, he asked God aloud what He had planned for his humble servant. The next thing he saw was "West Africa, as though it was laid out before me." He was hired at $20 a month and he and his pregnant wife, Eliza, immediately moved to Farmington where he began teaching the Amistads who remained on the farm.

In early September, Tappan was persuaded to bring the touring Amistads back to Farmington for a "regrouping." Jocelyn had reported that many of the tribesmen believed Singbe, Grabeau, and the others had actually been transported back to Africa and the rest had been left behind. They were becoming unruly and refused to take lessons or work in the fields where food had been planted to help them get through the winter. Tappan, too, was growing wary about the actions of Singbe and some of the others who were on tour. It had gotten to the point where Singbe would do nothing unless spectators first handed over money. He was also caught several times asking men and women for a dollar when they came up to shake his hand. When Tappan admonished him for doing so, Singbe shrugged.

"You say we need money to get back home, Mr. Tappan. People want see me, shake my hand. I ask for money. What wrong with this?"

Tappan spoke about manners and decorum and the way things should be done, but he could see his words were not making an impression. A few days later, at a stop in a Connecticut mill town, Tappan again scolded Singbe for soliciting and demanded he apologize to the people and return their money. Instead of demurring politely, Singbe shot back angrily.

"No! I want money! I want go home!"

Someone in the crowd yelled out that Tappan had trained his monkey but could no longer control him. Tappan turned angrily toward the mob but was met by a sea of laughs and jeers. He decided to cut the blacks' performance short and leave. After they had returned to Farmington, Tappan recounted the incident to Jocelyn.

"Lewis, we nearly have enough money," Jocelyn said. "Perhaps it is time we sent them home. With Cinqué back among them, I can see a change. At first they were very happy when he returned, and they gladly went back to the fields. But now they grow more restless, almost defiant. It is obvious they do not want to be here any longer."

Tappan nodded sadly. He had hoped that in the end the Amistads, especially Singbe, would want to stay in America and help the abolitionists in their attempts to secure freedom for slaves nationwide.

"Cinqué would have been such an excellent spokesman for our cause," Tappan moaned. "The press love him."

"Perhaps he shall yet be a spokesman, albeit for the cause of Christianity in his native land," Jocelyn said. "But I fear they must all return, and soon. As it is, some are quite depressed over being here this long."

Tappan nodded, although he wondered aloud how any man could be surrounded by the culture and beauty of such a place as Connecticut and want to leave.

A few days after his conversation with Jocelyn, Tappan told Singbe that he would not have to tour for money anymore, that enough had been collected and arrangements were being made to secure all of them passage back to Africa. Singbe and the others were excited by the news and the next morning they returned to the fields to prepare for the harvest. However, when he came back to the barn that night, Singbe received terrible news. One of the tribesmen, Fon-ne, had drowned while swimming with a few of the other tribesmen in a nearby canal.

"He was with us and then decided to swim up around the bend," Burnah said. "He was good swimmer, the best of all of us. So Mr. Raymond say it okay. But then we leaving and we no find Fon-ne. Then Mr. Raymond find him near shore, face down in water."

While Jocelyn declared it a tragic accident, many of the tribesmen commented on how depressed Fon-ne had been, how, despite Tappan's promises, he kept saying that they would never return to Mende. Some speculated that his growing depression drove him to taking his own life. Tappan considered their words, but he also turned over in his mind what Pendelton had said about people wanting to kill the Africans. The thought stayed with him only for a second, then his dismissed it. A week later, though, his suspicions were reignited by a second incident.

Singbe and Grabeau had been working in the field where the tribesmen were growing vegetables. It was dusk and they had both stayed longer than the others picking corn. They grabbed the burlap bags filled with ears of corn and began walking the two-mile-long dirt road that led from the field back to the barn. After a few moments, Singbe realized he had forgotten his boots. He went back into the field to find them while Grabeau walked ahead slowly. At the first curve in the road, about one hundred yards up from the field, two white men leapt out and began beating Grabeau. He fought back, but they knocked him to the ground and were kicking him yelling, "Dumb African!" and "Murdering nigger!" They did not see Singbe come out of the field until he was almost upon them. The big one turned, ready, but Singbe swung his kerosene lantern into the man's head, knocking him down. Grabeau kicked the other man in the knees, sending him to the ground.

"We flog them both good with our feet and hands, Mr. Jocelyn," Grabeau said while holding a rag to the gash in his head. "I know it not Christian to beat men, but I no feel sorry."

"I understand," Jocelyn said, "*and* you should always try to resist the temptation of raising your fist against another." Jocelyn paused, and then reached out and touched Grabeau on the shoulder. "Then again, my friend, the good book also says 'the wicked shall fall by their own wickedness.' I think you and Singbe may have given these men a taste of that."

The town's sheriff was brought to the place where the attack had occurred, but not much could be done.

Still the two events coming so close together worried Tappan. There had been persistent rumors that some Southern plantation owners had paid men to come up North with the charge of kidnapping or killing Singbe and any of the other Amistads they could get their hands on. There were also many people in the North who would not be disappointed at seeing the Africans swinging from a tree by their necks.

Tappan had hoped to go back to Singbe one more time and try to convince him to stay in America with his fellow Africans, at least through the winter, until a better financial base had been built up for the mission. But now the abolitionist saw that any more delay might be too dangerous. In October, he signed a contract with a shipping agency to transport to Freetown, Sierra Leone, passengers consisting of thirty-two free African men, three free African girls, and a missionary contingent of Mr. and Mrs. Raymond and child, the Reverend James Steele, and the West Indian-born mulatto minister Henry Wilson and his wife, a former slave named Tamar. The ship, a large four-masted freighter called the *Gentlemen*, would leave New York City on November 27, 1841.

During the next month Tappan tried to work with the federal government to insure that *Gentlemen* would receive a guarantee of safe passage to Africa. The Spanish were still outraged over the Supreme Court ruling and continued to lodge diplomatic protests and demanded retribution for the blacks. However, Secretary of State Webster refused to even respond to Minister Argaiz's entreaties for a meeting. As far as the U.S. Government was concerned, the affair had ended. As for an escort or guarantee, Webster informed Tappan that the *Gentlemen* would receive the same protection afforded all other ships sailing under an American flag, and if the Spanish dared to interfere in her voyage, it would be construed as a hostile act and responded to accordingly by the U.S. government. There would be, however, no special escort provided to the *Gentlemen* by the U.S. Navy.

The passenger manifest grew by one the week before the *Gentlemen* was scheduled to leave. James Covey, who had been granted a discharge by the British Navy, asked if he, too, could return to Freetown. He was not sure if he wanted to go back to Mende, but he felt he needed to get back to Africa. Tappan made the necessary arrangements.

The tribesmen were brought to New York for a grand send-off at the Broadway Tabernacle. Tappan, Jocelyn, and several esteemed guests gave speeches to a capacity crowd of more than four hundred people who had paid fifty cents each to benefit the newly formed American Missionary Association. The Africans performed readings, and Singbe, for the last time in America, told his tale of capture, slavery, and redemption. The night before the voyage, Tappan learned from a British Navy captain that the task of establishing the mission or even returning the Amistads back to their native land had become decidedly more difficult. The nation of Mende was at war again with their ancient enemy, the Timmani, whose lands lay between Freetown and Mende. Tappan told Singbe, who nodded gravely but said nothing.

On the frosty morning of November 27, under gray skies, the *Gentlemen* left New York. Tappan and Jocelyn rode in a pilot boat alongside the ship until it cleared the harbor and lowered all her sails to catch the 22-knot wind blowing down from the northwest. Despite the cold, Singbe and many of the others stood on deck until the land called America was completely out of sight.

There was great excitement among the tribesmen, but also a measure of anxiety and fear. They remembered well the terrifying storm that had nearly capsized the *Amistad*. They had also heard enough of the whispered talk among the whites to know that the people of Pepe Ruiz and Pedro Montes were still angry and might try to retake them as slaves. Many of the tribesmen declared that they would throw themselves into the sea before they would be in chains again. Singbe, Grabeau, and Burnah carried the same apprehensions, but the three leaders put on brave faces and spoke happily and confidently of how they would all be in Mende soon.

Soon would be about six weeks. For Mendemen, whose measured time in days, phases of the moon, and the seasons, six weeks was not considered very long. However, the years spent away from their families and their country, and the traumatic events that each had endured during their capture, enslavement, liberation, and imprisonment among the Americans, had conspired to twist their casual sense of time so that the weeks stretching before them on the sea now seemed like an eternity.

The missionaries, knowingly or not, helped defray some of the impatience and anxiety of the tribesmen by keeping them busy. Raymond ordered that instruction in the scriptures, reading, and writing take place for six hours each day. Steele, who insisted that the Africans refer to him as, "Mr. Steele, sir," conducted many of the lessons and proved to be a strict task master who did not tolerate impertinent questions or the wandering attention of his pupils. He was also fond of reminding Singbe and Grabeau that it was he, Mr. Steele, and Mr. Raymond, who would be in charge of the Amistads now.

"I know you will be anxious to see your kinsmen, but we are doing the Lord's work here. Our first priority will be getting our supplies to Mende safely, locating an ideal spot for the mission, and erecting the structure. Once that is done, you will of course be reunited with your families and friends. I know you may be distressed over the delay, but the Lord has seen you this far, and a few more months toiling in His honor will be a gift made through His glory and grace."

Whenever Mr. Steele gave such speeches to Singbe, Grabeau, and the others, which was often, the men would smile and answer softly with the same utterance: "Yes, Mr. Steele, sir."

They continued east southeast. The weather warmed, slightly at first, and then, after the third week, all at once so that the tribesmen could abandon their greatcoats and take their lessons on deck each day. They did not see another sail on the water until the morning of the thirty-fifth day, when the sun came up revealing three large sails and cannon mounts of a military ship less than a half mile away. A British flag flew on the mast. It came in close and both captains spoke through large conical megaphones. The British ship was on anti-slave patrol. When its captain learned that the famous Amistads were on board the American barque, he declared that he would provide them with escort into Freetown harbor. Ten days later, just past noon, on January 11, 1842, the tribesmen arrived back in Africa.

The *Gentlemen* was piloted to a mooring. The passengers rushed to the gangplank but Mr. Steele stopped them, insisting they all kneel and thank the Lord God for their safe arrival. He led them in a prayer of forgiveness that lasted nearly twenty minutes. When he finished, he was nearly pushed overboard by the jubilant tribesmen who ran down the gangway and the docks, falling to their knees and kissing the ground of Freetown. Many of the men began singing in Mende and dancing. They peeled off their fine coats and shirts proudly revealing their marks of Poro. Mende people, passing on the street, quickly joined in. Steele, Raymond, and Wilson were unsettled by what they saw as a decidedly pagan celebration. Steele began running through the dancing men, extolling them to get ahold of themselves.

"Gentlemen! Gentlemen! Remember who you are! Remember that you are Christian gentlemen! Joseph! Joseph Cinqué! Get control of your people! Joseph! Joseph!? Where are you?"

Steele and the other missionaries looked all over the docks, but Singbe and Grabeau were not be found. More desertions followed. Within three days, all of the Mendemen had deserted the missionaries.

Home

Freetown was exactly what Steele would later refer to it in a letter to Tappan: a Sodom, pure and simple. Singbe and Grabeau knew it was a dangerous place when they strayed away from the missionaries' care. Two black men, even dressed as finely as they were, could easily be waylaid, kidnapped, and sold into slavery. This was even more likely if they came across a group of Timmani men. But Singbe and Grabeau were willing to take the chance. Some would say it was a foolish move since the missionaries had supposedly negotiated a safe passage into Mende. But neither man could wait. They knew that they had to get home now, not days or weeks or months from now when the missionaries decided it was proper.

Despite the rashness of their actions, they did have a plan. Before leaving Freetown they passed through the bazaar. Singbe had nearly thirty American dollars with him, pieces of copper, silver, and gold, "handshaking money" that he had never passed on to Tappan. He had kept it hidden from everyone and only just shown it to Grabeau the night before they made port.

"It will be enough to see us through."

They used the money to buy a pistol, powder, shot, a small coil of rope, two large knives with sheaths, four flasks of water, some dried fruit and meat, and two blankets. Just before nightfall they made their way out of the city and traded their fine top hats to a man, who had never seen such things or fur of that type, for a canoe. They got in and paddled their way up the river under the light of a three-quarter moon into Timmani country. They didn't speak a word, but Singbe tingled with adrenaline as the stink and din of the city gave way to the warm heavy breath and wild sounds of the jungle.

They paddled until dawn and then drew the boat into a thicket and covered it and themselves with leaves and branches. Singbe took the first watch, letting Grabeau sleep until the sun was directly overhead. As they ate some of the meat, Singbe handed Grabeau the pistol and lay back gently in the leaves and closed his eyes. Within minutes he was lost in a thick, black, dreamless sleep.

Singbe awoke to a push against his shoulders and a hand over his mouth. He moved to struggle, not knowing where he was, but then saw Grabeau and the darkening sky. Grabeau winked but said nothing. They ate some fruit, drank from the water flasks and then pushed the canoe into the river and began paddling again. Sometime after midnight, Singbe felt Grabeau's hand tapping on his shoulder. He stopped paddling and looked to the back of the boat. Grabeau pointed with his oar at a small inlet in the river to the left. A fallen tree stretched from the bank into the water, the base of the trunk and roots resting on the shore. At the fattest part of the trunk, just above the twisted, tangled roots that reached into the moonlight, a leopard sat feeding on freshly killed prey. Grabeau smiled broadly. Singbe nodded his head.

Just before dawn they saw the great hills. On the other side was Mende. They found a sandy landing and got out and beached the canoe. Grabeau took out his knife and cut great holes in the bottom of the hull while Singbe stood watch. Satisfied with his work, Grabeau pushed the boat back into the river. They watched the current carry it for a few yards until it filled up and disappeared beneath the dark waters. The men turned and disappeared into the bush.

They reached the top of the great hills just after noon. They had seen no one. Exhausted, they found a small rocky overhang, covered it with brush, and fell asleep.

The next day, before the sun had begun to light the sky, they were on the road to Kawamende. It was not much more than a well-tramped path framed on either side by thick brush. They reached the first crossroad about an hour after dawn. Grabeau's village was ten miles to the east, Singbe's almost the same distance to the north.

"This is the road where both of us were taken slaves," Grabeau said. "It does not seem possible that we are back here again after all this time."

"I know, my good friend. I barely believe it myself."

"Singbe. Do not lie to me. You never doubted it. You, me, all of the tribesmen are alive because you never stopped believing that you would be back here in Mende one day. You were our strength, our courage, our hope. If you ever doubted, do not tell me now. I will not believe it."

Singbe smiled. He could feel a tightness in his throat. He took a quick breath and let out a great laugh to mask his tears.

"Grabeau, my conscience, my very good friend. We are brothers forever."

"Yes. Forever. Now, it is by your will and strength that I have come this far. Let me accompany you to your village."

Singbe nodded. They turned up the road to the north.

The sun rose and quickly grew warm and bright. They took off their fine American shirts and boots and wrapped them in their blankets, which they strung along their backs like packs. Neither man said anything but both men wore great smiles and more than once they burst into laughter. After a while, though, Singbe grew quiet and serious. Grabeau sensed the change and talked quickly and happily about the beauty of Mende. He ached to tell Singbe that everything would be all right, but he did not want to risk lying to his friend.

As they walked out of a broad curve, the thick bush alongside the narrow road gave way, revealing a long green valley with a line of trees following the banks of a shallow river. Singbe stopped. His lips quivered and tears began to fall from his eyes. Grabeau went to put his hand to his friend's shoulder, but Singbe leapt forward and began to run. He threw off the blanket, sending the shirt and boots in different directions. Grabeau tried to follow but he could not keep up.

Singbe ran through the fields, falling twice. He ran past a small thatched hut that stood near the treeline without slowing down or looking inside. His eyes were fixed straight ahead. Grabeau, still chasing, saw him disappear into the trees by the river.

By the time Grabeau reached the trees his chest was burning badly and his head spinning. He fell down exhausted at the muddy waterside, exhausted and gasping wildly for air. He leaned forward, his shaking hands reaching out to the river, and splashed the cool water into his face. As he looked up he saw Singbe in the middle of the river hugging a sobbing woman. Three children, a boy and two girls, clung to their legs. Laundry and an old brown basket floated down on the slow, steady current.

Epilogue

The *Amistad* was refitted, renamed, and sold to pay off the salvage claims of Lieutenants Gedney and Meade. No one knows what became of it. A full-sized replica is being built at the Mystic Seaport Museum and supported by Amistad America. When completed the ship will serve as both a tourist attraction and a sea-worthy mobile classroom about slavery. For more information, contact the Mystic Seaport Museum in Mystic, Connecticut.

The Legacy of the Amistad Trial can be seen at the New Haven Colony Historical Society in New Haven, Connecticut. The society has actual documents, articles, and the famous painting of Singbe-Pieh (also known as Joseph Cinqué) done at the time of the trial by Nathaniel Jocelyn. Contact the New Haven Colony Historical Society for more information.

The Spanish government continued diplomatic pressure regarding the *Amistad* incident until the 1860s. The United States never paid the damages demanded by the Spanish government.

Pedro Blanco's Slave Factory was raided by the British a few months after Singbe was sold in 1839. The slaves held captive there were liberated and the factory was burned to the ground. Blanco escaped prosecution, however, and retired a millionaire.

The Mende Mission was established in 1842 by William Raymond after James Steele and Henry Wilson decided to return to America. After a rocky start on a damp, disease-ridden site, the mission was relocated to the drier highlands of Mende and christened the Mo Tappan Mission. A saw mill was created on the mission grounds to provide revenue and a school was built. The curriculum included reading, writing, arithmetic, geography, scripture reading, catechism, and geography. Instruction was made available to children and any of the local tribesmen. By 1846, the mission reported having more than sixty-five regular students. Some of the original tribesmen from the *Amistad* returned to perform missionary work or act as translators, including Kinna, who took the name Lewis Johnson, and Fabanna, who called himself Alexander Posey.

The American Missionary Association (formerly the Amistad Committee) not only established the Mo Tappan Mission and others in Sierra Leone, it also went on to found a number of colleges for black Americans in the United States. These included Dillard University, Fisk University, Hampton University, Howard University, Huston-Tillotson College, Talladega College, and Tougaloo College.

Andrew T. Judson remained the Judge of the First Federal District until his death in 1853.

Seth Staples continued with his successful law practice and cofounded the Yale University School of Law.

Theodore Sedgwick returned to Philadelphia and continued his successful law practice.

John Quincy Adams continued to be reelected to the House of Representatives by the voters of his district. In 1844 he succeeded in getting the House to repeal the gag rule. In 1848, while debating a colleague on the House floor, Adams suffered a stroke and died a few days later.

Roger Baldwin continued with his successful law practice. He was twice elected governor of Connecticut and later became a U.S. Senator from the state. In 1861 he led a National Peace Convention in Washington, which sought to revise the U.S. Constitution to avoid the American Civil War. He died in 1863.

Lewis Tappan continued pursuing his cause of abolitionism and after the U.S. Civil War worked to establish civil rights for blacks. He also established New York's first mercantile agency and presided over it until just before his death at the age of eighty-five in 1873.

Margru, the oldest girl from the Amistads, took the name Sarah Kinson, returned to the United States, and attended Oberlin College at the expense of the American Missionary Association. She returned to the Mo Tappan Mission and worked as a missionary until she was nearly eighty. One of her sons went on to graduate from Fisk College and the Yale Divinity School.

Burnah divided his time between serving as an interpreter and teacher for the mission and working as a blacksmith in his native village in Mende. He did not return to the mission after 1847. It was rumored that he married a Mende woman from a prosperous clan and had eleven children.

Grabeau returned to his farm, married, and never set foot outside his village again.

Singbe-Pieh remained in Mende after being reunited with his wife, children, and father. Together they worked the small family rice farm. A few times after his first four years back in Mende, Singbe traveled to the Mo Tappan Mission and provided his services as a translator and tutor. However, after 1846, no one at the mission saw him again until 1879 when he appeared at the gates one morning, withered, frail, and extremely ill. He lived a week longer in the missionaries' care and then died. His last wish was to be buried at the mission. The funeral service was performed by a black American missionary, who had been born a slave in the United States.

Sources and Resources

This book is a work of historical fiction; that is, the majority of the facts surrounding the *Amistad* case are true as presented here, although I have created some fictional and composite characters, compressed and abridged certain events, and constructed fictional dialogue. For those who want to read nonfiction accounts of the events surrounding the *Amistad* Case, two excellent books have been written, both of which served as invaluable background for this novel. They are *Mutiny on the* Amistad - *The Saga of a Slave Revolt and Its Impact on American Abolition, Law, and Diplomacy* by Howard Jones, published by Oxford University Press, New York, 1987, and *Black Odyssey—The Case of the Slave Ship* Amistad by Mary Cable published by Viking Press, New York, 1971.

Though the newspaper quotes in this book are fictional, they accurately depict the journalistic language, sentiment, and content of the time. The actual newspaper accounts and excerpts, especially those in the *Hartford Daily Courant* and the *New Haven Register*, made for fascinating reading and background.

Microfilms of the *Courant* and other newspapers covering the *Amistad* case can be found at the University of Connecticut Library and the Yale University Library. Arthur Schlesinger's *The Age of Jackson* also provided excellent background about life in the 1830s.

For background information about slavery conditions, the middle passage, and treatment of African slaves, two books are especially helpful: *The Transatlantic Slave Trade* by James A. Rawley, published by W. W. Norton & Co., 1981, and *Without Consent or Contract: The Rise and Fall of American Slavery* by Robert W. Fogel, also by W. W. Norton & Co., 1989.

The Amistad Case/The Basic Afro-American Reprint Library, Johnson Reprint Corp, 1968, includes the complete text of John Quincy Adams's masterful Supreme Court argument on behalf of the Amistads and all of the papers in Congressional Document 185. Adams's opening and closing in his argument before the Supreme Court as it appears in this novel have been partially quoted and paraphrased from the actual court transcripts.

Also fascinating are the *Memoirs of John Quincy Adams*, published by J. B. Lippincott & Co., 1876. In Volume X, Adams ruminates on the *Amistad* affair, from his first notice of the slave ship reaching American shores to his wondering on the eve of his Supreme Court argument whether he can provide an adequate defense for the Amistads.